Every child could sleep easily that night. Every kid in the world could impress his parents with his sudden and stable bravery by going quietly to bed and to sleep without insisting his father check the closet, swish a broom under the bed, or even allow the tiniest light to remain shining. There would be no noises in the dark, no faint and glowing eyes blinking within the crack of the open closet door, no grimy claws to pitch forth from beneath the bed at little feet just trying to scurry to the bathroom. The boogieman wasn't going to be there.

Instead, he was standing in the narrow crevice between two apartment buildings in Los Angeles, holding Nick in his grimy claws and wiping the drip from his fetid nose onto Nick's shoulder.

Nick screamed...

Other Books by Joshua Dagon:

The Fallen Series:
   Marbas the Black:
–   *The Fallen*, Fall 2006
–   concluded in *Demon Tears*, Spring 2007
   The Heir of Linos:
–   *The Beautiful People*, Spring 2008

Into the Mouth of the Wolf, Fall 2007

the fallen

†

joshua dagon

BREUR
MEDIA
CORPORATION

Published in the United States by Breur Media Corporation, Lutz, Florida.

ISBN-13: 978-0-9789955-0-8
ISBN-10: 0-9789955 0 3

Printed in the United States of America

Cover photograph: Joshua Dagon
Cover design: Breur Media Corporation

BREUR
MEDIA
CORPORATION

Breur Media Corporation
18125 Hwy 41 N, Suite 208
Lutz, Florida, 33549

813-868-1500
www.BreurMedia.com

"I think we as gay people have more space to dream... in that liberation, that freedom from structure, lies the possibility of nothing happening: being in a void that you have to fill with parties and poppers, which is a trap that some gay men fall into. If we have nothing to do but service our own pleasure – because society has taught us that's all we're worth and we're exiled from positions of authority from which we could actually shape society – then we just become hedonists."

    – Clive Barker

"The beautiful know they have power."

    – Anne Rice
    Merrick

"That is just the way with some people. They get down on a thing when they don't know nothing about it."

    – Mark Twain
    The Adventures of Huckleberry Finn

For Arthur and for Kristie.

Angels. Both of 'em.

the fallen

PROLOGUE

†

Rome, Italy
A small chapel on the Borgo Vittorio, northeast of the Piazza San Piatro

†

"Get on with it," the demon said. "This is too intrusive."

"I'm sorry," said the man. He didn't want to be around her any longer than necessary either. "However, I have to know what will happen if this doesn't work."

"I will be destroyed."

He raised an eyebrow before he could stop himself.

The demon hissed at him. "You would not remain unscathed in that process, I assure you."

"How —?"

"The Beast also has his law. There is but one consequence for breaking it."

"And he would be aware?"

"Only if we fail. Then all would be subject to his punishment."

"Meaning me right along with you."

"Yes."

"As well as the mortal you will eventually find? The one who'll give voice to your spell?"

"It is not my spell. Yes, though. All."

She was sitting in the corner, on the floor. The sound of her skin moving against the wallpaper and over the carpet made his already queasy stomach lurch.

He could smell her too. She could take a pleasing form, he knew. Why didn't she? At least the lights were dim. They were just about out, really.

"And the skotos?" he started, trying to ignore the churning in his gut. "How will you find him?"

"I do not answer to you."

"If I'm to suffer along side you should our endeavor fail, then I think —"

"The problem would not exist had you but followed my instructions from the beginning!"

He backed away from her, again, before he could stop himself, retreating further into the shadows within his study.

Regretting having summoned her, regretting everything, he stopped backing away. No place was safe anymore.

"Don't chastise me," he said, hearing his voice tremble, hating it.

"Why?" she asked. "Is that a sin?"

"And now you mock me."

"I'm tired of you. I'm leaving now. Do not summon me again."

"I am not powerless," he said, sounding to himself a bit steadier. "You would do well to remember that."

"Don't ever say such a thing to me again, stupid man. You can't even follow simple instructions. Real power is obviously beyond you."

The man took a deep breath. His pride wanted to boast further to her. His common sense kept him from it.

"Be on your way then," he said after a moment. "Consider, though, my order will continue to search for the skotos as well."

"Keep them well out of my way," she said, hissing. "It would be such a shame for still others to have to suffer along side me."

The shadows rippled before him and she was gone.

CHAPTER I

†

That Which Comes From the Darkness

Before I go whence I shall not return, even to the land of darkness and the shadow of death; A land of darkness, as darkness itself; and of the shadow of death, without any order, and where the light is as darkness.

-Job 10:21-22 (KJV)

Los Angeles, California
An alley just off of Highland Avenue, between Romaine Street and Santa Monica Boulevard

†

Nick was only slightly alarmed by the idea of seeing a gargoyle in the alley. He thought he was hallucinating. A little side effect of mixing the wrong drugs, perhaps. It wasn't common for him to get warnings about possible negative interactions from freelance dealers in, let's call it, 'amateur pharmaceutical services.'

Even though the first bump of Special K that his boyfriend gave him back inside the club probably would have been more than enough—considering that Nick had already downed two doses of the GHB he'd acquired that afternoon—he didn't refuse when Darren went on to say, "Take two. They're small."

So, he took another hit of K. However, since he didn't think the little plastic bullet was working correctly, he did three more after that.

Had Nick waited just ten minutes before snorting the additional hits of K, he might have reconsidered. He might have given himself the chance to notice that the two compounds were enhancing each other significantly—both of them being essentially central nervous system depressants—and he was getting very high, very quickly.

Then again, Nick didn't know the specific chemical distinctions. He knew that K, or Special K, was a dried cat tranquilizer, which, oddly enough, made club dancing, among other things, a euphoric pleasure for people. Also, he'd heard that GHB was really just a liquid amino acid supplement, but was suffering from incredibly bad press in the States. He didn't understand why. He thought the stuff was wonderful, and couldn't possibly imagine ever having sex again without first indulging in a little G-cocktail.

Although Nick was new at using it, the dealer he'd seen that day did explain how to portion the GHB so it wouldn't knock him out. Nevertheless, it was a very busy weekend, and this very popular amateur pharmacist's apartment soon contained two more customers, both of whom were consistently semi-bulk buyers. Consequently, in his haste, he'd neglected to mention to Nick that mixing G with K might make him sick—or even very, very sick—and that mixing G with alcohol might kill him. Oops.

Darren didn't know Nick had taken the GHB or he likely wouldn't have offered him any Special K at all. Nick wasn't in the best of moods. He took the second dose because Darren was acting like such a jerk. No, Nick wasn't going to refuse any additional drugs. So far, his evening really hadn't been very pleasant, and any assistance in that area was therefore more than welcome.

Not only did Nick's boyfriend not know what he'd previously taken, he also didn't notice when both the letters, the notorious G and K, started to fight with each other inside of Nick and sent him running to the men's room.

The men's room in a popular Hollywood club on a Saturday night is the stupidest place in the world to which to run if you think you're going to be sick, unless you feel like getting the crap beaten out of you for heaving all over the guy in front of you in line. Suddenly noticing this, Nick took a deep breath, wiped the sweat off his face, got a reentrance stamp from the bouncer, and ran outside to puke. He just barely made it up the street two blocks, around the corner, and into a secluded alley before he started vomiting uncontrollably.

The majority of the drugs had already been absorbed. Nick's awareness was quickly becoming considerably slim. He didn't notice when his knees buckled and he collapsed onto an empty cardboard box, or that he'd already destroyed his four-hundred dollar pants, or that there was an exceptionally large demon sitting in the shadows.

He was extremely disoriented and becoming rather light-headed, having vomited the as-yet unabsorbed contents of his system in several consecutive bursts, mostly Evian and Diet Sprite. He then had to suffer his body's vigorous attempt to continue vomiting for the next several minutes. So, when the creature eventually spoke to him, he certainly wasn't ready to sprint away in fear. He did register shock, but nothing near panic or terror, at encountering the apparent apparition, and all the while felt only temperate curiosity that he was talking to it.

He'd managed to collapse into a comfortably isolated alley, as far as he could tell. It wasn't the main alley, which dissected the block and ran directly behind the building. That one would have been much, much larger, complete with a wet and slimy central gutter, ancient wooden telephone poles, neatly spaced metal dumpsters, and the biting smell of urine. It was also equipped with screaming halogen floodlights, which the genius city officials believed would reduce the occurrence of muggings, drug deals, and back-alley pavement quickies. However, what the lights actually did was create very dramatically shadowed recesses and lightless hollows; perfect for such goings-on.

The main alley directly behind this particular club was actually a very busy place, as would be well known to any club regular who ever cut through it on their way from a secluded parking space, which was why Nick had run up the street to look for someplace more private.

A short distance north, he found a much smaller alley very near the end of the next block. He wanted to make sure he ran down the street in the opposite direction of the already forming line for entrance to the club. This little side alley contained only one metal garbage dumpster, a dry cement gutter, and no lights at all. Though, it was fenced across in its center, which was the genius city officials' only attempt to prevent the criminal element from using it to make continuous rounds in the area.

It was here that Nick collapsed in his on-coming stupor, right where the light from the distant street died in an angle across the gutter, right where the dumpster blocked the north half of the alley, six and a half feet from where eight-hundred and seventy pounds of winged nightmare silently rocked back on its haunches and held its breath as the wayward nightclubber stumbled around the corner.

The wings were what initially made Nick suspect he was delusional. After he'd finished his first round of retching, he caught a very brief glimpse of them in the rapidly passing glow of some distant headlights. He could only see their tips. The light didn't travel far into the alley, and it really was only for an instant, but he knew immediately what they were, or what he *thought* they were.

He'd seen gargoyles before, both the medieval stone guardians themselves as well as any number of contemporary artistic representations of them, and these wings appeared similar enough so that they came to mind. This set of gargoyle's wings, though, were solid black against the washed-brick building, and Nick could tell they weren't made of stone because they had fur on the edges, and, of course, because they moved.

The wings quivered a bit for the half-second that the light hit them and they were visible, as if their owner had been startled or shaken. It was just enough for Nick to register that they also resembled the thin leathery wings of a bat. Although, from the size of them, and how high they were, if this bat was sitting on the ground, then it was about seven feet tall, and the tops of its wings were eleven feet high.

He was still staring up into the blackness of the inner alley, trying to reconcile what he thought he'd seen, when something bumped the metal dumpster, rolling it halfway out into the light.

Nick held his breath, but he couldn't hear anything. The dumpster, unlike the giant bat, was obviously real. So, whatever had bumped into it and sent it rolling three feet on its casters, Nick reasoned, must also be real. Maybe the wings had been a trick of the light—and his chemically compromised eyes—and it was just a dog or something in the alley.

Yeah, it was just a dog that knocked into a solid-steel trash dumpster, which normally required a hydraulic truck to move, sending it further out into the light so he could see it better. Nick didn't know if he was more frightened by the possibility of an imaginary, seven-foot flying rat or of Cujo the Wonder Pooch.

His fear, though, was soon overwhelmed by the growing eclipse of his normal senses.

"Hello?" Nick cautiously said to the darkness.

He held his breath again. Nothing answered him, not that he'd expected anything to answer him. He didn't hear a thing actually; no panting from the super dog and no giant bat sounds, whatever those might be.

"Hello?" he repeated, a little louder this time.

Despite the quiet, he was becoming uneasy. If he'd been sober, he might even have fled, just to be on the safe side. Although, if he'd been sober, he wouldn't be hurling his guts out in some grit-riddled alley in the first place.

The thing that bothered him the most, while he still had the mental resources with which to focus on it, was that there wasn't even an echo. Nick thought there should have at least been an echo.

It might have been the drug's increasing obliteration of his reasoning, or just brazen stupidity, but before the chemicals could completely debilitate him, Nick thought he'd try to get up, just for a second, and poke his head a little further into the shadows to reassure himself that he was alone. He'd just cross the line where the light ended and make sure he wasn't sharing this cozy little secluded alley with anything furry that might also weigh more than his car.

He sat up and scooted forward about a half a foot.

"I think you'd better stay where you are," said a voice out of the dark.

Nick froze. His mind desperately attempted to decide if he'd actually heard anything. Meanwhile, his testicles seemed to have leaped into his chest.

The voice had been quite clear, both its auditory quality and its instructions. Nick wasn't going to move.

He would have been much more upset, but maybe because he'd shifted his body or maybe because he'd forgotten to breathe, the dry heaves returned. The first couple were dry and painful. The next few were suspiciously damp, and very, very painful. He didn't think about the voice for a minute. He was in pain and much more concerned with his possible drug overdose than he was with an imaginary voice giving him directions. At least for the moment he didn't think about the voice. He didn't think about it, that is, until he heard it again.

"That was charming," the voice from the darkness said. It was quite deep and actually had a pleasant resonance. Nick thought it sounded like the guy from all the movie trailers. Though, it was soft enough to avoid any echo between the walls of the buildings.

"Wha...?" Nick was trying to speak, but he realized he wasn't breathing.

"I suppose I should be grateful that you missed me before you ran out of juice," said the voice.

As if to contradict it, Nick coughed up some more goo, wiped it on his pants, and then sank against the wall.

"Lovely," came the voice again, deeper, reverberating. What was James Earl Jones doing in an alley?

"That'll never wash out," the voice continued. "What are those? Versace?"

"What?" Nick managed. His head was beginning to swim and even the brick wall behind him didn't feel quite stable.

"Your pants, brainy. You got puke all over your pants."

Nick felt all the wetness in his lap and on his chest. "Oh, crap!"

"Are they Gianni or Donatella?"

"What?" He was concentrating on his stomach and wondering if it was done trying to send out all of his other organs. "Oh, um … they're Versace."

"Yes, thank you. I see. However, do you know if they're by Gianni or Donatella Versace?"

"Oh god, um, I don't know." The ground began to tilt slightly to the right. Nick leaned against the wall so he wouldn't slide into it.

"How much did you pay for them?" the voice inquired.

"Oh, holy crap, my fucking head," Nick stammered, pressing his fingers to his temples.

The wall began tilting right along with the ground. Nick crouched down into the corner, wondering if he'd eventually slide up to the roof. If the tilting continued, the whole building would be upside down in a few minutes. It would probably hurt to slide across the old bricks, he thought, not to mention most likely flying right off the top of the building and straight up into the sky.

"Were they expensive?" came the voice again.

"What?"

"Your Versace pants. They look expensive."

"Oh, my god! I ruined my fucking pants!"

"As noted."

"Who are you?" Nick squinted into the dark.

"What were they? Two? Three?"

"Four," Nick answered, "and a quarter."

"Ouch," the voice winced. "And they look like they're Gianni to me. What a shame."

"Who…? What…?" Nick was still struggling quite a bit just to breathe.

"You should relax for a minute, kid. You're pretty messed up."

"I'm fine," he insisted.

Nick could barely tell that he was sitting down. He pressed his back hard against the wall to assure himself it was still there. It was, although it was still slowly tilting backward along with the ground, but not enough to send him tumbling up the wall. In fact, it hadn't seemed to have made any significant progress at all in its effort to flip upside down. That was good.

"Really, I'm fine," Nick said again.

"Uh-huh. Yeah." The voice was, apparently, unconvinced.

"It's nothing," Nick insisted. "Maybe I'm coming down with the flu." It was an automatic answer; he would have given it to anyone.

"Well, buddy, 'nothing' seems to be kicking your ass right now. So, just take some deep breaths." Then he added softly, "I'm not going to hurt you."

Nick wasn't worried about that. After all, there really was no voice. He was imagining it. Even so, he decided to take the advice of the considerate delusion and try to settle down for a second. Even if he was able to stand up, which he doubted explicitly, he didn't need to be wandering around, especially if he was going to be encountering giant talking bats everywhere.

He closed his eyes and tried to consciously control his breathing.

"Good boy," the voice said in a soothing whisper.

Although he'd decided it wasn't real, Nick answered the voice again. Just because it wasn't real didn't mean he had to be rude.

"Thanks," he muttered. "I think."

Nick tried to take a deep breath. He managed one, and then half of another before the nausea returned. He held his breath and winced when it made his stomach cramp. He held it though, until he knew he wasn't going to barf again.

"You need to keep breathing," the voice offered.

"Actually," Nick said, gasping a little, "I'm just hoping the heaving will stop."

"Keep breathing and don't talk so much."

"Are you always so bossy?" Nick asked with a smile. At least he thought he was smiling. He had to concentrate specifically on his face in order to be aware of what it was doing.

"Quite often," the voice said. "More so with young men who can't handle their illegal compounds."

"I told you, I'm just a little sick, I haven't—"

"Save it." The voice stopped him. "I can smell it in this mess. There's keteset, and enough butyrate for two people."

"How…? Oh, my god, what the fu—?"

"You should really space that shit out more, the GHB. It's very unforgiving, from what I hear. You haven't used it before, have you? You're not going to take any more tonight, are you?"

"Hold up, hold up, hold up." Nick didn't know if he was amused or irritated. "What are you talking about? How do you—?"

"I told you. I can smell the chemicals in this crap you shot at me. Sheesh, there's a lot of keteset. You're quite the little Hoover."

"Oh right!" It was coming back to him suddenly. "Riiiight!" He nodded and shook his finger in the direction of the voice. "You know what I took because you're it! I mean, you're from it. Whatever. I'm just imaging you and this little lecture." Nick was relaxing a bit now that he'd put it together again. He'd almost forgotten that he was just humoring an apparition. He *had* forgotten that he'd never known the 'B' in 'GHB' stood for butyrate.

"Okay," it said.

"No, don't 'okay' me!" Nick laughed. "You little fuck, I'm on to you!" He was beginning to slur.

"Yup. You sure got me pegged there, Einstein."

"No, no, no, no, no! Admit it! You're a gargoyle! Like from France!"

"France?"

"Yeah, France! I seen 'em! Lots of 'em. On the big church. The one with the thingy... the, you know... you know... the thingy..."

"Notre Dame?"

"Yes!" Nick slapped his knee for emphasis. "Fuckin' Notre Dame! I saw the gargoyles on the church, and I'm feeling guilty and shit, so I'm hallucinating you." It came out sounding like 'halooocinatin'.

Slurring or not, the clarification made perfect sense to Nick and he was glad he'd been able to explain it to the illusion.

"Okay, whatever."

"So, you can stop lecturing me, because you're gonna be gone in a minute."

"Look, don't feel guilty about the drugs. Everyone takes drugs. It just depends on how you look at it. Alcohol is a drug. Every cup of real coffee is a drug. The sugar in your Pop Tarts is a drug. If you want to feel guilty, do so because you're an idiot."

"Oh... what?"

"You're an indulgent, spoiled, little idiot. Look at you. You've obviously either trusted the wrong people or you're too ignorant to trust yourself. Here, you're paying for your lack. Now, whether that's a lack of appropriate caution or a serious degree of intellect, I'm not yet sure. Either way, you're sitting there because of doing something rather stupid. You're in a lot of danger right now. So, like I said, you need to relax until it passes."

"I thought you said you wouldn't hurt me." Nick thought about getting up, but he didn't want to try that until the ground and the wall stopped moving.

"And I won't. But you're very likely to hurt yourself if you don't sit still for a few minutes. I don't care if you think I'm a hallucination, just sit still and breathe."

"I'm not going to hurt myself." Nick raised himself up only an inch or two before slipping back against the wall. He thought it was really comfortable right where he was, suddenly, and tried to remember why he'd been attempting to move in the first place.

"Fine." The voice sighed. "But if you manage to get up and to walk back into that club, looking like that, not to mention smelling like that, the bouncer is either going to call the police, beat the shit out of you, or both."

"Bossy. Bossy."

"Neither of which would be a very productive development in your life, I assume. No one is around, so sit still."

Even in this dreamy state, Nick knew the voice was right. All he needed was for some grouchy, underpaid, and under-bribed, door guy to decide to use him to work out some hostility. He'd seen it happen to people he knew and, although he'd wanted to help them, he knew he couldn't or he'd just end up in the same mess.

Still, he thought it would be a toss-up. He was on friendly terms with enough of the security guys at the club to maybe get away with it. He tried to recall if he'd recognized any of them either on his way in, or during his rather rapid exit.

Nick's boyfriend, Darren, knew just about everyone who worked at the club very well; he promoted large parties there from time to time. The manager was a close friend of both of theirs. The real problem was that there was no guarantee either of them would be anywhere near the front doors. Even if they were, Nick wasn't eager to put them to the test and embarrass them like that.

No, Nick didn't want to stagger into the club smelling like vomit and gutter filth. Darren might be able to keep anyone from calling the police, but even so, Nick would never hear the end of it.

He decided he could spare some time and at least hang out long enough to sober up and crawl into a cab. Once he got back home, he could shower, change his clothes, take some far more familiar drugs, and come right back. That decided, he closed his eyes and tried to relax again.

"You're a really bossy gargoyle," he said.

"I'm not a gargoyle," the voice huffed.

"Shut up. Yes you are."

"I'm not a hallucination either, little boy. Though, I doubt you'll be able to make that distinction tomorrow. You'll be lucky to remember where you live later."

"You're a big, fat, ugly, flying, hairy, bossy, gargoyle."

"If you're trying to retaliate because I called you an idiot, you're not going to wound me with names. And you're certainly not going to affect my opinion by insisting that I'm a gargoyle."

"You're kinda bitchy, too."

"Oh, I'm hurt. It's so terrible to be berated by a half-conscious junkie."

"You know, you can go anytime. Why don't you just fly away?"

"I can't."

"I saw the wings, Batman!"

"Yes, I suppose you did at that," the voice admitted. "That's why I can't leave at the moment."

"What?"

"I'm visible, it seems, which isn't my intention just now. Maybe I only need to rest as well. Maybe it will pass."

"Knock it off!" Nick clutched his head again. "You are an illusion! God, I almost wish I'd just pass out, or something."

"No, you don't. You know that wouldn't be a very good idea. I wouldn't hurt you, but I couldn't protect you either."

"There ya go! I know that! You can't do shit! Like some mugger is gonna be scared off by my delusion." Nick laughed a little at the thought.

"Look, I'm not a delusion, and it would be better for both of us if I didn't have to confront a mugger or anyone else. You're bad enough. So, maybe you should keep your voice down. In fact, I think that that's crucial at the moment. You should be very, very quiet."

"Yeah, right. I wouldn't want anyone to hear me talking to myself."

"Okay, whatever."

"I'm so sure that a gargoyle is going to say stuff like 'whatever.'"

"Just like you're so sure that I'm a gargoyle." The voice sighed. "Just like you're sure I'm a figment of your imagination, a remnant image from your adolescent jaunt to Europe."

"Fine, freak. What are you then?"

There was no reply.

"Come on!" Nick tried to slide himself across the ground closer to the line of shadow. If he could move another foot into the alley and get just his head out of the dim light, maybe he could see it again.

"You know I saw you! Why wouldn't you—"

"Do not come any closer!" the voice hissed angrily. There was a sudden breeze. A warm gust of wind threw dirt and trash out of the alley and into Nick's face. It was harsh and brief, making him close his eyes to it as it died. He heard the sound of a heavy tarp, or a tent flap, fluttering in the wind.

"Your glimpse of me was an accident," the voice whispered, "but if you gain the full sight of me in this state, by choice, then I cannot honor my earlier words. My promise to you will mean nothing."

Nick stopped. "Meaning...?"

There was another sigh, a touch of breeze, and barely a whisper, but Nick heard it clearly. "I will have to kill you."

Nick looked away, down at the pavement, which was still heaving like the deck of a ship, and decided not to push it for now. He rolled back and slid across the cardboard of the box he'd crushed. He leaned back and felt the comfort of the now-familiar wall. He wasn't in exactly the same spot, but he wasn't in the dark either.

"It's very important that you understand," the voice went on, just a little louder, "at least for now, I am not a figment of your imagination. I'm not an image that your drugged-out mind has called forth to punish you for your indulgence, and it would be a very bad thing for both of us, as matters are at the moment, if you were to actually see me."

The wall and the ground were still moving. Nick realized there was very little he knew for sure right then. He knew he was outside and it was night. He knew he'd messed up with his evening's party favors and was experiencing a degree of influence he'd never had before. He'd had mild hallucinations, the heaving ground or a slowly spinning dance floor, far away voices when he was alone in the quiet after he'd gotten home, but nothing ever visited him. He'd never stumbled upon giant, gothic creatures in the night.

"What are you?" he decided to ask again.

"It is not important. What is relevant—"

Nick started to move again.

"Stop!" the voice commanded.

Nick stopped, staring into the dark and seeing nothing.

There was a sigh from the shadows, long and tragic. It was followed by a grunt, the fluttering tent, the shuffle of gravel, and the dumpster again, creaking on its casters as something very big bumped it.

"Well?" Nick tried to sit up and have a better look around his dream. This *had* to be a dream. He'd overdosed, and this was a damn dream.

His friends had told him about their own hallucinations, usually from drugs for which Nick wasn't ready or even interested in exploring, such as LSD or mushrooms. One such acquaintance described a baboon running through his living room. Another detailed how he'd watched the fruit at the supermarket get up and dance. They'd been laughing at the memories, thoroughly at ease, thoroughly amused. Nick thought it sounded frightening. He couldn't think of anything more frightening.

"I am a demon."

Except that.

Nick sat back against the wall and closed his eyes tightly.

"I think you should shut up now," he whispered.

"That won't change what I am," said the voice in a brusque, smug tone.

"Okay, whatever." Nick giggled at the quote.

He still wouldn't open his eyes. He was just going to ride this out. Pressing himself against the wall again, he ran his hand along its rough surface behind him and, despite the feeling of subtle motion, he was glad for it; he could be certain the motion wasn't real, but the reality of the wall was clear enough.

"What's the big deal?" he asked the voice. "Why don't you want to be seen?"

"Do I need to threaten you again? I assure you, although you only saw a tiny portion of me, I am quite large, and rather capable of killing you very quickly."

"No doubt."

"Little boy, if you only knew what kind of situation you're in right now—"

"I have a name."

There was another grunt. "I'm sorry. You have not mentioned it."

"What?" Nick feigned shock. "You don't know it already, oh mighty demon?"

"I said I was a demon. I didn't say I was 'mighty.' And no, I don't know it already. You know, I can see that, as well a sarcastic little junkie, you're also a very typically assuming human."

"Okay, okay, um, if you're not an illusion or a hallucination from my head or whatever, and you are what you say you are, then I thought you guys could, like, read minds and stuff. I thought—"

"Yes. That's true. I can do that."

"Well, shit! Then what's my name?"

"I can't do it from here."

"Oh, dear god." Nick shook his head. This was getting silly.

"I'd need to touch you."

"What?"

"I'd need to touch you, you'd need to allow me to do so, and then I'd know the contents of your mind. With your permission, if I simply held your hand, or touched your skin, just for a few moments, I would understand what you believe to be the truth. I'd know you. I'd know you better than you know yourself, better than anyone else knows you now or ever will."

"Golly."

The darkness issued a disgusted grunt.

"What do you mean by what I 'believe to be the truth?'"

"I mean I'd know and understand your image of yourself, the world, and your relationship to it."

"My image of the world?"

"Yes," the voice said, sighing again. "Everyone has one, and they're all quite different."

"Like an—"

"Yes, crude little boy," the voice huffed. "Very funny."

"No, no." Nick chuckled. "I was going to say 'opinion.'"

"I'm sorry. As I said, I'd have to touch you first. And no, not really like an opinion. It's much more powerful than that. It would be what is the source of your opinions, what shapes them, what powers them. I'd know your opinions as well, of course, but I'd also know why you had them, how they were formed."

"That's an awful lot of shit to know about someone."

"Yes," the demon agreed. "Yes, it is."

"I'm not sure I'm comfortable with that."

"Not many are."

The butt of a cigarette had stuck to the dampness of Nick's shirt. It had lipstick all over it. It looked fresh and was dark and very red. He flicked it off.

"So, I'd have to *let* you touch me?"

"Again," the voice began, sounding irritated, "yes."

"So, if you just, like, jumped on me—"

"I'd only be able to rip the beating heart from your chest and chew it like a piece of gum before you had the chance to piss yourself," the voice calmly said, "but, no, I wouldn't be able to glean from you the name of your childhood teddy or whether you hated your mother."

Nick just stared into the dark. The alley echoed with the sounds of the city's summer night; the whisper of far away cars and the muffled throb of the music from the club nearly two blocks away.

There was another long and lonely sigh. "You know," the demon said, "you can be a little annoying."

Nick decided not to respond.

"Look," the demon went on, "I have no reason to hurt you. Not at the moment. I'm in a difficult situation right now because I'm very tired, and being so drained is why I think I'm still here, still visible to anyone, despite my best efforts. I know you couldn't possibly comprehend any of this, much less relate to it, but please do try and understand. It *is* rather stressful."

Nick was still somewhat shaken by the image of a seven-foot winged monster standing over his eviscerated torso, chewing his heart like a piece of Juicy Fruit.

"Perhaps before it gets too late I'll be able to phase out," the demon said, "or at least change form. Then I'll be able to leave this alley, and the darkness, without gaining any further witnesses."

Nick closed his eyes against another cramp. This one was worse than the others. He felt the bile rising, stinging his throat, but he managed not to vomit.

"Besides," the demon continued, "it will take a least another hour or so before..." He stopped.

"Before what?" Nick asked.

The dumpster creaked, the tent flap fluttered, a burst of dust flew from the cement into Nick's eyes. He blinked.

"Nothing," the voice answered. "Just before anyone starts to leave the club and wander around. Don't worry. In the morning this will perhaps seem to have been just a dream." He sighed again. He did that a lot. "This will seem like a dream, and we'll both be free."

Nick's head was still swimming. The ground and the wall were still heaving dramatically but, fortunately, they hadn't yet flipped the building.

"You keep calling me 'little boy,'" he said tentatively.

"I'm sorry. As I said, I'd—"

"It's Nicholas."

"Nicholas," the demon repeated. "Well, I suppose it's nice to meet you then."

"My friends call me Nick."

"How interesting."

Nick rubbed his shirt, smoothing it. It was very wet, and sort of sticky. He tried to swallow, afraid he'd start retching again, but he didn't. His mouth was dry, his jaw was trembling, and his teeth felt gritty.

"Are all demons as bitchy as you?" he asked.

"I really wouldn't know."

"What's yours?"

"My what?"

"Your name."

There was a long silence. Then—here it comes, Nick thought— another long and anguished sigh.

†

Darren Jacobson bobbed his head to the music and fingered the contents of his pockets: a black leather wallet, his keys, the receipt from the gas station next to his apartment building, a plastic bullet full of Special K, and a tiny clear baggie containing his second hit of ecstasy.

The bangs of his blonde hair swayed with his movement. He really liked the song currently blaring through the club, but he wasn't on the dance floor because he enjoyed watching the crowd more.

He was in the club's first room, next to the one containing the dance floor, watching the activity in and around the main bar, which was an island in the middle of a sea of people. Four bartenders clamored up and down its inside length, two on each side, dodging each other and the occasional bar-back, who always seemed to be weighed-down with a huge rack of still-steaming, dripping, clean glasses.

Each bartender stopped every few feet, leaned almost all the way across the top of the bar itself, turned an ear to the customer on the other side, nodded a moment later, and stepped back to make the order. They seemed very enthusiastic. Who wouldn't be? They pour twenty-five cents worth of alcohol into two cents of ice and juice/soda/water, charged six dollars and got a dollar tip. Sweet.

Darren knew it was a business necessity that the club charge excessive amounts both at the front door and for the drinks. Otherwise, they'd never turn any kind of profit. He understood it. The club was mostly filled with people like him, who would not buy a drop of alcohol all night.

His first hit of ecstasy had started to come on for him about thirty seconds ago, and he would not be thinking about any kind of alcoholic beverage for quite some time. He'd need water, though, and lots of it, come two or three in the morning. The ecstasy could dry him out, which had the potential to be dangerous. That's when the bar would get him; in that bar, a bottle of water cost nearly as much as a lap dance, and you could be sure there weren't any drinking fountains anywhere. He'd buy one, a lap-dance-value bottle of water, and refill it whenever he needed to in the men's room sink. Fuck 'em.

The crowd contained the usual Hollywood elite—although few of them; it was still early. Each room was flowing with flawlessly beautiful and expertly attired young actors and actresses, models, studio and production personnel from page to executive, musicians, authors, photographers, attorneys, agents, high-priced escorts, both male and female, drug dealers, club owners, and party promoters. Peppered among these were the ever-present children of wealth, who knew nothing but hedonism, got regularly scheduled maintenance at the Betty Ford Center, and never lived a day past thirty-seven.

They all maneuvered around, toward and away from each other in a turbulent designer sea on their way to one of the club's three bars, the dance floor, the restroom, one of the lounges, or just in the throws of a flirtatious cruise. No one headed to any of the exits, though. It was way too early for that. During this part of the evening, the front hall was strictly one-way.

The walls of the club were covered with a very tasteful array of dark, rich paints, heavy hanging drapes, and lusciously textured fabrics. Though, no matter the room or conceptual décor, just about everywhere one would be able find lots and lots of mirrors. There were two reasons for this: mirrors made the already enormous space look even more enormous, and the inhabitants of this world required a reminder of their youth and beauty every few seconds.

There were at least five places within the three-story club where the walls had been mirrored from top to bottom and corner-to-corner. Beginning in the early evening and continuing through the late morning there would never be a minute that those mirrors didn't contain the reflection of at least one patron checking the line of her skirt, the position of his collar, the prominence of her cleavage, the size of his biceps, the condition of the fall of fake hair cascading down her back, or the truth to the endurance claims of the gel currently making his hair-style more immobile than that of Malibu Ken.

The club's owner, Maxwell Hertz, known to all simply as 'Max,' was well aware of the dynamics of his unique clientele. Every assistance was given in their aesthetic endeavors. Special wattage and colored lighting was installed throughout the interior in order to keep the pickiest starlet looking and feeling young, glamorous, and like sticking around and being seen. The ceiling fixtures were strategically placed. They provided the male models a highly appreciated boost to their already prominent pectorals, even if it was only through a favorable trick of shadow. This specific component would be of special value around one-ish, when the club was way past capacity, the air conditioning was struggling to keep people from passing out, and most of the guys' shirts came off, spending the rest of the late night and early morning hours hanging, nearly forgotten, from their pockets.

Both Darren and Nick always arrived at the club wearing outfits of very pricey designer shoes and pants, which they topped with ten-dollar T-shirts. They'd each lost their share of highly fashionable shirts before they learned the two most important rules of club attire for guys: stuff your shirt down the *front* of your pants, so it hangs where you can see it, and never wear one that's too nice to use as a face towel.

The club assisted its patrons wherever, whenever, and however possible, in both obvious and not-so-obvious ways. There were always plenty of security guys at the front door to make sure no one was granted entrance without either being on the guest list, a recognized regular, a recognized celebrity, being swift and discreet with a fifty-dollar bill, or waiting in line longer than it took to finish dental school. This all but insured the consistent exclusion of any low-glam element; anyone that might not represent a flattering aspect of the club, should any of the evening's moments be captured digitally and subsequently published, which happened just about nightly.

Less visible inside the club—yet just as necessary—were a number of conveniently dark and secluded areas. These were sufficient for slipping your dealer a thin stack of large bills and receiving in return a plethora of powerful social chemicals, a brazenly common and generally agreed requirement of big city club life.

Dark halls and corners were also very good for getting to know new, let's call them, 'friends,' in a manner not achieved as easily through the efforts of conversation alone. Luckily, the club didn't have a policy restricting its specially selected security guys from wearing dark sunglasses while inside, which, while looking cool—or unquestionably stupid, depending on who you asked—had been known on occasion to conveniently hinder their view of these areas.

Of course, Darren only utilized the more dark and private spots for casual, but intimate, mingling. He never purchased anything inside the club from anyone other than a bartender. Even then it was never anything other than a bottle of water. Of course, judging by the price of the water, it was obviously attained from a spring in the Holy Land originally called forth by Moses himself.

As he'd recently explained to Nick, although it was tempting and easy, buying one's party favors after arriving at the club was never advised. Such a thing should only be the final resort of those poor souls who where perhaps encountering a rare and unforeseen disturbance in their normal methods of acquisition, such as their usual source being on a mandatory federal vacation. Darren felt it was crucial to always have a source or two (or five) with whom one was familiar enough to do business at a safe location, and always in advance. Any other way was just foolish.

However, shit happens, as they say. Though, in the event of an unfortunate hindrance in standard practice, Darren normally—and wisely—opted to stay home and not chance the unknown. Less worldly club patrons ran the risk of purchasing tablets of plain old vitamin C, which might be masquerading as ecstasy from the hands of an alarming array of nameless opportunists. Scoring some crushed Excedrin masquerading as cocaine was also a staggeringly frequent occurrence.

Sometimes the lure of easy money was just too overwhelming and it moved the more feeble-minded to attempt such a ruse. A number were even so enabled by greed they could actually complete the transaction with a straight face. While Darren had never personally fallen for this, his friends weren't always as sensible. Thelma, for example, seemed to be tripping over this obstacle way too often.

Thelma's real name was Theo. He hated being called Thelma, which was why Darren did it. He was a twenty-four-year-old Anglo-Puerto Rican, daytime personal trainer, adult video star, nighttime club-hopper, and frequent scam victim. Darren thought Theo's size would have been enough to discourage the wannabe dealers from selling to him. He weighed-in just over the normal range for a boy his age—if that boy also happened to be holding a lawn tractor.

Theo's big dream was to compete as a bodybuilder at the international level, which he certainly had the body to do. However, no one had yet been able to convince him that it might help his athletic career if he were to, oh, perhaps keep his ass out of gay porn movies, among other things.

It was always endearing to be around Thelma, though, who had an unconscious habit of overextending himself to insure that everyone liked him. The funny thing was, people would like him even if he never opened his mouth and just showed up; he was beautiful. He was also, unfortunately, dumb as a tree. He spent an enormous amount of energy trying to please everyone he admired. This included an entire spectrum of favors, though mostly it was sex. Darren tried to keep an eye out for Thelma; despite being so huge, Theo would never hurt anyone. Not even a brainless putz who'd sold him some imitation narcotics.

Thelma and Eddie were always on hand. Eddie was a twenty-three-year-old fine arts student at UCLA. He worked out with Thelma religiously, though he was nowhere near his size. Even so, he was muscular and extremely well proportioned; a significantly formidable image.

Eddie was very popular at the club because he was nice to everyone, always high, and notably prettier than most women. Even so, the women still loved him. They'd hang on him all night and twitter at his every utterance. Then they'd pout, whine, and argue, because he didn't ever sleep with girls. Even so, each one thought she could change him. Each one thought that, if she just batted her eyes at him enough, rubbed the back of his neck while pressing her cleavage against his triceps, and pouted in just the right way, she'd be able to make him hard. Each and every effort only made him laugh.

Darren thought Thelma and Eddie were the nicest, most loyal, most fun, and possibly most naive guys he'd ever known. At least Theo was all of those things. Eddie was guilty by association.

Both of them, however, would bend over backward—or forward, it was rumored—for anyone, if they thought they were cool enough. Still, even together they barely displayed the aptitude to brew a cup of tea.

Thankfully, it had been business as usual for the past couple of months and Thelma was able to easily procure any desired compound without complication. He hadn't had to whine to the smaller muscle-boys about being ripped off.

Recently, supply was good with the authentic dealers. Darren even had the opportunity to stock up a little, which meant that there were two extra hits of ecstasy at his home, each secured in a tiny plastic baggie in the sock drawer, and two ounces of GHB stored in a saline solution travel bottle in the medicine cabinet. When he had Special K left over, which was extremely rare—Darren loved a full bullet—he kept what was left in the 'Left' side of an extra contact lens case. Personally, he thought that was pretty clever.

At that very moment, Darren spotted a couple notorious dealers of counterfeit contraband lurking between the lounges. Some of their victims would never know the difference, of course. Not for a couple hours. Not unless the scam-dealers were markedly brazen and the pills they tried to push were shaped like Barney Rubble.

It made Darren think again about his own supply for the night. He felt the little baggy in his right pocket for the eighty-fourth time. He assured himself it was still there, that it hadn't slipped out as he was retrieving his VIP card for the new door guy. The new door guy had been trying to charge Darren the regular thirty-five dollars for the privilege of admittance. Darren even had to wait while the new door guy phoned upstairs and asked what a black VIP card meant. Someone had obviously forgotten to explain to him that, sure, the regular gold VIP cards got in for only twenty-five dollars, but the much more rare *black* VIP cards just got a big smile, and a nod. Despite the audacious lack of deference, Darren had remained calm. It was, after all, possible that the new kid had not yet received the appropriate training: *You won't see very many black cards. So, be polite, don't ask to see their ID, and for the sweet love of Jesus, don't try to charge them anything.*

Darren was relieved for the eighty-fourth time when he felt the little baggy, still safely planted beneath his wallet at the very bottom of his pocket, where he normally kept it.

In his left pocket he fingered the little plastic bullet he'd secured underneath his keys. Any casual frisking—which never, ever happened—from any official individual, police or security, would likely not reveal the bullet within the tangle of keys and key chain. That was what Darren told himself. It made him feel better. Though, any officer, blessed with at least half the sense God gave a poodle, would be able to feel and identify the telltale shape right through his pocket. But he'd never have to worry about that. As long as he didn't overindulge and retained the veil of discretion, he'd never call unwanted attention to himself, and therefore never face the legal component of his entertainments. Besides, what were the odds? Ninety-nine out of a hundred of the members of this crowd had the same kind of things in their pockets, or worse. Some of them even much, much worse.

That was what Darren told himself. It made him feel better.

The ecstasy already in his system was slowly gaining momentum and his smile widened. It sent a wave of euphoria that swept through him like a glistening tease of the evening to come. He was ready for it. It had been absolutely forever since he'd been able to go out and indulge. At least two weeks.

No matter how many times he did it, no matter how often the wonder drug known as ecstasy sent Darren to the same gorgeous, libidinous kingdom, he suffered serious anxiety between the time he dropped the first hit and twenty to forty-five minutes later when the chemical first took affect. He was always nervous until the X began to lick tiny tingles up the back of his neck. *What if this X doesn't work? What if I've built up an immunity? What if it never works for me again?* He'd stand in a secluded corner or against a wall and not even make eye contact with a single soul until he was sure he was going to be on the ride with everyone else. It would be a cruel, cruel turn to get into the amusement park and never make it onto the roller coaster. He couldn't handle that. He'd leave.

Well tonight, as of three minutes ago, he could stop worrying. The familiar sensation was roaming through his fingers and running up his arms. He inhaled deeply, held his breath for a moment, and a shimmer of heaven sprinted from behind his eyes, split down over his shoulders, and back up to camp under his scalp. He was almost sure the whole room could see his hair standing up as goose bumps marched down his back and around his legs. His second deep breath brought another assault, stronger this time, running around his chest and raiding his stomach. He arched his back against the wall and was overrun from head to toe. He was being invaded, but he offered no resistance, surrender was inevitable, and he needed no mercy.

Now he just had to make sure to keep it going all night. He had to stoke the fire, occasionally, but resist the temptation to throw all the logs on at once. That was an amateur's mistake; indulging in a barely confinable inferno right away, and after it died down, shivering for the rest of the evening around the sparse and failing embers.

No, he'd wait to drop the second pill. He'd have to wait if he didn't want to accidentally overwhelm himself. Taking the second hit too soon wouldn't really be an overdose, but it could still cause an uncomfortable couple of hours where his senses were so bombarded by stimulation that he couldn't enjoy it. So, what would be the point?

He wouldn't risk it. It was better, he'd learned, to stop and take pleasure during these initial subtle moments, instead of rushing for the edge and risk toppling right over it. Less was more, as the saying went. Though, that lesson had been hard learned.

The first little pill would get him past at least one-thirty, and if he kept his cool, if he maintained his grasp on his mantle of moderation, he wouldn't toss the second one down his throat until at least two-thirty (or two, or maybe one-thirty, tick-tock, tick-tock). Darren's major concern was that if he didn't roll the dice, everyone would be having a much better time than he. Despite standing right in the thick of it, he'd miss the party.

Two-o'clock would be okay. That'd be respectable. Even if Nick ended up flying higher (Darren could tell when Nick's drugs were really working for him: he'd get up and dance on a box, always without his shirt, but once without his pants, which was a story that Darren never got tired of telling), he was going to resist the urge to try and get up there with him by dropping his second hit too soon.

That was his plan. Drop the second pill at two. That would take him through the night and insure some chemical influence would be left for the last hours and protect the euphoric value of the inevitable prime time of the morning. He'd save some rollin' for the last, magnificent hours.

Though, just in case he didn't make it and jumped back into the pool too soon, which was a very real possibility, despite his resolve, he still had his bullet full of K, which could rescue him immediately from the cold, cold fingers of a sober morning, forsaken among the club's remnant crowd.

The remnant crowd, he knew, would still be considerable, even at five or six in the morning, a few hundred strong, and would still be rolling in the throes of their designer potions. All the drinkers would be gone, all the 'just-say-no'-ers would be long asleep, the prudes long shamed into retreat.

He loved being a part of that time. Darren loved the fondness of the crowd that had spent the night together, danced in a dream together. It was impossible for him to ever walk out on that. Impossible to try and settle into the quiet stillness of his apartment, knowing the party would still live on without him. Impossible to even try to lie there, in his silent bedroom, alone, listening to the echoes of the music crash around inside his head when he knew there was still a crowd on the dance floor.

It was impossible unless he walked out in the tow of a warm-blooded, enthusiastic companion or two. That was always a welcome distraction. However, Darren wasn't above racing back to the club if the distraction didn't live up to his high—pun intended—expectations. Yes, sir. He'd just wait until the door closed behind them after they left, pop back into his pants—make sure they were the same ones, can't have anyone noticing he'd changed pants—wait until their car turned the corner, and then sail back to the club. He'd get a better parking space, check on his hair, indulge in a bump or two, and get back to the party.

Leaning against the wall, Darren absently reached underneath his shirt and rubbed his stomach. Ripples of the usual tingles exploded throughout his body. Yeah, this was going to be a good one. He could tell. The night was stretching out before him like a promise fulfilled, like a dream in motion, like the first building chords of a fanfare, gallant and dauntless. It had only been twenty-five minutes and he was already rollin' strong.

"Your abs are still there."

Darren turned. Eddie had stepped up next to him.

"Edwardo, mia bella!" Darren blossomed into a smile and threw his free arm over the shorter boy's shoulders, keeping his other hand under his own shirt.

"What does that mean?" Eddie asked with a grin.

"It means, 'Eddie, you fuckin' stud, you!'" Darren liked Eddie. Eddie was twenty-three, but damn if he didn't look like he was seventeen.

"Where did you get that great skin?" Darren blurted. "That's really fuckin' great skin, man. Really smooth, dude." If not for the ecstasy, Darren would have been mortified at the idea of telling another guy he had smooth skin. Instead, he brushed a finger up Eddie's cheek. "Don't let Cher see you with that or she'll knock you out and take it."

"Please. Cher has the skin of a twenty-year-old."

"Yeah, and her name was Becky!"

Eddie laughed hard and loud. One of the bartenders turned his head and smiled at them.

"How old are you again?" Darren asked.

"Twenty-three."

"You are a liar. You are a liar, and liars burn in hell."

"Yeah, well, so do homos, I'm told. I guess I'm fucked anyway. See, lyin' isn't gonna be what sends me to Hell."

"I guess I'll see you there then, baby"

"Yeah, you can save me a spot."

"Okay." Darren nodded, smiling. "Unless someone cuter comes along. Then you're just gonna have to burn somewhere else."

Darren slowly leaned his head back against the wall, closed his eyes, breathed deep, rode the wave, dropped his jaw, smiled like a lantern, and said, "Oh, gaaawd."

"You dork." Eddie tossed him a dazzling grin. "You're the happy-man already. What're you ridin'?"

"Duh." Darren giggled as paradise assailed him. "You can be a tad dense, babe. No offense."

"Fuck you." Eddie laughed, punching Darren in the arm.

"This shit is prime, pretty boy." Darren shook a finger at him. "You better keep an eye on me, so I don't go-off lickin' any skanky people." He hooked his finger into Eddie's gym pants and snapped the waistband.

Eddie patted him on the chest. "Don't worry," he said, "if you need something to lick, maybe I'll be charitable."

"Ha!"

Suddenly, both of them were rubbing Darren's torso, to his utter delight, but he had to put a stop to it; he didn't like getting too physical with friends. Well, not with *all* of them, for cryin' out loud. Though, it was frequently a major temptation. He'd broken that rule once with Theo, and constantly with Nick, of course. Nick was far more than just a friend, though. Unless someone asked. Then they were just friends.

Darren's trysts with Theo didn't count, however, because everyone did it with Theo, and it hadn't changed anything. It would probably be the same story with Eddie, but why risk it? Darren had learned that if he wanted to increase the chances that a friend would drop out of his life forever, all he had to do was sleep with them.

He stepped away from the Eddie, doing a quick turn-around. "Who's here?" he asked.

"No one. It's early." Eddie slumped against the curtained wall in Darren's spot, still grinning. "I don't even know what we're doing here. By the way, you never answered me. What're you ridin', freak?"

"Well, Missy and I started talking a few minutes ago," he said, referring to the ecstasy with their own coded anthropomorphism. They referred to the drug with a phonetic abbreviation of 'Miss Ecstasy,' or 'Miss E.' – 'Missy.'

"She behaving herself?"

"Actually, she's being really sweet." Darren put his finger to his lips. "She's just whispering right now, but I believe we're getting geared up to have ourselves quite a heavy conversation."

"Do you know where I can find her?"

"No, you fool," Darren answered, looking around.

"It's not for me."

"Sure." Darren smirked.

"Really," Eddie said, looping his finger in Darren's pants and pulling him closer. He whispered, "It's for Theo."

"Where is Thelma, anyway?"

"Wandering, I guess. Looking for Missy too."

"He won't have any trouble, but he'll have to wait. It's just the B-crowd right now. Tell him to wait."

"He's chompin' that he's not going to find her."

"He will," Darren said. Though, he could certainly relate. "But it's too early. Go get him and tell him to wait."

"He's fine. Where's Nicky?"

"No, really," Darren said, scanning the B-crowd. "I just saw a couple of those scam-twerps. Thelma's likely to shell it out again for vitamins or birth-control pills, or something."

"That would suck!" Eddie laughed knowingly. "But it'd be great!"

"Tee hee. Laugh it up, Barbie Boy. 'Cause you're the one who'll have to handle two-hundred and thirty-five pounds of severely pissed off, whiney, sober muscle all night."

Eddie stopped laughing.

They both craned their necks to try to peer over the masses. The B-crowd was large, but Theo wouldn't be too tough to spot. Six-foot-three and a half inches, probably wearing something shiny (or luminous, if he'd been to Disneyland recently), shoulders the size of a coffee table, prettier than Salma Hayek, he was like Ricky Martin on massive doses of Human Growth Hormone.

They couldn't see anything in that room but the milling mish-mash.

"Balcony?" Darren asked.

"Yeah." Eddie pointed to the hall that led to the stairs. "Go baby."

It wasn't a balcony, really. That was just what everyone called it. In reality, it was a very wide, railed catwalk that circled over the main dance floor and the adjacent back-bar and lounge. At the west end of the building, the walkway became a large carpeted platform and offered two booths from which could be had a prime view of a major portion of the second floor as well as the dance floor below.

The booths were always full of those the A-listers quietly referred to as 'B-crowd babies,' earning them their own nickname among the A-listers, 'the B-crowd booths.'

The B-crowd babies gathered at these booths because they thought they'd staked-out the club's most prime and exclusive area; the VIP spot. They were clueless to the locations of the actual *secret* VIP rooms, one on the first floor and a second high up on the third floor.

The first floor's VIP room was the larger of the two by far. It had a two-way mirror, which looked out at the main dance floor from behind the back-bar. It was always crowded with the young Hollywood up-n-comers that the club wanted to make feel particularly special. All of them would be displaying their most disarming personalities—more plastic than Tupperware—as they waited their turn to stoop over the enormous glass coffee table, which was usually covered with fine quality cocaine that had been cut into lines as thick as a finger. This was the real candy land, boys and girls. Just be polite, avoid any observable loitering, and you'd get as many opportunities to use your personal straw as your dignity allowed.

The secret room on the third floor was smaller, but much more opulent; the *true* place for VIP's. Anything that happened behind its door *stayed* behind its door, no matter who was involved. In the club's six-year history, it had achieved a reputation for offering that secluded sanctuary, where anything was possible. Celine Dion could have three-way lesbian sex with Halle Berry and Condoleezza Rice after they all shared needle drugs with Prince William, and neither Renee, Eric, George, or Chuck would ever hear a word about it.

There was always a specially selected security guy standing in front of each room's "hidden" entrance wearing a black everything, dark sunglasses, an electronic communication ear-piece, a cheap buzz-cut, and an expression like someone just farted on him. Most of the security guys carried around roughly the same amount of weight as Theo, and a good number of them even got their steroids from the same dealer.

From the top of the stairs, Darren and Eddie could see a healthy portion of the enormous club, including a very nice view right into the DJ booth, which jetted out over the north side of the dance floor, halfway between the first and second floors. At the moment, it contained only the DJ himself—who Darren didn't recognize; maybe this wasn't going to be such a great night after all—which was unusual. Typically, the long balcony held four or five or more of the DJ's entourage, who were conspicuously absent at the moment; another bad sign. It was early, though. Maybe they were still getting doped-up.

The dance floor was packed, but the box tops were empty of go-go girls or boys, and even any enthusiastic patrons, with the glaring exception of one silly queen in the back corner who'd obviously snorted a shit-load of crystal meth—way too early—and now apparently thought he was Janet Jackson. At least he hadn't brought any flags or musical instruments to play with—one dork brought *bongo drums* all the time, for god's sake, but they still let him in, which meant he was rich.

Darren and Eddie pressed right over the rail and spent ten minutes peering into the convulsing throng below them. Unfortunately, it didn't contain any beautiful Latin muscle boys.

Darren was getting light headed and leaned back again. The tingles were becoming ripples, which weren't just marching through him, they were starting to stampede. He needed to find a couple of cozy friends and a place to camp with—and on—them before the ripples became waves. If the waves became billows before that happened, he was going to have to grab Eddie, go someplace dark and, friend or not, cling to him.

He looked over at Eddie, who was staring right back at him, that same impeccable grin on his face. Motherfuck, he was cute.

"What're you lookin' at, pretty boy?" Darren couldn't help but smile back big. The thought of kissing Eddie ran through his mind for an instant before he could stop it. Between Missy and this shapely little gym rat, Darren was going to be in serious trouble if he didn't find himself some kind of a distraction soon. He knew if he started kissing Eddie, he wouldn't be able to stop. They were still in a very well lit and traveled area, and although this was a notoriously mixed bar, some of the more throwback breeder-boys got very nervous around same sex public displays—unless it was a female/female display, for which they cheered enthusiastically. Plus, it was just tacky, which was no doubt the best of all reasons to resist, even more so than the fact that Eddie probably really *was* seventeen.

"You, big happy-man," Eddie's plump-little-temptress-vixen-lips said.

"Oh, god, please don't start with me." Darren sighed. "You know, if I didn't know better, I'd think—"

Wait a second, Darren thought to himself. Eddie's pupils were the size of train tunnels.

"Fuck, Eddie!" Darren quipped. "You're rollin', you little shit!"

"I told you it wasn't for me!" Eddie laughed. "I dropped before I came in. I'm just trying to get Theo hooked-up."

"He's such a load of baggage," Darren said. "And you're on my list now!"

"All right!" Eddie ran his fingers up the back of Darren's neck, which almost sent him to the floor.

He stepped away laughing, pointing a finger at the younger boy. "You stay at least five feet away from me!"

Eddie giggled mercilessly. Holy motherfuck, he was cute.

"We gotta find Thelma, and I mean right now!" Darren backed away two more steps, still laughing, staring into Eddie's train tunnel eyes. Then he spun, dashed around the catwalk's corner, and headed to the booth side, not looking to see if Eddie was following. He knew that he was, of course. Duh.

Darren was even more eager to find Thelma now. Since he'd

discovered that Eddie was affected too, he either needed to pawn him off on Thelma before their ride got too intense, or he needed to add some company to their experience.   They both needed some distractions to keep them respectable.

Ecstasy worked differently for different people. Everyone's unique body chemistry reacted in various ways. Though, it generally put just about anyone in the mood to be touched, to touch other people, and basically be exceptionally physically affectionate.   It also made spending time on a crowded dance floor an experience rivaling the achievement of Nirvana; bodies moving together, holding each other, two or three (or five), boys, girls, doesn't matter, skin on skin, just a groove, just a swaying in an ambient, hypnotic rhythm, hours go by, days maybe, who knows, who cares, just roll with it, baby, rollin' was the way.

Darren, though, was in a bind. Darren was staring straight into the eyes of his sixth year of consistent and regular indulgence; a relatively long relationship with Missy. Missy and Darren knew each other well, had spent many glorious nights together, dancing, swooning, loving each other, loving everyone. The dance floor was their first place, of course. It was where they met, where they fell in love, and as will often happen with very passionate relationships, they burned bright and hot, exploiting fuel and warming the night. They'd already gone through quite a bit of fuel, actually, and Missy and Darren needed more now. See, as a couple, they were developing. They were moving forward.

What Darren was developing with Missy was much more demanding. When he got together with that swanky bitch he still needed to be held, he still needed to hold someone, but not soon after all that had started, he needed to get down and dirty, plain and simple, nasty and gritty.

He wasn't satisfied anymore to sway on a dance floor for hour after hour with just Nick's head on his shoulder, or Karen's, or Matt's. That had all been fine and dandy the first year or two, but the demands of the fantastic Miss E were much more complicated now.

First of all, everyone had started to think that Darren and Nick were together, which was true, but he didn't want everyone to think it. It wasn't like they were in a *relationship*, lord in Heaven help us, or that they were exclusive or anything. He and Nick were just friends, really.

Okay, Darren and Nick had a pretty intense 'friendship.' Maybe it was even an intimate one, and a friendship *is* technically, if you want to get literal here, a relationship. Nevertheless, friendship was still the more appropriate term. Certainly, it was more appropriate than something like 'boyfriend', which didn't feel right at all, and not '*lover*' either, for the love of God Almighty, the very thought of which made Darren want to punch someone.

No, things were different now. Things were in transition, in motion. He and Missy needed to work things out. Darren needed to better control his environment when he was with her. Now all Missy seemed to want to do was skip right to the good part, go right for the gold. Darren had to keep that in check. He knew once he let her take him to that nasty, sexy place, he'd be on a very slippery slope.

Nick was bad enough. Darren's life with Nicky was confusing as it was, so he hadn't let Karen step into Nick's life and make it worse, and he wasn't going to let Eddie start that ball rolling in his own life either. Nope. No way. Find Thelma, right now, and maybe even a crowd of people, a gang of distractions. Find a group that was fun and frivolous, that was loud and affectionate. Find something, anything, that *wasn't* Eddie, or Nick for that matter, in the dark and all alone. Find Thelma and grab a gang along the way.

Darren and Eddie jogged down the catwalk toward the opposite end of the club. The B-crowd babies were spilling out of both huge booths and gushing all over the place. It was only eleven-fifteen and they were already drunk (beginners), and dressed as if they were at the Emmy Awards and each one of them had been nominated for 'Best Set Background-Baby' for their stand-in or background/extra work that week on whatever prime-time teen-drama it was to which the high school drop-outs were selling their futures for a hundred and seventy-five dollars a day and the too, too remote chance of being noticed by Jerry Bruckheimer. Darren thought they should just buy lottery tickets; their chances for success would be so much better.

Nick was an actor, true, but he sure wasn't a B-crowd baby. Nick had modeled pretty successfully since about the time he'd learned to walk, and had even landed himself an enviable number of national commercials. Just a few months ago, Nick appeared in a commercial that would probably set him up for the next several years—if he didn't, say, go and buy mass amounts of real estate in Miami, or something. Nick had a very decent agent, studied acting privately, and would not ever walk around anonymously in the background of any movie or TV-show, any more than he'd attempt to remove his contact lenses with salad tongs.

"'Scuse me, baby." Darren gently pressed his hand on the back of a short blonde girl to politely inform her that she was in his way. She was lost in some dramatic moment as she spun out a presumably fabulous and momentous anecdote to the two other girls standing with her, each with the expression of one who was receiving crucial, life-saving information that must be memorized on the spot, instead of what the Second Assistant Director on the set of *CSI: Minneapolis* had the nerve to say after mistaking her for background when she was clearly *principal fore*ground.

The short-ish, blonde girl shot an initial look of horrified irritation over her shoulder at Darren. Then she smiled abruptly, apparently recognizing him. He gave her a closed-mouth smile; he didn't waste flashing his porcelain on wannabes. She, however, had no problem beaming the whole of mommy and daddy's orthodontic investment at Darren, giving him a double bat of her eyes, and inhaling deeply for maximum cleavage display.

"Hi, Darren," she cooed.

"Hi," he said, not having the faintest idea who she was. "How's it goin'?"

"Great." She flashed more orthodontia and actually blushed. If she really did know him somehow, it obviously wasn't very well.

"Cool." Darren nodded.

She just smiled at him, evidently trying to let her cleavage do the talking.

"Uh..." he went on, "we're actually looking for Thelma."

"Oh." She pouted. "Well, where are you going to be? I'll send her there if I see her."

"Um... okay." Darren barely stifled his laughter. Eddie wasn't doing nearly as well. All three girls were giving him funny looks as he snorted to himself.

"Sorry," Eddie said, covering his mouth with his hand. "It's nothing. It's not you." Eddie was probably used to this sort of thing and most likely thought it was wonderful to see Darren getting some of the aberrant attention for a change. His efforts to hide his amusement, however, where wholly ineffective.

"We'll be behind the back-bar," Darren lied. He never went behind the back-bar. Eddie snorted some more.

"Great!" The blonde B-crowd baby beamed. "Toodles." She flickered her fingers at him in a little wave.

Darren was still staring at her in disbelief when Eddie put both hands on the back of his shoulders and forcibly marched him through the group. They almost knocked two skinny, teen-looking boys right over the railing in the process. They would have deserved it, though;

they were wearing *ties*, lord help us all.

"Did she actually say, 'Toodles?'" Darren's eyebrows were smashing together dramatically. Eddie burst into a full-throated belly laugh and continued to push him down the catwalk.

"Five feet, temptress!" Darren laughed. "Stop touching me! Five feet! You're on my list!"

"Whoo hoo!" Eddie sang.

They moved through the upper lounge as quickly as they could in the growing crowd, all the while attempting to be conscious of whether Theo or Nick happened to be anywhere in sight, but Darren and Eddie were laughing a lot, and Eddie was looking mighty nice. This was going to be a close one.

Darren was starting to recognize people. The A-list was filtering in, apparently. Oh, joyous day. Yawn.

Then they saw one of their lost sheep. Theo was standing around the corner from the coat-check counter, nodding his head at something being explained by the black-attired, electronic-ear-pieced, buzz-cut, security guy, who was stationed in front the upstairs secret VIP celebrity room door. They didn't appear to be arguing or anything. It looked like the security guy was reviewing something important, and Theo was pretending to comprehend it.

Theo was standing in his usual I'm-Listening-Very-Closely pose; hands clasped in front of him, slightly stooped to get his ears closer to the person speaking, and giving an occasional nod to indicate periodic acknowledgement. Though, Darren quickly recognized Theo's I-Have-No-Idea-What-You're-Talking-About expression. Darren thought he should get over there and see if he could help Theo out. Some people got sort of pissed-off if they thought Theo wasn't paying attention. At least they were pissed off until they realized they'd really just been talking to a very attractive stack of muscles with nice hair.

Theo spotted Darren as he and Eddie pressed through the line to the coat check area. He smiled at them, obviously glad to see familiar faces.

"What's goin' on, babies?" Theo chimed.

"Hey, big guy." Darren nodded at him, smiling back. He couldn't figure out how he'd missed Theo when he came in; he was wearing three hollow plastic necklaces with luminescent chemicals inside. They were all purple, this time.

The security guy stopped talking. "Mr. Jacobson," he said, offering his hand to Darren.

Darren shook the security guy's hand, but he didn't recognize him right away. They shook for a second or two before it started coming back. He hated having to think when he was in this state.

"Brady, right?" he asked, pointing at the security guy.

"Brad," corrected the security guy.

"Oh, so close!" Darren snapped his fingers. "You're new, right? Didn't you start last month? I thought Karen put you right on the front door?"

"Alex couldn't be here tonight."

"So she stuck you in his spot, way up here? Is she mad at you? Crap. That's gotta suck."

Brad the Security Guy nodded.

"Well," Darren said, "you're much bigger than Alex. You know, more intimidating."

"Hooray for me."

"This is hardly as, um, exciting, I'd think, as the front door might be, I guess," Darren said sympathetically. He winked, though, as both men knew that by 'exciting' he really meant 'profitable,' as in the grease that flowed out of the pockets of the more impatient and/or underage line-occupants.

"How're you holding up?" Darren asked.

"I've only been here for a couple minutes. Ms. Alanson just went inside with Mr. Hawthorne. The room was locked up before that."

"Karen's inside with who?"

Theo piped up. "It's Troy. She's talking to him for me." He gave Darren his secret You-Know-What-I-Mean look. Though, that particular expression was fairly easy for anyone to decipher, as long as they had the necessary equipment, such as eyes.

"Is she getting you some candy?" Darren asked, smiling brightly.

Theo went white as a sheet and shot a worried look at Brad the Security Guy.

Darren looked at him too. "She's getting him some candy," he said, nodding.

"Duh," said Brad the Security Guy, pulling off his dark glasses, rolling his eyes. Eddie snorted.

"I hope we're not interrupting anything..." Darren started, suddenly smirking, shifting a pointing finger between Theo and his new friend.

"No, no," said Brad the Security Guy. "I was just telling Mr. ...?" He raised an eyebrow at Theo.

"Theo," said Theo. Eddie snorted again.

"...Mr. Theo about what it's like working in New York."

"Pretty different?" Darren asked.

"No. Not really. People are just as rude and full of themselves out here. They just have better tans."

Theo looked hurt. Darren laughed while Brad the Security Guy smiled at him.

"It's Ramon, by the way," Eddie said. "His last name isn't Theo. It's Ramon. He's Theodore Ramon."

"But he likes to be called 'Thelma,'" Darren offered.

"Shuuut uuup," Theo whined.

Brad the Security Guy gave Theo a funny look, who shrugged, then reached around Darren and gave Eddie a little shove to his forehead. Eddie laughed.

Brad the Security Guy looked at Eddie. "And you are ...?"

"Eddie," he said, offering his hand. "Eddie Thornton."

"It's nice to meet you, Mr. Thornton." He shook Eddie's hand. "And," he said, shifting his eyes to Darren, "in case you don't recall, I met you in Mr. Hertz's office right before that little fashion show thing here at the club last month." Brad the Security Guy gave Darren a knowing smile.

"Oh god, that's right!" Darren clutched his forehead. "I can't believe they did that! That's not typical, man. Though, that Creighton guy was cool. We liked him."

"You mean it wasn't one of your events?" Brad the Security Guy grinned at him. He obviously knew damn well it was not.

"Bite your tongue!" Darren laughed. "Don't get on my bad side now."

"Is this one of your nights?"

"No. Not tonight either, but I'm still going to enjoy myself."

"I can see that."

Darren decided to let that go.

Brad the Security Guy went on. "Did you get a date out of Mr. Hertz?"

"Yeah. A Saturday in mid-November."

"Not bad."

"It's crap, you dork." Darren laughed again.

"True," Brad the Security Guy laughed with him. "I just didn't want to make you feel worse."

"He wouldn't even give me the Saturday before Halloween! I asked for Thanksgiving weekend, of course, but he wouldn't even give me the frickin' stupid Saturday before Halloween! And Halloween's during the fucking week this year!"

"I understand Mr. Hertz can be very difficult with his holiday weekends."

"Max can just be plain old difficult."

"Those dates were taken? The ones you wanted?"

"Yeah, I guess. By Mark Holland."

"Perhaps Mr. Holland had a couple of good concepts."

"Yeah, sure." Darren smirked. "Or he was more willing to bruise his knees."

Brad the Security Guy tilted his head, frowning. "I thought Mr. Holland was straight?"

"Yeah," Darren quipped. "Straight to bed for a quarter-bag."

Brad the Security Guy laughed harder. Darren decided he liked him and he could stay.

"Well," Darren said, "I'll just have to pump it out in mid-November. No stress. Though, Alex or not, I think I'd be more comfortable with you at the front door."

Brad the Security Guy seemed pleased.

"Where's Nick?" Theo asked.

"I don't know," Darren said. "On the dance floor, probably. He's with Kelly."

Darren referred to the code-name/personified female moniker for Special K, which was 'Kelly.' Though, he just did it out of habit. He knew he wasn't fooling Brad the Security Guy.

"Already?" Eddie said, looking surprised.

"Yeah," Darren said. "You know Nick. He was getting kind of grumpy, so I bumped him up and patted him off."

"I guess he didn't hook up with Gina then," Eddie said, referring to GHB with its own code name/female personification.

"What?" It was Darren's turn to look surprised.

"Who's with Gina?" Brad the Security Guy was suddenly very serious.

"No one." Darren stopped him. "Eddie's just confused."

"He went to see Troy this afternoon," Eddie continued. "I thought he was going to try to meet up with Gina."

"No," Darren said. "He doesn't talk to her." At least not outside of Darren's bedroom. "And if he did, he certainly wouldn't bring her here." He shot Eddie a look he prayed the little guy would understand. All of a sudden, Eddie wasn't quite so cute anymore.

"I must have misunderstood him," Eddie said.

Good boy, Darren thought.

"No one has invited Miss Gina to the club tonight, I hope," Brad the

Security Guy said, deftly displaying his clear understanding of the personalized code words for the more popular party drugs.

Somehow, all the most common chemical compounds that could be found in nightclubs had attained female code names: 'Gina' being GHB or G, 'Tina' being Crystal Meth, 'Kelly' being Special K or Ketaset, 'Mary' was marijuana, 'Lucy' was LSD — duh, and the famous Missy, of course. Not only did they each have a female nickname, they also seemed to have distinct personalities; some of them got along with each other rather well, some did not.

"Don't stress, Bradley." Darren smiled at him. "Everyone knows that Gina is a temperamental bitch. It's common knowledge she doesn't play well with others."

Brad the Security Guy nodded. Maybe he wasn't completely pacified by this response, but he didn't ask any more annoying questions. Darren didn't think he would; the front door on one of the events that Darren produced, even one on a crappy date, was still very lucrative.

The door to the VIP room opened a bit and Karen stuck her head out. "The doctor will see you now, Theo." She saw Eddie and Darren. "Boys!" She beamed a smile, coming halfway out the door, though being careful to keep it as closed behind her as possible, concealing the room's occupants and content. "Well, I guess we could squeeze you in as well. What do you think? Feeling all right? Need anything? A prescription perhaps?"

"We're wonderful, beautiful lady," Darren said, popping right into Mr. Charming mode, "and a check-up is never a bad idea."

"Come right in then, Blondie." She stepped aside a bit. "I think I've got a rectal thermometer around here somewhere."

Theo and Eddie laughed and trotted inside. Darren sauntered in after them, sharing a moment with Brad the Security Guy as they rolled their eyes in unison.

†

The demon giggled a little when Nick asked again for his name. That was the only description Nick could come up with for the sound, even though it was a little weird to think of a demon giggling.

The demon, or illusion or whatever, certainly was amused, though. That was obvious. Nick had apparently tripped over some major, primordial joke. A demon's true name was apparently a very big deal. If you knew a demon's name then you had him by the balls, so to speak.

The demon wouldn't tell Nick his true name, of course. However, he said he had no problem listing a few of the names that had been assigned to him by various mortal sources over the years. Although, he couldn't really be sure if they were just for him.

Due to the rarity of an entity's undisguised manifestation, mortals tended to get them all mixed up. They'd name the same entity several times by mistake and often assign the same name to different demons, generally getting them completely and hopelessly confused with each other.

"The Beast and Beelzebub, for example," the demon explained, "have commonly been thought to be references to a single entity. The truth is, though, they're very separate beings."

"Really?" Nick asked.

"Yes.   Both were very powerful seraphim before The Fall. Beelzebub was among the first to band with the Beast, and stood as a very convincing example for others."

Because they couldn't see them, or they were more truly what the demon called "selectively observant," mortals were left naming demons in very creative, although ultimately human, ways. The most common was based upon the demon's behavior or perceived actions. If there was a plague, for instance, and someone decided it was the work of a demon, they might give that demon a name that reflected the earthly results of the demon's attentions, such as Bringer of Death, or Bearer of Boils.

"Or, 'The Sniffling, Sneezing, Coughing, Aching, Stuffy Head, Herald of the Migraine?' " Obviously, Nick was still very messed up.

"Sure," the demon agreed.   "My, what a terrifying monster that would be."

"Or how about 'The Super Duper Way Sarcastic Bitchy Bossy Batman?"

"That's only my formal title."

They laughed a little bit together. Nick had no trouble imagining that a demon would laugh outright, as opposed to giggling, but he was surprised, however, it was such a pleasant sound.

An action-based name would mark the demon's work and at the same time allow them to be remembered and blamed. Humans would name the individual demon they thought was responsible for a plague, even though it might have been the work of several.

"Or none at all?" Nick asked.

"No," the creature answered.   "Where there is plague, there are demons."

Another way demons were named was based upon their assumed individual area of residence, such as The Hall of Cocytus, or Hell's Mountain.

However, the final and most efficient way a demon was named, was through clairvoyance. "Through those who can see," said the demon. "Those mortals who have been blessed with that sight and have chosen to use it."

"You mean psychics?"

"No. They don't have to be psychic. Just clairvoyant."

"I thought that they —"

"No, they're not the same. Clairvoyant means 'clear seeing'. Nothing more."

"And they would know your real names?"

"No. It's possible for them to discover the manner in which some entities might refer to each other or how a few are addressed individually by the angels, but no, not our 'real' names."

"So, you guys have to use fake names?"

"It's not like that. These people, these clairvoyants, they might have some limited understanding of our world or the ability to recognize us even when we're not in our true form. They may hear any number of demons addressed, and record the name, and it would be the one that belonged to that demon. But it would not be a name of power they would hear. It would not be the demon's true name. That is another matter completely and would take time to explain."

"Well, then what's the name that other demons call you, or whatever, and isn't the one that would freak you out?"

"I'm afraid I won't tell you that either."

"Oh, come on!" Nick slapped his knee. "Why not?"

"Although that name wouldn't entitle you to possess any genuine power, it would allow you to identify me to those who did."

"And I guess that would suck for you?"

"Yes," he said quietly. "Although, it could turn out to be most unpleasant for you as well."

The demon ended up rattling off a list of ancient nicknames instead of his own, true name. He recited names that had been, at one time or another, assigned to him by people. He didn't mention anything given to him or used by any divine source. He didn't mention anything of power.

There were quite a few nicknames, each of which in what Nick thought were very old languages, such as Hebrew, Greek, Latin, and even what the demon identified as Sumerian. There weren't any names in English, to say nothing of Contemporary American English. The demon said that no one had thought to give him any new names for quite a while. English was a relatively new language, in the overall span of mortal history, and he'd yet to be labeled with it. He only had English translations of names from older languages.

Finally, Nick stopped him and asked what name mortals had most often used to identify him. The long list of appellations had begun to blur together. Nick was getting a headache and finding it difficult to concentrate. What he really wanted to do was think about getting up and out of the alley, maybe think about going home.

Nick hadn't even really planned on going out that evening, but Darren had been insistent. Nick originally wanted to stay home with a book and a pint of sorbet, maybe rent a movie. Though, whatever the components that might have allowed the situation in which Nicholas now found himself, sitting in a dark alley in the most desolate hours of the morning, it was happening and he had to deal with it.

Despite the creature's assertions, Nick still told himself that he was speaking with a drug-induced delusion. It was simply the least dangerous explanation. He'd had mild auditory hallucinations before. Though, his previous experiences were nothing more than very faint and barley distinguishable whispers, a jangle of separate monologues from very far away, or the subtle white noise that haunted the silence of his bedroom whenever he'd spent the night with Kelly, happily snorting-up too much of her special magic. Those sounds were obviously the residual effect of the chemical and so familiar by now as to be almost entertaining. He'd lie there and listen to them as he tried to go to sleep. He'd listen to the tangle of voices, some distant, others right there in the bedroom, seeming to come magically out of the ceiling. Nick would listen to these phantom voices, but he could never make out anything the voices might actually be saying.

This experience tonight, however, was altogether new and unexpected. There was only the single voice and Nick could not only understand every word, but he was answering back and the voice was responding to his answers. Nick wasn't just listening to the sound of the drugs leaving his mind; he was having a conversation. The voice was very clear and it even sounded as though it was coming from just a few feet away, out of the darkness, right where he had thought he'd seen the wings. It was a very convincing package, as hallucinations went, Nick thought.

Nick only considered for a moment that maybe it might just be another person in the alley with him, that maybe it was just someone messing around. For that to be true, it would have to have been someone who happened to be sitting in the blackness of a Hollywood alley at eleven-thirty at night, holding or wearing some fake, though very convincing, giant bat wings—which he'd maybe gotten from some movie studio somewhere—and telling random strangers that he was a demon. However, Nick just wasn't sober enough to allow himself to accept that possibility. It would have meant major trouble. Specifically, it would have meant that he'd spent the past almost sixty minutes sitting and speaking with a complete lunatic. That would have meant there was real danger, which would require real, immediate, and coherent, not only thought, but action. He was far from ready for such an idea. It was better to stick with the hallucination concept for now; it didn't get his heart racing so fast.

Sitting in the tiny portion of dim light that managed to seep into the entrance of the alley, Nick hoped he wouldn't be conspicuous to any passing cars, but not so obscured that Darren couldn't eventually find him if he did end up passing out. He was wishing that he'd driven, instead of riding with Darren. If he'd driven himself to the club, Nick could have endured his chemical error without worrying about barfing in Darren's new BMW. He could have relaxed in the relative safety of his own familiar car instead of suffering delusions alone in the night.

It was very dark, even with the halogens from the street. Actually, Nick thought it was beyond very dark. There in the alley, further than the line of shadow, it was like a fog of blackness. Nick couldn't get his mind away from that idea. A fog of blackness. Then he corrected himself. The only fog was in his head, which was certainly also the source of this mystery voice.

"I'll answer your question and do you one better," said the voice/demon/lunatic. "I'll tell you the name with which I've most often been addressed, as well as the one that I believe is the most appropriate, as they happen to be the same."

"All right," Nick said.

"For three centuries I was almost convinced that 'Exousia Skotos' was uttered by the faithful from the Aegean Sea to beyond the Judean Desert in order to put a name to me, and me alone."

"Skotos." Nick whispered it back. Just saying the word chilled him.

"It's Greek," the voice offered.

Nick waited a moment, not sure what to say next. Was Exousia his first name? Was it a title? Should he call him Mr. Skotos? Nick had no idea where to go from there, so of course he blurted the first tangible thought he could develop.

"Skotos kinda sounds like 'Scott.'"

"Scott?" The demon sounded amused again. Nick went with it.

"Yeah. Why not? It could be your first English name." Nick was talking out his butt, of course. He had no idea if the name Scott was English or not. For all he knew, it could have been Chinese.

As the delusion waited somewhere in the blackness, as Nick sat simply trying to breathe, almost feeling its gaze, he had an abrupt and sickening insight. It was a sense of his own terrible insignificance, like a dreadful weight, a black and ancient curtain falling onto him, dark and smothering. He might have just been sobering up, but he was able to glimpse, for only a brief second, still another possibility. He glimpsed the possibility that the voice in the alley might not be coming from his head or from another person at all. He was able to consider for an instant with whom, or with what, he might actually be speaking.

Nick suffered what he would later describe as an eternal instant. It was as though the expanse of infinity itself blossomed for the briefest of moments. This happened as the recognition of speaking directly to an entity from the very dimension of divinity presented itself to him as a possible reality.

He was ultimately able, once again, to dismiss the notion as comical. Though, he noticed with trepidation that it was getting more and more difficult to do that. The smile fell from his face.

"I guess if you haven't been given a name for a while," Nick muttered to the illusion as he fumbled to believe himself, "then Scott is as good as any."

There was no immediate answer. Nick shivered again, though he thought it was probably from the wind through the narrow space. Had there been more wind? He looked around, but didn't see anything; no trash, no discarded gum or Big Mac wrappers, nothing to give away any movement in the air. Even if there'd been a breeze, it wouldn't have been cold. Not in Los Angeles in late August. Still, he crossed his arms and rubbed his hands over his skin to fight the chill.

He thought he could feel the wall vibrating slightly with the beat from the music in the club on the next block. He was grateful he'd settled on the cardboard remains of a crumpled box and not on the pavement itself. At least there wasn't any oil or worse on his pants. Maybe the delusion didn't know anything about the maintenance of designer club-wear anyway. Nick was hoping he'd be able to find a good drycleaner who could rescue his pants. He was also hoping he'd find the strength to get up soon, before Darren got too worried and decided to look for him.

"Do you know anyone named Scott?" the voice came again.

Nick closed his eyes and clenched his teeth at the sound. He couldn't figure out exactly how long he'd been there or been talking to himself. As hallucinations went, this one was beyond intense. Nick was tired and wanted to go home. He took another deep breath and strained at forcing himself to get a grip.

The voice of the demon was a gentle baritone. Nick thought it even had a slight dialect. He didn't like to travel much, not lately anyway, but from what the creature had told him about his name, he assumed its accent was also Mediterranean. He smiled at the thought of having a delusion that had been imported for him all the way from Greece.

"Are you awake?" the voice asked.

"No," Nick blurted. "I mean, yes, I'm awake. No, I don't know anyone named Scott."

"Well," the demon said, "now I suppose you do."

†

Troy leaned over the table in the corner of the VIP room, carefully measuring out some crystal meth for Eddie. Theo was a little distracting, dancing seductively by himself between the couch and the table. Darren was relaxing on the room's sofa with his head in Karen's lap. He looked lost. He looked lost in her lap. Karen was running her fingers through Darren's hair, starting her perfectly manicured nails above his eyebrows, then sliding them through his thick hair to the back of his skull. Darren probably wouldn't have been able to move if he'd wanted to.

Theo looked quite happy as well. Troy knew from experience that it didn't take much to put that gorgeous boy on the moon. Just twenty minutes after swallowing the little white pill Troy had sold to him, Theo began rubbing his hands together, breathing in deep, sumptuous breaths, and rolling his head around with his eyes at half-mast. The moon had a new visitor.

Troy didn't usually bring anything to sell while he was at the club. However, Karen had told him she anticipated some special company from San Francisco. She practically begged Troy to come with a load of supplies for them. Karen hadn't been all that sure of exactly what her San Francisco guests would want, but she had a pretty good idea and provided Troy with a little list.

When her guest's plane was delayed the first time, and they called from the airport, Karen told Troy that they were still optimistic about being able to get into LAX, shuttle to West Hollywood, check-in, change, and still be at the club before things really got moving.

The second time they called they weren't in quite as good a mood and were considerably less optimistic. Although they were still stuck at San Francisco's airport, they were relatively sure they'd make it to LA that night, and confirmed with Karen that they *really* wanted something worth while waiting for them when they finally got to the club. They'd need something to lift their spirits.

Karen hadn't been around to take their third call, but she told Troy that as soon as she heard the frustration in the voices recorded on the club's voice mail system, along with the airport sounds in the background, she knew she needed to figure out how to get Troy unloaded, or he was going to be pissed. She'd said she knew that Troy would be somewhat irritated, to put it mildly, and she totally understood.

Normally, Troy conducted all of his pharmaceutical business out of one of his homes. Specifically, his gorgeous apartment in the Wilshire district. Troy's building boasted the past residence of the likes of Elizabeth Taylor and Katherine Hepburn—if you believed the property manager and two of the far-too-chummy nighttime security guys. The building had beautiful hardwood floors in every unit and hallway, a very rickety elevator, still with it's manually-operated iron gate, and a lobby security desk, occupied twenty-four hours a day by very old, and very bored, retired men who, for one reason or another, felt much more comfortable sleeping behind the security desk of Troy's building than at their homes.

Troy's pharmaceutical business apartment was fairly lavish, and furnished with the kind of trappings one could also find in Troy's little furniture store at Beverly and La Brea. One could almost fall asleep in the ever-so-comfy living room, sitting on the luscious antique sofa, or in his way, way comfy designer chair, while waiting for Troy to finish bagging a freshly weighed eight ball of either coke or crystal for whoever had gotten there first. One could fall asleep, if not for the normal two or three additional 'customers' seated there as well, patiently waiting for Troy to stick his head out of the bedroom and say, "Next."

Troy Hawthorne was fairly young and, as yet, relatively untouched by the ravages of either time or indulgence. How he'd managed to create such an enterprise to finance not only his demanding lifestyle, but also a chain of esoteric baby businesses was a mystery to all. But why should they care? Really, as long as he was functioning for the benefit of all concerned, why should anyone care how he did it?

Usually, to purchase any party chemicals from Troy, it had to be at his place, there had to be a telephone call first to let him know the individual was on their way, and he had to know said individual personally. One never just *brought* someone along with them over to Troy's place that he didn't know. One never just *showed* up. Plus, one never approached him outside of his home in search of any kind of transaction, unless it only involved a floor lamp, a maybe some end tables.

Tonight, for Karen, he'd made an exception. First of all, Troy and Karen were very close friends, but that wasn't even one of the top two reasons. When the manager of the biggest club in Los Angeles called and begged for a really big, big, big, big, favor, and then started pleading in her Helpless-Little-Girl voice, it was very difficult to refuse her anything. Still, that wasn't even the primary reason he'd obliged her.

Troy couldn't imagine how many helpless little girls would ask him to bring a sample platter of ecstasy, crystal meth, cocaine, GHB, and Special K, and he *should* have refused. Troy should have known that something was going to go wrong. As soon as he stepped out of his apartment he'd felt as though he had the words *Intent to Sell* tattooed smack in the center of his forehead in luminous lavender.

After he'd been sitting in the back-bar lounge for a half an hour, and still hadn't seen any sign of Karen, Troy knew he should have refused. Then, when she'd finally come clicking across the dance floor and sat down with him wearing her Stupid-Standard-Hostess smile, cocked her head, and said, "There's been a little glitch," Troy should have said, "Of course there has," and run straight for his car.

But, no. No, instead Troy had let Karen talk him into offering what he'd brought with him to Theo and the gang in lieu of the stranded San Francisco boys. Sure, he already knew Theo, Nick, Darren, and Eddie. Sure, they all had his super-secret pharmaceutical business number. Sure, he thought they were the hottest things walking, and sure, he'd even seen one of them that very afternoon, but this just wasn't his normal procedure, and it all made his palms sweat. However, Troy had decided not to be a jerk, to aim for a more Zen perspective, and was therefore trying to roll with it.

"Darren," he chirped from the corner, "do you want a baggie?"

"No, baby, I'm cool." Darren didn't lift his head from Karen's lap or even open his eyes.

"You sure?"

"Hey don't pressure me, man!" Darren mock wept.

Troy grinned. Darren was a good guy. Darren was a funny guy, as well as a hot-as-motherfucking-shit guy. In fact, all three of these boys were quite an eyeful.

Actually, Troy knew Theo quite intimately. Who didn't? They'd gotten to know each other one lazy Sunday afternoon. Troy had been in no frame of mind to go around remembering where he'd first seen anyone, and he sure-as-shit didn't realize who he'd brought back to his apartment until both of their pants were practically off. That's when he'd made the connection between the muscle boy on his couch and several of the DVDs stacked next to the television in his bedroom. No big deal. He'd let the guy work out some of his energy, express some of Miss Tina's influence. At least for a little while anyway. Who'd know? Troy didn't need to ask him out on a date afterwards or anything.

Now, Eddie and Darren were another story altogether. Darren Jacobson was beautiful beyond reason. Seeing him with Eddie Thornton, who was a no-shit, walking-magazine-cover, was only a vision outdone by seeing Darren with Nicholas Reynolds, who, in Troy's opinion, was god-glorious, hands-down the most beautiful man he'd ever seen in person, print, or on screen, praise Heaven above us, glory to the Lord, halleluiah!

Nick was the only person on whom Troy'd ever had such an enormous crush. He knew, however, that he had a snowball's chance in you-know-where to actually land someone like the immaculate Nicholas Reynolds. Therefore, Troy opted instead to simply shoot for the barely attainable goal of remaining conscious while in Nick's presence.

Nick appeared to Troy like one of those guys who maybe knew he had it majorly goin' on, but then again, just maybe didn't. He wasn't gorgeous in a 'constructed' kind of way, like just so many other boys in this part of the world—and, oh Becky, wasn't that the truth—but maybe just in a 'moderately manipulated,' kind of way.

Nick had very light, sandy brown hair, cut very short in a haphazard, natural-ish style that could have been done in ten minutes at Fantastic Sam's, but on him looked like a four-hundred dollar job sheared on location in Barcelona by Creighton himself. Nick's eyes were a luminous hazel with what Troy would describe as a genuine twinkle—if Troy were a total dork and used words like 'twinkle.' Nick had a very modest deportment, which was first introduced to his admirers by his five-foot-ten stature, and then it was driven home because he really *was* modest.

Still, a couple parts of Nick did appear to Troy as though they'd been distinctly planned and managed: his teeth and his physique. Firstly, although charming, Nick's smile was an obvious rendition in porcelain veneers. Secondly, even though he'd never win any muscle man contests, Nick's torso was certainly, what Troy called, 'sculpted.'

Troy normally had to make sure he was holding onto something so he wouldn't swoon when Nick took his shirt off on the dance floor. Nick's chest seemed to be just a touch too big to be supported by his little waist; two perfectly rounded pectorals with those big, flat nipples that looked as though they'd been painted on.

Practically hairless below his chin, and always with a soft, casual tan, Nick could have been twenty-two years old, or thirty-two years old, or frickin' nineteen, jeez-Louise, what kind of motherfucking moisturizer did he use?

Nicholas "Nicky" Reynolds was one of those guys who easily achieved the Fresh-College-Athlete-Who-*Could*-Be-Straight look that so many of the West Hollywood masses spent so much time and so much money attempting to attain. Some of the WeHo masses came close to succeeding with that look. Some of them managed to scrape by, but most fell far, far short. The thing was, with a look like that, you either had it, or you didn't. It simply could not be purchased at The Beverly Center.

What made it all worse, though, what gave the whole weapon of Nick's appearance such a sharp edge as to slice Troy's heart to shreds, was that, in addition to his heavenly form, he was genuinely nice. Believe it or not, former male supermodel Nicholas Reynolds was as nice as the day was long.

Without doubt, all the WeHo residents truly expected a guy who looked like Nick to be the queen of the egotistical bitches. In fact, they hoped for it, they *needed* it, as such a characteristic instantly brought a person of Nick's physical beauty back down to a human level. It would pull them right off of Olympus, planting them squarely back into the mortal plain. Nick Reynolds, however, to the absolute disappointment of many a wannabe circuit-stud, was nowhere near aloof, or stuck-up, or spoiled, or any of the other standard labels that every jealous brat who ever caught Nick's passing likeness would have loved more than anything to slap on him. He was polite and genuine and quiet and sweet. Troy, right along with everyone else who ever met Nick, just about got a toothache from merely talking to him.

Nick had to know that he was no ugly boy—duh—but talking to him, listening to his deep—okay, *somewhat* deep—husky purr, while he smiled, nodded at Troy's points, laughed at even his most meagerly passing humor, couldn't for a second lead Troy to believe that Nick was even close to being aware of just how beautiful he really was, or just how much Troy ached from the very center of his soul at the mere glimpse of him.

Yup, Troy had the most incredible crush on—or obsession with, whatever—Nick, and was more than a little disappointed that he wasn't with the group at the moment. Troy was downright pissed, actually.

He'd seen him that afternoon, however, at which time Nick had mentioned he'd be at the club tonight, which, truth be told, was the second and most compelling reason Troy had been so obliging with Karen. Frankly, it was the sole reason he'd shown up at all.

Seeing Darren and Nick together was only outdone by seeing the two of them with Eddie Thornton thrown in for good measure, which happened all the time, which drove Troy completely nuts, because no one seemed to know the whole story, or even anything even remotely credible. Was Nick's boyfriend either Darren or Eddie, or was he single, or what?

Troy had thought about asking Nick that very question earlier that day, as Nick sat on Troy's couch in Troy's living room, waiting to purchase the two ounces of GHB Troy was pouring into a little bottle in the bedroom, and the gram of cocaine he was weighing. Okay, he'd thrown in a little extra, which he never ever never did for anyone, not even Theo, who blew Troy fairly regularly. It was Troy's little way of making up for the fact that he knew, despite the major detail that Nick had been alone with him in his own home, that he'd never work up the balls to say anything to Nicholas besides, *Here you go. Thank you very much. Please come again.*

So, the extra powder was Troy's little secret love message, which clearly said, *My god, you're the hottest guy I've ever seen, and even though I'm a hopeless mutt, please notice me and also possibly love me!*

Besides, before Troy could even finish all the necessary compound measurements, he'd gotten the call from the desk that there were two more guys on their way up to see him, guys who'd made appointments days ago. Maybe Troy used it as an excuse not to be assertive, or maybe he didn't want Nick to see just how big a dealer he really was—a detail about which Troy was quite proud around some people and quite reluctant to divulge around others, go figure—but he'd quickly finished measuring Nick's stuff, answered the door, seated the new-comers in the study, quoted some arbitrary (and low) amount to Nick, collected the cash, and then rushed him out the door.

Anyway, they hardly ever talked to Troy, the tantalizing trio, Darren, Eddie, and Nick, much less gave him any indication that there was any chance he'd ever spend any kind of leisure time with them. Not Theo-style time, at least. Not any style, more likely.

Troy was their dealer, their supply line. If he wasn't that, then he knew they'd never look at him more than once, if at all. He was no muscle boy, nowhere near their aesthetic genre. Troy was so skinny he could move through a crowded dance floor without ever having to say, "Excuse me," which kind of came in handy, actually.

Troy sighed, being careful not to blow any of the freshly measured meth off the table, and looked at Darren where he lay in Karen's lap.

Troy wondered what was up. Was Nick Darren's boyfriend or pal or love-slave or what? The question made Troy's neck itch.

Darren was apparently lost to the world at the moment. He was obviously riding very well on the stuff he'd gotten from Troy last weekend. Karen knew how to work it and seemed to somehow get off on tripping up the ecstasy boys.

"He's so cute," Troy heard Karen observe. She was referring to Theo, who was quite happily doin' the funky-boogie by himself.

"I swear he just followed me home," Darren said without opening his eyes. "Can I keep him?"

"Sure, honey." She grinned. "But you have to feed him."

"That's the way, baby!"

"But, if he's bad, I get to spank him."

Theo shot her a grin, but kept dancing. He had to test out the gravity on his new planet.

"So, Darren, honey," she started, "what's with the 'totally gay' thing?"

"Don't fuck with me, Karen," Darren whined. Troy perked up. This was getting interesting.

She rubbed her hands across his torso. "I mean, just feel this chest. Not too small, not too big. Well, maybe a little big. And these abs! You bastard, I could do my laundry on these abs of yours."

"No, I tried that when I ran out of quarters. I got a rash from the fabric softener."

"Oh, and I heard…" She slipped her hand underneath his shirt and slid her nails down his stomach to the top of his pants, running them along the belt line. Troy held his breath and lost his jaw. "I heard," Karen purred, "that you're pretty blessed—"

"Easy, Tigress!" Darren laughed and grabbed her hand. "I'm ticklish!"

Troy exhaled.

"You're a tease." Karen pouted. Troy thought she sounded like she needed a bump.

"You know, Karen," Troy said, about to give away his eavesdropping, "how many guys have called *you* a tease when you wouldn't fuck 'em?"

She sighed. "All of them, I guess."

Darren lifted his head off the arm of the couch. "You mean *both* of them?"

She slapped his stomach.

"Motherfuck, knock it off!" He laughed, though. "Do I need to get up? You were being so nice. Are you going to be nice?"

"Shhhh! Fine, asshole. Shut up." Karen pouted some more, but then ran her fingers tenderly across his head.

Darren gasped and lay back down.

"Men just so overwhelmingly totally suck," she said.

"That's the way, baby!" Darren crooned.

"Where's Nicky, anyway?"

"Sweetie, I really don't know."

"He told me earlier that you'd talked him into coming tonight."

"Yeah, he's here." Darren sighed. "But I hardly twisted his arm."

"Did Nick come with you?" Troy asked. "How come he's not in here?"

"I dunno, man. His leash broke and I totally lost track of him. Hey, Troy, you didn't see him this afternoon, did you?"

"Yeah, why?"

Darren sat bolt upright, his eyes abruptly the size of wall clocks. "When?"

Oh, shit. Troy had messed up. He stopped what he was doing and looked at Darren, feigning in surprise. Theo stopped dancing and Eddie suddenly went pale.

"What's up, Darren?" Troy asked stupidly.

"How much did you sell him?"

"Darren, you know I'm not going to—"

"How much, Troy! Don't tell me you don't know what I'm talking about, or give me that little 'privileged information' crap you like to play, or whatever! You're not Sam Waterston!"

Troy waived him off and went back to what he was doing. He didn't put up with Darren when he tried to show off his testosterone.

"Huff and puff all you want, Darren," Troy said, pleased with the serenity in his voice. "You know the rules. Nick's a big boy."

"Troy, did you fucking tell him that Gina and Kelly don't get along?"

"He didn't—" Troy caught himself. "I would have told him whatever he needed to know."

"I'll bet."

Theo looked very confused. "Darren, I thought you said—"

"Thelma, please shut up." Darren closed his eyes and pressed his fingers to his temples. "Really, I don't want to be mean or anything, but just stop, okay?" He stood, then went to sit next to Eddie. Theo replaced him on the couch next to Karen.

"Come here, baby," she cooed at him as he lay down in Darren's old spot. "He's a mean ol' meanie."

"Shut up, Karen," Theo said, laying his head in her lap.

"Theo, honey…" Karen grabbed a healthy chunk of Theo's hair. "I love you and everything, but I'm going to shove this coffee table right up your cute little ass if you ever talk to me like that again, all right?"

Theo stared at her for a moment. "Okay. I'm sorry."

She let go of his hair and started running her fingers through it instead. "That's okay, sweetie," she cooed. "You know you're my big muscle-muffin. You just spend too much time around big blondie dickhead over there, that's all."

Darren stood up again. "Eddie, what did Nick tell you?" he asked, pacing. He was going to try to get what he wanted out of Eddie. Troy just started putting all his little baggies away and didn't even look at him.

"I told you," Eddie said. "Nick told me that he wanted to try and hook up with Gina."

Troy saw Darren staring at him out of the corner of his eye.

"Don't even ask it, Darren," he said, not looking up. "If it were you, you'd kick my ass."

"Troy, this is a little important," Darren huffed. "I bumped him up with Kelly earlier and I haven't seen him since."

Troy stopped. Some people could mix Kelly with Gina and have no problem. Most people got violently ill. Some required medical attention.

"Troy?" Darren was going to push this.

"I don't know, Darren." Troy still wouldn't look at him. He wanted to get everything put away and then maybe rush it all home. "How much did he do?"

"A bump or two."

"Or…?"

"Fuck, Troy!" Darren spun on his heal, rolling his eyes. "He was pissing me off! I just handed it to him. I didn't fucking count anything!"

Troy carefully folded the big plastic baggie that held all of the little plastic baggies and put the whole sterile jumble inside his little nylon pouch. He zipped it up, popped it under his shirt, and slipped it snugly inside the front of his pants.

He looked at Darren. "Maybe we should all take a nice walk then."

†

"Why can't I see you?" Nick asked.

"It might be dangerous," Scott answered. "And I don't think you'd want to."

"How do you know that?"

"I'm almost four-thousand years old. I've picked up a thing or two."

"Oh, I understand." Nick nodded. "You haven't been taking care of your skin. I guess I wouldn't want to be seen either."

"Once you've seen me like this, you cannot un-see me. It could change you. There could be additional consequences as well."

"I think I have some Olay Sunscreen in the —" Nick had a sudden stabbing pain just beneath his ribs. His breath caught in his chest and he gagged as he tried to inhale.

"Nicholas?" Scott said.

Nick started to cough, and it hurt. He rolled over onto his knees and hung his head very close to the ground, clutching his chest and wheezing painfully.

"Nicholas?"

He couldn't answer him. Nick was barely catching his breath. He closed his eyes and winced against the pain. There was a tiny fire in his chest and it was all he could feel. For the moment, it was all there was. He gasped in a breath, and another, held it, but the pain burst forth and he coughed harder. He screamed as the fire ripped up from his stomach and exploded in his throat.

"Nicholas, what's happening?"

Nick coughed again, winced; the pain was not subsiding. He rested his forehead on the pavement and began to cry. "I don't know," he managed, feeling drops of moisture fall from his lip. "It just hurts."

"Can you breathe?"

"Yeah, a little." Tears began to run down his face. He opened his eyes and watched one fall to the cement and mix there with blood.

Nick raised his head a bit. There was blood on the pavement in front of him. He looked at his hands. There was blood there too.

"Oh, my god…" he said.

"Nick you have to try to stay calm—"

"It's blood. It's coming from me—"

"I know."

"What do you mean?" he wailed.

"I can see it."

"There's blood coming from me! Oh, my god, what's happening?"

"Nicholas… Nick… you have to calm down. You're going to make it worse."

"What do I do? Oh, my god, what do I do? I have to get up…" He started to look around. He needed something to hold, something on which to pull himself up.

"Nick, don't move. If you try to stand you will fall and you will die where you land."

"Oh, god!" Nick flopped back over against the wall. He couldn't tell before in the dim florescent light, but his pants had blood on them. He pulled his shirt away from his body and it was soaked in it.

"Did you know? Did you see this? Smell—?"

"Yes. I'm so sorry. I did, Nicholas. I'm so sorry I didn't tell you, but it wasn't very bad at first. It wasn't bad, and… well, I wasn't quite sure what to do about it. I didn't want to panic you. You were really in no condition to be walking around. Frankly, I didn't think you could stand. You were even unconscious for a couple of minutes—"

"What?"

"Yes." Scott sighed. "You were unconscious. You passed out about thirty minutes ago, while I was listing my names. Just for two or three minutes. But then you suddenly woke up and started asking questions again. You asked me what I'm most often called. I wanted to keep you from moving around and making things worse. If you'd gotten up and fallen, or wandered into the street—"

"Oh, my god—"

"Your first cough, a moment ago, it was much worse than any of the others. It sent up most of the blood. Now, though… now you have to sit still. You can't try to move. You will fall and you will not be able to get back up. Maybe in a minute or two—"

"Oh, motherfuck, Scott, what's happening? What do I do?"

"Stop. Just breathe a moment. Don't panic—"

"I'm dying! Oh, fucking crap, I'm dying here, in this sewer!"

"Nick, you have to stop. You have to calm down!"

"Do something! Can't you do something?"

"I cannot."

"Oh, fuck this!" Nick was beginning to sob. He felt the pain start to build. He was lightheaded. The pavement hadn't stopped moving and he was very aware that he couldn't tell if he was still sitting up.

"Scott, what's happening? Scott, help me—"

"You cannot ask that of me! Do not ask that! I cannot help you!"

"Why the fuck not?" Nick screamed, though it burned his throat. He could feel the blood running down his chin. "Do something, you fuck!"

"I have no power." Scott's voice was flat, anguished. "I'm so sorry, Nick. I have no way to help you. There is nothing I can do."

"Oh, motherfuck!" Nick squeezed his eyes shut. "I'm dying in a sewer and begging a mirage—"

"I am not a hallucination, Nicholas. You must calm down now."

"Oh, right! What're you gonna do? Eat me? Fuck off!"

"I have no power to help you. I am so sorry, Nicholas. I'm sorry. There is nothing I can do."

"You're really nothing then. You're really not here. It doesn't matter anyway. You have no power. You're nothing! You're a hologram from my head!" He coughed again, fresh blood ran down his face. Nick wiped at a tear and smeared blood and slime across his cheek.

"I have to be *given* power," Scott said quietly. "It has to be offered to me. Power must be offered to me freely, once I've lost it. It doesn't take much, and it lasts for some time, but I've been fighting and…" He grunted. "You just need to relax for a moment."

"You're a fake! You're a fake from my head and this is going to kill me, isn't it?"

"Nicholas—"

"What does it take?" he screamed. "What does it take for you to help me? Have you just been sitting there waiting for me to die? Why have you been talking to me? Why didn't you just kill me?"

"Nicholas, no, I didn't—"

"You fuck! Just do it! Just kill me! Get on with it, you freak!"

"Nicholas, that is not my way. I will not kill you and I cannot help you. I'm sorry." There was a rumble of gravel beyond the threshold of the darkness. "I'm so sorry."

"Why not?" Nick cried. "Why can't you do something? I thought you were a demon! I'll bet you've been sitting there just waiting for me to die!"

"Don't be a fool."

"Oh, my god, help me!" Nick was panting, rolling his head from side to side.

"You do not know what you are asking."

"Help me, you freak!" He coughed violently, clutching his chest. When it was over he saw all the blood. He felt his mouth. The blood was beginning to fill his mouth. He retched, vomiting a torrent of bile and blood onto the cement.

"You have to understand what you're doing." Scott's deep voice rolled out of the shadow. "This is not a game. You must listen to what you're saying. You have to know in your mind and your heart that you are facing a demon and asking its help."

"What?" Nick grimaced. His chest was on fire, an agony. His breaths were short and horrible. "What then? Then you take my soul, or something?"

"No." Scott grunted. "No, that's not my way. I do not need your soul or anything from you but your request. I will not harm you. I will not take your soul. I am not the Beast."

"Scott, what is this?" Nick tried to lay his head against the wall— maybe it was the ground, he couldn't tell. "Is this a trick? Did you know this was going to happen? Did you do this?"

"Nick, please. No. I did not know. I knew there was the chance… I thought you should rest, that there was a chance…"

Nick's chest burst with fire. He screamed and blood flew from his mouth. He began to cough and to vomit and there was blood everywhere. He doubled over onto the ground and wrapped his arms around his stomach. His body cramped and tore with pain. The blood was pouring in a thin stream from his mouth. He shut his eyes tight and began to sob.

"Nick!" Scott shouted.

Nick couldn't answer him. He couldn't breath. The pain lunged and gripped his heart. He felt the fire rage from his stomach, rip through his chest, and tear up his throat. A fresh pool of blood filled his mouth and he spit it out. It splattered onto the cardboard beneath him, running off onto the pavement. Nick collapsed into it.

He rested his head on the ground. The pain was going away. The fire was going out. He was drooling blood into the dry cement gutter.

"Scott?" Nick could barely whisper.

A breeze touched his face. Nick could smell the ocean and a campfire. It was sweet and dark.

"Yes, Nicholas," Scott answered calmly.

"Help me."

Nick closed his eyes. He heard a great fluttering, and a wind as warm as summer, a warm, summer gale, blew over him. The wind blew the thoughts from him, blew the fear from him. He relaxed.

Someone turned him gently onto his back. Someone touched his face softly, stroked the hair from his eyes and the tears from his cheek. Someone lifted his head in their hand.

Nick opened his eyes. There was a man kneeling over him. He appeared to be near Nick's own age, with hair to his shoulders, very wavy dark hair, thick and blacker than the night behind him. The man's eyes were as blue as the sky in a dream, shining as if they were a light unto themselves.

Nick was shocked. Shocked and surprised at both the unquestionable presence of him and at how beautiful he was.

"Scott?" Nick barely breathed it.

"Shhh," the man whispered. "I'm here."

"Scott?"

"You're going to be fine. Everything is going to be fine."

He leaned down and placed a gentle kiss on Nick's forehead. Nick could feel the beautiful man's soft lips above his eyes, soft and tender. All of Nick's pain was gone. The pavement slipped away beneath him.

Nick was floating in a warm and delicious breeze, touched by the scent of a lazy campfire on the beach.

CHAPTER II

†

Demon Spit

What then? If some did not believe, does their unbelief nullify the faithfulness of God? Absolutely not! Let God be proven true, and every man a liar, just as it is written: "so that you might be justified in your words and will prevail when you are judged."

- Romans 3:3-4 (KJV)

Yorba Linda, California
A modest church, atop a small hill west of Imperial Highway, south of Buena Vista Avenue

†

The church sat facing a large sun-beaten parking lot, which, unlike most late Sunday afternoons, was filled to its limit. The funeral had started over an hour ago and Bishop Patrick had to park at the supermarket down the street and pray no one would tow his rented Hyundai Sonata.

He walked the half block to the church entrance and then up the steep driveway to the grounds, passing beneath the massive statue of Saint Sophia standing at the corner of the bluff and gazing majestically across the eastern sprawl of central Orange County, California.

The day was hot and clear. Just two visible clouds, sparse and thin, streamed from north to south, indicating there were winds high above, though offering no relief from the heat to those on the ground. With his briefcase in his hand and his blazer slung over his arm, the bishop trudged up the drive, hoping he wouldn't sweat so much as to soak his dark shirt or saturate his collar.

He waded through the pool of sparkling sedans, mini vans, and sport utility vehicles to the entrance of the church. Like so many suburban temples in Southern California, it was in a contemporary style with just the suggestion of Spanish influence. A single story structure, awnings of darkly stained wood, pronounced cobblestone walkways, heavy oak doors, and long brass doorknobs. The adjacent rectory, to the east of the main building, was a trailer unit, although the surrounding foliage was well tended, granting it a sense of solidity.

On the cobblestone path to the church entrance, underneath the main wooden awning and shadowed in rails from its slatted beams, stood a painter's easel on which was displayed an enlarged photograph of the deceased. It was taken during his sophomore year at USC, from what the bishop had been told. From it, the local boy gazed out at the silent, gleaming cars, as he smiled with the glow of the young and the faith of the innocent. Beneath the photograph, barely noticeable through the dense collection of resplendent bouquets, was his name in bold black letters, 'Alexander Richard Monroe'. He died two months shy of his twenty-second birthday. The circumstances of his death were both alarming and confusing, as well as the sole reason Bishop Patrick had traveled to this tiny part of the world.

The church's grand main doors, which had been closed to the heat, opened as the service ended and the mourners slowly began to file out. Robert couldn't have planned his arrival any better, unless he'd allowed himself more time to cool down before his meeting with Alex's parents.

He found a shaded spot between the church and the rectory where he could catch his breath and wipe his forehead with his handkerchief, out of the way of the exiting assemblage, before he had to put on his jacket. Bishop Patrick was a young man, only forty-one, and in excellent shape. Still, the jaunt up the little hill had winded him.

He heard the faint conversations of the gathering along with the quiet click of their shoes on the cobblestones, but the most conspicuous sound was from the sobbing still inside the chapel. The bulk of the assembly were very young adults, some in their late teens, but most in their very early twenties. A tragedy of this sort was always difficult to bear. When it involved the young, though, the promising innocent, it inevitably intensified the suffering.

They streamed outside, young men and women, still crying, their faces still reddened with the heat of their grief. They stood in groups of three and four, arms over and around each other, embracing, holding, giving and taking comfort. It was a far too familiar scene, one that Robert had been asked to endure far too many times. He found the same familiarity that had deadened his sympathy so long ago now fueled his anger.

"Bishop?" said a voice behind him.

He turned to see a short, older priest approaching along the walkway from the side exit. He wore no vestments, just black denim with a short-sleeved black button down shirt, and the white collar. He was bald but for some thin white hair circling the sides and back of his head. Thick bifocals rested at the very tip of his nose, which stood prominently above a broad and disarming smile.

"Yes, hello," the bishop answered, extending his hand while switching his jacket to his other arm. He was glad the priest wasn't wearing a blazer, as it meant he didn't have to worry about putting on his own.

The older man shook his hand. "I'm Father Talbert," he said. "Eric Talbert."

"Oh." Bishop Patrick was a little surprised. "I thought you'd be giving the service."

"No. Father Manning is close to the family and I thought it would be appropriate for him to say the mass. Besides, I wanted to catch you right away, Bishop."

"Please, call me Robert."

"Yes, yes," the shorter man said. "Robert."

"There was no need to watch out for me. I would have found you."

"Yes, yes, I'm sure, but I wanted to be certain to speak with you before the service was over."

"Is there a problem?"

"I don't know yet."

"I came as soon as I could."

"Yes, yes. Uh… could we go into the office? I'd just like to ask you a question or two, if I may."

"Of course."

Father Talbert turned and motioned for Robert to follow him around the side of the church. They stepped up over a small porch and into the hallway leading to the office. The air-conditioning was nothing short of heavenly.

"Father Talbert, forgive me, but the family..." Robert started. "Aren't they leaving for the cemetery right away?"

"They may. That's what I'd like to speak with you about. Please, come inside and sit down. I don't believe this will take very long."

They went up another two steps and Father Talbert unlocked the door of wood and smoked glass, on which was stenciled just the simple word 'Office.' The room itself was small and filled with stacks of un-filed folders and papers. A high-backed, leather swivel chair held dominance over the entire room from behind a single, humble desk. Two smaller, low-backed, though matching, chairs faced the desk. Two tall gray filing cabinets filled the far end of the cluttered room. The rest of the interior consisted of a long and disheveled bookcase and a small plaid sofa against the far wall, which seemed alarmingly out of place.

Everything was in pristine order despite being of obvious early eighties manufacture. There were two modern-ish items in the office: an Apple computer that looked as though it did little more than serve as a glorified calculator that could produce an occasional dot matrix letter or flyer, and a combination thirteen inch television/video cassette player.

"Please have a seat," said Father Talbert. He swept around the desk and landed in the swivel chair. "I know it looks like a mess in here, but I'm assured by our administrator that there's an intricate system at work."

"My office is no better," Robert lied. His office in New York was immense, lavish, and immaculate.

"I have to tell you, I didn't expect anyone to actually come in person."

"Well, the cardinal was very interested in the names—"

"Yes, yes. Uh… what I mean is, really, I didn't expect anyone this soon. I understand that the letter caused quite a little bit of commotion, but I didn't think for a moment that it would have been the catalyst of such, I assume, attention? You haven't actually taken any official action yet, have you?"

"No, not really." Robert tried to make himself comfortable in the small leather chair, finding a place to lay his briefcase on the desk. "Aside, of course, from coming here for the interview. As you know, there are some issues that, despite the seeming controversy, we must take very seriously. Especially—"

"I understand," Father Talbert said. "Although… uh, I'm just concerned about anyone speaking with the family this soon. Isn't there a way we can give them a chance to finish the day? Maybe even complete the burial and just get a chance to let all of this settle a bit? A day or two?" He raised his eyebrows. "Maybe a week?"

Robert was a bit startled. "What?"

"I think we should give the family some more time, Bishop Patrick."

"Father, it's very important that I be allowed to—"

"Yes, yes. Uh… Bishop Patrick—"

"Robert."

"Yes, yes, Robert. Uh … I'll just come right out and say it. I think that's probably going to be the best way. There's just no sense in beating around the bush, I guess. You see, this is a very touchy subject right now, for all of us, and we've been very careful not to make any assumptions or do anything drastic. Do you know what I'm trying to say?"

"Father?"

"Yes?"

"Please try and relax. I'm really not here to disrupt anything. "

"Yes, yes, thank you. The thing is, I really don't want you to speak with the family for quite a while."

"I'm sorry?"

"Actually, I'd be much happier if you didn't speak to the family at all."

"I don't understand."

"I don't want you to speak with the family at all." Father Talbert let out a breath of what Robert assumed was relief and retreated into his high-backed-nineteen-eighties-leather Chair of Power.

Robert nodded slowly and raised his eyebrows. "I see."

"The poor boy's body was just returned yesterday," Father Talbert began. "You must understand, there's been delay after delay because of the investigation in Los Angeles. Then with all the questions and intrusions here as well, I'm afraid the family is rather shaken. They don't know up from down. Alex's mother sat here this morning, before the service started, and just wept and wept. He's been gone since last month, but she just broke down, frantically, and well, near hysterics, I believe, and I'm afraid she's still simply too distraught to be very rational. The boy's father sat with her and was very supportive, of course, but he's quite, well, I'd say, uh... impassive. I suppose it could be from shock, even after this much time. In any case, I don't believe he'll be of much help either."

"Father, it was the family, Alex's mother in fact, who addressed the letter to Rome. She demanded the involvement of Cardinal Matine himself, whose interest—"

"Yes, yes, I know. I'm sorry about all that. The cardinal must have been at a loss, I imagine. As I said, Alex has been gone since July, *early* July, and there's been no word at all that anyone is any closer to understanding what happened. His poor mother insisted she didn't want to simply have a memorial, but that she wanted to wait until his body was here, which I couldn't understand, as there was no way they were going to be able to have an open casket, anyway."

"I know." Robert looked at his hands. "Donna talked to me briefly about that on the phone, but I didn't feel it was the really all that appropriate, over the telephone, that is, to—"

"His father had to identify him, you know. A few weeks ago. Even then, from what I understand, it wasn't a very easy thing to do. I thought it was horrible they had to ask him to do it at all. There must have been some other way. Then, the sensitivity of the authorities involved in all of this has been detestable, from what I understand. Imagine having to see your own child after such a thing. I suppose, when one falls from a height such as that, one can't expect to be able to—"

"Father Talbert," Robert interrupted. He was trying to be patient, to be nonchalant and easy with the little suburban priest, but his practiced comportment was being tested. "I came all this way because I felt it was important that I speak with the family immediately. I came as soon as I could. His mother invited me to the service, but I just didn't feel it was very proper that I attend. She's a sweet woman, but it might have been awkward. I never knew Alex, of course, and the chapel is filled with all these kids, all his friends. Be that as it may, I really would like to speak with Donna and Ted as soon as possible. As I explained to you on the phone this morning, they're expecting me. They've agreed to meet briefly before they go on to the cemetery."

"I understand," Father Talbert said. "But, uh... I can't imagine how they'd be at all helpful. I don't see how they could be. They don't understand anything about any of this. No one in the parish does. It's downright freakish, to be perfectly honest. Well, I'm sure you do, being who you are, and all, and seeing this sort of thing all the time, I suppose.

"And really, you know, the boy lived in Los Angeles and wasn't back here very often, from what I understand, even though it's no more than an hour drive.

"His parents were of absolutely no help to the police. The detective made that quite clear to me. Rather rudely, I might add. It's very possible... uh... more than very possible, I'd say, that they won't be able to offer you anything either. At least nothing that would be of any practical use. I was fairly certain you'd just want to view the tape, which you could have easily done from back east, couldn't you?"

"You have the tape then?" Robert didn't like where this was going. Usually, small town congregations were fairly bright models of faith and didn't give him any trouble. He liked that. He liked the faithful. He didn't like the city clergy, whom he considered to be nothing more than faithless academics masquerading as priests.

"Yes, yes." Father Talbert nodded quickly. "I don't understand why you didn't just ask for a copy to be sent to New York. You could have reviewed it at your leisure. I'm sure you could have forwarded a copy to the cardinal and to anyone else that may have had an interest. Surely, you could have done any necessary examination at the archdiocese before deciding if an interview was really necessary."

"Father Talbert, I sincerely felt…" Robert started, then stopped. He needed to find a way to keep the older man from stalling further. "Actually, both the cardinal and I felt that it was important for someone with some official credential in this area to speak personally with the boy's parents right away. So much time has gone by already, and we need to get their understanding of the tape and maybe—"

"They *have* no understanding of the tape!" Father Talbert said abruptly. "Or much else, frankly. His mother simply refuses to even consider the possibility that poor Alex may have had a problem, that he could have been at all ill. She's positively irrational on the subject. So, of course she wrote to the Vatican itself, of all things. It was a mother's quite understandable attempt to make some kind of sense of what had happened to her son. She needed to make sense of what he'd been saying. She's fishing for some validation, nothing more. She's looking for comfort. It's really very simple. She wants something more emotionally acceptable than the scenario the police ended up being so quick to accept."

"I was told he had no history," Robert said. "Alex had no prior behavior that could have been linked to either drug abuse or mental illness."

"It was his third year away at college." Father Talbert frowned. "Even his mother could hardly say much about Alex's regular behavior."

"Well, I'd like to go over some of the possibilities with her. Just the essentials, whatever might be pertinent. I can at least give her that. When Alex was at home over the spring break, she said he was perfectly normal. She didn't notice anything out of the ordinary. After speaking with her, I don't believe there could have been any kind of psychological deterioration that would have—"

"Robert, no one's saying the boy was completely crazy. I don't personally believe that, at any rate."

"So, he might have been only slightly crazy?"

"There's the possibility he could have been slightly delusional, perhaps. Neurotic, maybe, but I don't personally believe that he was psychotic."

"You're basing that on the tape? Alex's neurosis?" Robert squinted at the older priest. "Just the tape? You're taking the same road the police have chosen?"

"Well, who knows what he'd been doing up there, away from his home and his parents for so long?" Father Talbert shook his head and gazed down at the desk. "Who knows what he may have gotten into? Just the good Lord, I suppose. You know, I hear so many horrible things about those campuses. God in Heaven only knows what those kids today are doing to themselves."

"They screened him for toxins, right? No one found anything, isn't that right?"

"What?" Father Talbert raised his eyes. "Oh, I didn't hear that. But that doesn't mean there wasn't anything to be found. You know, any archaeologist will tell you, 'absence of evidence is not evidence of absence.'"

"The medical examiner found no toxins or chemical compounds," Robert said. He was getting irritated. "They found no drugs, no alcohol, nothing that could have been considered an impairment, correct?"

"Again, I can't honestly say. They may very well have failed to find anything like that, but still, it's very possible Alex could have been—"

"He went through the window, didn't he?"

"Well, yes, but I've been trying to tell you—"

"Why on earth would he hurl himself through the glass?" Robert asked, trying to keep his voice flat, to remain unemotional. "Alex could have simply opened the window. He could have just opened it and stepped out onto what I understand was a pronounced ledge. That would have been much more consistent with the behavior of a suicide, even when drugs are involved. It's highly unusual that he wouldn't take the time to reflect, to ponder his decision while he faced it."

"But what you're suggesting is that someone may have thrown the boy through the window," Father Talbert said, almost whining. "The police, brash as they were, were never able to even remotely establish that anyone else had even been in the room."

"I'm not suggesting anything. I'm just asking questions. I need to ask these questions because—"

Father Talbert interrupted again. "One, there was no sign of any kind of struggle. Nothing was out of place." He counted off his points on his fingers. "Two, not a single friend, relative, or student interviewed by the police was able to suggest any plausible scenario other than one that indicated suicide. Three, you're suggesting that the Los Angeles Police Department, over a five-week period, missed a gamut of evidence. You're suggesting that they missed evidence indicating someone just picked up this boy up and threw him out the window." He laid both his hands flat on the desk before him. "Now, Robert, for one thing, Alex was a rather large person—"

"Eric, I'm not suggesting anything at all. I don't think he was thrown out. I really don't. I believe he jumped, but—"

"Didn't you just *say* that suicide was highly unlikely!"

"And it is! I suppose, in its strict definition, it is. But please hear me out. There are other components to consider."

"Why else would he have jumped if he didn't have some degree of mental illness and he wasn't on any kind of drugs?"

Robert snapped his fingers and pointed at the older priest. "That's exactly the question I believe we need to concentrate on!"

"Bishop, please! Let's not mold this into something it simply is not! It was a suicide! Leave him alone! Leave his parents alone! I don't know the exact manner in which Alex was disturbed, or what possible... oh... indulgence might have played a part, but it's been determined that—"

"How can you be so ready to accept that? How can you have known this boy all his life, known his family, known his friends, and still allow yourself to look his mother in the face and tell her that Alex died that day only because it was his choice?" Robert stared at the older man, breathing angrily through his nose. They sat motionlessly in the small office, the sounds of a shuffling crowd outside the door.

"Did you tell her that?" Robert continued. "Did you look at Alex's mother and tell her you believed her son died freely and of his own design? Are you telling me that you've granted a funeral in this chapel, despite the sin of suicide? I don't understand why you're so eager to believe he had such a developed mental deficiency that he could have thrown himself from a six-story window, right through the glass, without leaving a note, without so much as a single word to anyone. I'll remind you also that the medical examiner found he'd been completely sober."

"But what about the video tape?"

"It's my understanding that the tape says nothing of suicide! His mother told me it doesn't sound like he was saying goodbye at all!" Robert sighed, leaned closer to the desk. "There are no apologies, no accusations, no should-haves, could-haves, or would-haves. She said he's pleading, he explaining, and that he's terrified. She said that it sounded to her as if he wanted to—"

"Bishop, you forget that I've seen it!" Father Talbert leaned back in his swivel chair, away from Robert. "It's a child's rambling, nothing more. It's the foul ravings of a young man who was caught up in that urban nightmare and couldn't find his way out. It's gibberish."

"He used her name!" Robert pounded his open palm on the desk. The bald priest jumped, despite being the one in the Chair of Power.

They stared at each other across the desk for over a minute, not speaking, hardly breathing. Robert didn't know where to go from there. They'd come to it, their dilemma: Father Talbert didn't believe. That was the issue. It wasn't the proclaimed sensitivity of the boy's parents, no matter how hard he tried to push that issue. He just didn't want to believe. He didn't believe and he didn't want the archdiocese swooping in and giving the boy's mother any more fuel for her denial, any more ammunition against his advantageous logic, or any more reason to question his judgment.

It was clear that Father Talbert had decided the boy had lost his mind, through using drugs or through some other big city seduction. Father Talbert had decided that Alex Monroe threw himself through the glass in his own apartment window because he was too disturbed to determine any other course of action. Alex had done it all by himself, all of his own volition. He'd done it alone, because he'd been disturbed and corrupted, but not because of what he'd claimed on the video tape he'd made immediately before his death.

The good father was sitting there, trying to face Robert down, trying to stall him long enough so that the pressures of the day forced the family to move on to the interment without meeting with him. It was obviously important to this little man that he not allow the authority of the archdiocese, the authority of the Church, for that matter, to lend any credibility whatsoever to a notion beyond his capacity to fathom.

Robert wouldn't let him have it.

"I'll speak with his mother now," he said quietly, sitting back and averting his gaze.

"Bishop—"

"I'll speak with his mother now, and afterward, I'll see the tape."

"I really must insist—"

"Father Talbert, please don't make this any more awkward than it has to be. You can either bring them in here, or to some other more comfortable place..." He looked around at the clutter. "...and you'd be welcome to sit-in on the meeting."

The older priest hesitated; he wasn't making any move at the moment, to go and get Alex's parents, or even to get out of the chair.

"I'm sure it's not your intention," Robert said, "to stall me here so long that the funeral party leaves for the cemetery before I speak with Alex's parents." He leaned forward to the edge of the matching leather, though low-backed, chair. "I'm sure that's not your intent. I'm sure you're not consciously trying to manipulate me, father. Though, that may just be the result of our little meeting if you don't go and get them right now."

Unfortunately, this sort of thing happened to Robert from time to time. He tried his best not to be a disruption. If a local parish was involved, he tried to allow them to cope with the phenomena—if there really *was* any kind of phenomena—in whatever manner offered the most comfort—and, of course, in whatever manner afforded Robert the most discretion. However, he couldn't allow their sensitivities to hinder his work. He couldn't allow those who sat idle in the comfort of their capricious faith to encumber the momentous responsibility assigned to him by the cardinal, not to mention the very Church itself.

Robert not only had to get at the truth but he had to do it very quickly and completely. Sometimes that meant being very direct, which often meant being a bit abrasive. Or worse. Sometimes he had to step on some toes.

Or worse.

It was a shame. It really was a shame so many of the clergy had such small vision and such small faith.

The spectacled priest drummed his fingers on the particleboard desk. "They'll have guests to tend to."

"I'm sure there'll be plenty of time after the interment."

"The air-conditioning in the rectory lobby is very bad—"

"I'm sure they won't mind sitting down in the chapel for a—"

"—and the casket is still in the chapel, so I don't think they'd be at all comfortable in there. It'll be carried out to the hearse soon enough, and then everyone will wonder why they're all still waiting around."

"A quick meeting in here then. Right now. That will be fine. You can either sit-in or wait outside, but please decide now. If they leave before I get the chance to speak to them we'll both have wasted a lot more than time."

Father Talbert gave Robert one more icy glare and then rose from his chair. "Please wait here. I assume you can trust me to bring them in."

"Father, again please, this doesn't have to be any more—"

"I'll be back with them as soon as they're ready. I'll tell them you're here and ask them if they'll come in."

Robert folded his hands in his lap. "That's all I'm asking."

†

Trying to maneuver the BMW out of his parking space was going to be a challenge; Darren was still feeling a little sloppy. So far, the car was both scratch and ding free, but Darren knew it was only a matter of time before he slid the entire driver's side across the metal beam that just happened to don the rear left corner of his assigned space. That was going to be a sad day. Why couldn't he have the space in the middle that didn't have one of those obnoxious obstacles? The guy that parked there drove an old Rodeo that was already banged up a little on the driver's side. Maybe he could get him to switch.

He slowly, very slowly, inched his new baby out of the parking stall. He'd have to accomplish something like a six-point turn before he could head out of the driveway with any kind of confidence. Why couldn't he have been assigned motherfucking center space?

This was Nick's fault. It was Nick's fault that Darren had to drive anywhere at all today. It was that little shit's fault for being alive and not in the hospital or at all in any kind of trouble. Okay, Darren was elated that Nick wasn't dead or hurt, but he could have had the decency to at least have been arrested or mugged or something acceptably dramatic.

The very first thing Darren had done when he woke up this morning—well, this afternoon—was to call Nick. Okay, it wasn't the first thing, but it was at least the third or fourth or some other number that was still very high up on the list of things-Darren-did-when-he-woke-up-even-though-it-was-Sunday-and-all-that-he-wanted-to-do-was-sedate-himself-and-sleep-'til-Wednesday.

Just being showered, dressed in a clean outfit, and behind the wheel of his car was something Darren considered to be over and above the call of duty on days such as this. This was the type of day that didn't produce any guilt in him, even if all the accomplishments of his conscious hours were limited to meagerly feeding himself, flipping between VH1 and the Sci Fi Channel, and successfully getting out of bed to pee.

Nick was at home. At home! And he was by himself. At least it sort of maybe sounded like he was by himself. Darren didn't ask directly. Half the reason he'd said he was coming right over was so that if there was someone else there, Nick would have to toss their clothes at them very quickly while he stammered for some polite way to ask them to leave. *Thanks for last night. Um… please get out.*

Yes sir, Darren had to rush right over there. Nick was all right and didn't need bail money or a transfusion or a kidney or anything, so maybe he didn't have to exactly rush, but it had still been a very long night to have to worry about the jerk, and he wanted to see him. Not that he'd missed him or that it had ruined his night or anything. After all, he'd been with Missy, who was very nice as usual. Sure, his second hit never made it out of his pocket, but it certainly wasn't because Darren was disappointed that Nick hadn't been there and didn't want to waste it without him. Nope, Darren just hadn't felt like taking it, for some odd reason, that's all. He'd save it for another night, and there'd be plenty of those.

Also, Darren had only done a couple of bumps of Special K while he was dancing with Eddie and Thelma, which meant he was almost totally sober right before he went home at five-thirty. So, of course he was tired now. Of course he was a little irritated. At least Nick was all right. Why was he going over there again?

He began his six-point maneuver and hoped none of his neighbors would want to either get in or out of the tiny parking lot before he'd finished. He was in no condition to contend with any of those movers-and-shakers who might be hurried and honking at him while trying to park a Suburban the size of a supermarket. How the hell did they get those things into those little spaces?

Actually, Darren was in a much better mood than he should have been, a state with which Ms. Gina had a great deal to do. He'd talked to Gina already today, though still waited the obligatory two hours before driving. However, earlier, when he'd finally gotten around to calling Nick, Gina had initially made him a little belligerent.

"What the holy motherfuck happened to you last night?" had been the very first words that zipped out of Darren's mouth the second Nick picked up the phone and before he could even start to pronounce the second syllable in *Hello?*

"Darren?" Nick had sounded sleepy and distant, which probably meant he'd had a great time the previous evening, the little prick.

"No, it's Cloris Leachman," Darren said. He'd been relieved to hear Nick's voice, and suddenly didn't want him to know it. "You're a

total dick. I hope you're intensely aware of that today. You had no
less than ten of your closest friends spending the entire night, which
they should have been allowed to enjoy, lord knows they deserved it,
scouring, and I mean *scouring*, that entire club looking for you all
night, which is three floors mind you. Three floors, you dick!"

"Oh, my god, Darren, why were there ten—?"

"Ten, seven, five, whatever."

"Why were all those people—?"

"All right, so I didn't exactly count every one of them, dickhead!
There were a lot, though! Too many! One is too many if we're talking
about wasting someone's time shuffling around in a crowded bar
worried sick about some dickhead that just up and leaves and doesn't
tell anybody, not even the person he rode with, who was expecting to
count on his company, which was why he asked the dickhead to come
in the first motherfucking place!"

"What time is it?"

"Are you listening? Do you even care that me and Eddie and
Thelma and—"

"Are you high?"

"Don't change the subject!" Darren quipped. He had been pretty
high, though, or at least getting there. Boy, nothing leveled out the
Day After Depressions like a little G- cocktail. Missy was the chick to
kick it with when you were on the town, but Gina was the queen of the
morning, the only girl for whom he'd get out of bed, or pretty much do
anything else during these types of days, for that matter.

And so what if Darren had done a little more than just level himself
out? It wasn't like he had to go to a meeting or do any work or
anything. Sure, it was late Sunday afternoon, but Monday morning,
and the responsibility that came with it, was still a long, long way off.

"You sound kinda like you're swooping," Nick had said.

'Swooping' was a word Nick had made up himself to describe the
unique way people sometimes slurred when they'd taken a drop or
two too much of that particular drug. If they had done enough, it
sometimes made them walk in a swoopy sort of way as well, which
really made the term stick.

"You are not in a position to lecture me, Nickydick!" This had been
the only spot where Darren had gotten close to actually getting
seriously miffed. "You spent exactly five minutes with me last night
before you disappeared completely. So, you're either the world's
biggest dickhead or you're the city's most prolific slut. Which is it?
Maybe it's both, I don't know." Darren was bent on playing this card.

Never mind that bumping Nick up with Kelly had been Darren's idea. See, Nick had been a little irritable, and Darren had hoped the stuff would make him hit the dance floor for a while and stop bagging on him.

"I just got really sick. Sheesh, chill Darren."

"What?"

"I got pretty sick. I was hurling all over the place."

"When?"

"Right away. I thought your bullet wasn't working and I did like five bumps before I thought I'd gotten anything—"

"Oh, my god."

"—and then I realized it was working the whole time and I must have really overdone it."

"Well, golly, that's awful, Nicky."

"I can hear the sympathy just dripping from you."

"You know, Nick, I would be sympathetic. I would be more than sympathetic. I'd be holy fucking commiserating if it weren't for one little thing. One minor detail, one tiny component. One little, itsy-bitsy—"

"Is this going to take long? Do I have time to make a sandwich?"

"—little thing. Okay, you are a dork, and what the hell were you doing buying from Troy and not telling me about it?"

"What makes you think—?"

"Okay, you can save that, because Troy told me—"

"Don't give me that crap, Darren! Troy didn't say squat! Unless you tricked him, or beat him up, or something. You didn't hit him, did you? Don't you call me and start cussing and throwing names if you've been going around punching people again!"

"I didn't hit anyone. I didn't have to. And stop trying to change the subject. Just tell me one thing. Did you go over there before or after I asked you to come to the club with me?"

"Darren, you always have your own—"

"Okay, I always share it with you, and more important—"

"How do I know what you always do?"

"—is that I could have told you not to mix that shit with Kelly."

"What?"

"You're such an ass. We've done it here, what, two times? You're an expert now? Next time, just tell me. I don't care. At least then I won't bump you up with something that's going to make you sick. Oh, and by the way, if you mix it with alcohol, you could die."

"What? Really?"

"Yeah. Total mess. Coma. Death. Stuff like that. Absolutely ruins your whole day, is what I hear."

"No shit?"

"Totally."

"I didn't drink, though. I never drink."

"Yeah, instead you snorted enough Kelly to put down a mountain lion."

"Oh, my god, Darren, you'll never believe what I did! I destroyed my pants." Nick sounded like he was waking up a little; he'd stopped yawning through his words, so Darren hadn't jumped on him again about his sudden subject shift. Though, that's when he'd made up his mind that he needed to trek over there.

"How did you get home anyway?" Darren had started trying to put on his shorts without letting Nick know he was getting ready to leave.

"My four-hundred-dollar Versace pants! There's puke and—"

"Your brand fucking new, 'drive-me-to-San-Diego-I-have-to-have-these-pants!' Versache pants?" He'd chosen one of the two clean T-shirts in his drawer, the one that was folded, and put it on. Nick's voice trailed out of the receiver when Darren tried to switch hands to maneuver into his clothes.

"—well, stuff all over them. I can't even take them to the dry cleaners, they'll think someone—"

"What happened?" Darren asked once he got the receiver back to his face. "Did you slide all the way across town on your pants?" He'd been trying to dress quickly and without alerting Nick so that he might be able to surprise him a few minutes before he was expected, maybe also catching a glimpse of any frantically retreating company.

Darren had tried to open the third drawer as quietly as possible; he had to have clean socks. Even on those rare occasions when he wasn't wearing underwear, he still had to have clean socks. There was an unopened plastic package of six pairs in the drawer, the kind with the gray patches on the toe and the heel. When he picked up the new package and saw the little plastic baggie underneath it, he'd suddenly remembered that he'd left his other hit of Missy in his pants, along with his bullet full of Kelly.

There was just so much of which to keep track. Darren sighed. So many compounds, so little time.

"—I don't even know what they'd think" Nick's voice poured out of the receiver. "See Darren, I try to take care of something expensive, something nice, and… fuck!"

Darren decided to start the clock. "Hey, I'm coming over." He slipped on his Vans and started scanning the floor for his keys.

"I think I took a cab or something," said Nick. He wasn't even listening.

"Are you dressed? Because I'm coming over there."

Darren's keys had to be on the floor by the bed, which was where almost everything ended up when he got home from a club and didn't have company. He ended up crawling around, flipping clothes everywhere, and gazing under the bed for a full two minutes before he stopped to think where he might have left them when he got home.

"What? You're going where?"

"Put on some Calvins and brush your teeth," Darren said into the phone, trying not to sound like he was getting up off the floor, as he was getting up off the floor. "I'll stop and get a movie or something, but I'm coming over there to convalesce." He'd found his keys in the living room. That morning, coming in from the club in what could only be described as a sober funk, he'd dropped them onto the end-table after throwing his shirt on the fake ficus tree.

"Should you be driving?"

"Shut up. Do you have any left or should I bring her?" Even as he asked, Darren had been grabbing his bottle of saline solution, which was actually filled with his two remaining ounces of the stuff.

"What? Who?"

"Gina. I am not going to face a recovery day without Gina. Is your building's pool heated?"

Along with his left over drugs, he'd also found his wallet in the pants he'd worn, which were hanging alongside the towels in the bathroom.

"Um… yeah, I have... uh..." Nick was muttering.

"Okay, bye. See ya in about sixty."

Darren had tried to quickly fish his wallet out of his pants, along with his bullet full of Kelly and his extra Missy (now he had three), which he promptly put away in the sock drawer with the rest of his stash, as he wouldn't be needing them until maybe next weekend at the earliest.

He paused for a second, looking into the sock drawer, Nicholas droning on about something in his ear, and decided to snag a bullet full of cocaine to bring along. One never knew what the day had in store. They might wanna have themselves a little pep later on. Nick could be really fun when he had a little pep.

Darren stashed the saline bottle of Gina and the bullet of coke in his designer backpack—Abercrombie, duh—and made a run through the apartment to make sure he hadn't left any lights on or the stereo playing. It would have taken him even longer to get to his car and get going if he'd stopped to contemplate why his old pair of socks were in the medicine cabinet, but he knew better than to waist time with such pursuits.

"Darren...!" Nick suddenly blurted out the earpiece.

"What, baby?"

"Um... Gina's here. You know I'll share."

Darren had stopped for a second and grinned at that. "I know. I was teasing. I'm just glad you're all right. I'll see you in an hour." It would be more like twenty minutes, but Darren wanted to surprise him. He would have just shown up and not told Nick that he was coming over at all, except that he didn't want Nick to decide to go somewhere.

"Darren... ?"

"Dude, what? I'm hanging up now, 'cause I've gotta, um, get into the shower." It had started to sound suspiciously like Nick might have been trying to stall him.

"Um... Okay, um ..." Nick stammered.

"Do you have soda?" Darren asked. "Do I need to stop for cola? 'Cause you know I can't take her with just juice." GHB had to be mixed with something sweet, as it was the most vile and bitter crap he'd ever tried to swallow. After tasting her the first time, he'd never have done it again if it didn't make him feel so incredibly euphoric and like fucking anything with a pulse.

"Oh, god yeah, there's plenty of that. With my club card I got—"

"Okay! Great! I'm in the shower!" he lied. "Okay? Hugs and kisses! I'll see you in about an hour!" He'd hung up on him, which he would normally have hated to do, if not for the slight possibility that Nick was trying to stall him.

He'd already showered, of course, all the better to get there faster than Nick expected. Maybe he'd even get a chance to see the other person, if there was one, which he doubted, but just in case.

Darren pushed his sunglasses back up on his face and stared at the traffic on Fountain Avenue. Nick had sounded mostly like himself, but Darren still had a sick feeling that something was up, something that required his attention. Although, it didn't really matter what it was because Darren was going to go right over there and smooth everything over. He was going to take charge and work it out. Something was up and it made itself known to him in the form of a little knot in the pit of his stomach. It was just a little knot, not something catastrophic, just a push, just some pressure, telling him not to be by himself today. It was also telling him not to let Nicky be by himself today. Actually, this particular little knot was clearly communicating specifically to Darren that he shouldn't let Nick be without *Darren* today.

He'd remedy that, and if he could smooth out whatever was up, whatever was knotted up in his stomach, and at the same time cure poor Nicky of his loneliness, well all the better.

It was Nicky who was lonely, of course. He must be the lonely one right now, going on and on about his pants, and after being sick last night and maybe having a stranger in his home and everything. Yes sir, Nicky needed some familiar company, and Darren was just going to flip a couple right-hand turns, track down Sunset, pick up some scary movies, maybe some passion fruit sorbet—Nicky's favorite—rush right over there, and spend the rest of the day, and maybe a good portion of the night, making sure Nick had what he needed.

Maybe Darren would relax down to his own Calvins and watch the movies from his favorite of all comfy-cozy places, the curve of Nick's leather sectional. He'd have the air-conditioning breathing softly on his shoulders as Nicky fell asleep with his head in Darren's lap.

If Darren could just traverse the length of the driveway and safely make his way into the late Sunday afternoon West Hollywood traffic, that's exactly what he planned to do.

†

"He's coming over here," Nick said, hanging up the phone.

The black-haired guy sat stiffly on the far end of the sofa closest to the television. He was examining the remote.

"That's for the TV," Nick offered. "It's that glass box against the wall."

"Yes, thank you, I've seen one," the guy said. "Do you have satellite?"

"Uh... no. Sorry. Basic cable."

"HBO?"

"Sorry."

"I suppose renting movies is okay. No biggie. Your computer plays DVDs, right?" He put down the remote and looked at Nick. "How do you feel?"

"Uh... okay, I guess," Nick answered. All of it had come back to him in a rush. He'd been in a dead sleep in the bedroom. Then, jolted up by the phone ringing, he'd run into the living room to answer it—

he'd left the frickin' cordless in the living room again, damn it—
fumbled with the handset trying to click the 'on' button in his
evaporating stupor, and noticed the familiar-looking guy sitting on his
couch. By the time Darren hung up, the whole night, and the identity
of this quiet man, had flashed itself back into Nick's memory. Just
about every detail.

"I'm sorry the phone woke you," the familiar-looking guy said.

Scott. One last major detail. Nick had called him 'Scott' when he'd
come to him, and he'd kissed him on the forehead, and then...

"I've been asleep this whole time?" Nick blurted. "Oh, my god,
I've been out this whole time!"

"What do you remember?" Scott asked.

Nick thought for a second. "Everything, I think."

"That's good."

"I mean, at least up until I passed out in the alley."

"Yes, of course."

"I passed out, right?"

"Yes."

"Was I—?"

"Are you dizzy at all? Take a deep breath for me." Scott stood up
and gave Nick a closer look.

"Scott, was I, um...?"

"What?"

"Um... I don't know. Was I dying?"

"Yeah," Scott said, holding Nick by the chin and staring into his left
eye. "I'm fairly positive you were."

"Did I... oh, ah... god... did I...?"

"No." Scott shook his head. "No, you didn't die. I couldn't have
helped you if you had." Apparently satisfied, Scott picked up the TV
Guide, spun, and plopped back on the sectional. "That sort of thing is
far, far beyond me."

"What happened?"

"I'm not sure what the medical term is," he said, gazing at the
cover photo of the current American Idol, "but the best I can figure is
that a hit of ecstasy was stuck in your esophagus."

"You're kidding."

"It most likely burned a hole in the esophageal wall. You've got to
be more careful." Scott tossed the TV Guide back onto the coffee table.
"You have to drink a lot more water when you do that shit. And
really, Nick, you simply cannot mix compounds the way you do.
That's bad enough all by itself." He picked the remote back up. "In

any case, your lungs were filling with blood."

"Oh."

"Anyway, don't worry. I fixed it."

"Um, okay. Yeah. That's good."

"I'll just bill MediCal."

"Okay." Nick needed to sit. Glancing down, he suddenly noticed he was standing there in his underwear.

"Your pants really were a horrible mess," Scott offered. "I threw them in your bathtub, but I think you're going to want to dump them."

"How did we get here?"

"Well, if what you told Darren was true, then we took a cab."

"Oh."

"And you owe me twenty bucks."

"Okay."

"I'm kidding, Nick."

"Okay."

"Nick?" Scott got up and went to him.

"What?"

"Come sit down." Scott took him gently by the hand. He guided him past the coffee table and sat him gently on the couch. "Look at me."

Nick raised his head and looked at him. There was just the touch of a smirk on Scott's lips.

Scott touched him again on the chin. "No, no. Look at my eyes," he said.

"Why?"

"Nicholas, just look right into my eyes. The left one, actually. I want you to look really hard. Can you? Just for a second?"

Nick needed to pull himself together. There was a lot to take in and he'd only had a couple of minutes to try and manage it. Last night, he'd almost been able to convince himself that the conversation outside the club had taken place entirely in his head. Now, here was this gorgeous raven-haired guy, the one he'd seen before he passed out, sitting with him in his apartment, complaining about the entertainment center, explaining to Nick why he was only in his underwear, and telling him to look into his eyes.

They were breathtaking eyes, though. They were the color seen on very big maps to show the shallow oceans. They were the darkest tint of a glacier, ice at its most dense, most solid, the only hue that could escape the frozen prism. As Nick looked at them they actually seemed to get brighter. Their blue tone burnished before him like a late

August morning.

Scott's eyes contrasted dramatically with his hair, which was very thick, very black, and jumped from his forehead, arching backward in dramatic waves to end where it met his shoulders. The black waves framed his face in a striking divergence to his skin, which was pale, even with its Mediterranean tint. There was age in his face. There was age, but within a profound calm, held there, within skin that was tender and almost seamless. Looking at him, he appeared a flawless blend of simple contradictions; light and dark, color and blackness, wisdom and youth, menace and beauty.

Nick looked at him in silence and felt his breathing slow. He blushed. It was a very warm blush, and he felt it distinctly around his eyes and lips. He closed his mouth and filled his lungs through his nose, feeling the air rouse and stretch his chest. When he exhaled, he smiled. It just popped onto his face and he giggled at it in surprise.

Scott giggled with him. "Better?"

"What are you doing?" Nick asked through his smile.

"Nothing." Scott smiled back at him. "I'm making you happy. That's all."

"You can do that?" Nick laughed.

"Sometimes. Not always. But I know you want to ask me something and you're anxious about it." He raised his eyebrows at Nick. "Are you still anxious?"

Nick thought for a moment, slowly smiled, and shook his head. "No," he whispered.

"Ask me then."

Nick thought for a second, suddenly not sure if he really did have anything to ask. Then, "Did you, um… did you touch me?"

Scott nodded. "Of course. Last night, and I've done so a few times since you've been awake. I thought you would have noticed."

Nick's smile faltered a bit.

"But," Scott continued, "I didn't really take anything."

"You didn't—?"

"You were very clear about not being 'comfortable' with it. So I didn't really take a look at anything."

"You touched me, but you didn't read my mind?"

"I like to call it 'gleaning,' and yes, I did, a very little bit. It was almost impossible not to, last night especially, while I was carrying you, dressing you. After we got here, I had to find something for you to wear. I mean, once I got your pants off—"

"Oh… my… god…!" Nick blushed so hard he started to sweat and covered his face with his hands. He hadn't been wearing underwear the night before.

"Really, I didn't read your mind," Scott continued. "I just got very minor details. You know, where you live, your last name, your age, nothing that isn't on your driver's license. I also picked up some names from your family, though, and the names of some cities, but nothing else, nothing instrumental. I didn't follow anything."

"I thought… well, I thought you'd want to—"

"Oh, and I picked up your language." Scott closed his eyes and counted off on his fingers. "Plus a little cultural background, and I noticed some very sticky-sweet thoughts about that guy you just hung up with, because I think you might have been dreaming, which really doesn't mean anything, but I didn't follow those either. Really, don't stress over it."

Nick gasped and blushed some more.

"It's not something I go around doing all of the time," Scott continued. "Gleaning is a lot of work. Not the process itself, actually that's quite simple. A parlor trick really. It's difficult not to glean *something* when I touch someone, when they let me, which, technically, you did. And, of course, after someone allows me to touch them just once, then I don't ever need their consent again. I can glean from them at any time, should I choose to do so. But, Nick, really, all that information can be a seriously odious burden."

Nick covered his face and groaned from beneath his hands. "Oh… my…"

"Really, though, I don't want it all. You can't imagine all the clutter that's already in my head. I mean, all the centuries of crap, from—"

"What do you mean, 'my language?'" Nick was trying not to think about how he'd gotten into a clean pair of boxer briefs and tucked into bed. "Weren't you speaking my language last night?"

"Yeah, English, I guess, sort of, but I gleaned it from an American I'd known in Greece. Actually, I just got a little adjustment from you. Semantics, that sort of thing, I guess. It's like linking two computer languages, I think." He scratched his head. "Is it? Actually, I don't know. I'm very likely talking out my butt."

Nick realized that even the slight hint of Scott's Mediterranean accent was completely gone. His voice was even a little different. Still the same deep, resonant tone, but just a bit lighter, more casual.

"Scott, buddy," Nick said, "I never use words like 'odious.'"

"Perhaps not, but you know it. And I didn't say I completely taped over everything that was already in my mind. I just, well, pushed it aside, sort of. Stored it, I guess."

"All right, so my language, or dialect, or phonetics, or whatever—"

"Good one!" Scott put his index finger on his nose and pointed the other one at Nick. "That's a good one. That too. Semantics and phonetics, definition and dialect. All of those things, within me, are now linked to you. My vernacular, parlance, jargon, lingo, all that fun stuff."

"Okay." Nick had to sit down again. "Wait, wait, wait, wait, wait—"

"Are you all right? Are you getting anxious again?"

"Oh god, Scott, just hold up a second!"

"I borrowed some of your clothes this morning to go shopping. I hope you don't mind," Scott said. He was wearing Nick's denim shorts and his white Powerpuff Girls T-shirt. "The shoes are mine, though. I hit Payless this morning while you were sleeping."

"Scott! Oh crap!" Nick had a horrible thought. "What were you wearing last night?"

"Nothing."

"And we took a cab?"

"I didn't say we took a cab." Scott lifted his eyebrows. "*You* said we took a cab."

"Well, how the—?"

"I think maybe now I should explain how we got here. Um, you see—"

"Didn't you also have wings at some point last night?"

Scott put his index finger on his nose and pointed the other one at Nick.

†

After Father Talbert seated Donna and Ted on the ugly sofa, he nodded to the young bishop, indicating that he should begin. If the pompous New York cleric was determined to go through with this nonsense, then the very least he could do was to get it done quickly.

Father Talbert didn't offer anyone anything; water, juice, or coffee, which was unthinkable under normal circumstances. These circumstances, however, were far from normal. He would do all he could to make sure the young bishop didn't further upset the Monroes. That included trying to keep the meeting, which was completely inappropriate in the first place, as absolutely brief as possible.

The more he thought about it, the further he got from being able to deem the meeting as merely inappropriate. As Father Talbert considered it now, it was nothing short of insane.

He didn't sit down in the second leather swivel seat in front of the desk, the one next to Bishop Whipper-Snapper. He thought it would have looked and felt too much like he was a part of this, as though he agreed with whatever it was this arrogant young man was going to say. Instead, he retreated to his comfort zone, to the plush, executive chair behind the desk. From there, he could watch and listen, as well as appear uninvolved in any of the maneuverings of the archdiocese.

Father Talbert crossed his legs, rocked back so that he could see Donna and Ted around the bishop, pushed his glasses back up on his face, and unconsciously rested his chin on the steeple of his fingers as they came together in the habitual position of prayer. Staring at Robert, he couldn't help but feel guarded, cynical. How on earth did this man ever become a bishop in the first place? What was he, thirty?

"Donna," the adolescent bishop said, starting right in, gazing solemnly at the tiny woman. "I know this has already been a very long and demanding day and, were we dealing with conditions of any other nature, I would never dream of making it any more difficult."

"I know, Father." Donna Monroe nodded. All the color on her face had long since been cried away, poor thing. She held a clot of tissue in her right hand, clumped and wet with tears, and her husband's hand in her left.

"However," Robert continued, "as I'm still relatively unfamiliar with the specifics of the case, I must assume an element of urgency and proceed with some degree of sensitivity to time."

Father Talbert said a silent *Amen*.

"I understand." The mother of the dead boy lifted her head, took a deep breath.

"Before we begin, though, I'd like to make sure you're aware that I'm not here to either acknowledge or discredit any of the components of this issue on behalf of the Church. At least not today, at any rate. It's not my intent to assign or discount any likely possibility or to allocate any authority. I can't speak to the authenticity of any of these elements. I'm merely here to better appreciate as much of the situation as possible."

It was the same speech Father Talbert had heard recited by Bishop Patrick over the phone at the disrespectfully early hour of four-thirty that very morning. Father Talbert knew it was a canned speech, he knew it was rehearsed. It was a very clear red flag, the first indication that Donna's letter might have sparked a bigger fire than he originally thought, one that was obviously going to take much more effort to extinguish quickly.

The phone conversation had only gotten worse when the bishop first told him—not asked, *told* him—that he was flying out there to meet with the Monroes.   Now, here he was, sitting in the administrative office, determined to undo everything Father Talbert had done to allow Donna Monroe any hope of peace.

The afternoon had cooled a bit as it drifted toward evening, but most of the heat inside the building hadn't yet been smothered by the air-conditioning.   It made the office heavy in the quiet.   Even the rocking of the high-backed desk chair made no sound.   Outside, however, there was a great deal of commotion from the multitude of family and friends, no doubt wondering why they hadn't yet proceeded to the cemetery.

"With that in mind," Robert said, "I'd still like to take this time to address the issues to which I am able to speak.   Though, I'm afraid my assistance may be limited.   As I said, I know this has been a long ordeal, but I wanted you to be able to bury Alex without questions."

"We really just have a few minutes," Father Talbert said. "Everyone's ready to go."   He knew well enough that this man from New York hadn't come all the way across the country on behalf of getting answers for anyone but himself.   Answers he may or may not eventually pass along to the archdiocese.

If Father Talbert were keeping track of the manipulative lies he was expecting to hear, the lies he expected this servant to the hoity-toity Cardinal Matine to tell these grief stricken parents, the score would have just gone up to one.   Bury Alex without questions, indeed.

"Donna," Robert went on, "when we spoke on the phone you said you'd never heard Alex mention any of the names before, the ones on the video tape.   Is that correct?"

"Well," she said, "of course I knew Laura's name, but I'd never met her.   And he'd mentioned a couple of the people he worked with before."

"But the odd names, the two you mentioned specifically in your letter, had he ever used them before?"

"No. He never did. But I looked them up, on the Internet, when they found the tape, and they're—"

"Yes, that's what you said in your letter.   You told me on the phone." Robert turned to Alex's father. "Ted? Had you ever spoken with Alex about those names, or did he ever mention them to you?"

"No," Alex's father replied, shaking his head. His eyes stayed focused on the carpet.

"I assume that Alex was baptized?"

"Oh, yes." His mother nodded quickly.

"As an infant?"

"Yes." She nodded again. "Is that important?"

"Yes," Robert said, sounding surprised. "Yes, of course it is. Father Talbert should have explained all this to you."

"Oh, well, certainly. Father Talbert's been wonderful. He's been quite a comfort."

"Now," Robert began, looking again at Ted Monroe, "tell me why Alex couldn't have killed himself. Tell me what you believe."

"I, uh…" Ted looked at his wife. "I just, um… I knew my son. I knew that he…"

"Ted." Donna squeezed his hand. "Tell him. Tell him about the…" She squinted, pressed her lips together, and looked down at her lap.

"Is this really necessary?" Father Talbert asked.

"Go on," Robert whispered, ignoring him.

Alex's mother looked at her husband. He met her eyes and his lip quivered. They looked at each other for another second, then he shook his head.

"It was his face," Donna said, turning to the bishop, speaking for her husband. Her eyes welled with fresh tears as Alex's father squinted his shut.

"The wound on his face," Robert said. "The one you told me about."

"Yes," she whispered, nodding her head as the tears rolled down her cheeks for the hundredth time that day. "At first, they said it was from the glass, but…" She closed her eyes, shook her head.

"From the window." Robert nodded.

"But they only just decided that a few days ago." Donna looked up at Robert. "Before that they said the… the wound… they said it wasn't 'consistent.'"

"It wasn't consistent with the fall?" Robert pressed her.

"No, not with anything. There was no glass in his face, no splinters, nothing, and he landed on his back. Also…" She stopped.

The bishop gave her a moment. Then, "It's all right, take your time."

What a saint, thought Father Talbert.

"They said it might have been older," Alex's father offered.

"Who? The police?"

"Yes. Well, the medical examiner's office. They said the wound on his face could have been there before he died. Maybe even by an hour or more. When I first saw him, when I went there to identify him, it was the first thing I saw. It was the first thing anyone would have seen, right down the side of his face. At first, I thought there was something on him, like a ribbon or a piece of cloth, or..." He shook his head. "I don't know."

Father Talbert would have stopped him. He would have told Ted he didn't need to go through all this again, except it was most likely something the young bishop was waiting to hear. They might as well get through it quickly.

"I don't know what I thought," Ted continued, "but it was a stripe right down the left side of Alex's face, right next to his eye." He paused, touching his own face. "That's when I realized, when I saw his eye. I realized it wasn't something on his face." He stopped again, took a breath. "It *was* his face."

Donna was crying silently, heavy streaming tears, fast and steady. She wiped at them angrily with her dirty tissue.

"A stripe, or a strip, of skin was missing from his face?" Robert asked, emotionless.

"Yes," Ted answered, "from just below the line of his hair down the left side of his face. Just left of his eye and his mouth, past his chin, there was a thick line of missing skin, at least an inch wide. It... it looked..." Ted Monroe's eyes wandered back to the floor.

"And no one could explain it?" Robert asked.

"No," Alex's father said, gazing at the faded carpet. "No one. At first it was the whole reason they wouldn't let us bury him. They said we couldn't take him because they couldn't explain why the wound was there. They said it was 'inconsistent.'"

"But then they found the videotape?" Robert asked. "They found the tape in his room?"

"Yes." Ted nodded. "They found the tape, and as soon as they heard him, as soon as they heard what he'd been saying, about the... when he said the names of the ..."

"The demons?"

Alex's father nodded. "Yes. That did it. That ended it all."

Once the police had seen the video of Alex Monroe ranting about demons and monsters, the authorities had all just washed their hands. The tape was very clear: Alex sincerely believed that not only his ex-girlfriend, but also at least one other person with whom he worked, were demons.

Both individuals had been thoroughly interviewed, but no progress was made. In truth, the investigation became a joke in its entirety once the tape was discovered. It even got out to the press rather quickly. The Los Angeles Times printed a small story with the headline 'USC Student's Delusions May Have Caused His Death.'

Consequently, the police decided they weren't going to be able to resolve the case. So, they released the body. They'd decided that, even if they eventually found evidence of foul play, which everyone doubted at that point, there wasn't a defense attorney west of the Mississippi that wouldn't be able to use that tape to produce reasonable doubt, even blindfolded, with their hands tied behind their backs, with a lobotomized jury that didn't speak English. No, once the tape was discovered, it was all over. Solved or not, the case was closed.

"It had been very frustrating for them, I suppose," Donna explained. "They were getting nowhere and everyone was becoming more and more upset. Then, when they found the tape, I guess that just gave them an excuse to stop. It was permission to close the file and forget about it."

"We all tried to accept it at first," Ted continued. "Everyone was so tired and we just wanted it all to be over. Then, after we saw the tape ourselves and had a day or two to think about it, we realized what they were saying. They were saying he was crazy. Simple as that. They thought there was nothing more they could do. Even if someone had hurt him, there was nothing they could do if the tape showed Alex had lost his mind or taken drugs or whatever else they might infer from it."

"Did he ever take drugs?" Robert asked. "Did you ever know Alex to take any kind of drugs?"

"No." His mother shook her head. "No. He was very excited about school. We spoke all the time. I couldn't imagine he'd... Well..." She sighed, stopped for a moment. "Oh, of course, I think, once or twice, when he was still in high school..." She looked at her husband.

"He'd been smoking marijuana with some of his friends," Ted admitted, "and every so often he'd go out and drink. We were furious when we found out about the marijuana. Absolutely furious. It happened two or three times, actually, now that I think about it. I can't say for sure if he ever completely gave it up."

"Oh, I'm sure he did," Alex's mother insisted. "I'm sure he didn't keep doing that once he got to USC. He was getting very good grades, all the time. I just don't see how he could have been doing so well and—"

"Nothing else?" Robert pressed them. "You never knew of him trying anything else? Cocaine? LSD?"

"Oh, no, no." Donna shook her head vigorously. "Never anything like that. Someone would have known. We would have known, or one of his friends, or someone. The police would have found someone who knew about things like that."

"Did he attend mass?" Robert asked.

Father Talbert hadn't seen that one coming. He squinted his eyes, pursed his lips against the tips of his fingers. What was Bishop Whipper-Snapper doing?

"Well, no," Alex's mother started. "I don't... He did when he was here, of course, attend mass. Oh, and I think he went to a church in Los Angeles once when—"

"Regularly?" Robert crossed his legs, folding his hands in his lap. "Did Alex attend mass on any kind of regular basis?"

Neither of the Monroes answered. They just looked at the bishop for a moment and then shook their heads.

"No," Ted finally answered. "He didn't attend mass regularly. Not since he was a boy."

"What kind of religious education did he have?" Robert continued.

"What do you mean? He went to public schools."

"He had scripture classes," Donna offered. "He went to all the scripture classes here. Though, I guess they don't call them that anymore." She looked at her hands. "He went to camp, to the Church's camp."

"Oh, that's right," Ted agreed. "He went to a religious youth camp when he was a freshman in high school."

"Nothing else?" Robert said.

"What else do you mean? What were we supposed to have done?"

"After youth camp," Robert said, looking down at his own hands, his neatly laced fingers, "did he attend any kind of class with ecclesiastical interest?"

"There aren't really any here for the older kids. Except maybe at the catholic high school, but—"

"Did he take anything at USC that had any kind of religious component? Anything at all? It doesn't have to be something like hermeneutics or Biblical etymology, but any basic theology or even philosophy?"

"Oh, um, no, I don't suppose--"

"But he was baptized and confirmed?"

"He went to all the church classes before his confirmation," Donna said. "All the classes before his first communion and his confirmation. We sent him to everything available." Donna leaned across the short distance between her and Bishop Patrick. "Father, were we supposed to have done something else? Was there something that Alex should have done, something he should have known?"

"Donna," Robert said, "your son believed in God? Is that something you can say with certainty?"

Father Talbert sat up in his chair. "Robert, of course the boy believed in God! What are you doing? Let's not—"

"Did Alex," Robert barked, raising a finger into the air to silence him, without taking his eyes off the boy's parents, "ever say or do anything that would indicate to you that he'd ever questioned his faith?"

Both of the Monroes looked horror stricken. Father Talbert could tell that such a thought had never crossed their minds. They were visibly stunned and shaken. Donna appeared as though she was attempting to answer, searching her memory, but no words came out of her.

Father Talbert didn't know what to say either. He didn't understand how any of this could be relevant. He didn't understand at all.

No one said anything. The moment crept on, the office dead in its silence. Father Talbert thought he could hear a growing, perhaps impatient concern in the rustle of the people outside.

"It's all right," Robert finally said, settling back again into his chair, re-lacing his fingers. "I'm sure Alex believed. If he was having any serious doubts, I'm sure it would have been known to you."

Clear relief appeared on both of the Monroes. Father Talbert frowned.

"Does this all have something to do with the tape?" Donna asked.

"Yes," Robert said. "Of course."

"Do you think..." Her eyes began to glisten again. "Do you think...?"

"What, Donna?"

"Do you think he was..." She leaned forward slightly as a tear rolled down her cheek. "Do you think he was... possessed?" The boy's mother could barely whisper the word. It obviously embarrassed her. She scarcely gave it voice, gave it life.

"No, that's not possible," Robert answered simply. "That's not possible if he was baptized."

Donna Monroe stifled a sob. She nodded, wiping at her cheeks.

"Father Talbert didn't discuss any of this with you?"

"There was nothing to discuss," Father Talbert said quietly.

"Did you ever speak with Alex yourselves?" asked Robert. "Did you ever discuss religion or your faith with him?"

"It didn't come up very much," Ted answered.

"Even when you brought him to mass? When he was here? When Alex was visiting from school, and you brought him to mass with you, you didn't discuss it with him?"

"Maybe, but I don't really recall having many conversations about—"

"None at all?" Robert put his elbows on his knees and leaned forward once more. "Do you remember discussing anything recently? The last few times he'd been here? Any sermons? Scripture?"

Donna shook her head while Alex's father gazed at the floor.

"Anything at all?" Robert repeated. "Can you remember just one conversation you had, or may have had, about your faith or religion or spirituality, since Alex left for school? Anything in the past three years? Perhaps even a conversation just between the two of you, something he could have overheard?"

"I can't really think right now," Donna said. "I know we must have discussed something, when he was here, when he came to mass with us. We must have talked a bit, but I just can't think right now." She wouldn't look at Robert.

"There must have been something," Ted continued. "I'm sure at least at Christmas or maybe at—"

"Yes, at Christmas, of course," Robert said, leaning back into his chair, abruptly gazing at the wall.

The young bishop rocked back and forth in his small swivel chair for a moment. Father Talbert watched him, could hear him breathing through his nose, his bottom lip rising absently over his teeth.

Another awkward, silent moment. Father Talbert thought about ending the meeting. This was going nowhere.

"Do you remember any specific questions he may have had?" Robert turned back toward Alex's parents. "Perhaps you can recall some religious issue in particular about which Alex might have been curious?"

"Oh, Ted!" Donna looked again at her husband. "Remember in the car that day, that day we had to drive to Riverside? It was in the old Toyota, you remember. Alex asked you about the angels?"

"Oh, right." Ted nodded again. "He wanted to know, uh, he was asking about, um…"

"He was asking about guardian angels," Donna said, "and he wanted to know if Grandpa Sam was a guardian angel now."

"Right," Ted agreed. He looked at the bishop. "My father had passed away about six months before that and Alex was curious about it."

"How long ago was this?" Robert touched his lips with his fingers, swiveling in his chair carelessly.

"Oh," Donna said, gazing up, pouting, "it must have been fourteen or fifteen years ago. She looked at her husband, who gave a tiny nod.

"That wasn't recent," Robert said. "He was, what? Eight? Nine?"

Mrs. Monroe nodded slowly, wiped a straggling tear from her eye. "Yes. I think he was about nine or so."

"And you told him, of course," Robert said, looking at the wall above their heads, "that people don't become angels."

"What's that?"

"When Alex was nine, in the car that day, you corrected him. You must have explained that human beings do not ever become angels, of any kind, when they die. You must have explained to him that it was a common, though definite, misconception. What did he say?"

He'd silenced them again. Father Talbert watched as Donna Monroe stared at the young bishop with open embarrassment. The look of fear and anguish on her grieving face was audacious. It broke his heart.

Father Talbert would have cried with her, if he could. He pursed his lips instead, pressing them almost painfully onto his steepled fingers.

The crowd outside the door presented more of a building rustle, a reminder of the task at hand. The bishop drummed his fingers against the particleboard desk and glanced back at Father Talbert, who happily leveled his best I-Told-You-So gaze at him.

"Do you think he was crazy?" It was Donna. It was Mrs. Monroe who finally cut right to the chase.

Robert turned slowly to look at her. "I don't know."

"Why did you come?" she asked. "There must have been something. There must be something you want to know, or something we can tell you." She began to cry, but made no move to wipe the tears, as if these she didn't feel. "What was it that we missed?" She leaned closer to him. "Tell me, father. As parents, what did we miss? How did we fail?"

Robert reached out, and after a moment Alex's mother took his hand. The three of them moved closer, Donna, Ted, and the bishop, tighter into their circle. The tears fell freely down Donna's face as she looked at Robert questioningly.

Here we go, thought Father Talbert.

"It's not my place to say what happened to Alex, Donna," Robert told her. "It's not for me, here, today, to decide if your son was ill, or if he was a victim of something else. I want to answer as many questions as I can, but maybe that's going to be of little value after all. I'm sure that Alex was not possessed, as to be so, he would have had to be an un-baptized soul, and that was not the case."

"But the demons," she whispered. "He said he knew them. He said there were monsters where he worked, he'd spoken with them —"

"Yes, I know." Robert nodded solemnly. "That's not uncommon, believe it or not. All throughout history people have been confronting demons, whether real or imagined. Whether or not they were real for Alex, I can't begin to say with any certainty. However, it's highly unlikely."

"I thought, well... Father Talbert —"

"Yes, it's best maybe that we all listen to Father Talbert," Robert said softly. "For now, perhaps. For today."

"But you traveled quite a bit, didn't you? You came all the way from... where was it?"

"Your letter to the archdiocese was rather compelling, Donna. Also, I happened to be relatively close to Los Angeles when it was decided someone should come. It was no trouble for me to stop here to see you."

Father Talbert decided those should be added to his tally of the young bishop's manipulative lies. Unless one considered New York City to be 'relatively close,' and a last-minute, two-thousand dollar seat on a red-eye flight, plus a two hour drive, to be 'no trouble.'

"I needed to know," Donna said. "Alex died believing that..." She took a deep breath. "My son thought there were demons coming for him. He thought there were monsters, demons, and that they were coming to kill him. Oh, he was so upset, so distraught. His language... I've never heard him talk like that, not ever, he was so upset, so scared..." She covered her mouth, squinted against her grief.

"I know," Robert said, taking the tissue from her hand. He threw it away and pulled three new ones from the box on the desk. With them, he touched the clear streaks of tears on Donna's face.

"I know it's hard," he said. "If I could bear any of this burden for you, I would take it in an instant. To have suffered and died in the process of such delusions, of such imaginings, must have been very frightening." Robert threw away the tissue, took two more, put them in Donna's hand. "But consider, Donna... I want you to honestly consider the alternative."

She looked back at him plainly, then nodded slowly as fresh tears ran the tracks of the old ones. She squeezed her husband's hand as he continued to gaze quietly at the floor.

"The reason I came," Robert continued, "was because of the two names your letter said Alex used. Actually, both are commonly thought to refer to the same entity, to the same creature."

Both the boy's parents looked up at him. Father Talbert unconsciously stopped rocking in his chair.

"There is a very ancient demon," Robert said thoughtfully, "a female demon, that is said to prefer the souls of children—"

"Oh, God," Alex's mother gasped.

"Shh." Robert touched her hand. "Listen now. Listen carefully. There's very little known of her, really. As far as anything scriptural, there's just the tiniest mention in the Book of Isaiah."

Father Talbert groaned.

"In reality," Robert continued, "she may only be the result of centuries of superstition, and the tales of grieving mothers in the ancient world."

He's up to six, Father Talbert thought.

"She may only be a name spoken in the grief of women when their babies died in their sleep." Robert took a deep breath. "This was very early history, early Israel, Egypt, and Assyria. Early, early stories, born in the land of Haran and Canaan. Those early people, they knew nothing of crib death, of course, or SIDS, or any of the other modern names we give to such things when they happen today. So, quite understandably they'd see those things as the work of a demon. They would speak of those tragedies when they all sat together after the sun had set, in the dark quiet of the wild lands, and they would give names to the tragedies in their lives. Each type of misfortune had a personified designation."

Donna's eyes widened. "You mean—"

"Do not speak her name." Robert stopped her, raising his finger again. "Do not mention her, or give her attention, especially inside the temple structure, or at all, if you can."

Donna nodded nervously.

"At any rate," Robert went on, "that's what we believe is the relevance to the names Alex mentioned, the names he repeats on the videotape. Still, before we jump to any conclusions, we have to consider all the facts.

"First, you must understand part of the nature of a demon. Demons are limited creatures. Unlike God, they can only be in one place at one time. With that in mind, we can consider some of the things that we know with some certainty.

"Please don't take this the wrong way, but it's very unlikely that this demon, if she exists at all, would have bothered with Alex. She really is one of the most ancient and illustrious of demons. Her name has been recorded for many thousands of years and she's been credited with no less than the destruction of whole civilizations. She would hold regard for nothing and no one, with the exception of the Beast himself. Lucifer alone commands her, and his favor is the only reward she desires.

"Although a child of God and, as I understand from you today, a blessed and special boy, I can see very little possibility that Alex was in any way a part of this demon's attentions. Only being able to be in one place at one time forces these creatures to act, when they act at all, in the most efficient manner possible. If their plans included the manipulation of a human being, you can be sure it would be one of profound and widespread influence."

Robert reached out and took both of Donna's hands, looking at her and her alone. "Harsh as it may be, terrible as it sounds, the best possibility is that your son simply heard these names somewhere. He could have seen them in a book, or heard them used in a movie or on television. Somehow they slipped into his subconscious. Somehow, his young mind, which was innocent of these matters, caught the sound of these names, and they slipped from him in his illness.

"Although the circumstances are questionable, although this answer may not be the most satisfying, it is the most probable, and frankly, I'm relieved."

Seven lies, thought Father Talbert.

"But you believe in them then?" Donna asked.

"In demons?"

She nodded.

"Oh, yes." Robert nodded sternly. "Yes, of course."

Donna touched her eye with her new clean tissues. "But you don't think that he was...?" She bit her lip.

"Donna, I don't know," Robert whispered. "From what I understand about demons, and from what you've told me about Alex, the chances are just so remote. I would even go so far as to say that they're nonexistent."

Eight. Father Talbert was still counting.

"I want you to tell me if you change your mind." She began crying again. "After you've seen the tape, after you've listened to him, I want you to tell me if you come to any other conclusion."

"Donna, really, I—"

"You have to tell me." She grasped his arm. "Please, I need to know."

Robert nodded, looking at Donna's hand where she was gripping his wrist. "Yes, of course."

Father Talbert decided he'd heard enough. He stood, ending the meeting. It was getting very thick in that little room. Maybe the Monroes didn't know the degree of trouble and expense incurred to send Bishop Doogie Houser out from his post at the archdiocese in New York all the way to Orange County, California, but Father Talbert knew. Such a thing would never have happened if the archdiocese believed the probability of demonic activity to be at all remote. Nonexistent, indeed.

Father Talbert ended the meeting before the bishop had the chance to increase the number of his manipulative lies any further.

†

"Oh, man," Nick said, lying down on the sofa.

"It was a very quick flight," Scott said. "You don't live far from where we—"

"But you had wings, then you didn't!" Nick covered his face with his hands. "You had these big, big, black, leathery wings! I didn't see anything but the tips of those big, big, huge—"

"Well, of course, if I wanted to fly, I had to phase back to that form," Scott explained. "It was just the fastest and least complicated way to get you home. I stopped the bleeding, cleared your lungs, and got you breathing again. Then I thought, as I kept saying last night, that you needed some rest. So, we came here. You were unconscious, so I didn't worry about you seeing anything."

"We flew?"

"No one saw anything. It was very dark. I was able to land right in your building's courtyard. Okay, I didn't see the pool right away, but I changed form again, got you out, dried you off—"

"What?" Nick sat bolt upright.

"Nick, there was no better time. It was the quietest time of the morning, at least that can be had in this city on a Saturday. Honestly, there was no one on the street. No one saw anything, believe me.

Certainly not when we took off or while we were flying, anyway. Someone did look out from the second floor while I was pulling you out of the water, but by then I'd been able to phase back to this form again—"

"Where? Which apartment? What time was it?"

"I don't know the answer to all of those questions. I'm sorry, but—"

"My landlord lives on the second floor. If she was awake it might have been her."

"I can point out the apartment." Scott closed his eyes, raised his arm and indicated toward the kitchen. "It's on this side of the building, about two doors that way, above your place."

"Okay, that's not my landlord, thank God," Nick huffed, draping his arms dramatically next to him on the couch. "That's Alison and Marlon. Four to one they'd been slamming meth all night, got paranoid, and were watching the courtyard for militant democrats." Nick pushed himself up and draped his head back over the sofa. "Oh, my god, this is going to sound horrible, but I really hope they were slamming meth."

"You're not getting anxious, are you?"

"No." Nick jumped up and headed into the kitchen. "I mean, yeah, okay, a little, but that's all right. Really. I don't need for you to do your little eye-thing again." He stopped, tilted his head. "Well… no, maybe later." He opened the refrigerator. "What I think I really want right now is a beer. Do you want a beer?"

"No, thank you. Neither one of us should have any beer."

"I have Corona, or there's this Lite stuff—"

"Nick," Scott barked. "Neither of us want any beer."

Nick popped his head over the refrigerator door. "Why not?" he asked. "Oh, you don't drink or something?"

"Nicholas…" Scott shook his head, chuckling. "You really do need to pay better attention. Darren is halfway here and he's bringing… um… I assume you're going to want to indulge in…" He churned his hand in the air, waiting for Nick to catch up.

"Oh yeah!" Nick shut the refrigerator. "Oh good." He headed back into the living room.

Sitting down again, Nick squinted at Scott. "So, how did you…? I mean, did you glean, or whatever, all this stuff about Gina and everything?"

"Well, you remember," Scott explained, "I just came from New York. Information about drugs like GHB is extremely easy. The minute I shake hands with someone, I know whether they're being influenced by any chemicals, alcohol, or even a high-protein diet. I can tell you if they've done smack, or crack, or whatever, G included, and I can tell you if they mixed it with diet or regular cola. So, yes, I know all about Gina. And Missy, and Tina, and Mary, and Kelly, and Lucy. I'm well aware of all the more popular nightlife chemical-sisters."

Nick quietly shook his head, folded his arms across his bare chest. "He's halfway here?"

"He was getting dressed while the two of you were still on the phone."

"He told me he hadn't even showered yet."

"Well, if not, then he was planning on doing that with his clothes on, because I distinctly heard him getting dressed. He was going through all his drawers and he even opened a new package of something. Plastic. I'm not sure what it was. It could have been underwear, I think."

"You could hear...?" Nick started. Then he just shook his head. "Oh, fuck, of course you could. Listen, Jamie Summers, um, I do have one more question."

Scott had gotten up and was strolling around the back of the couch, looking at the framed photos on one of the bookshelves. "Shoot, babe."

"This may be a really lame question, but I have to ask it. I mean you can't blame me with all the movies and stuff, and what with all the different crap religious people tell you, or don't tell you, rather—"

"That's okay, go ahead," Scott said, gazing intently at the photos on Nick's living room shelves. "This is Darren with you here, isn't it?"

Nick looked over his shoulder. Scott was holding a five-by-seven, framed, color glossy. In it, Darren was beaming his Mr. Charming smile from behind Nick, his arms wrapped around him affectionately. It had been taken at the Mandalay Bay in Las Vegas the previous spring. Darren loved that picture. He looked great in it, but Nick didn't like having it out. Sure, it showed them both smiling. It at least appeared as though they were having a good time. The truth was, Theo had snapped it only a few minutes after they'd arrived. It didn't really reveal anything at all, anything real, about that trip. That photo certainly didn't even hint that Nick had ended up staying in the room with Eddie the very first night because Darren was being such an asshole. It didn't show any of the bags he'd developed over the four nights from not sleeping. They should have snapped the photo right after they'd checked out; Darren hiding behind his mirrored sunglasses, unable to even produce a Mr. Charming twitch, much less a smile, and Nick looking absolutely emotionless.

Where Darren was concerned, after that weekend, Nick had been resolved never to talk to the big, self centered, fuckhead again.

He turned back around, sank back into the couch and faced the blank television. "Yeah," Nick said. "That's Darren."

"He's beautiful." Nick heard Scott replace the frame on the shelf.

"I suppose," he said. "That's all anyone ever sees."

"You see a lot more than that, Nick."

"Okay, whatever."

"What did you want to ask me?" Scott said. Nick heard him move along the shelf, gazing at all the photos, picking them up and putting them back down again.

"Oh, yeah, um..." Nick started, trying to remember his question. "I know I asked you to help me and everything, and well, I guess, I mean—"

"You don't owe me a thing."

"What?"

"You don't owe me a thing," Scott said, casually. He didn't even turn around. "I told you before, I'm not after your soul or anything else. That question was the first thing I got from you when you woke up. Actually, it's the only thing I've gleaned today. Again, I wasn't trying to do it, but you practically screamed it at me. I just brushed your face to get a better look into your eyes and there it was, in neon. That's what I thought you were so anxious about in the first place."

"You did all that for nothing? You saved me just because you—"

"Nicholas," Scott said, turning so he could look at him, "you saved *me* last night. I can't explain how. Actually, I can, but I'd really rather not talk about it. Suffice to say that I was the one who was dying, hours before you ever showed up. I couldn't ask you to help me. That would have been wrong. I couldn't do anything. I've never, not in more than thirty-nine centuries, been in a situation like that before. I had no idea what to do, other than sit there, in the dark, and wait."

"What are you talking about?"

"Please..." Scott knelt down and looked at Nick for a moment before going on. "It's all very, very complicated. There really isn't any more I can give you right now that you'd understand. Nick, believe me, that's all you would want to know anyway. It's all that matters. Everything else is just so much trivial melodrama. You found me and now I'm here. Yes, I cured you. That's something I'm able to do, but you were the one that made it possible."

Nick looked down at his hands. "I thought demons were totally

evil and there'd be some huge and horrible price to pay for all of this."
Scott sighed. Nick couldn't help smiling at the familiar sound.

"Nick," Scott whispered, "good and evil are something that I'll be happy to discuss with you. I'll tell you everything that I know. But if you're asking me whether or not I'm evil, that's a question I can't answer, any more than you could answer the same question of yourself. If you want to know whether I've done evil things, the answer is yes. It's as simple as that. Yes, I've done evil things. I've done terrible things. Horrible things." Scott stopped for a moment, biting his lower lip. Then he took a breath, shook his head. "I think I've also done some wonderful things, though. I think I've been decent and even virtuous. But the balance, Nick..." He bit his lip again. "The balance between good and evil, so far, hasn't really been for me to determine."

Nick thought he understood. He nodded.

"Now, though," Scott said, "I want you to ask me if I'd lie to you, because the answer would be no. After you've asked me that, I want you to ask me if I intend to cause you, or anyone you care about, any harm of any kind, and the answer would, again, be no." He sighed. He did that a lot. "The fact is, you're going to have to make a decision, Nick. You're going to need to decide whether you believe what I've just said or not. If not, just say so right now. Tell me if you have doubts, or if you're afraid of me, and I'll go. I'll go, and you'll never see me, or be affected by my actions, again."

Scott stopped for a moment, looked at the carpet, at his hands.

"But if you believe me..." He whispered even softer, looking back down at the carpet again. "If for some reason you do believe me... If you do, then, if it's all right, if you don't mind, I think I'd like to stay for a little bit. If that's okay, of course. If you believe me, that I won't lie to you and that I'm not going to hurt you, then I'd like to stick around for a bit. Actually, I really think I'd like that very much."

Scott didn't look up. He just stared at the carpet, half kneeling against the sofa.

The apartment was way too quiet. Nick could hear the courtyard gate slamming and the jingle of his neighbor's keys as he passed the door. There was an argument going on in one of the units upstairs, and someone across the pool had their door open and was blaring something by Courtney Love for the communal enjoyment of anyone who happened to live in Los Angeles County and was not yet deaf.

Sunlight streamed onto the couch through the blinds, but it wasn't hot in the room. Scott must have known just as much about air-conditioning as he did about satellite broadcasting and DVDs.

"Scott?"

Scott looked up at him. "Yes?"

"Would you lie to me?"

The hint of a grin touched Scott's lips, which Nick thought made them much more beautiful.

"No, Nick." Scott shook his head slowly. "I will never lie to you. Nor have I."

"Scotty?"

The demon chuckled. "Yes?"

"May I call you 'Scotty?'" Nick smirked.

Scott's grin was no longer anywhere near subtle. "Of course." He shut his eyes and nodded solemnly.

"Scotty?"

"Yes," he answered. Nick was even seeing some teeth in the grin now.

"Will you ever hurt me, or anyone I care about?"

Scott took a deep breath. "No, Nick. I would face the flames the Lord intended for the damnation of the Beast himself before I hurt you or anyone upon whom you've granted your affection."

Courtney Love finished her tune and then Nick's neighbor decided that For An Angel by Paul Van Dyke was an appropriate follow up.

"Scotty?"

Scott couldn't help but laugh. "Yes?"

"Just so you know… I would never use a word like 'suffice.'"

Scott stopped laughing, but his lips were holding the most scrumptious smile. "Oh," he said, nodding slowly, "but I think you would."

They laughed together, loudly and freely. Nick jumped up from the couch.

"Okay," he said, "there's so much more I want to know. Do you want a soda? I'm getting a soda." He went back into the kitchen. "And since you said you'll tell me the truth and everything—"

"He's here," Scott said.

Nick popped back around the corner. "Who? When? That's what…? I'm getting a… Darren? He's here?"

Scott stood up and walked to the window. "Was I speaking French?"

"You're an ass." Nick laughed.

Scott peeked out between the blinds. "He's got a grocery bag with him."

"Oh, crap," Nick whined. "He must have stopped for some

apology sorbet."

"Apology sorbet?"

"Oh, my god, Scott, what the motherfuck am I going to tell him about you?" Nick was standing in the archway between the living room and the kitchen. The sudden realization that, at that very moment, Darren was walking up to his front door hit him like a punch in the stomach. How the motherfuck was he going to explain why he was alone in his apartment, wearing nothing but gray boxer briefs, with some guy that Darren had never met?

Nick pressed both his hands hard on his forehead while the situation hit home. He held his hands to his face as though trying to keep it attached to his skull.

"Don't worry about it," Scott said, going back to the bookshelf, looking at more photographs.

"Oh, my god!" Nick gasped. "Scott, this is serious!"

"No, I'm serious. Don't worry about it. Here." Scott grabbed a small framed photo of Nick and his older brother off the very top shelf, licked his finger, ran it along the image of Nick's brother, and then handed it to him. "Put this in your bedroom, face down, on something hard, like the dresser. It's very important that it's face down."

"What the hell are you talking about?"

"The countertop in the bathroom will work too," Scott said.

There was knocking at the door and the buzzer was pushed several times.

Nick turned to rush into the bedroom. From the corner of his eye, he saw Scott take off his shirt. Nick was about to ask him what he was doing but the sight dumbfounded him. There wasn't an ounce of fat anywhere on Scott's body. It was the most perfect example of a proportioned male torso that Nick had ever seen, anywhere, on anyone. He was hairless, except for a very black treasure-trail that slid up to end at his navel, the sight of which, for some reason, had the same affect on Nick as headlights on a deer.

Darren started knocking again, very insistently, which would have snapped Nick out of his hypnosis, except that Scott then took Nick's t-shirt and began eating it.

Scott saw Nick staring at him. "Wha...?" he said, the cotton T-shirt hanging from his mouth.

"Why... are you...?" Nick mouthed the words of his question absently. "...putting my shirt in your mouth?"

Scott dropped the shirt. "Nick, for crap's sake! Would you please just put that photo in the bedroom and shut the fuck up?"

"Okay, okay!" A little startled, Nick took the photo and headed toward the back of the apartment just as there was even louder knocking at the door.

"Oh," Scott said. Nick stopped and turned back around. "You'd better be wearing more than just your underwear when you open the door. I pulled some khaki shorts and a blue T-shirt out of the drawer. They're folded on the night stand."

"You know," Nick said, turning back down the hall, "you're a really bossy gargoyle."

Before he rounded the corner into his room, Nick saw Scott start eating the t-shirt again.

He ran into the bedroom, taking note that it was much cleaner than he remembered leaving it. Nick looked at the picture of him and his brother at the beach. He'd forgotten it had been up there. There was a faint line of saliva running down the glass over Tom's face and body, from the top of his head down to his bathing suit, where Scott had touched it.

Eeew, Nick thought, and laid the frame, demon spit and all, face down, on the dresser.

He could hear the knocking at the door get louder and Darren's voice, very faintly saying, "Hellooooo!"

As the knocking got even louder, Nick fumbled into the clothes Scott had pulled out for him. He went back to the dresser quickly and grabbed a pair of socks. If he wasn't wearing socks, Darren would know he'd just gotten dressed. With the exception of the shower and the beach, they both always wore socks. Always.

He ran back into the living room. Scott was sitting on the couch, right where Nick had found him after the phone woke him up. He was wearing a different T-shirt, though. It was one Nick hadn't seen before. It was white, like the Powerpuff Girls shirt Scott had eaten, except it had an X-Files TV-show logo on the front instead. *The Truth Is Out There*, it said.

Even louder knocking, and Darren's voice, quite strident this time, "Hellooooo! Niiiiiiiiickyyyyyyyyyy!"

"Just a sec!" Nick yelled at the door. "Stop fuckin' knocking, you dork!"

The door went quiet and Nick looked at Scott and rolled his eyes.

He opened the door.

Darren was standing with his feet together, both hands holding onto the paper handles of his Ralphs bag as it hung in front of him. He was running his tongue along his teeth underneath his upper lip, the way he would when he was exceptionally annoyed. He was wearing his mirrored sunglasses, the same ones he'd worn in Las Vegas, the ones he liked so much because he could watch people checking him out without them knowing.

"I'm going to just throw this in the freezer, 'cause it's been in the car with me for several miles," Darren said, stepping into the apartment, "and now, because I've been standing outside since Reagan was president, I think there's a good chance its become sorbet soup."

Darren took two steps inside the apartment, started toward the kitchen, saw Scott, and stopped in his tracks.

"Hi," he said.

"Hi," said Scott. Darren didn't move.

"I thought you wanted to get your peace offering into the freezer," Nick said, shutting the door.

"Aren't you going to introduce me to your friend?" Darren turned slowly toward Nick. He thought it almost looked like Darren was gloating.

"Um, yeah," said Nick, waving his arm in the general direction of the couch. "This is Scott. Scott, this is Darren."

Darren smiled sarcastically and extended his hand.

Scott stood and walked to him. "I'm Nick's cousin," he said.

"You're what?" Darren blinked as Scott grabbed his hand and shook it.

Nick closed his eyes and slowly bowed his head.

"I'm Nick's cousin," Scott repeated.

Darren looked over his shoulder at Nick, who felt instantly nauseous. Then Darren turned to the kitchen and started to laugh. He laughed as he slowly walked to the refrigerator. He laughed loudly and viciously. Nick couldn't help but chuckle right along with him, though.

He glanced at Scott. He was not chuckling.

Darren went on like that as he shuffled across the kitchen floor, turned on the light, and opened the freezer door.

Scott mouthed a barely audible whisper to Nick. *I'm going to lie. Play along.*

Nick mouthed silently back. *No shit.*

"Okay, okay," Darren said, not bothering to look at them while he put the two pints of sorbet into the freezer, "let me just understand what you're telling me. You're Nick's cousin, that he's never mentioned, and you just happened to show up here today, between the time I hung up the phone and drove over here." Darren closed the freezer door, turned and glared at Nick over the counter. At least Nick thought he was glaring at him. He couldn't tell while Darren was still wearing those stupid mirror sunglasses.

"Is that it?" Darren said with a smirk. "Am I gettin' this?"

Nick looked at Scott.

"I hope I haven't caused any trouble," Scott said. He was gazing at Darren with a worried, but subtle, sincerity. "Nick didn't know I was coming. I called this morning from the hotel, but no one answered, so I thought I'd stop by after my appointment. I've only been here once before, so…" He chuckled nervously. "I'm actually a little surprised I remembered where his apartment was."

"Uh huh." Darren hadn't stopped staring at Nick.

"I should go, I guess." Scott blinked. "Nick, I'm sorry. I didn't mean to intrude. Anyway, let me give you the number to the Mondrian." Scott patted his pockets as though he was checking for a pen. "Just call me tomorrow morning, or something, and we'll arrange for that dinner."

"Hold up a second, Cuz." Darren raised a hand at him, still looking at Nick. "What's the deal? Couldn't you two finish up in time to get him out before I got here?" He walked around the counter and came back into the living room, approaching Nick. "Am I going to see empty condom wrappers in the bedroom? Was it so good that you just kept going until you had to make up the lamest story ever? What? Did you flip a coin? 'Let's see, heads you're my cousin, and tails you're the cable guy?' "

Nick rolled his eyes. "Darren, can't you enter a room without mortifying everyone in sight?"

Darren waded right in. "You cannot seriously be asking me to—"

"Okay, um… I'm going to let you two settle this," Scott interrupted, raising both of his hands, one toward Nick, the other toward Darren. "Nick, I'm just in town until Wednesday, but I'm going to try to have lunch with Uncle Alan before I leave. It'd be fun if you came too, but we'll talk more about it tomorrow, I guess."

"Oh, that's classic." Darren folded his arms. "I'm not impressed, though. So you at least finished in time to tell him your father's name." He turned to Scott. "All right, Cuz, since you're having lunch with 'Uncle Alan' this week, where does he live?"

Scott sighed. "In Burbank."

"Mm hm."

Nick really wished that Darren would take off the stupid

sunglasses. They made him feel like he was going to write them a citation at any moment. *Do you two know why I stopped you? Do you have any idea how fast you were screwing?*

"And where does 'Uncle Alan' work?" Darren asked.

"He's the Human Resources Director for Cigna Healthcare," said Scott.

Darren looked at Nick again, who shrugged.

"Okay…" Darren squinted at Scott. "What does Nick's mother —?"

"She manages a movie theater in Santa Monica. Can I go now? Look, I don't mean to be rude, but I really didn't come here to play Appease-The-Jealous-Boyfriend. So, if you'll just —"

"He's not my boyfriend," Darren huffed, with a condescending nod.

"Oh? He's not?" Scott chuckled some more. "Well, it looks like I've goofed again. I thought that was why you're standing between me and the front door, and why you're arms are crossed so tight you're about to pop a rotator cuff."

Darren uncrossed his arms. "He's not my boyfriend and I don't really care —"

"Whatever," Scott went on. "I'll just go back to the hotel and let you guys wait for your sorbet to refreeze."

Nick started to join in. "Scott," he said, "please don't leave. He pulls this crap all the time."

"Okay. Right there." Darren finally took off his sunglasses. "Who's pulling crap? How did I become the crap-puller here?"

"Nick, really, it's no big deal," Scott said. "I should have just tried to get you on the phone again."

"If anyone in this room is guilty of crap-pulling," Darren continued, "it's most definitely not me."

"Wait, wait. Just a second." Scott squinted his eyes and pointed at Darren. "I think I saw you out last night."

"You what?" Darren squinted back.

"Yeah," Scott said, nodding. "You were dancing with that really young guy in those thin gym pants."

"Who was that, Darren?" Nick asked, crossing his own arms.

"I don't know," Darren started. "I mean, where were you? Um, are you sure it was —?"

"Oh yeah." Scott smiled. "You were wearing those black D&G's. I remember 'cause you had this really cheap t-shirt stuck down the front of them, right above your zipper."

"Okay…" Darren shook his head nervously. "I don't …remember…"

"That really pretty girl was with you a lot of the time too," Scott said. "I remember her because you're both almost the same color blonde. At least it looked that way in the club light last night." He glanced at Nick. "It's so hard to tell what people really look like with nothing but twenty-watt bulbs fifty feet above them."

Nick scowled at Darren. "Karen was with you last night? Was she working?"

"No," Darren said, then shook his head quickly, squinting his eyes. "I mean, yes, she was with me. No, she wasn't working."

"Boy, that kid looked like a teenager," Scott went on. "I would have thought he was your boyfriend, the way you guys were moving, but then I saw him dancing the same way, later on, with that huge muscle guy. You know, the one with the glowing purple necklaces from Disneyland."

Nick started to laugh. "Darren, was Thelma wearing some of his Chernobyl jewelry?"

"Just a few of those necklace things." It appeared Darren couldn't help smiling. "I think some guy was giving them out when he got there, or something."

"All right," Scott said, looking at Darren, "so, if the teenager wasn't your boyfriend, were those other two guys together? The teenager and the gigantic, muscle guy?"

"No," Darren said. "They're just friends. And Eddie's not a teenager. We're all just friends, really. And I don't—"

"Boy, Darren," Nick said. "It sure sounds like you were 'scouring' the club for me. I'm sure glad I have such devoted friends to watch out for me if something ever happens."

"Hey," Darren said, "we *were* looking for you, but—"

"What? Did you think I was hiding in Eddie's pants?" Nick asked, smiling.

Darren rolled his eyes. "Oh, my god, here we go."

Scott looked at Nick. "Were you at the club too? I don't remember seeing you. That would have been funny."

"I was there for about five minutes," Nick said, throwing Darren a smirk. Nick was loving the bewildered look developing on his face. This was turning out to be fun. "Scotty, if you were here yesterday, why didn't you call me then? We could have all gone to the club together."

"I thought about that." Scott beamed a smile at him. "But I wasn't able to check in until after ten, and I figured if you hadn't planned on going out, that you might already be asleep."

"Time-out!" Darren yelped. "Hold up a sec! Time!" He crossed his open palms together in a T-shape.

"What time did you get there?" Nick continued. "To the club, I mean." He was going to start laughing if he kept this up, but he couldn't stop himself.

"About midnight." Scott was still smiling.

"Did you have to wait in line?"

"I would have, but luckily I had my VIP card on me."

"Okay, right there!" Darren looked like someone had slapped him. "You have a VIP card?"

Nick just about lost it.

"Yeah, sure," Scott said, smirking. "It's green and it has Benjamin Franklin's picture on it."

Nick simply couldn't help laughing at that. He and Scott howled while Darren crossed his arms again.

"Who was at the door?" Nick went on, merciless. "Was it a huge bald guy?"

"No." Scott shook his head. "Though, there was a huge bald guy just inside the door, patting people down. I didn't know they frisked you so thoroughly at that club."

"It's an election year." Nick shrugged. "They've gotta put on a show for the city, look like they're tough on drugs, blah, blah, blah."

"Okay, um, Cuz, Cuz…" Darren's head was oscillating as though he was watching a tennis match. "Have you been at the club before? Would I … excuse me, *should* I know you?"

"We haven't met," Scott said. "If that's what you're trying to ask."

"But, I mean, I haven't even seen you, and like, I think I would have seen…" Darren stopped. He was staring at Scott's crotch. "Okay, dude, um, aren't you wearing Nick's shorts?"

"Motherfuck!" Nick yelled. "Yes, Darren! You caught him! As you know, The Gap manufactures denim shorts exclusively for me! No one else in the whole fucking world is allowed to purchase them! They're restricted!" He turned. "I'm sorry Scott, he's too smart for you. You're going to have to pay a very heavy fine now, maybe face some jail time."

Scott was cracking up. "You know, you can be kind of sarcastic."

"You have no idea." Darren rolled his eyes and shook his head.

"Show him the picture, Nick," Scott said.

Darren stared at Nick, who stopped laughing.

"What?" he said.

"The picture. The one from the beach?" He looked at Nick from the corner of his eyes. "Hello! The one I just gave to you?"

"Oh, yeah!" Nick's eyes lit up and he ran back into the bedroom.

He rounded the corner and headed for the dresser. He could hear Scott talking to Darren back by the front door.

"I've been trying not to be offended because he put it in the bedroom," Scott was saying. "I mean, maybe it's not as nice as the one of the two of you guys in Las Vegas, but—"

"Holy...!" Nick was looking at the photo of him and his brother. Only it wasn't of him and his brother. Not anymore.

Right there, on the film, where a clear likeness of Nick's brother Tom had been just two minutes earlier, was a very flattering image of Scott, sans shirt, wind blowing his wavy, black hair. The image of Scott had been captured as it laughed along with the image of Nick, sharing some intimate and jovial moment that had never happened.

"What?" Darren shouted down the hall.

"Nothing," Nick said, walking back around the corner. He suddenly felt very drained. "Nothing. Here." He handed the photo to Darren while he was staring at Scott, who smiled.

"This is cute," Darren said. "When did you take this?"

"It was in Santa Monica," Scott said. "I think it was the last weekend in... April?" He raised an eyebrow at Nick, who just stared back at him.

"Well, anyway," Scott went on, "my ex-boyfriend took it. Nick you remember him, Todd, who we will not discuss, so let's move on. Anyway, I thought it was cute too." He looked at Darren. "So, I brought a copy to Nick, who promptly put it away, back in the bedroom, but I'm not offended."

"What?" Nick said.

"Sheesh, Nick," Darren said, taking the photo over to the bookshelf. "This should go out here. It's nice. Don't hide it in the bedroom."

Nick couldn't take his eyes off of Scott. He'd expected as much. Really, he had. Still, for some reason, when he actually saw it, the change on the photograph, he'd been completely stunned anyway.

It hadn't really sunken in when he saw the t-shirt, but it was magic. That word was bumping around inside Nick's head like a roving cue ball on an empty pool table.

Magic.

"So, Cuz," Darren said, arranging the photograph on the shelf next to the Las Vegas picture, "are you in town on business?"

"No." Scott was still smiling at Nick.

"Oh, vacation?" Darren turned, hopped over the back of the

sectional, and kicked off his shoes. "You're off work for a while?"

"No, no." Scott looked at him, shaking his head. "I don't work at all. I'm very, very rich."

Nick leaned against the front door so he wouldn't fall down.

"Cuuuzzz," Darren crooned. "Want some sorbet?"

†

The bishop slid the videotape into the combination TV/VCR. The Monroes had left it with him and he'd promised to make a copy when he got to New York and send back the original. Father Talbert left muttering something like, "He had to get it up to ten," whatever that meant.

Robert thought the meeting had gone rather well, despite the fact that Donna and Ted Monroe really knew very, very little about their son's life. Still, with the information that was available, Robert had decided that Alex fit right in with the other victims.

For quite some time, bodies had been piling up around the world. They were always determined, by local authorities, to be murder victims. What made them important to Robert, though, was a very specific list of characteristics: each victim was between eighteen and thirty-five years old, single, with a Catholic baptism during infancy, little to moderate religious education, not practicing, and no significant continuing religious influences.

And then there were the wounds, of course.

The telltale wounds: missing strips of skin on the bodies like stripes drawn along the corpse. The discovery of Alex Monroe made three victims so far in the United States; two in New York, and now the one in Los Angeles.

However, in Europe, as well as the Middle and Near East, the mutilation of victims had been much more severe. Whole sections of skin were missing from the faces and arms of the bodies, and sometimes large sections of the torso. A thirty-two year-old man in southern Turkey had strips, three inches think, of missing skin starting at the small of his back, just below his hips. The wounds ran up his back, over his shoulders, down the front of his torso, across his stomach, and finally tapered out below his belt line.

The victim's family had told Robert that he'd gone completely insane in the days before they found him, ranting about demons, tossing around names such as Uphir, Alastor, and Gillulim.

There had only been one name, though, that really mattered to the cardinal. One name alone brought the attention of the Church to the victim's village in southern Turkey. It was the name his wife repeated to her priest at the victim's funeral.

The name had incited Cardinal Matine, prompting him to pull Robert out of Italy and send him to the Near East. The Greek word, the name the Turkish man uttered before his death, was the most important name to the cardinal and everyone in the synod. In English, the name meant 'darkness.'

Robert rewound the tape. Now he'd see if they had found the evidence the cardinal sought. Now, for the first time, perhaps he'd hear the names finally spoken by a first-person witness.

The VCR clicked and a white lettered message of 'Stop' appeared on the blue screen, indicating it had reached the beginning. Robert pressed a button, and the white letters changed to 'Play.'

He reclined into the low-backed, rocking, leather chair as the blue screen turned to black. On the tape, the lines of static danced themselves out.

The screen changed to a very fuzzy, out-of-focus, face. A pair of out-of-focus arms reached over to the sides of the frame, adjusting the angle of the camera's view. Leaning back, Alex Monroe came into focus, sweating, breathing in quick, panting heaves.

Alex was a quite big kid, Robert saw. Though, muscles or not, tall or not, he was still just a child.

And he was terrified.

"I don't know if I have any time," whispered the tiny, video-image of the dead boy. "I don't know if she'll come here first, or to the club." He wiped the sweat from his forehead with the back of his arm. Alex closed his eyes, appearing to Robert as though he were trying to get himself to breathe more slowly.

"Maybe she'll send Gil to find me," said Alex's video image. "I don't know. I don't know. I know she's coming, though. Fuck, she's fuckin' comin', man." He raised his face in alarm, perhaps at a noise in the hall. He frowned with painful agitation and his eyes opened wide in his panic.

Robert could see how this tape might concern the police; the boy was sweating profusely, highly agitated, and sounded fairly paranoid.

On the screen, Alex rushed out of focus as he reached for the camera again. Everything became a fuzzy swirl as he moved it across the darkened room, Alex's Fourth Street apartment, and settled again against a far wall, facing the entrance. Robert could tell the only light in the room was the one shining from atop the camera itself. He couldn't help thinking it looked like *The Blair Witch Project* meets *Seventh Heaven*.

"I know how this is going to sound," Alex went on, whispering to the camera, sitting against the wall, barely back in focus. "I know what you're going to think. Okay, guys. I know, I know. But this isn't a joke, okay? Really, I'm not fuckin' around, man! I swear to God, man! This shit is real! It's fuckin' real, and I'm in it deep. Oh, crap, I am fucked! I think I'm really fucked!"

He was panting, looking up at the door. "So, okay, like, even if you don't believe me... then, like, just listen, okay?" He frowned again, but this time it was despair. This time it was resolved desperation as the young man broke down. He cried for a moment, brushing his eyes with the palms of his hands, sniffing and wiping at his nose with his shirt.

"It's Laura," he said, taking a moment, swallowing. "It's my girlfriend, Laura. Okay, my ex-girlfriend, whatever. Um..." He squinted. He was crying, trying to shake it off. "She's, um... okay, guys, just listen, okay? Really! Please... just listen. Laura, she's... she's a thing. She's not a girl. She's like, this monster, or something. I dunno. She's, like, a demon, or whatever. I don't fuckin' know."

He wiped his eyes one last time and looked into the camera. He took several deep breaths, looked into the lens as if he saw some familiar eyes, someone he trusted, someone he knew who could perhaps comfort and help him.

"She's, um ... she's a demon, I think. She's 'Lamia.' Gil called her that. Ya know, that little runt guy at the club? That little fuckin' runt guy that's always acting like he owns the place? Well, he's a fuckin' monster, too." Alex swallowed. "He's a monster too, right, but he called Laura 'Lamia,' or something. That's what he called her, that's what Gil called her.

"Okay, at first, they were just arguing, ya know, like people, or whatever. They were arguing and shouting at each other. He was saying stuff to her, about how she was wasting her time, and that she'd have to answer for all the wasted time, and she just kept calling him names like 'puny' and 'imp.' I didn't think anything about it, really, but I didn't interrupt them. I just stayed back by the door, in the dark. They didn't know I was there. I thought I'd wait. I'd wait until they finished and he left. I thought this fight was a long time comin'. They were always bickering. They were always digging at each other and stuff like that.

"Gil works for Laura. Well, he works for their boss, but Laura always treated him like he worked for her, like he had to do what she said.

"She even hit him sometimes. Right in front of everyone. She'd smack him in the back of the head, really hard. He never hit her back, though. He never touched her.

"I always thought she was his boss. I always thought he was hanging around the club because he worked for her and he was there to help her, ya know, like a gopher or an assistant, or something. I don't know, I never asked her. I didn't like him, but I never talked to her about him. He always seemed to just make her upset. He only pissed her off. He just always made her fuckin' anxious and bitchy.

"Anyway, so I go to the club, because I have to see her, ya know? She maybe didn't want to see me, but I just had to try, ya know, I had to try one last time.

"I go to the front doors, but they're locked. They're usually locked, but if she's there sometimes they're open." He stopped, wiped his face. He was no longer crying, he was explaining, working it out.

"But they're not open, they're locked, though. So, like, I knock and I waited for a bit, and then I knocked some more, really loud, even though I thought maybe I'd piss off Max or someone, but no one came. So, I went to leave, and then I thought I'd just check the side door, the one down the hall from the bathrooms on the lower floor, the emergency ones, down the hall where there's almost no lights, and stuff, and where people are always bumpin' up or gettin' busy, and stuff.

"So, this is really rare, but they're open, and so I just went in, ya know? Really quietly, though, 'cause, ya know, I didn't know if anyone was there or what they were doing and I didn't want to, like, stumble on, like, a drug thing or somethin', 'cause you never know, and stuff. But I didn't hear anything for a couple minutes and it was totally dark, so I was about to leave when I heard Laura screaming.

"She wasn't screaming like she needed help, or nothing, she was screaming at Gil, and I swear she never sounded so motherfuckin' pissed off before. She was blowin' off, man! I mean, she was rakin' him over, and I was just totally shocked and so I stood there, listening. I just wanted to find out what the little fuck had done, ya know, like, what he fucked up, or whatever, so I just stayed there, back by the door. She was fuckin' blowin' off!

"But..." He frowned again, tears welling, shaking his head. "But, her voice... her voice was ... oh, my god, it was like... I don't even know! I could tell it was her, but it screeched and shrieked like nothing I have ever fuckin' heard before, like nothing I think anyone has ever heard before.

"She's shriekin' in this high pitch and I can barely make out the words. It sounds like she's even screaming into a microphone, and she's got, like, some weird effects on it, or something, but she's not, it's just her, and I can hear Gil, I knew it was Gil, and he's shrieking back, but it's much lower and not as loud, and he sounds kinda scared, almost, I think, you know?

"So he starts screaming back to her that she's, like, gotta answer to Lilly, or Lilitu, or Yulitu, or Yuliti, or some African shit like that. He yells at Laura that she's 'just the lamia' and she's gotta answer to Lilitu. And this Lilitu, or whatever, is coming, and pretty soon, I guess, and Laura isn't ready, and Gil is really givin' it to her that she's not ready, and she's going to be really fucked up if she doesn't get her shit together. So, she like just tears into him with this fuckin' vicious, screaming shriek, but I could still tell it was her. I could, like, still tell it was Laura." Alex begins to sob. "It's Laura, and she's shrieking at Gil, saying it's his fault, and he's a maggot, and she'll serve him to the Lilitu. 'Soft little maggot,' and shit like that."

Alex broke down. His breathing was very loud and he was sweating again. There was another noise in the hall, or in the apartment, or somewhere, because he stopped breathing altogether and raised his face in alarm.

He began again once he was certain there was no one around. "Oh, my god, I didn't know what was going on. I was just totally freaked out at her voice and at what they were saying and I'd never heard her mention this person, or whatever, before, the Lilitu or Yolitu, or whatever the fuck they were screeching back and forth at each other.

"But, now I know. It's some kind of monster. It's some kind of thing, a demon, like Gil, man. I saw him, man. He's, like, this monster thing. A demon, I think. I know that's what Laura is too." He began to cry again. "I know that's what she is. I know it. She's this, like, thing, just like Gil, and she's going to…" He stopped, swallowed, wiped his face.

"She was always too cool. She was always the one that would make me want to stick around, even after I was done and everything, and the floors were swept, and all the crap was put away, and the DJ was gone, and Max was even gone. She'd put something on the turntable and she'd whisper to me to stay with her for a while. I would, ya know. I mean, like, fuck, who wouldn't? You've fuckin' seen her, man! Motherfuck, she's like, hot! She's, like, the hottest! And she'd just whisper to me. She'd, like, fuckin' whisper, man.

"I couldn't ever figure out why she wanted me, man. I never got it. Why the fuck Laura Shah would want to hang out with me, but she did, she fuckin' did, and I loved it. I loved it when she'd whisper to me.

"She was always talkin' like that, like it was just for me, ya know. She always made me feel like she was just for me and like everything we did, everywhere we went, was for me, like she'd seen all the movies before, and eaten at every restaurant, and walked in Malibu at night a million times before, and stuff, like it was all just for me. She was just doin' it for me. I never understood it. I never fuckin' got it.

"Then we'd be together, at night, late, late at night. Sometimes in the morning, the sun hitting my blinds. I'd hang my comforter up on the blinds to keep out the sun.

"She'd kiss me and say, 'Just whisper to me.' She'd say, just like that, 'Just whisper to me. Tell me a story.' And I'd make something up, anything, and she'd smile, and we'd just lay there, and I'd just talk and talk, and she'd just listen and smile.

"Then... man, you know. You know the story. You know the saga. Then the bitch just ran out on me." He frowned again, shaking his head. "She just up and ran out on me! She stopped calling. She stopped seeing me. She wouldn't even see me at the club. She was never there when I was working. And Karen always told me I'd 'just missed her,' or some other crap like that, but it was crap, and I knew it was crap, and they knew I knew, but they gave me the crap anyway.

"I tried to just be cool with it, ya know? Like, the worst thing you can do when some girl dumps you is, like, act all crazy and shit. Especially when you work in the same place, and everything.

"I tried to be all like I didn't need her or like it didn't bother me, and stuff. I tried to be all cool, and I thought if she heard that I didn't care, that she'd maybe talk to me at least. Like, if she heard that I wasn't freaking out that she didn't want to see me that she'd, like, at least be at the club one night when I was working.

"Max didn't like us to be there when we were off. He didn't like any of the guys to be at the club when we were off. He said it just avoided trouble, because we could go out, we could go to some other club, and we could get rowdy and shit like that, and it wouldn't reflect on him, but if we got rowdy at his club, then he'd have to fire us, and he said that all that shit was a just a total pain in the ass. So, he just preferred if we just went somewhere else on our nights off so he didn't have to worry about it and we didn't either. We could get crazy, or whatever, and it wouldn't matter.

"So, I was only there when I was working. She always knew when I'd be there and she was never there at the same time. Even though I wasn't freakin' out or anything, she was never there. Karen's all, like,

'You just missed her,' and shit, but it was shit.   Karen's cool, an' everything, ya know, but she can be a bitch too, ya know?

"I started to really go nuts. I mean, I didn't think I was in love with Laura or anything, I mean, like, when we were together, it didn't seem like I needed her so much, or whatever, but after she'd been gone for a while, I started to go a little nuts.

"I missed her, but it wasn't like, ya know, I'd miss my mom or anything. It was really weird. I missed her, and it really sucked, and I was just thinking about her, all the time, at work, and at home, and like all the time. It was creepy.

"So, ya know, I just wanted to talk to her, ya know, just a little bit, and I just wanted to, ya know, see her, 'cause I hadn't even seen her, not even across the motherfucking room, ya know, since she bailed, since the bitch ran out on me.

"I used to think about places I might find her. Ya know, like where she might be, other than the club, and stuff. I was almost sure I could find her.

"I tried again to just let her go. I tried that a lot. I tried again and again. I'd lay awake and I'd make myself just say goodbye and let her go and she wasn't all that, and stuff. I tried to pretend like she'd just been visiting, like we hadn't been dating, or screwing, or anything. I tried to pretend like she and I were just casual friends and that I was okay and complete without her. Like I didn't need her. Like I could go on like we'd never met. She'd just been visiting and we were just friends, just talking, and I had a life above and outside of her.

"No dice, though, man. You know the saga. It was too hard, though, to just let her go. I couldn't just let her go, just go on, without me, without me seeing her, or talking to her. After she'd run out, she wasn't really with me, but she was. I could still hear her. I could still make out what she'd say if she were there. She still echoed in me. 'Just whisper to me,' she'd say. 'Just a little bit. Tell me a story. Just whisper.'

"I could lay around for hours just listening to her, even though she wasn't there. Sometimes it didn't matter if she'd run out or not, I knew I could find her. But sometimes, while I listened, I thought I'd really go and find her. I thought I'd really go out and look. Not at the club, not the club, but where I thought I could find her, the other clubs, the other places, downtown, the other clubs.

"I started to try. I started to walk and to drive around and to try places. It was a game, sometimes, trying to find her. First, I'd check around to all the bigger clubs, to all the really glam places she might go, but if she wasn't there, I had to keep looking. That was pretty bad, though, when I ran out of ideas. That was really fucked, trying to find her in the street or in some club I didn't know, where I didn't know anyone.

"I went by her condo all the time, but there's that fuckin' security, and shit. Man, I couldn't cruise by there anymore, ya know? They were, like, going to nail me for stalking, or something.

"But I kept trying, ya know, out and about. I could hear her laughing sometimes, or I'd see people she knew and I could tell they'd been talking to her. I knew it. I'd ask them, 'Have you seen her, do you know where I can find her?' Sometimes they thought they knew, sometimes they didn't. Sometimes I thought they knew, and they just said they didn't.

"So then two nights ago, Thursday, was when I thought I'd try the club again, ya know, our club, but early, when it was still closed, to see if I could catch her in the office, maybe. I knew it might piss her off, or Max, or whatever, but I just wanted to see her, ya know?

"So that's when I heard her screeching and shit, and I got really freaked out and just bailed. That's when I heard them, but I didn't see nothin', though. Not then, not that day. I mean, I was totally freaked about hearing that shit, but I didn't see nothin', so, like, I didn't know yet, right? Not 'till I fuckin' saw Gil, man. I saw him tonight, when I was working. I fuckin' saw him, man!

"Okay, so ..." Alex's breathing began to quicken. He started to pant. "So tonight, like, I'm at work, right, and Gil comes up to me, and he wants to go into the room upstairs, right, and so I can't let him, ya know, and he's like all huffy and shit, and then he calms down, and he starts acting really cool, and stuff, and then he says he's going to go home. He says he's going to just chill at home and he tells me to have a good night. He's suddenly all, like, Joe Manners, and shit. He goes to, like, shake my hand and tells me to have a good night.

"But then, like, I nod, and I shake his hand, and he gets this funny look, this totally fucked, crazy look in his eye. He fucking smiles at me. He gets this like crazy, motherfucking smile on his face, and he says, 'Oh, you'll see her.' Just like that. 'Oh, you'll see her, all right,' he says, nodding his head with that crazy fuckin' smile, and shit. 'You'll see her very soon, I'm sure.'

"So, suddenly, like, I knew. I just knew. I knew that he knew I'd heard him, that I'd heard them. I don't know how, I just fuckin' knew. He knew I'd heard them, and he was going to tell Laura. He was going to tell her, and she was going to, like, fuck me up or something.

"So, Gil just leaves. He grins this big, stupid grin at me, and he nods his head, and he walks away. Only I saw him get to the stairs, and he turns around and looks at me again, and he starts laughing. He's fuckin' laughing, and then he runs, he *runs*, down the stairs.

"So, I'm all, like, 'fuck this', man! He fuckin' knew something! He knew it, and he was going to do somethin', man! I don't know, he was going to do somethin'!

"I just bail, right. I just go, 'fuck this', and I bail. I have to go to the office and get my keys and leave my ear-piece and shit, and so I go into the office, and it's, like, dark and everything. Max wasn't there, he was at the door, or something like that. So, I don't even turn on the lights. I just leave the door open and I toss my ear-piece and the volume-box on the desk, right, like I fuckin' quit, right, and I go to the mail boxes and I grab my keys out of the box, and turn around.

"Fuckin' Gil is in the doorway. The door's wide open, right, and there's people walking through the hall behind him, and shit, so I can't, like, really see his face, not right then, but I can tell it's him.

"Only..." Alex stopped and exhaled loudly. There was a tremor in his voice, in his breathing. "Only, he, like, he's smiling and suddenly I can see him. I can fuckin' totally see him, even though there's no light in front of him. I can just barely see his face, mostly his eyes, though, like they were lights, or something.

"I can see him smiling, and I can see his eyes, only they're not brown anymore, they're like, fuckin' gold, or something, and they're really bright, and he's smiling and he's right in the door, right there." Alex's eyes were glazed, lost, he was far away. Sweat ran down his face, down his neck, into his shirt.

"Then he, like, tilts his head, he, like, cocks his head." Alex tilted his head in demonstration. "And he's smiling and I could see his fuckin' teeth. They were, like, fuckin' like, vampire fuckin' teeth, man, only all of them, ya know? Not just the two front ones, like fuckin' all of them were like these sharp, fuckin' sharp vampire teeth, right?

"So, I'm like crappin', man. I'm like dumpin' right there, ya know, and he starts laughing. Not like laughing, but like chuckling, only it's not even like that, I don't fuckin' know, it sounded like an animal, like some fuckin' animal standing there, laughin', fuckin' growling or chuckling or fuckin' I don't know, man!" Alex was almost panting now, racing out his words.

"Then, fuck man!" Alex looked right into the camera. "I can motherfucking smell his breath! I was like, eight feet away, or something, and I can, like, fuckin' smell it from across the office, and I can even feel it, it's even like hot, or something, like it's steamin', or whatever. It's, like, rank, and it's steaming!

"Gil's like, breathing hard, and doin' his laughin' thing, ya know, and like he knows I can smell him, and on the desk, by the door, right on the desk, my volume-box, my fuckin' box, it starts to smoke. There's fuckin' smoke coming off of my volume-box, that I just put on the desk. I can just see it against the light behind Gil, and it's fuckin' smoking!"

Alex, looked up at the door behind the video camera, saw nothing, pulled up the bottom of his T-shirt, wiped his face, reached for the camera, adjusted it, and took some deep breaths.

"Gil's right in the door, right, so he goes, 'She'll want to see you now.' Only, it's not his voice, though. I can fucking tell it's Gil, except for his, like, gold eyes and vampire mouth, and shit, but it's him, only it's not his voice. It's like this rough, scraping sound, like he has rocks or marbles in his fuckin' throat.

"That's all he says. That's it, 'She'll want to see you now.' Then, he just turns around and walks away. He just turns into the hallway and walks away. I can see his face in the light, and even though, it's a little dim, it's way brighter than the office, and I can see that it's him, it's normal him, it's Gil, he looks the same, he totally looks the same.

"Man, I don't know what I did then. I don't know. I just bailed, man. I don't remember seeing anyone. I don't remember what fucking door I used. I don't think I went out the front, 'cause, ya know, I thought Max would be there, and I'd have to say why I was leaving and stuff, like I was quitting and stuff, but I couldn't do that. I just had to get out.

"I don't know what's up, man. I don't know what I'm gonna do. I think I'm goin' to church, man. I think I'm going to try to get to a big church, a big fuckin' church, ya know, like that one down on Franklin, maybe.

"I don't know what to do, man. I don't know what's going on. I don't know what I'm going to do, but just..." His breathing stopped, then hitched. "Oh, fuck!"

Alex reached suddenly toward the camera. His image blurred, then became silent static.

Robert sat there for a moment. He sat there, watching the static become a black screen. As he watched, he could hear a vacuum in the chapel. He could hear a voice outside the office door, leaving through the side of the church, greeting someone on the walk.

He sat that way for a long time, just listening to the sounds of the church, listening to the staff as they cleaned and fixed and went about returning the building to its former state, before the funeral, before the body of Alex Monroe was blessed and mourned and taken to rest.

He'd mentioned the lamia. Alex had mentioned the lamia, and Robert, even knowing what he knew of them, couldn't be sure if the boy had meant the demon's name was Lamia, meaning she was *the* Lamia, or that she'd been a lamia demon, a simple succubus.

This was important, it was different than Donna had said in the letter. There could be a simple lamia involved, which would mean there was an even higher probability Alex might have actually encountered one. Perhaps if he knew something, or had something, or could get her something, something she needed. That was most likely the case, if there was a lamia in Los Angeles. That might explain why she wouldn't see him, why she'd stopped their relationship. She didn't need him anymore.

Or maybe she did. Maybe she needed him but not right away. Maybe she just needed to keep him close, keep him available. That was perhaps why she let him live so long. Long enough to discover her.

Though, there was also the remote possibility that she was the Lamia. If that were the case, and Alex had overheard and recounted the conversation with Gil accurately, then there were two entities after all. Because, yes, the other name Alex had heard was Lilitu.

The name he'd heard from the arguing beasts, the bickering henchmen, the name of the ancient one, the old and prominent demon, whose involvement Robert had explained to Donna Monroe as being an utter improbability. Alex had heard her name, in almost its oldest Hebrew form, Lilitu, the Assyrian nightmare, the ancient bane of the mothers of Israel, Lilith.

The tiny screen changed again, from black to blue. The machine clicked and whirred as the tape Alex made, the recording of his desperate, and final, ramblings, rewound. As if Robert would watch it again. He would not.

He stood, picked up his briefcase, and opened it on the desk. He'd make room for the tape; the cardinal would want to see it. The cardinal would want to hear it for himself.

There was his binder of notes from New York, containing the two files. There was his home-made directory of entities. A directory of possibilities, of probable demonic phenomena.

Beneath that was a photograph of the artifact. The artifact that was still in Rome in the care of Cardinal Matine. The ancient treasure of the Church that only he, the cardinal, and four other bishops knew, could be, and had been, opened. That is, since the Babylonians did it the first time, a thousand years before Christ walked upon the Galilee. Not even the Pope himself knew what only those few knew: the artifact was truly authentic, it could be opened, and it hadn't been, but now was, empty.

The cardinal would tell him what needed to be done. The cardinal would know how to proceed after considering the possibility of Lilith herself.

Robert picked up the directory, flipped through its pages. There she was, page 15.

> ISAIAH 34:14   Wild animals and dogs will meet there, and a goat* will call to it's neighbor, Yes, the screech owl** will rest there, and will find for themselves a resting place.
>
> *or Satyr
> ** This is in Heb: tylyl, or Lilitu, the Assyrian/Hebrew Lilith.

She was coming, apparently. Lilith was coming to California. There were demons there preparing for her arrival. There was at least one lamia, if not the Lamia, and at least one other, a familiar perhaps, or even a homunculus. Though if he were serving the Lamia herself, it could be any of a number of higher demons, an imp or a loubin. Add to all that the notion that Lamia and Lilith might not be the same, as well as the possibility that the two would soon be together, apparently after the same prize, working at the same goal.

Of course, there could be many, many demons out west. The suspicions of the eastern fundamentalists might be right on the money; the city of Los Angeles could be positively infested with demons.

He would have to tell the cardinal. He would tell him that it was possible there were two; that Lamia was something to be considered on her own. They would discuss it. They would reconsider the materials, the artifacts, the stories. Lamia, a separate and viable demon, just as the legends told, just as he'd first been taught.

And, of course, now Lilith as well. Lilith was coming. She could be coming, and she'd of course be after the same prize, the same objective as the cardinal. She was looking too, searching for the prize of the age, which was, of course, the skotos. The darkness.

Robert replaced the binder, stacked the tape on top, and closed his case. Whatever the specific instructions from Rome, he knew he'd be going to Los Angeles.

Chapter III

†

A Six Pack and the Secrets of the Universe

And he answering said, Thou shalt love the Lord thy God with all thy heart, and with all thy soul, and with all thy strength, and with all thy mind, and thy neighbor as thyself.

- Luke 10:27 (KJV)

West Hollywood, California
A small, open façade bistro on Santa Monica Boulevard, between Larabee Street and Palm Avenue

†

"Can I ask you a question?" Theo stared at Scott as though he'd never seen blue eyes before.

Nick watched him, stirred his iced tea, pulled out the straw, sucked on the end, and then raised his eyebrows at Darren, who winked.

"Of course." Scott beamed a smile at Theo, who was sitting on his left, leaning on the table toward Scott, as if no one else would hear.

"Where does your family live?" Theo stirred his own iced tea, although he wasn't paying much attention.

"Hey, Helen Keller!" Eddie pulled the glass away from him. "You're getting tea all over the cloth."

"Don't make me slap you in public," Theo said, taking back his drink.

"Who do you mean exactly, Theo?" Scott asked. "My parents?"

"Yeah," he said, snagging the last Equal from Eddie, who squinted at him.

"They're buried in Greenwich, Connecticut. Just outside of New Canaan. I still have the house there, but it's so frickin' hot this time of year, who can deal with it?"

"Oh." Theo stopped in mid packet-rip. "I'm sorry."

"No stress. They've been gone a while."

No one spoke for a moment. They all listened to the sound of straws diving through clumps of ice, someone speaking very angrily in Spanish in the restaurant's kitchen, and the husky purr of early evening traffic out on the boulevard drifting in from the restaurant's open patio.

"Is it a big house?" Eddie chirped. "Can we see it?"

"Sure." Scott smiled. "Didn't Nick tell you? I'm having the jet fueled-up right now."

"Right on!" Theo sang, to the utter delight of the rest of the table, who laughed with heartfelt abandon.

"He's kidding, Thelma," Darren said. "I'm so sorry."

Theo slapped his head and giggled. "You guys suck."

"That's the way, baby!" Darren crooned, rousing the laughter back to pitch. Even their waiter was smiling.

It seemed as though they'd been laughing all the way from Nick's apartment. Everyone was in a great mood. Eddie and Theo had shown up before any scary movies were popped into the VCR, and their unannounced — though, not unwelcome — arrival had changed the planned course of the evening.

After a round of introductions, then a very pleasant, lazy afternoon in front of the DVD player, an early dinner in Boy's Town seemed very appropriate for all the general good humor. Of course, Darren had doled out four doses of G from his saline bottle before they'd piled into his bimmer. Nick was thoroughly surprised when Scott even indulged in a portion of the compound, but he seemed to be enjoying himself.

Once the valet had the car, and they were seated at the restaurant, Darren wasted no time in spiking his own soda and joining the group's state of mind.

Before they left Nick's apartment, Theo had been visibly miffed when Nick and Eddie made him sit up in the front seat of the car, away from Scott. He was just too big. Three people trying to ride in the back seat was difficult enough without one of them being a genuine bodybuilder. Though, Nick noticed that Theo still managed to keep a very close eye on everyone's hands during the whole ride. Apparently, he didn't want anyone taking any fun little liberties in the back seat without him, not with this pretty new addition to their lives. Theo had a horrible crush, and Nick thought it was the cutest thing he'd ever seen.

At the restaurant, Theo stood back until Scott had chosen his seat at the big, round table. Then, he muscled Eddie out of the way in order to sit next to Scott. Who was going to argue? Theo's pectorals alone weighed more than Eddie.

Currently, Theo was destroying a lemon wedge over his iced tea, but not getting much juice inside the glass. Eddie was wiping his face with a cloth napkin and squinting at him again.

"Where does your family live, Theo?" Scott asked, nodding and then silently wording a *thank you* to the waiter as he put another full glass of cola in front of him. Nick thought the guy should have put down the other refills first, as he looked like he was going to dump the whole thing and faint when Scott smiled at him.

"Puuueerto Rico..." Theo sang the opening four notes to *America* from West Side Story.

Eddie and Darren joined him and made it a trio. "Jouuu lOvely island! IslAnd of tropical breezeees..."

"All right," Nick said. "If this is how the evening's going to be, I'm gonna need another hit."

Scott was laughing and clapping, completely amused. The song ended quickly, as, thankfully, the singers found the moment so amusing they broke into laughter themselves.

"Darren," Nick said, "do you have any candy?"

"Why, of course," he said.

Grinning, Darren reached into his front left pocket and, being careful to keep everything under the tablecloth, pulled out his bullet. Then, very discreetly, he handed it to Nick, who was sitting right next to him.

Darren could usually be counted upon to have, somewhere on his person, at least something mildly uplifting. Today, Nick assumed because of his recent tryst with Kelly, it was likely to be cocaine.

None of them knew any cute little anthropomorphic appellatives for cocaine. At least Nick had never heard any. Even so, the standard 'coke' was just so appropriate there was really no reason to habitually use any other moniker. It had its popular terms of course: snow, blow, and possibly some other rhyming nickname. Though, why would anyone use any of those when they could refer to one of the world's most famous illegal compounds by slamming home its historical ties to a major international corporation?

"What're you doing?" Eddie grinned at Darren.

"Nothin'." Darren grinned back.

"Well, um... you either just groped Nick right here, or you handed something to him under—"

"Shhh!" Darren gave the room a worried glance. "You know Eddie, you are just sooo subtle. Not since the Northridge earthquake has this city seen anything quite as subtle as you."

Eddie grimaced and covered his eyes in embarrassment. A second later, when Theo got the joke, he began to giggle a bit, only he was sipping iced tea at the time, causing it to blow back out his mouth and also, most unfortunately, his nose.

All the other guys at the table laughed so loudly that the cook stopped screaming and peeked his head into the dining room. Luckily, it was still fairly early. The boys were only one of two occupied tables in the tiny sidewalk restaurant, the second being a cozy deuce in the back, the occupants of which simply smiled and shook their heads at the commotion. The jovial little band of boys wasn't in much danger of being disciplined.

Darren was hanging his head backward over his chair with his laughter, practically supine. Nick was laughing more at him than at Theo. Scott, laughing almost as hard as Darren, was trying to grab some napkins for Theo, who was now shaking with laughter himself, blushing brightly, hopelessly embarrassed, holding his hand over his nose and mouth, probably afraid that more of his drink would escape through his face.

There was a little iced tea running down Theo's arm and dripping from his elbow, but he couldn't even breathe or open his eyes, much less attend to the mess. The waiter walked out and set a stack of white paper napkins, about six inches high, right in front of Theo. That, of course, roused the whole group into yet another vivacious outburst.

The street outside rang with their clamorous merriment. Couples strolling the sidewalk looked at each other, smiled and continued on.

Darren grabbed a napkin to wipe at his eyes. Eddie and Scott teamed up and applied all the paper products in reach to Theo. He was breathing again, but still chortling while he sponged napkins into his crotch.

A trickle of iced tea had run down Theo's white shirt. It left a stain that Nick knew from experience wouldn't be noticed until Theo either got in front of a mirror or someone told him. Since no one was going to tell him—one, they wouldn't want Theo to be uncomfortable during dinner, and two, it was just too funny—Nick knew Theo wouldn't know about it until he visited a men's room, which might not even be until they'd moved on to a crowded bar. At least then, Theo could just take the shirt off, instead of making Darren run by his apartment for a clean one. People would be staring at his chest, but then again, people were always staring at Theo's chest. He wouldn't notice a thing.

"Oh, my god, you are such a dork!" Eddie wiped a napkin over Theo's face, still smiling and laughing. "I can't take you anywhere."

"So, Theo," Scott said, "how long have you had this drinking problem?"

Finally, after the waiter had taken away the tea-soaked napkins, and Theo was satisfied he'd absorbed as much of it from his crotch as possible, everyone settled back into their seats.

"Are you okay?" Nick asked Theo, whose face was still as red as a September sunset.

"Yes," he said, looking down at the table.

"It's very rude to drown during dinner, you know."

"I know, I'm sorry," Theo said. He was still having some chuckling aftershocks.

Eddie sweetened Theo's new iced tea for him. "You're going to have to change your shirt before we go out."

"Eddie!" Nick glowered at him. "Now he's going to be self-conscious all through dinner!"

Theo pulled out the front of his shirt so he could see it. "Shit," he said.

"Out?" Scott looked around the table with raised eyebrows.

"Oh, yeah," Darren said. "Sometimes we hit one of the smaller though chic clubs on Sunday nights for a little bit. Sometimes we don't. But since Nick's um…" He tapped his nose. "It's probably already been decided."

Darren looked at Nick. "Have you done that yet, by the way? Can I have it back?"

"I was laughing too hard," Nick said. "I didn't get a chance."

"Okay, I'm trying to be subtle." Eddie leaned over to Darren, who was on his left, and whispered in his ear. "What the holy fuck are you two doing and why aren't you sharing it?"

"He's just getting a pick-me-up," Darren whispered. "Don't stress, baby, there's plenty."

"That's not Kelly, though, right?"

"Good gravy, no!" Nick answered. "I learned that the hard way last night."

"What…?"

"It's coke, but, shh! Jeeze, call CNN! I don't think you're getting us enough attention."

"Me?" Eddie looked at Nick in surprise, then lowered his voice back to a whisper, this time leaning over Darren's lap toward him. "You're the one who's snorting from a bullet full of snow in public."

"Calm down," Darren said, gently pushing Eddie back into his seat. Then he patted him on the head. "Watch this." He looked at Nick. "Is it loaded?"

"Yeah." Nick had his arms under the tablecloth.

"Go boy."

Hidden under the table, in his lap, Nick put the plastic bullet into the cloth napkin. Then, raising the napkin to his face, he snorted the contents of the bullet's chamber. Immediately, both the cloth napkin and the bullet went back down to his lap. The entire move took about two seconds and didn't appear to anyone, even within a couple feet of him, as if he'd done anything other than wipe something off of his upper lip. Only the guys seated around him were able to hear the telltale sniff.

"Holy motherfuckin' shit, Nicholas Reynolds!" Eddie sat back and crossed his arms. "I am very impressed. I've never seen anything like that. You are a pro."

"Darren taught me," Nick said, grinning.

"Of course," Theo chimed. Darren laughed.

"He taught me in the worst possible way," Nick went on. "You should have seen us, we were a mess. The bullet was full of Kelly, though, at the time, only Gina wasn't with us that day, so it was okay. We were at this restaurant off of Third Street in Santa Monica last summer, with some of Darren's friends, guys visiting from Miami."

"Oh, my god, I remember this!" Darren covered his face. Scott leaned back in his chair, smiling, listening intently.

"Okay, so, the service is excruciatingly slow," Nick said, "and, Darren gets the bright idea that we should all bump-up with Kelly. There're eight of us, but he's got a full bullet."

"Of course," Theo said, sipping his new tea.

"I guess these guys from Florida are really major Kelly-heads, so they start to pass around Darren's bullet under the table and each one takes a turn putting it in a napkin and doing a bump or two. Well, I'm totally shocked and in awe, and I want to learn how to do this. So, Darren, who already indulged a bit himself, decides to teach me."

Darren, still covering his face, was laughing through his fingers.

"We're in the back room by ourselves," Nick continued, "which at first pissed us off, because we thought they were putting the faggots in the back, but then we were happy, 'cause, you know, we realized we could do drugs."

Eddie and Scott were mesmerized while Theo and Darren both chuckled, shaking their heads knowingly.

"There were still some tables in the place that were close enough to see us," Nick went on. "So, you know, we couldn't cut lines of coke, or anything, right there, but Darren wasn't so worried about being seen that he didn't want me to try doing some K with the bullet."

"Oh, my god," Darren whispered through his hands.

"And let me tell you," Nick said, starting to laugh, "it took *quite* a few tries before I got the hang of it."

Everyone was laughing again. Theo was shaking his head and rubbing his index fingers at Darren. *Shame! Shame! Shame!*

"By the time the food got there, of course I was so trashed I couldn't eat a frickin' thing and I was falling, I mean *falling*, all over the other seats and the other guys. I couldn't even talk."

"I'm sure all those nice boys from Miami took real good care of you," Eddie said.

"Sure," Nick nodded, "but the problem was getting me out of the restaurant. All I'd had was regular iced tea, so the waitress wasn't going to think I was drunk or anything normal like that. Darren and the gang had to figure out how to get this mess they'd made to walk out of the place without falling onto a bus boy."

Eddie giggled. "Why would you *not* want to fall onto a bus boy?"

"They stalled for a while, hoping I'd maybe sober-up enough to not be noticed, but the waitress actually came back and saw that I'd barely touched my food. She asked me if I was feeling all right and when I looked up at her she just said, 'Oh, guys, he looks like he's had some bad fish. Did he have the salmon? Oh, yeah, oh geeze, he's got it, oh, boy...'"

Darren was busting a gut.

"She started stammering, poor thing," said Nick, "saying she should go get the manager and all that."

"She thought you had fuckin' food poisoning?" Eddie's jaw dropped.

"I guess so," said Nick. "I guess they'd had problems with the fish before."

Theo shook his head while Darren and Eddie laughed with delight. Scott stirred his soda with his straw, watching Nick, smiling.

"Darren jumped right on it," Nick said. "He told the waitress not to worry about it, that I had a bad stomach to begin with, and that they just needed to get me back home. The manager let us leave through the emergency door in the back and even took care of the check."

"Oh, my god." Eddie shook his head. "I don't believe it."

"The old Jacobson luck," Theo said.

"We ended up walking back to their hotel," Nick said, "and lying around in our bathing suits in the air conditioning, talking, snorting K, and laughing our asses off for the rest of the day."

"Those guys are crazy," Darren said.

"We were all lying around on the two queen sized beds talking about discrimination and employment law, of all things, but it still seemed funny as hell for some reason. Two of the guys were lawyers."

"Didn't Philip end up tearing off on roller-blades?" Darren asked.

"Oh, my god!" Nick slapped the table. "One brain surgeon grabs his own bullet of K, straps on his roller-blades, knee and elbow pads, and an MP3 player, and races off down the boardwalk toward Venice. We could see him from the balcony, waving his hands in the air to the music."

"What a freak." Darren laughed.

"He was a brain surgeon?" Theo asked.

"No," Darren said. "He's a stock broker, but we all thought he was going to *need* a brain surgeon."

"We were all seriously worried," Nick agreed, "but none of us were in any condition to stop him. Though, he came back a couple hours later and didn't have any head trauma, thank heaven. He'd only managed to scrape himself up a bit on the shins and on his shoulder, I think. He didn't end up breaking any bones or anything, unless they were in someone else's body."

"Lemme try that," Eddie said, reaching under the table toward Nick.

"Wait, one sec. I want to do one more."

Everyone watched as Nick flawlessly repeated the napkin maneuver. They rewarded him with mild applause. Nick bowed his head at them. "Thank you. Thank you. You're too kind. Thank you."

He passed the bullet to Darren under the table.

"Now, I'm just going to load it for you," Darren said. Then, "Oh, actually, I need one."

Grabbing a napkin, Darren wiped at his nose and briefly sniffed into it.

"Oh, my god. Did you do one?" Eddie's eyebrows were almost lost in his hairline.

Darren nodded at him, then stared at the ceiling and whistled, all the while keeping his hands under the table. Then he suddenly wiped his nose again.

"Another?" Scott asked.

Darren nodded, whistled some more, and handed the bullet to Eddie under the table. "It's loaded," he said.

Eddie grinned, looking at everyone sheepishly.

"Here," Theo said, putting a cloth napkin into Eddie's lap.

"Thanks," Eddie said. He was staring blatantly at his crotch as he arranged the little container of cocaine in his napkin.

"Subtle," Darren said. "Just like the Northridge quake."

"Shut up," Eddie said.

"Don't try and do it too quickly the first time, Eddie," Nick offered. "If you drop it, we're all going to jail."

"Okay," Eddie whispered. "Here goes."

He slowly lifted the napkin to his nose and *sniiiff*. He lowered the napkin back to his lap.

"Well?" Darren asked.

Eddie nodded and sniffed again to make sure everything went where it was supposed to go. "Any residue?"

Darren squinted at Eddie's nostrils. "Nope. Want another? Need me to load it again?"

Eddie nodded and passed it back to Darren. Theo watched the lesson with rapt attention.

Nick was tapping his front teeth with his finger. He looked over at Scott, who was smiling at him. "My teeth are numb," Nick said. Scott nodded.

"Go boy," Darren said to Eddie.

Once again the napkin came up, though this time there was a little adjusting required with the other hand. Eddie looked at Darren in alarm.

Go on! Darren mouthed.

Eddie sniffed again and the napkin went back into his lap. He wiped under his nose with the back of his index finger and sniffed again, just to be sure.

"Good boy," Darren said, taking the bullet back.

"Me, me, me, me, me, me, me!" Theo was practically hopping up and down in his seat. Scott squinted his eyes shut and grinned.

"I don't know." Darren smiled. "I think *you* need a sedative."

"I'll help him," Scott offered. Still grinning, he reached across Nick's lap to get the bullet from Darren.

"It's not loaded yet," Darren said, handing it to him.

"I got it." Scott nodded.

Nick looked at him in surprise. "You know how to…?"

Scott sighed. "Foolish mortal."

Laughter all around. Darren was watching Scott and Theo, resting his arm on the back of Nick's chair, brushing his fingertips against his shoulder. Nick smiled.

Scott grabbed his napkin and put it under the table. He whistled for a few seconds, then brought it back out.

"You've got something on the bridge of your nose there," he said, then put the napkin to Theo's face.

Sniiiff.

Nick looked back at Darren and Eddie and they laughed in surprise. Eddie was tapping his teeth.

"I don't think you got it all," Theo said. Giggles all around.

Scott put the napkin under the table, whistled, put it back to Theo's face, allowing his nose a second go at the cargo.

"There you go, big guy," Scott said bringing the napkin back down. "All clean."

"Thanks," Theo said, sniffing and rubbing his nose with the back of his finger. Nick looked at him closely; he thought Theo was blushing again.

Scott raised his eyebrows at Darren. "Do you mind?"

"Go boy." Darren nodded.

The napkin went to Scott's face. He wiped at his nose. *Sniff.*

Darren nodded again. "Take two. They're small."

With his arms under the table, Scott whistled the Jeopardy theme, then wiped his nose. *Sniff.*

"You know," Darren said, shaking his finger between Scott and Nick, "it's amazing how much you two have in common."

"Isn't it, though?" Scott passed the bullet, now considerably less full, back across Nick's lap to Darren.

The waiter arrived with a huge tray stacked with plates of teriyaki chicken and sides of spinach salad. Nick was suddenly very glad he hadn't ordered a lot of food. Although the G tended to make him hungry, that appetite was curbed by the cocaine.

The good humor, however, didn't suffer with the arrival of their dinner. The five guys had to keep their cloth napkins handy to quickly cover their mouths each time they laughed. An evident giddiness filled the little restaurant, which was drawing in quite a crowd. A small line of people gathered at the host's podium to wait to be brought to tables, smiling as they eyed the five gorgeous, giggling men in the center of the room.

None of the boys noticed the rest of the tables filling up, or that their waiter stopped by less and less as he became more and more busy. They ran the bus boy ragged and drained soda after soda and iced tea after iced tea, laughed and giggled, squinted and shook their heads, as they struggled to breath and talk and laugh and eat and all at the same time. The bullet was passed around again underneath the table, which was much more exciting now, what with the added danger from the crowd of eyes around them.

The din in the room grew to match them as outside the day retreated. Early evening came to claim the tiny West Hollywood neighborhood. Passive summer light lingered to fill the streets and invite the town to enjoy the season's tranquil hours. Sunday nights and work on Monday mornings weren't normally a significant deterrent for the locals. The bars would be filled until closing time. Although it got an earlier start than on Saturdays, the little Californian city would be filled with traffic, sparse of parking, the sidewalks would be teeming, and the joints would be jumpin'.

Anecdotes were the language of the moment as the four old friends instinctively brought Scott into their group. Nick found it impossible to tell what Scott already knew and what he didn't; he seemed genuinely entranced by each story, by each perspective, and the enthusiasm of each storyteller. The animation of Nick's friends was that of the eagerness of children getting a rare chance to tell a familiar tale to a new and rapt listener.

"He didn't have very good air-conditioning," Eddie was saying, "and a lot more people had shown up than he'd planned."

"This was the party last summer?" Scott asked.

"Yeah." Eddie nodded, smiling.

Now it was Theo's turn to bury his face in his hands and laugh. "Oh, my god, no, no, no, no, no, no, no!"

"I remember this!" Darren clapped.

"Shut up a sec!" Eddie barely kept himself from bursting. "So, okay, Sean didn't have great air-conditioning or anything in the apartment, but he had this huge, industrial-type fan, right?"

"Oooh, my *gaaaaawd*," Theo groaned.

Nick and Darren had started laughing already. Scott needed to lean over Theo to hear Eddie's story.

"Theo is totally trashed already, and the place is filled, it's *filled*, with people, wall to wall, packed! We're standing behind this enormous floor fan talking to Karen. That fan is really the only thing keeping the apartment cool and it's on its highest setting, right? So, Theo's standing there behind the fan with us and he's playing with

Karen's keys, for some lame-ass reason."

"Oh *GAAAAAWD!*" Theo moaned. Nick and Darren were almost hysterical.

"Karen and I are talking," Eddie went on, "and Theo's tossing around her keys and he suddenly flips open her pepper-spray and goes, 'What's this? Hairspray?' And he hits the button and it shoots all this pepper-spray *right into the back of the fan!*"

"Ha!" Scott burst out, covering his mouth with his napkin, shaking his head. Nick could still hear him laughing through the cloth.

"He pepper-sprayed the whole fuckin' party!" Eddie was barely able to continue speaking through his laughter. "The whole frickin' party is standing in front of that fan trying to keep cool! Sean is absolutely beside himself that so many people showed up to his new place and were having a good time, and then our cruise director, Julie McCoy here, pepper-sprays everyone! Every-frickin'-one! He doesn't just squirt the thing for a second. Oh, no! He sprays a very hearty blast right into the back of the fan, effectively dispersing a lethal dose of pepper-spray throughout the entire room!"

"Hey... I didn't... it sort of stuck, I think," Theo stammered. "It stuck... I think..."

Eddie ignored him and went on. "There're all these people screaming and cussing and there's total confusion and Theo just hands Karen back her keys like nothing happened and goes into the kitchen. People are running out of the apartment and Sean's running around screaming, 'What the fuck? What the fuck?' The poor guy's little surprise miracle party success disintegrated in seconds! He's got tears streaming down his face, and I don't think it was entirely from the pepper-spray!"

"Oh, Theo, Theo, Theo, Theo," Scott said, shaking his head with a smile and a chuckle.

"Well," Theo started, "I didn't know what—"

"Oh, jeez, Theo," Eddie whined at him. "How many people do you know that carry hairspray on their—"

"—it was! I don't know! I'd never seen one before! Shut up!"

The rest of the table laughed affectionately as the two went at each other.

"So it was real smart," Eddie said, laughing, "to hit the button when you didn't even know what it was!"

"*You* know Karen! I thought it *had* to be hairspray! I didn't think she'd carry mace, or whatever. I asked her before if she was afraid of being at the club late at night, if she was afraid of being raped or something, and she goes, 'Only by someone ugly.'"

Even Scott laughed, but it hardly seemed out of place. Their table was surrounded now; the little restaurant was full of laughing people. The boys were merely the hub.

"I don't think he ever found out what happened," Darren said.

"Who?" Nick asked. "Sean?"

"Yeah."

"No one ever told him?"

"I don't think so," Darren said. "Theo's still alive, which probably means Sean never found out." Darren smiled and nodded at Theo.

"*I* told him," Theo said.

"What?" Eddie looked stunned.

"Yeah," Theo explained. "I told him the next day. He was really upset and I just couldn't walk around feeling like an ass, so I told him."

"And…?" Nick raised his eyebrows at him.

"And he laughed his head off."

"Sean's a good guy," Nick said, nodding.

"Yeah, he is." Darren agreed.

"He's not still going out with Brent, is he?" Eddie asked.

"Not for a while now," Theo said.

"How's Brent doing, by the way?" Nick asked. "Does anyone know? Is he outta rehab?"

"Yeah." Darren nodded, sipping his tea. "I think so. It was his second stay, you know."

The waiter came by and started clearing the table. He leaned between each of them, gathered cutlery, stacked napkins, took everything away.

"I saw Brent at the club a couple weeks ago." Nick shook his head. "He didn't look all that rehab-ed to me."

Darren shrugged.

"Does he have a big problem?" Scott asked.

"Well," Darren began, "that depends on how you define 'problem,' and how you define 'big.'"

"Mm." Scott nodded.

"Frankly," Nick said, sighing, "we *all* have a big problem."

The waiter came back and showed the group an enormous tray of plastic desserts. They laughed, of course. Then he offered coffee, which they accepted.

"I can't believe I didn't see you at the club last night," Theo said, looking at Scott.

"I was behind the back-bar most of the night," he said. "I saw you, though."

"When?"

"You were dancing with Eddie. I thought you two might have been together."

"We're not," Eddie offered quickly.

"You just have sex?" Scott said, smiling.

"Oh, lord help us, no!" Eddie laughed. "Not anymore. Once was quite enough."

Scott shot a smirk at Theo.

"Looong story," Theo crooned, his eyes wide with his You-Don't-Want-To-Go-There look.

"You won't get any judgments from me, Theodore," Scott said.

"Only my mother calls me that," Theo said, carefully setting his iced tea back down on the table.

"But no one calls you Ted?"

"Nope. I hate that."

Scott nodded.

"I hate to be called Thelma, too." Theo flicked the end of his straw at Darren.

"Skank!" Darren smiled, ducking under some unseen flying iced tea molecules. "You know you love it."

Theo smiled, replaced his straw, and absently stirred the ice in his practically empty glass.

"Darren says it with love," Scott said.

Theo laughed and shook his head. "Oh, that's not at all true."

Scott smiled at Darren. "Yes, it is."

"What're you talking about?" Theo chuckled.

"He knows it bugs you," Scott went on. "He thinks it's cute. He thinks it's sweet that you care so much about what he calls you. He's flattered. He thinks it's sweet that you even give a rat's butt. If you didn't hate it, he'd never call you 'Thelma' again."

The table went quiet and Nick looked at Darren. He was squinting and grinning at Scott.

"Isn't that right, Darren?" Scott asked, folding his arms, sitting back so the waiter could set a steaming cup of coffee in front of him.

Darren only smiled. The waiter set down Theo's coffee, Eddie's, then Darren's, who looked up and nodded a *Thank you* at him.

Theo just stared at his full cup of coffee, an expression of serious discomfort blooming on his face.

"You're extremely important to him, Theo," Scott went on, not taking his eyes off Darren. "He's happy when you're around."

Darren didn't say anything. He silently blew across the top of his coffee, cooling it.

"You're an only child, aren't you, Darren?" Scott asked.

Eddie gasped. "Oh, my god, that's so cool! How did you know that? Nick, did you tell him that?"

Nick slowly shook his head, shot a glance at Darren, and smiled. Darren glanced back at Nick, who winked.

They all sat there for a moment, their coffees cooling on the table, the laughter in the room rolling over them, washing through their silence.

Scott shook his head, reached for the sweetener, breaking the moment. "I'm just fuckin' with ya, Darren. Sorry, buddy." He smiled, cocked his head.

Darren folded his hands in his lap, licked his lips, and leaned across the table at Scott, almost all the way across Nick. "You're a little prick," he said with a quiet smile. "I like that about you."

Scott leaned over in front of Nick from the other side. Their faces almost met. "You're a big prick," he said, smiling back. "And, I love that about you."

The two of them stared at each other while the others at the table watched in silence. Meanwhile, the busy restaurant roared around them. The coffees cooled, the waiters sauntered, the glasses clinked, while outside the traffic purred.

"Okay," Eddie finally said, raising his hand, "am I the only one here with a raging hard-on right now?"

Laughter erupted again. Darren and Scott relaxed back into their seats.

Darren had left his hand on Nick's knee, which surprised him. Nick reached down and laid his on top of Darren's. He was even more surprised when Darren laced his fingers through his and held them.

"Who else was in the back-bar, Scott?" Theo asked.

Scott chuckled. "It was mostly just some young actor-slash-waiter-slash-models, I think. I didn't get a chance to talk to very many of them. I ended up sitting there listening to this girl tell me about her day working on some television show. She was sweet, and I didn't want to be rude, but I couldn't get her to shut up."

"It was probably the Toodles Girl," Darren said, nodding and smiling at Eddie.

"Who?" Scott smiled at him.

Eddie burst a big guffaw. "Oh, my god, that's right! You sent her behind the back-bar!"

Nick started giggling again. "Darren, what did you do?"

"Nothing," he answered. "This chick accosted me in front of the B-crowd booths when we were first looking for you guys. I didn't know who she was, so when she asked if she could meet up with me somewhere else later, I told her I'd be behind the back-bar."

"You *are* a big prick!" Nick laughed.

"Was she in a black shoulder-y thing?" Scott asked. "With serious cleavage?"

Darren squinted, laughing silently, nodding. Eddie roared and clapped.

"Well," Scott said, "you owe her some cash."

"What?" Darren asked.

"You owe her a little money. She had to grease the door guy quite a bit to get in. He wasn't being at all friendly. Apparently, she even tried dropping a name, someone the guy should have known. I assume it was yours, she didn't say, but it didn't work. So, she ended up greasing him considerably."

"Oh, crap." Darren almost looked genuinely disturbed. "You're kidding, right?"

Scott shook his head. "I'm afraid not."

Darren took a deep breath. He looked like someone just accused him of kicking a puppy. It was a vulnerability that Nick had seen before, although it was exceptionally rare. In fact, this was something of a surprise, in that similar situations had never evoked any reaction even remotely sympathetic from Darren. Pretty much the contrary, actually. It wasn't normal for Darren to be so affected by the consequences of his actions.

Nick suspected Scott was lying, of course. Though he could certainly have picked the image of the Toodles Girl out of Darren's head, Nick couldn't figure out how Scott would have known what happened with the girl the rest of the evening.

It said something about Scott, whoever, *what*ever he was, Nick thought, that he would test Darren this way. It was kind of cool, actually. Spooky, but cool.

Darren leveled a gaze at Scott and sighed. "I'm really not a big prick, you know."

Scott nodded.

"I'll find out who was at that door," Darren said. "No, actually, I'll find out who the B-crowd chick was and get her added to the permanent list for that room. Maybe a couple of her chums too."

"I feel kinda bad now," Eddie said, sipping his coffee. He glanced at Theo and grimaced.

"You should, you ass." Theo elbowed him and tried to give him a very stern look, but he was smiling too much.

"You didn't know her, Darren?" Nick asked.

"No," he said. "I guess she knew me, though. I mean, she knew my name and everything."

"That happens a lot, actually," Nick explained to Scott. "Darren has promoted a couple of really big events at the club and people come up to him all the time and know who he is and he doesn't know them." Nick gave Darren a gentle punch in the arm. "He's usually at least polite, though."

"Well, I didn't have you there to kiss her ass for me," Darren quipped.

"Yeah, Nick," Theo said. "We were kinda worried for a while."

"You mean, all the way to the dance floor?" Nick laughed.

"No, man," Theo said. "Darren made us comb the place. He was giving Troy a really hard time, actually. So, the systematic search was Troy's suggestion."

"You actually combed the place?" Nick looked at Darren.

"Yeah," Eddie chirped. "Top to bottom. More than once, actually. Darren even sent Troy behind the back-bar."

"You *know* I would not have been behind the back-bar, either." Nick shook his head at Darren and smiled, but he was embarrassed. Not to mention more than a little ashamed for giving him such a hard time at the apartment.

Darren shrugged.

"Actually," Theo said, "we were more worried when we left."

"Why?" Nick asked.

"Well," Eddie said, "there were all those police and everything. When we couldn't find you in the bar we just thought you'd gotten pissed and left, or something. But there were all those police outside when we left, so we got a little worried again."

"What police?" Darren looked confused.

Nick risked a glance at Scott, who frowned a little and shook his head.

"Well, I guess you left a lot sooner than we did," Theo said. "Maybe they hadn't shown up yet."

Eddie went on. "There were, I think, three squad cars and a news van parked about a block and a half up the street when we left. They'd taped off the alley two blocks south of Santa Monica."

Nick felt the blood drain from his face. He sank into his chair.

"What was that all about?" Darren asked Eddie.

"I don't know," Eddie shrugged. "We were fucked up and waiting for our cab. We weren't about to go trotting up to three squad cars and ask 'em stuff."

"Duh," said Theo.

Darren looked at Nick and Scott. "Did you guys see anything?" They both shook their heads.

"Maybe tonight we'll see someone who knows what happened," Theo said. "I'll ask Karen, if she's around. Or Matt."

"Probably some dork passed out or something in the alley while he was puking," Eddie suggested.

"No." Darren shook his head. "You'd have seen an ambulance right next to the squad cars. Actually, if someone had just passed out, there wouldn't have been any squad cars at all. This was something worse. Someone was really hurt, or dead, or there was a gang-bang, or some really heavy frickin' shit like that."

"Oh, crap," said Theo.

"I hope not." said Scott. "But there wasn't anything on the news earlier today. You said you'd seen a news van too, right?"

"Yeah," Eddie nodded. "Definitely."

"Well, then whatever happened didn't turn out to be news worthy," Scott said, looking at Nick. "But if it really bothers you, maybe we could make a phone call or two."

"Oh, jeez, no." Darren gulped the last swallow of his coffee. "Let's go *out!*"

Nick smiled. "That's the way, baby!"

†

Sundays weren't anything like Saturdays, as far as business was concerned, but this was still LA, and it was still, technically, the weekend. Troy had barely closed the door on his last 'customer' when the phone rang again from the front desk. If his apartment building ever employed anyone at the—so called—security desk, other than silver-haired retirees who could barely remember their last names, much less that they sent a steady stream of young urban professionals up to the same apartment all day, he would have been out of business long, long ago.

Of course, there were other apartments in the building that received a suspiciously steady stream of guests, a good many of whom weren't all that professional looking. Well, not in the same way.

Troy's regular clientele were of a specific, esoteric demographic, which was narrow even within their own community. Yes, they were all men, and yes, they were all gay, but even more than that, somehow they also tended to be between about twenty and forty-five, in immaculate shape, quite high on the income scale, and maybe just a little bored with their lives.

Personal boredom was the only explanation Troy could find as to why, for example, a two-hundred and fifty thousand dollar a year real estate broker would park his Lexus four blocks away, walk through wind and rain—*rarely* necessary, this was California, after all—to his door, wait in his living room with any number of other six-figure-salaried west coast circuit-boys for anywhere from fifteen to sixty minutes for his turn to pad his pockets with enough contraband to put a buffalo into a coma.

Although the use of drugs to enhance the dynamics of one's life was far from typical in the gay community, or even its professional upper echelon, it was certainly a curiosity to Troy that, among his clientele, evident success was such a common feature. These guys, successful or mega-successful, were still looking for something to spruce up their lives, and they came to Troy to help them do it. Their cars weren't enough. Their hot tubs full of muscled twenty-something-year olds weren't enough. Their houses and condos with the views of Santa Monica and Malibu weren't enough. Their vacations in New York, Miami, New Orleans, and Sydney, all in the same year, somehow, gosh-darn-it-all, weren't enough.

At least this particular variety of chemical-user wasn't going to knock-off any liquor stores or mug any nuns in order to be able to buy. Also, they weren't generally the type to pound on Troy's door at five-o'clock in the morning on a weekday needing a fix. That was a fun little treat that, by sticking near exclusively with this particular customer type, he was able to avoid.

There was a drawback, though, to working with the beautiful, gay, white-collar type of clientele. At some point, they'd all apparently been convinced that they were a gift from Heaven sent to grace the earth with their image. When they weren't power lunching, or assembling six, seven, and eight-figure deals over their office headsets, they were down at Crunch or Gold's Gym sculpting bodies that far surpassed any Greek ideal. These were guys who could afford home gyms, to be sure, but they still showed up at Crunch everyday, nonetheless.

You had to hand it to them a little; they had discipline when it came to diet and exercise. Or perhaps 'obsession' is a better word than discipline. However, where diet and exercise left off, most of them employed science and technology, meaning surgery and/or performance-enhancing chemicals—the latter of which being another demand Troy was more than happy to satisfy.

He did have some clients that were outside of the snooty, circuit-boy spectrum. Although, they were rare. These other clients also represented a distinct type, which Troy called 'heavy hitters.' Not dealers themselves, but the absolutely most wonderful style of consumer: the kind that wasn't purchasing entirely for personal use, but *gave* away the surplus they acquired, as they were also in the business of keeping a lot of other people happy. These were folks who needed to cater to the esoteric tastes of their own target markets. These target markets were made up of a special brand of person who was not happy if they only found tootsie-rolls in a candy dish.

When Mr. Party Promoter wanted to get Ms. Major Celebrity to lounge conspicuously in the VIP area of his nightclub event, he sometimes came to Troy to get something fun for Ms. Major Celebrity to suck up her nose.

Troy might also arrange for Mr. Teen Heartthrob to be surrounded by some lovely B-crowd babies that have been indulging in something luscious, also supplied by Troy, which would help them relax, have a great time, and possibly also become more bendable and pose-able than a plastic action figure.

Karen Alanson was a heavy hitter. She'd managed to keep her job at the club longer than anyone had expected and it didn't look like she was going anywhere anytime soon. She wasn't one to be shy about arranging for those she cared about—and for some she didn't give a flying raccoon about—to have what they wanted, as Troy had learned on more than one occasion. He genuinely liked Karen, though, which made her occasional above-and-beyond requests of him quite a bit easier.

Actually, the club was the source of a number of these specific types. It was where Troy had met all of the regular party promoters, most of his heavy hitters, who weren't above using him to supply the frosting for their particular cakes.

His last meeting today was within that range, and although he hated this little jerk, he nevertheless resolved himself to cope with him. Karen had sent him, as a matter of fact, which was the only reason Troy agreed to the appointment. Though, this guy normally worked with one of the club's more successful event coordinators, Laura Shah. Normally, Laura personally scheduled and attended all the meetings with Troy.

Apparently, Laura couldn't make it today. So, Karen had asked Troy if he'd speak instead to Laura's assistant. Laura already introduced them at the club some months ago and suggested that Troy add him to his list of Folks-Allowed-Up-To-the-Apartment. At the time, though, Troy had instantly disliked the guy and only considered adding him to his list of Folks-Allowed-To-Speak-To-Troy-Only-If-He-Is-In-A-Good-Mood-and-Not-Armed.

The individual in question was just a lackey, just a runner, which made Troy a little nervous. Besides that, he was just odd. Still, odd or not, the guy seemed to have the right connections and the bottom line was the bottom line. The potential of this particular bottom line would put Troy so far in the black it made him giddy. When he was giddy, Troy didn't so much mind dealing with people who might be a trifle odd. After all, what would one appropriately call a gay, millionaire, ecstasy-junkie, if not 'odd?'

He picked up the phone on the third ring and the current front-door retiree grunted at him, "There's a real young fella here, he says he's—"

"Send him up," Troy cut him off, hanging up the phone. He immediately regretted it, because he couldn't remember the jerk's name. Troy could have asked the desk guy to get it. He spent a minute or two trying to remember the two times Laura had introduced them at the club. All he could recall was that the guy was really short, had a stupid name, and was so annoying that Troy had privately told Laura he wouldn't be allowing him business access. It took Karen a half an hour and the dangling of some very extreme numbers to change his mind.

Troy thought the guy had a name that sounded like Phil or Will. Why was he thinking that it was something especially stupid for a guy, like Jill, or something?

He contemplated the little electronic scale on his desk. It still had some snow on it, enough for a nice little line that might get him through this meeting without causing a headache or enough irritation to blow some important detail. Troy didn't normally do that kind of indulging. It wasn't normal for him to foster any bad habits outside of the direct enhancement of some deliciously hedonistic event. The thought of the obnoxious little runt currently riding the elevator to his door, however, made him look at the powder twice.

Not this time, though. With some effort, he turned away from the scale without grabbing his little straw. He grabbed his little calculator and a pad of paper instead.

The runt wouldn't be leaving with any product today. He'd just be giving Troy a more specific heads-up as to what would be needed—as those were things he and Karen simply weren't comfortable discussing on the phone—and when.

The living room was clean and tidy as usual, but Troy took a last sweep anyway, mostly to make sure there weren't any knick-knacks sitting out anywhere that might fit into someone's pocket. You never could tell with people these days.

Despite his initial effort at restraint, when Troy heard the elevator door open, every spec of personal discipline he thought he had rapidly abandoned ship. Knowing there were only seconds before the knock at his door, he tore back into the bedroom, grabbed his custom steel straw, set his nose on '**Shag**,' and cleaned every granule off the scale. He felt like a leaf-blower in reverse.

There was a knock at the door.

"Just a second!" he shouted, tapping out a little more coke onto the scale pad. Just a little more, that's all. He just needed to get through this meeting. This was rare, but motherfuck, the little runt kind of gave him the creeps, and he just needed a little bit more assistance from The Powder of Confidence.

He didn't bother to line anything up or make it pretty. He tapped out the straw, put it to his nose, and made like a DirtDevil.

There was more knocking at the door. That was all right. Troy was in control. He laid his finger against his unused nostril to close it and gave the open one a nice long cleansing sniff. When he was sure he'd gotten everything, he checked the mirror—couldn't leave any residue, no, no, no, no, no—and closed the bedroom door behind him.

"Coming," he said, only semi-loudly as he purposely slowed his pace. This was still his apartment, on his time, on his turf, and he was in control, dag-nam-it.

He moseyed into the living room and grabbed the TV remote, flipped on the power and hit the auxiliary button that would allow him to see from the tiny camera mounted in his front door's peek-hole. The television took just a second to warm up, but the image became clear pretty quickly. It was the runt—what was his fucking name, again? The runt looked pissed. Very pissed.

Troy rolled his eyes, turned the TV off, and dropped the remote. He didn't care if the guy was pissed or not, he told himself. Troy was fast approaching that lovely point where he didn't care about very much at all, with the exception of getting this crap over with so he could maybe go out and get laid. He casually ambled to the front door, absently tapping his front teeth with his finger, which were fast approaching the usual numbness.

As soon as he opened the door, the little guy, who'd been facing down the hall, whirled back around and blasted Troy with a big stupid grin, all evidence of anger gone immediately. Troy frowned.

"Troy-dude!" said the runt, through his big stupid grin. "I was beginning to think you'd fallen asleep. How you doin'?" He extended an open hand at him.

"I'm a little irritated today, Bill," Troy said, taking a stab at guessing the runt's name, just staring at his extended hand. "So, you'll have to forgive me if I'm not all that pleasant at the moment. Come in." He turned, put his hands in his pockets—Troy felt some of his personal power return just having watched the smile fade on the guy's face as he left his hand hanging there, open and unshaken—and headed back into the living room.

Troy couldn't stand this dork. He was seeing him because Karen asked him to, but that certainly didn't mean he had to touch him.

"Shut the door, would you?" Troy said, not looking back. He stooped to the coffee table, picked up his pad of paper and pencil, plopped into his overstuffed way, way comfy, custom chair, looked up at his guest as he entered the room, and motioned to him that he should sit on the sofa.

"It's Gil, by the way," said the runt. "Not 'Bill.'"

Gil sat on the edge of the sofa. If he'd tried to sit against the back cushion, his feet would have dangled there like some pygmy-male love doll. What was he, five-one or something? Good golly, that's little.

"Oh, yeah, sorry about that," Troy said, smiling, shaking his head, tapping his cheek with the eraser end of his mechanical pencil. "It's been one of those weekends, you know?"

"I hear you." Gil shot him another stupid grin. What a charmer.

Abrasive or not, Gil was very well groomed; Zegna shorts and a collared-casual, loose-weave Armani shirt, Ferragamo shoes, a Tag Heuer watch, light blonde hair slicked so tightly and so well it might have just been done by a tall cosmetologist in the elevator. Evidentially, Ms. Shah was very generous with her assistants.

It would have been a seriously refined look, had the runt been taller than your average mailbox. Also, there was a large portion of his right eyebrow that was completely white, which drew enormous focus. Jeez, Troy thought, anyone sporting a Tag Heuer watch should be able to manage a motherfucking eyebrow pencil.

"What can I do for you today, Gil?" said Troy. "It's Gil, right? With a 'G'? Like on a fish?"

"Heh, yeah." Gil nodded his big stupid grin, raised his eyebrows, the half-white one making him look like Spock the Elf. "Yeah, that's it, like a fish. You got it, big guy."

"That's short for... um..." Troy tapped his head with his eraser.

"Gilbert," Gil offered quickly. "My mother loved British opera and hated my guts."

Troy chuckled, in spite of himself. "That's terrible. Haven't you ever thought of changing it?"

"Wow, dude!" Gil laughed a little. "Now look, there you go, tall *and* smart. Where've you been, buddy?"

"Okay, okay." Troy nodded. "I'm sorry."

Spock the Elf had certainly heard all of this shit before, nothing new.

Yeah, he looked like he was about five-one, or so. Couldn't have been more than five-two at the most. Troy was a little shocked now that he saw him again, it was the third time, but it still shocked him. He was just short, really. He was proportioned rather nicely, actually, in every other way, but the guy was just short. In fact, he could have even been cute, maybe, if he wasn't, well, such a short, odd, little dork.

The poor guy was vertically challenged *and* had a seriously stupid name.

"This deal is gonna be a whopper, dude," the short, odd little dork said. "I'm glad you got your pad there."

"What? Is Karen inviting...?"

"No, buddy." Gil slowly shook his head, smiling. "Karen's just helpin' out this time. Laura too."

"Helping you?" Troy gave him a sidelong smirk.

"Heh, heh. Yeah. Good one, there. Yeah, me." Smile. Nod. "No. Lauren Isseroff's decided to ring in the New Year in LA. Don't ask me why. Somehow Karen managed to book her. Max nearly shot a load in his jeans when he heard."

"I'll bet."

"Lauren has a heavy hand in production, so Laura's taking a backseat to her, naturally."

"Wow. Karen didn't mention this detail. Lauren Ice is coming to LA?"

"Don't let her hear you call her that."

"I thought—"

"She fuckin' hates that, dude. No one calls her that, not in Europe, not in New York. I guess the LA kids haven't heard."

"I thought that was her name, what she wanted to be called."

"No, it's not. It never was. It was unfortunately printed by mistake on a promo flyer a couple years back. She totally went postal. I'm sure you can understand why."

"Right."

"Anyway, don't worry about it. She won't be here until the day before, maybe *of*, and I doubt you'll meet her."

Troy raised an eyebrow. Was he just insulted?

"You're talking about New Year's Eve?" Troy asked.

"Well…" Gil grinned. "That's probably the best time to ring in the New Year. So much as I've heard anyway, but if you suggest Valentine's Day or something, I'd be happy to pass it along. Though, I don't think—"

"Yeah, yeah, very funny. You're a quick one, you." Maybe it wasn't his last one just yet, but that was a nerve, and the runt was workin' it.

"Her real last name is Isser-what?" Troy asked.

"Isseroff," Gil answered plainly. "You pronounce a 'z' sound in the beginning."

"She needs an easier last name, like Laura's."

"Shah?"

"Yeah."

"Okay, well, that's an abbreviation. Laura's last name is Shahnazarov."

"Wow!" Troy couldn't help laughing. "Are they related? Or both, like, Russian, or something?"

"Yeah, sure, Russian, or something. That's probably it. Something foreign, like possibly Czech or Lutheran. Actually, dude, I don't know. Related?"

"Well, you know, 'Laura', 'Lauren'. If there were a third, don't you think she'd be 'Lana'?' " Troy smiled. Didn't the runt get this?

"A third what?"

"Never mind." Troy let it go. Why was he shooting the shit with this goober anyway? "I'm assuming I won't need to supply any product until after Christmas then?"

Gil slowly shook his head. "There's been an additional development. Lauren wants a small intro-type event produced in late December, mostly for promotion staff and some celebs. She wants to make sure the thirty-first is sold out, gone, flooded, out of print, not negotiable. She's hoping to manufacture that idea, like a rolling buzz, you know, in advance of things, so people are highly motivated to talk and the tickets go well before the day."

"A small event? What, at the club?"

"No." Gil shook his head again and smiled, but the look on his face clearly said, *Of course not, you idiot.*

Troy tapped the eraser against his ear. He didn't know how many nerves he had left, but Gil was working through them in record time. This was going to be a short meeting.

"Hey, you know what?" Troy said. "Why don't you just fill me in on all the particulars right now?" He shot Gil a tepid smile. "I think I mentioned back at the front door that I was PMSing a bit today, so don't make me guess anymore, okay? I'm not in the mood."

Gil leaned forward, laced his fingers, flashed his stupid grin. "At a private residence, I think somewhere off Sunset, on, like, Genesee or Nichols Canyon, or something, there'll be a small, but glimmering event. Strictly invite only. Strictly list, you know? A-list, man. There'll be big, big bouncers, big, bad, bouncin' booby-babes, maybe even some of those muscle-dancer-dudes for the bone smokers, I don't know, all this shit is so mixed these days, you know? You never know who's going to be checkin' out your ass."

"I'm sure you don't have a problem," Troy said, getting very, very low on nerves. So low his warning light was about to come on.

"Yeah, well, you know," the well-groomed, obnoxious Lilliputian continued, "whatever, man. Okay, so, this is happening the week before Christmas. Saturday evening. The second Saturday of the month, not the third, I think. And it's *the* deal, babe, catered, waitered, and tailored."

"DJ? Is Lauren spinning, dare I dream?"

"Okay, buddy, no." Stupid grin. "Not 'till New Years, dude, remember? She's not going to be here for the promo thing. She gets here, like, on the thirtieth, or the thirty-first."

"At the club?"

"You're catching on."

"Gil?"

"Yeah, dude?"

"See that window behind me?"

"Yeah."

"That's the way you're going to be leaving this apartment if you shoot one more idiot remark at me."

Gil's stupid grin fell onto the coffee table.

"Also," Troy went on, "if I hear one more derogatory statement about 'bone smokers,' or anything of that nature, I'm not going to throw you out the window. Instead, I'm going to take great pleasure in finding out just how long it takes to feed your screaming dwarf-ass to my garbage disposal. Am I clear? Is that a little easier to understand than my warning at the front door? Normally, the adults that come here tend to pick up on stuff like that, but it seems to have gone completely over your head. Oh, excuse me! Was that a short-crack? I guess it was but, then again, you have to deal with a short-crack every time you drop your pants, don't you?"

Gil just stared at him. Troy had tried to remain calm, he'd tried to stay professional, but he had to put his foot down. This was partly Karen's fault, however; she could have warned Gil. She could have made sure he understood that he was to be on his best behavior while he was in Troy's home and he was not to, under any circumstances whatsoever, make derogatory remarks about gays.

After all, being gay tended to make one a bit sensitive to such commentary.

Of course, there was the possibility that Karen *had* warned him, that she had made Troy's orientation known to the little bigot, but that the runt had chosen to use that information in an antagonistic manner. If that turned out to be the case, Troy saw a couple of very short and very broken legs in this boy's immediate future. For a little guy, he had a very big mouth.

Troy just watched him. He didn't let his tepid smile falter or allow his gaze to stray. He stared right back at him to let Gil know that, in no uncertain terms, he meant business; if his attitude didn't change, someone was going to be scraping Gil's stupid grin off the parking lot.

Gil didn't blink. He returned Troy's glare with fervor, but there was a slight twitch over his eye, underneath the bleach-white part of his eyebrow, actually, just the tiniest tremble to indicate to Troy that maybe Gil was working quite hard to fight down his temper and his ego.

After a breathless moment or two, Gil raised his hands, palms out, in surrender.

"I'm sorry, dude," he said. "I didn't mean to be offensive."

Troy closed his eyes, inhaled, sat back in his way, way comfy custom chair, and tapped the eraser end of his mechanical pencil against his forehead.

"You're going to want to have product all over the place at the private party," he said.

"Yes," Gil nodded.

"And you're just going to want the club's VIP rooms handled at the big event."

"Right. Plus the DJ booth"

"Tricky," Troy lied, posturing in order to increase his fee. "But do-able."

"Really, buddy, I'm sorry about all that. This is my first time taking care of any kind of chemical-catering."

"I'll tell you what," Troy said, tapping his knee with the pencil, "you never call anyone a 'bone smoker,' ever again, and I won't have you killed. How'zat?"

"Heh," Gil chuckled nervously. "Um, yeah, okay, sure dude. I didn't mean nothin'."

It took them another forty-five minutes, but they managed to hammer out the numbers, the dates and times, and the protocols. The runt didn't make any more lame comments, but Troy thought Karen still owed him big. He was pleased, though, that his violent bluff had managed to intimidate the guy into at least the appearance of respect, and didn't for a moment even consider the fact, much less feel guilty, that he thought of him as a runt, and had actually called him a dwarf.

†

Nick sat up in bed and wiped at his eyes. He looked over at Darren, who was sleeping soundly, breathing deeply and evenly. Just how the heck he managed to do that after spending five and a half hours dancing, laughing, cavorting, bar hopping, downing Gina and snorting cocaine, was a mystery that actually irritated Nick a bit.

Nick had taken an over-the-counter sleep aid, which did exactly nothing. An hour later he'd taken another, which at least managed to squelch the rambunctious coke-fuzzies bouncing between his ears, but didn't do anything to help him get to sleep. Instead, he just laid there and listened to Darren snore next to him in that little baby lion way that sounded so funny coming from such a big guy.

Nick listened for an hour or so, but when he saw the dawn begin poking at the bottom of his blinds, he decided to get up and find a stronger sedative.

Although it ruffled him a little that Darren was out cold, he didn't want to wake him up. So, he slowly swung his legs out from under the thin comforter and carefully lowered himself from the high stack of mattress and box-spring to the carpet. When he'd lifted his weight off the bed with just the most minimal squeak from the frame, he looked back, saw that Darren was still asleep and making little lion noises, and then quietly walked out to the hall.

He shut the door to the bathroom before flipping on the lights and squinted at the sudden brightness. He'd forgotten to take out his lenses and a kind of smeary fog covered his vision. Careful to be quiet when he opened the medicine cabinet, he took out his lens case and saline. While he was taking his lenses out, he wondered if it had been long enough from his last dose of GHB for him to safely induce sleep with the aid of yet another sleeping pill, perhaps enhanced with a large shot of vodka. Or two.

When the contacts were removed and he'd donned his glasses, he shut his eyes to get them used to the dark again, flipped off the light, quietly opened the door, and headed to the kitchen. The apartment was still very dark; the morning was only beginning to kiss the corners of his windows. Nick knew his apartment very well, though, and he effortlessly navigated his way past the end of the sectional and through the wall-arch into the kitchen without smashing into any walls or knocking the table lamp to the floor.

Even in the kitchen, he didn't bother with a light. The open refrigerator would be enough. He reached in and took out a two-liter bottle of cola, which was the only thing inside the refrigerator besides two six-packs of Corona. Then he opened the freezer, moved the remaining half pint of sorbet, and grabbed the only hard liquor he had, which was Absolute Citron—it was on sale if you had a Ralphs card. The combo wasn't going to be the next beverage craze anywhere. He was used to it, though, since he couldn't drink the shit straight. The fact was, he never kept any other hard liquor at home, and never thought to buy anything else with which to mix it.

He poured a generous amount of the booze into a large coffee cup and filled the rest with soda. Then he drained half of it, squinting at the horrible combination, and filled the cup again with cola. The rest wouldn't taste so bad.

He shuffled into the living room and lounged on the sofa. From there, he couldn't hear Darren or any other sounds in the apartment besides the soft hum of the refrigerator. The only sounds from outside were the drone of several air conditioners coming through the slightly open window on the courtyard side of the apartment, and the infrequent whisp of traffic on the street side.

The blinds on the windows were open just enough for him to see the growing light in the street and watch it begin to gleam on the cars at the curb, one of which being Darren's new black BMW.

After they'd gotten home, Darren tried to convince Nick that, since he was going to stay rather than try to drive back to his own apartment, they should swap spaces; the Beamer should be in the underground garage and Nick's older—by exactly one whole year—and less expensive—by five-thousand dollars—car should brave the street. Nick told Darren that his new car was going to have to learn about the outside world sooner or later and tonight was as good a time as any. Besides, Fountain Avenue wasn't as busy as Santa Monica Boulevard, but it sure wasn't a tiny, residential street that was deserted in the night and therefore more prone to break-ins or outright theft. Plus, since it was Monday morning—they'd gotten home around three or so—Darren was going to have to get up and move his car before eight o'clock anyway. If he didn't, the city would move it for him.

By eight, though, a number of Nick's neighbors would have gone to work and opened up some room in the garage, where Darren could put his new treasure should he opt to hang out for breakfast.

Nick hadn't worked in six months and was well aware of what his apartment complex was like during the week's business hours. It was empty, quiet, and very, very dull. The only sounds were of the single maintenance guy trudging around with his broom and wastebasket. Occasionally, he trimmed foliage or cleaned the pool. That was always exciting.

Work or no, Nick's bank account was dangerously full. Full, because the last time he'd worked had been in an international commercial, which had a market impact that exceeded expectations nicely, especially in Europe. The commercial hadn't stopped running yet, though its appearance was much less frequent. Still, that meant the residual checks were still coming in.

The money was dangerous because money meant freedom, and freedom meant indulgence.

Despite his indulgences, Nick had so far managed to keep himself out of jail, the hospital, and the morgue, while he waited around pretending to care if his agent called. The morgue, he realized later, had only been avoided with the somewhat divine intervention of, jeeze-louise he didn't even want to think about what.

It was difficult to look at Scott and see a demon. Impossible, actually. Even if he could view his new friend as a demon, what did that mean precisely? He wasn't exactly going around sacrificing children or possessing anyone and making them spit pea soup. During the entire time Scott had been spending with them, not a single person's head had spun completely around on their body. Nope, no red-eyed Linda Blair wanna-bes here.

Theo was in love with Scott. Eddie was delighted with his company. And Darren... well, Darren was acting a little strange. Darren was being nice, which was a little strange. Nick liked it, though, but it made him nervous at the same time because he thought it was capricious. He thought it was Darren's reaction to the novelty of Scott, just like Theo's tantrum about the front seat of the car. Darren might, at any time, go back to being Darren, which meant Nick would, well... Nick would do whatever he thought was appropriate when and if that happened.

That was a truckload of donkey-hockey, though. Nick never did what he thought was appropriate where Darren was concerned. He only did what he thought would be less painful, which was often quite *in*appropriate. Therefore, he hadn't suffered an intense broken heart, consequently skimmed the dregs of depression for a month or so, but then eventually picked himself up.

No, instead he'd opted to suffer the inevitable broken heart, which wasn't immediately intense, but drawn out over time, and paid for in regular installments.

It certainly seemed like each month or so, in one way or another, Nick had to find a way to handle the emotional expense of letting Darren stick around. Either by ignoring the fact that Darren didn't think it bothered him when he screwed around with other guys, or by allowing Darren to perpetuate the We're-Just-Friends façade that was so important to him—for some stupid, immature, motherfucking, asshole reason.

The We're-Just-Friends façade was very important to Darren, as a matter of fact, even around their own kind and in their own world. In the end, Nick thought all the compounded interest of anxiety and heartache was probably going to kill him.

Tonight—last night, actually, he corrected himself—had been kind of cool, though; very un-Darren-ish. It had started out sort of sweetly. Darren almost acted as though he maybe didn't care that anyone who saw the two of them might think they were together. It had started out sweet and nice and wonderful, but new-friend-novelty type influence or not, it turned out, inevitably, that Darren was still Darren.

Whooo, surprise, surprise.

They hadn't gone to the club, which was pretty much totally heterosexual on Sundays. They only went on Saturdays, when it was very mixed. It was very gay on Fridays, but it was a dorky kind of gay, which meant they normally stayed home and opted for sorbet and a rented flick.

At the club, Nick could almost understand why Darren didn't want to advertise that he was gay. It was a place that had done very well mixing the various orientations, sexual and such, that one found all over the City of Angels. Maybe it was important for his livelihood, which, after all, was promoting huge hedonistic parties that didn't cater to gays *or* breeders, but were vivaciously popular with both. Maybe it was important then, in that regard, that his social designation remain nebulous.

Nick had sat sulking in the club's upstairs VIP room one night during one of Darren's events the previous year. Nick thought that he should have been happier that Darren was having such a great success instead of wishing he'd picked another place, one that maybe didn't require Darren to avoid being seen with the homos that were completely 'out.' Never mind that he'd been sleeping with one of those homos, quite regularly in fact, for almost two years, and had also begged said homo, *begged* him, to be at his event because he needed his 'support.' Uh huh.

Most of Nick and Darren's friends, their regular crowd, knew that Darren was gay. Darren knew that too. He knew it very well, especially of the people with whom he worked. Darren had made sure that Karen was aware of every nuance of his relationship with Nick, for whatever reason—probably another stupid, motherfucking reason. Though, Darren also made sure Nick understood that the majority of the club's considerable patronage didn't know anything about him. Not with any degree of certainty, anyway. They might be talking about it, and maybe there was a story or two going around, but Darren insisted that no one outside of his immediate circle had a definitive understanding of his sexual orientation. It all just seemed like serious ego food to Nick.

That night at Darren's event, while sulking over his relationship and lounging in the VIP room, Nick ended up having a very enlightening conversation with one of *NSYNC's concert promoters. The guy had told him that sometimes it was better to "let everyone decide for themselves" when it came to the question of one's sexual orientation. It was better, when a public image was at all important, especially in the way of a person's income, to present as blank a canvas as possible and let folks fill-in whatever made them "the most comfortable." In other words, let them draw their own fantasy character, one to which they could most easily relate. The tactic was much more lucrative than showing them more than they needed—or wanted—to know, and therefore forcing them to see a picture of someone to whom they couldn't relate at all.

"Don't acknowledge or deny," the concert promoter had said. "Let the girls have their fantasies and let the guys think they know a very big secret. Everyone wins."

That was all right for the club, then, Nick guessed. The club was the club, but tonight it had really hit home, while they were hopping from bar to bar in the heart of Boys Town USA; West Hollywood, California itself. There, even within that most safe of atmospheres, when they'd gotten into a crowd, when they became the attention of people who were only the mildest of acquaintances or even complete strangers, Darren had still reverted to his habitual deportment of possible hetero-hood.

Nick was hoping that something had changed. Nick allowed himself that because Darren had actually held his hand at dinner. Okay, sure, it was under the table, where Darren had also passed around a plastic bullet filled with cocaine, but Nick still allowed himself to hope that maybe some little switch had been flipped.

It hadn't been, of course. No switch-flipping had spontaneously occurred.

It had hit home that maybe the problem was fundamental. Maybe it was going to be a major obstacle, even *the* obstacle. Maybe Nick should take action and protect himself from the eventually devastating reality. Maybe he'd do just that.

Yeah, well, maybe Streisand would win an Oscar too.

Nick sat there, gazing out through the thin opening in the blinds at the black BMW as the sun came up, swishing the vile combination of Coca-Cola and Absolute Citron around in the bottom of his Mickey Mouse coffee mug, pushing his familiar pain back into its regular place. He looked at it, at his pain, at his problem, in the same old frighteningly apathetic way he'd looked at it for the past two and a half years.

Then, he did what he always did. He took the easy route; he pushed the whole issue back out of his way, back away from the front of his thoughts, away from where he might have to consider it further, where it might suggest that things needed changing, where it might just blaze a neon beacon declaring that Nick was simply better off alone. But if there was one thing that terrified him beyond reason, beyond rationalism—beyond even the notion that he'd been skipping happily around Hollywood all day and night with his three best friends and some gorgeous new acquaintance from the underworld—it was the idea of being alone.

The very concept of erasing Darren from his future welled tears in Nick's eyes and spiked pain in his sinuses. He squinted and pursed his lips against it. It caused him to let his glasses fall into his lap so he could squeeze the tips of his fingers into the corners of his eyes. He squeezed the bridge of his nose as if he'd stop the tears that way. He pressed his fingers to his face and pursed his lips in defiance of this ache. He'd put the pain away. He'd put this burden of reality back on its shelf.

The tears, though, he couldn't stop. They were already rolling.

†

In his dream, Nick was walking down an impossibly long alley between buildings so tall their pinnacles were out of sight. He was walking into a looming, rolling cloud of darkness. The dark cloud was somewhat far off, but there was no other way to go except right into it. He would have turned around and gone the other way, except there was something behind him too. There was something closing in on him from behind, just as the darkness was moving toward him from in front. He was cut off in both directions and the obstacles were closing the gap.

He could see his shadow straight in front of him, long and crisp. Whatever was behind him, it was very bright. It was like a beacon or an enormous searchlight and Nick didn't want to even turn and look at it. It would have been like looking directly into the sun.

His long, long shadow began to shrink as the luminous thing approached him faster than he walked away.

Feeling a chill behind him, he knew it could only be coming from the light. The light was gaining on him, and in odd accordance with the wise advice given to little Carol Anne in *Poltergeist*, he didn't even want to turn and look at it, much less allow it to overtake him, or go into it, for cryin' out loud.

The darkness billowed far down the alley in front of him, its surface rolling and moving and actually reflecting the light coming from behind Nick in rapid flashes. There were bursts like lightning on the face of the darkness itself, but not *of* the darkness, it was reflection, clearly, from the approaching brilliance behind him.

He could feel his breathing become heavy and labored, as if whatever was behind him, whatever was giving off that horrible light, was also sucking the very air into its grasp. Nick began to pant and he could feel his heart rate quicken. He clenched and opened his fists and felt the sweat in his palms.

Nick was afraid. In his dream, not understanding why, Nick was terrified. Although he was having trouble breathing, Nick began to run.

He ran straight down the alley, straight toward the darkness, as a violent boom thundered behind him. Waves of sound rolled across the walls of brick until the sound overtook him, bringing an almost deafening voice.

"*Be you angel or devil?*" the booming voice asked.

Nick ran on, listening to his breathing, rasping quicker and quicker as it hurried in and out of him. The very sound of the question shook the ground and the walls around him. Cracks raced over the bricks and across the pavement ahead.

Another clap of thunder rumbled from behind and swept over him, presenting its question again.

"*Angel or devil?*" demanded the voice in the thunder.

Wider cracks flew across the walls and bits of sickly cream-colored brick rained down into his path. Nick stumbled but managed to keep his pace and stay on his feet. He raised his hands against the onslaught of falling debris.

There was another boom, a treacherous clapping rip, vast and explosive, though this sound did not come from behind him. It came from the cloud of darkness ahead and rumbled down the alley toward him. It brought, not a voice, but a roar, as if in answer or perhaps as a challenge to the light thundering its question from behind. A great bellowing roar clashed between the walls and swept into Nick, lifting his hair and brushing his face like wind. It was like a cooling wind that filled his lungs and gave power to his breath. Nick ran faster.

An explosion rocked the world behind him and he could hear the walls crashing in, great falling clusters of brick and cement. The echo of the question battered the alley as it shot toward him, unabsorbed by the rumble of cracking and falling stone.

"*Be you angel or devil? Angel or devil?*" it asked over and over, in a boom of vibration, pounding him from behind, louder and louder, as it swept to consume him.

Nick looked up at the billowing black cloud. It was rushing toward him, though still far away. He could feel the ground shuddering from behind and hear the great cracks in the walls and pavement pursue him. The question was thundering to a painful decibel and Nick pressed his hands to his ears and ran, pressing them forcefully to the sides of his head, running and screaming through the falling shards of brick.

Another clap of thunder, impossibly loud, rocked the world and shattered the very ground beneath his feet. With one more scream, he lunged toward the racing black cloud and fell.

†

Nick woke with a start on his own couch in his own apartment, shaken and a little sick from the immediate and horrible sense of falling. It was the quiet knock at the screen door that woke him and Nick realized he'd fallen asleep and was only dreaming. The Mickey Mouse mug was on the coffee table next to his eyeglasses, which he quickly grabbed to look at the time on the cable-box. It was ten minutes after seven, so he'd only been out for a few minutes, not even an hour.

More quiet rapping came from the front door, and Nick knew somehow that it was Scott. He got up, made sure he didn't bang his shins on the table in the still very, very faint morning, and went to the door.

"Scott?" he whispered through the slight crack in the courtyard window.

"No," Scott's voice whispered back. "It's Jane Fonda."

Nick beamed a smile and opened the door. Scott was grinning at him with his blaring white teeth.

"I could hear Darren purring from the cab," he said.

"I thought you were going to stay at the Mondrian?" Nick said, opening the screen door, careful it didn't squeak.

After clubbing, they'd dropped off Scott, at his insistence, in front of the lush Mondrian Hotel at quarter past three that morning. Nick didn't argue with him, even though he'd of course known the story about staying there hadn't been anything more than a spontaneous fabrication. He just figured Scott was going to work it out somehow. He'd chew on some leaves, or something, and spit out a couple of hundred dollar bills. Then maybe he'd lick some business cards into looking just like a driver's license and a major credit card. Demon spit seemed to be some pretty potent stuff. There was a very cute photograph sitting prominently on Nick's bookshelf to prove it. Also, Scott was still wearing the T-shirt he'd managed to suck on until its logo changed from the Powerpuff Girls to The X-Files.

"I got a room," Scott said, "but I couldn't sleep at all, so I grabbed a cab over here."

"I'm not going to ask how you managed all that."

"Yeah, that's fine. And don't ask me to do anything else for a while. That cocaine shit really dries me out."

They smirked behind their hands as if they were a couple of little girls who'd stumbled into a men's room.

"Shh!" Nick waved his hand at Scott, but he was already giggling. "I don't want to wake up Darren."

"Oh, my god, Nick, go brush your teeth." Scott waved his own hand in front of his face. "Coke and Absolute? Are you completely crackers?"

Nick had to cover his mouth with both hands as he squinted and puffed laughter against his fingers. Scott stepped inside and headed to the couch.

"I like the specs," he said in a boisterous whisper, pantomiming a set of frames on his face. "You look very studious."

Nick tried with all his might to stifle his laughter. All traces of his dream had faded away.

"Do you mind if I grab a Corona?" Scott whispered, pointing at the kitchen. He jumped up off the couch. "You said you had Corona, right?"

"Yeah," Nick whispered back, "but it's seven o'clock in the morning."

"Said the Citron Man." Scott smiled at him and disappeared through the dark archway into the kitchen.

Nick covered his mouth again. He watched the light from the refrigerator illuminate the living room carpet from the archway, saw it fade, heard the door close, the wisp of the bottle cap being removed, and the tiny clink as it hit the trashcan. A moment later Scott came out with his beer, a third of it already gone.

"Have you slept at all?" he asked, still whispering, taking another swig.

"Almost an hour," Nick said with a smile. "But then someone came a-knockin'."

"Ooh, crap." Scott frowned. "I woke you up?"

"That's okay. I'm sure it wouldn't have lasted much longer. Sleeping Beauty set the alarm for seven-thirty so he could decide if he wanted to go home to do some work or just get up to move his car."

"You could have moved it for him."

"Well," Nick whispered in a mock huff, "that might have been an option, *if* the butt-wad had any intention of ever letting me drive it. Actually, we thought we'd both be asleep."

"How did he manage getting to sleep when you couldn't?" Scott's beer was just about gone.

"I don't know. He has a tendency to do that, though. Is that helping at all?" Nick asked, pointing at the almost empty beer bottle.

"Oh, yeah." Scott grinned and nodded, then drained the rest in a gulp. He walked into the kitchen and Nick heard him quietly place the bottle in the trash. "I'm still kinda pinging, though," he whispered from inside the darkened kitchen. "I can't believe how often you guys pull this shit."

Scott popped his head back around the corner, out into what pale illumination the covered windows allowed from the encroaching morning. "I'm going to grab another one," he said. "You want?"

Nick nodded.

He walked over to the couch and partially lay back down at the far end. He heard the chucking of two bottle caps this time. Scott hadn't turned on any lights, but the darkness seemed suddenly soothing, like a blanket.

He came back into the living room. The blinds on the window, with the streetlights behind them, made shining horizontal stripes run up Scott's body as he moved. He extended the fat end of the open beer bottle at Nick.

"This'll be much better than that crap," he whispered, nodding at the mug on the coffee table, which was now illuminated with horizontal stripes of its own.

"Yeah," Nick agreed, "but it takes longer and it'll make me get up to pee more often."

Scott smiled, sat down close to him, and then whispered. "Well, cheers."

"Cheers," Nick said, barely tapping the neck of his bottle to Scott's. "Here we are again, I guess. You're in my clothes and I'm in my underwear. This isn't going to become a theme, I hope."

"I don't know," Scott smiled. "Your glasses go quite well with socks and boxer briefs."

"Shut up, you dork," Nick whispered. He took a sip of beer and smiled. "Scotty?"

"Yeah?"

"Did you really take a cab? Or did you... you know..." He flapped his free hand in the air like a wing.

Scott drained half his bottle. "I won't lie to you," he said plainly, shaking his head a bit and grinning.

"Oh, right." Nick frowned. "I'm sorry."

"I understand." Scott waved him off. "It's hard to start taking someone at their word with guys like Darren around. To him, I don't mind lying."

"I noticed." Nick grinned.

"Besides, it's so much easier than flying, to just hop in a cab, believe me. Changing form takes energy. It takes a lot of energy. Then I have to worry about being seen, yada, yada, yada."

Nick rubbed his forehead, let out a breath. "How many forms can you... I don't know... Can you be anything you want?"

"Oh, no, no," Scott whispered, shaking his head. "Three. I have three forms. Actually, nothing and no one has more than three forms. No human, non-human, or immortal entity, can assume more than three forms."

"Um... okay." Nick swigged his beer while he tried to keep from laughing.

Scott smiled hard. "What does that mean?"

"I have no idea how to ask these things." Nick smiled back. "You talk to me as though it's nothing, like you're explaining how to do the laundry."

"Well, it's simple. I don't know of any creature, any kind of demon, or anything else, that's able to change form and has more than three to choose from."

"Well, you know what?" Nick raised his eyebrows. "Neither do I."

They laughed into their hands in whispered bursts. Nick had to set his beer on the table to keep from spilling it.

"So..." he started, when they'd settled down a bit. "Can all demons change how they look?"

"I don't know. I know that quite a few can, and do."

"How many demons do you know?"

"Me, personally?" Scott whispered, giggled, licked some beer off his lip.

"Yeah, I guess," Nick said, containing his smile and braving forward.

"Um, gosh, I don't know. A few hundred or so, I think."

"Whoa," Nick gasped. He gave Scott a cautious look. "Well, how many are there all together?"

Scott looked back at him tentatively. He shook his head. "Tens of thousands. Maybe hundreds of thousands. I'm not sure."

Nick was stunned. "Oh, my god. Hundreds of thousands?"

"Well, it's nothing compared to six *billion* people."

"Wow. Okay, so you have this form..." Nick started counting.

"Right," said Scott. "And I have my true form, and then I can 'phase out.' That's totally weird, though. I hate to do it."

"What's that like? 'Phasing out?'"

Scott looked at the ceiling, pouted.   "Well, it's like becoming essentially nothing," he whispered in a furtive tone.   "All that I retain is a very thin strand of consciousness, like I'm almost dreaming.   I can't be seen or heard, and time seems to go by very, very quickly.   It's like I've been swallowed by a river, and I can barely see or hear the world around me.   I'm carried down a river of nothing that's rushing along, faster and faster."

"What do you mean, 'river of nothing?'   Where do you go?"

"Nowhere, or just about anywhere I want, anywhere I've already been at least once.   I can phase out and just *be*, or I can phase out and come right back, only somewhere else."

"You can, like, disappear and go somewhere else?"

"Yeah, mostly."   Scott nodded.   "It's just got to be somewhere I've been before.   It's got to be someplace I know.   Whenever I do that, though, it takes enormous energy.   Only entities with the greatest power are able to pull off that sort of stunt."

"It's that hard?"

"Well, actually, what takes the most energy is phasing back.   After I've phased out and want to come back into a solid form, the hard part is pulling myself back into being.   It's very difficult.   It's like trying to get back up a very steep and muddy hill, once you've slid down.   I have to be very careful, because if I don't have enough energy, I can't do it and I'm stuck."

"What happens then?"

"I just… I stay as nothing.   I stay as a whisper of an idea that hasn't been thought.   I drift.   I float around aimlessly, buffeted by whatever tides flow in such a place."

Nick smiled.   "Now you're fuckin' with me."

"That's all I know of it.   I don't know how to say it any other way."

"Wow."

"Nick," Scott said, setting his beer bottle on the coffee table.   "Look into my eye."

"Oh dear god, here we go."   Nick giggled.

"No."   Scott laughed with him.   "No, shut up.   Look into my eye and don't be a dork.   The left one.   Look into my left eye."

Nick took a gulp of his beer, set it on the table next to Scott's, and dried his lips with the back of his hand.   He gave Scott a timid smile, then gazed sternly into his left eye.

Instantly, Nick's vision blurred.   His sight melted in a rapid shift as if his focus were being pulled away in a pulsing pattern.   Waves of light rolled in front of his face and across the blurred image of his home like heat over the desert.

His vision cleared suddenly, almost as fast as it had faltered, but when it did, the couch before him was empty.

Scott was gone.

"Oh, my fucking—"

"Shhh," whispered a soft voice behind him.

Nick would have screamed, but Scott's hand was ready and quickly covered his mouth. Scott held him from behind and the fear flew away in an instant. Nick just laughed with shock instead.

"Shhh!" Scott said, his face next to Nick's. He laughed quietly into Nick's ear, holding his hand over his mouth. Scott's soft hair brushed against Nick's bare shoulders.

"Shhh!" the demon repeated. Scott giggled against Nick's cheek. "Shhh, baby, shhh! I'm sorry, I didn't mean to scare you."

Nick pulled Scott's hand from his mouth and turned to him agape. "Holy, fucking crap!" He turned all the way around toward Scott, trying to whisper, but hardly succeeding. "That was the coolest thing I've ever fucking seen!"

"I didn't mean to scare you."

"No way! That rocked!" Nick could barely contain his voice. "Do that again!"

Instantly, Nick's vision rippled before him over the space that had been filled with Scott's image. Nick gasped.

Once more, Scott's arms enfolded Nick from behind, across his chest and shoulders and around his stomach. "I don't need to cover your mouth again, do I?"

He didn't. Nick was covering his own mouth, happily screaming shocked laughter into his fingers. Scott giggled quietly against Nick's face and they both rocked together on the couch, trying to keep laughter from bellowing through the apartment.

Nick turned around again and looked at his friend. When he did, he felt a little woozy.

"Oh," he said, surprised at his sudden dizziness. "I've only had one beer. Oh, yeah, and the vodka earlier. Maybe that's it."

"No, Nicky, I'm sorry." Scott covered his face with his hand, embarrassed, peeking out at Nick between his fingers. "I sort of did that on your dime."

"What?" Nick smiled, his eyes wide.

"I just wanted to make sure I had it in me. Don't worry, it won't hurt you. I thought you'd get a kick out of it, though. The first time I did it, and I had you look at me, I used your power to do it. Your soul's power. The second one was all me, though."

"*I* did that?"

"Well, kind of. You were the battery. I probably could have done it, but I didn't want to fuck it up. Don't be mad, okay?"

"Oh, my god, I'm not mad! I'm just drunk." He reached for his beer, then thought better of it. "Why am I so drunk?"

"Oh, jeeze, I probably shouldn't have done that while we were drinking. I've never done that before. Oh, crap, I fucked up."

"No, no, I'm fine. I think you maybe just turned up the juice a bit, that's all. Don't you think?"

"You might be right. That could be it. I've never done that after I've been drinking. I should have been more careful. I'm kind of sloshin' too."

"Okay, new rule," Nick said, shaking his finger at Scott. "'Don't drink and phase!'"

Scott had to cover his mouth to laugh. When that wasn't enough to muffle the sound, he threw his face into the sofa cushion.

"Oh, my god, Scotty, that rules!" Nick whisper-screamed into Scott's ear while he tried to muffle his laughter into the couch. "That fucking rules the kingdom!"

Scott waved his hand at him to shut up, his face still buried in the couch.

"Do you know," Nick went on, chuckling deeply, "that David Copperfield would motherfucking *kill* to see you do that!"

"Shhh!" Scott turned to him, still smiling. "You're going to wake up Darren!"

"Oh, my gosh, that's so cool." Nick shook his head.

"Listen, listen," Scott said, "you need to know something about demons."

"What?"

"You have to be my battery. You have all the power. I can't hang around without your consent."

"What do you mean? You need me for when you want to disappear and stuff?"

"Yeah, sort of, okay. But really, it's much more than that. It's everything, really. You need to allow me to use enough of your energy to exist. I need your consent even to just sit here."

"I don't get it."

"See, we don't have souls, demons I mean, in the way that you do. We don't have that kind of energy. It's kinda complicated. Are you sure you want to hear this now? I could explain it tomorrow."

"Give me the Cliff Notes version."

"Well, see, I don't have a soul of my own—"

"What kind of fucked up—?"

"Shh! Stop it. This is important. It's listen time."

"Bossy, bossy." Nick smiled, sipped his beer.

"I need sort of a 'blank-check' kind of acknowledgement from you in order to hang around. I don't have the energy to do it on my own."

"What happens if you don't get the energy?"

"Well, first, I fall into my true form and can't change back, which really sucks cheese." Scott shook his head, looked at his hands. "Then I just phase out, with no energy at all, not a single drop. After that happens, I have no clue what comes next."

"Oh, my god. That's horrible. How do you even deal with—?"

"That's just the way it is."

"So, wait, if you're phased out, and not dead or anything, but you can't come back... well then..." Nick tilted his head, squinted. "Where do you go?"

Scott shrugged. "Nowhere."

"You're just stuck like that? Forever?"

"I have to be summoned back into being."

"Summoned?"

"Someone who knows how to do it has to call for me. They'd have to call me specifically, which would mean using a very specific spell."

"Trippy," Nick said. He picked up his beer and took a slow, easy sip.

"Be careful," Scott said, pointing to the beer. "Don't you feel woozy? I'm really woozy."

"Yeah." Nick lifted his beer bottle, glanced at the label for a second, then drank it anyway.

Scott picked up the other bottle, looked at it, shrugged. "Fuck it," he said, taking a drink too.

"Has it ever happened to you?" Nick asked. "I mean, where you couldn't come back by yourself?"

Scott nodded slowly. "Yes. Once. It was a long, long time ago."

"And someone cast a spell, or whatever, and called you back?"

Scott nodded again, smiling. "Duh."

"Oh, jeeze." Nick giggled and shook his head. "I think I'm too fucked up for this."

"It happened just at the beginning of the fifteenth century, in a cave, north of the Judean Desert."

"Fuck. So, wait, someone knew a spell that specifically called *you*? Only you?"

"Yes," Scott whispered, nodding. "Though, I don't know if it was intentional, exactly. I don't think the guy really thought it would work."

"Why?"

"Because he ran away when I appeared."

Nick smirked. "He ran?"

"Yeah. Like a bunny." Scott's gazed through the blinds at the light outside.

Nick chortled and shook his head. "This is too much, man. This is fuckin' too, too much."

"I think it was some kind of standard spell, for summoning, and he happened to know the right word. My name, I mean. He happened upon my name somewhere, somehow, and then he put the two together, the proper spell with my true name. Either that, or someone taught it to him. I can't believe that's likely, though, the way he reacted. It must have been an accident, at least partially. That's the only way that makes any sense. It's the only probable way he could have done it."

"He used 'skotos?'" Nick asked. "He knew the skotos name?"

Scott looked back at Nick with a tiny grin on his face, then slowly shook his head.

"Ooh..." Nick nodded solemnly. "He knew the big momma whoop-ass name."

Scott laughed, trying not to dribble beer down his shirt.

"Ssssh, dude!" Nick whispered loudly, waving a hand at Scott, smiling. "Now *you're* gonna fuckin' wake up Darren, you spaz!"

"Sorry!" Scott wiped his mouth with his shirt.

"And your 'true form?'" Nick raised his eyebrows. "Tell me about that. This isn't your true form? The way you look right now isn't how you really look?"

"No," Scott whispered, shaking his head. "I guess not."

"What do you really look like?"

"Well..." Scott sighed. "First of all, I think that's just a label, actually, 'true form.' I can't feel any difference between this one and that one. I mean, besides the physical, of course."

"I don't get it."

"Well, it's not like phasing out, where my whole consciousness is altered as well as my body. Both of my physical forms feel natural and easy and comfortable."

"This one and the one with wings?"

"Yeah." Scott grinned, drained his second beer. "Yeah. The one with wings."

Nick was only halfway through with his Corona. "I'm still sorta lost," he admitted.

"It's such a bitch to explain." Scott sighed. "See, I can barely notice any difference in the way I'm able to perceive myself or the world, regardless of whether I look like this, or I look like... well, you know, what I look like with wings."

"You like them both the same?" Nick asked. He chugged his beer.

"No." Scott shook his head slowly. "This form is my favorite." He looked down at his open palms, whispered even softer. "That's a no-brainer. This is my favorite form, by far."

In the growing morning light, Nick could see that Scott wasn't smiling any more. He was gazing at the sofa and rubbing his fingers along the palm of his right hand.

"Your favorite?" Nick said.

"Yeah." Scott nodded. He gazed at the couch, the floor, then looked up and far away. "This is the closest I can get to how I once looked. This is the closest I'm allowed to come to resembling what I was. This reflection, of sorts, of my former shape."

Nick held his breath.

Scott looked up at him. "This is as close as I'm allowed to get to looking like I did, the way I looked before I fell. It's as close as I can get to the image I had when I was still an angel of God."

A single, tiny tear rolled down Scott's face. He brushed at it, irritated, looking away.

"Scotty," Nick whispered. "I'm sorry, I—"

"Oh, no, Nicholas..." Scott shook his head, pushing Nick playfully on the shoulder, smiling again. Though, the thin wet track left by his tear was still visible. "You can just knock that off right now. How could you *possibly* know?"

Nick sighed, nodding.

"I wish I could just tell you everything," Scott said. "I wish I could explain all the secrets of the universe to you in five minutes. But *I* don't understand the universe. And frankly, I'd much rather sit here and drink beer with you than try and explain anything like that at all. It's much nicer to just sit here, enjoying this morning, this moment with you, than to try to describe such profound and ultimately tenuous things. It would be so tough anyway, to analyze the secrets of the universe, even the few things that I maybe *do* understand."

"I guess it might be a bit much," Nick said.

"It's not even that. Really, Nick, you don't *want* to know even a little bit of the crap I know. I wish I could tell you everything I've seen and everything I've felt, describe every century, every minute, but what good would that do? Would this beer taste any better? It's all too much for me as it is. Believe me, there's no purpose to you knowing any of this. There are no ultimate answers."

"I can't imagine it." Nick shook his head. "I can't imagine having been around for so long, seeing so much, and not even just of the earth, but of everything else. Heaven, or whatever. I don't know. Is there a Heaven? Oh, brother!" Nick slapped his forehead. "What a question. Holy crap, I don't know what I'm saying."

Scott smiled at him. "I guess there *is* an ultimate answer I can give you. Yes, there's a Heaven. Of course there is."

Nick looked up at him. Light from the ledge of the window was just touching Scott's chin, falling across the shoulder of the white t-shirt. A smile spread on his face as Scott tried to whisper even softer.

"You shouldn't be afraid to ask me questions like that," he said. "If I know the answer, then I'll tell you. Understand, though, that we're really not so different, you and I. We're both restricted creatures, sharing the same world."

"There's just the soul business?" Nick asked.

"Pretty much." Scott nodded, pouting. "We're of a different substance, yes. And of course, there's the soul business. But really the only meaningful difference in our natures is that we've been shown different things. We have different knowledge and a different experience of the same world. My understanding, as a whole, is probably no more profound than yours. I don't know everything. I don't even know very much."

"There's got to be more to it than that." Nick squinted. "I mean, good gravy, you've seen Heaven!"

"Yes, but you say that like you have too." Scott grinned. "You should hear the security in your voice. You use the word 'Heaven' as if you know exactly what you're talking about."

Scott lowered his face. Nick could see him raise an eyebrow, even in the dim morning light that managed to squeeze its way through the blinds.

"You speak of Heaven as though you know exactly what you're saying." Scott smiled, gazing at Nick pensively from beneath his lowered eyes. "Maybe you do know."

"You're wiggin' me, man." Nick smiled. "Okay, this was cool, but now you're wiggin' me."

"There's also the possibility," Scott went on, taking a sip of beer, licking his lips, "the place that's alive in your mind when you use the word 'Heaven,' might not be at all like the memory I have of it. Heaven might not be something that you'd think of as a 'place' at all, but something very different, very special, something you haven't considered. Stranger still, it might be something very, very close. It might be right in your lap."

"Okay, now you're *way* wiggin' me." Nick leaned back, smiling.

"Don't you remember it? Don't you remember Heaven?"

"Very, very vaguely." Scott set his beer bottle on the coffee table. "That was another life altogether. Another time. Another everything. You can't imagine." He sighed. "Do you remember going to preschool?"

Nick smiled again. "Very, very vaguely."

"But you know you've been there. You know it was real. What color was the swing set?"

"I don't know."

Scott chuckled. "You see? I have a simple answer for you. 'Yes, Nick, there is a Heaven.' Though, the comprehension of it is where our largest challenge lies. I wish I could just give it to you. I really wish it were within my power to explain it, but you can't look to me to help you completely comprehend something like Heaven. I can't help, because I don't comprehend it myself. I *might* have a more viable experience of it, I guess, or of a philosophy, or an understanding of what you might think of as Heaven. Though, its truth, its reality, is as ultimately fragile to me as it is to you and everyone else."

Scott raised his shoulders with a deep, contemplative breath, and then dropped them with a heavy sigh. Nick giggled.

"I'm a limited creature, Nick," Scott continued. "That much I know for sure. I can't comprehend infinity, or eternity, or the mind of God. I can barely remember just a shade of Heaven, and I don't think there are any who truly understand it, other than God, the Creator, himself."

Nick glanced down at the floor. He pressed his lips together, nodding.

"I do know, however," Scott went on, "that there are two who can ultimately grant you the proper comprehension of Heaven, the Kingdom of God. No angel, no demon, not the Beast, or any creature of this world or any other, can give you that key. It's something that comes only with the allowance of the Lord of Heaven himself." Scott nodded at him. "And with you."

"What?"

Scott closed his eyes, remembering, and recited, "'The Kingdom of God cometh not with observation, neither shall they say, 'Low here!' nor 'Low there!', for behold, the Kingdom of God is within you.'" He leaned forward and set his empty beer bottle on the coffee table. "That's from the book of Luke in the King James Version. Chapter seventeen, verse twenty-one." Scott grabbed Nick's beer, took a swig. "Oh, and a little part of verse twenty, too."

"Verse twenty-two?" Nick said, taking back his bottle, finishing it.

"No," Scott whispered and chuckled. "Verse twenty, *also*. Excuse me."

"You're quoting the Bible?"

"Oh, yes, of course." Scott nodded. "The truth is in there. It can be a bit poetic and it's been buried within itself, but it's there just the same."

"Really?"

"Absolutely." Scott nodded again, pressing his dark black eyebrows together. "But the thing is, and don't go spreading this around or someone's likely to call you a heretic and possibly some other much nastier names, the Christian Bible is by no means the only divinely inspired work of truth."

Nick squinted at him.

Scott squinted back, smiling. "I've noticed here on the lip of the twenty-first century that people haven't changed much since the days of Moses. They're still only able to take comfort in a divine revelation if that same revelation is denied to just about everyone else. That's why I don't think it would do any good to run around to all the Christians, the Jews, the Muslims, even the Buddhists, and maybe to a whole kettle full of others, and let each of them in on the fact that the same essence of the Divine, the same glorious and simple message of life and what it's really about, is actually at the core of each of their faiths. It might be wearing a different outfit, but it's the same truth."

"Why couldn't you tell them that?"

"Because such a message would awaken the Church."

"What church?"

"Oh, good gracious Becky, here we go." Scott rolled his eyes and stood up. "The Church is a *whole* other story. You know, I think I want another beer."

"Really? Wow. I would have thought—"

The alarm suddenly went off in the bedroom. It was brief, though. They heard Darren smack it rather hard and several times.

"Oh, crap." Nick frowned. "He's going to be grumpy."

Nick looked up and saw Scott heading into the kitchen. He pushed himself up off the couch and padded across the carpet after him.

"But, Scott," he whispered.

"What?" Scott turned and yawned. Nick almost howled with laughter; between the beer and the phasing, Scott had gotten seriously buzzed.

Nick shook his head and smiled.

"So," Nick whispered, "if the truth is in the Bible, then we're really screwed, I guess, huh?"

"What are you talking about?" Scott turned and went into the kitchen. He opened the refrigerator and brought out two more beer bottles.

"It says we're sinners." Nick lingered in the arch leading to the living room. "The Bible says that being gay is a sin."

Scott had to cover his mouth to laugh. He set the beer bottles onto the kitchen table and held them there, shutting his eyes and laughing.

"What?" Nick smiled. "What's so funny?"

Scott just shook his head, still obviously trying to keep himself from bellowing his amusement.

"You're making me feel pretty stupid here." Nick crossed his arms.

"No!" Scott finally said, smiling broadly. "No, the Bible most certainly does *not* say that! Good gravy, that's a wide-spread crock!"

"But… I thought… everyone always said…" Nick stammered while Scott, still grinning and shaking his head, opened both bottles of Corona and handed him one.

"Listen," Scott whispered at him in the slowly illuminating kitchen. "Nowhere in the Bible does it say that being gay is a sin. That's just simply not true." He guzzled a third of his beer. "Everything you've heard is based on an incredibly vast and hideous misinterpretation of sacred literature. It's not only horribly unfair, but it's been that way since the late thirteenth century. In fact, I'm beginning to believe that the very vastness of this particular screw-up has actually become one of the major contributors to its common acceptance."

"Okay, um…" Nick frowned, rubbing his eyes. "I did not understand a single word you just said."

Scott chuckled softly. "Never mind." He patted Nick softly on the cheek, brushed the hair out of his face. "Just know that the Bible doesn't say that. It doesn't say that being gay is a sin. And I wouldn't lie to you."

"Then…" Nick shook his head, pressing his eyes shut. He was

beginning to feel a little sleepy. "Then I'm not a sinner?"

Scott laughed again.

"Shhh! You spaz!" Nick laughed, waving his hand at him.

"Oh, my gosh, you have a lot to learn," Scott said.

Nick shook his head, rolling his eyes. He took a swallow of beer.

"Okay, look," Scott said, taking a breath, sighing again. "You're a sinner all right, most definitely, but not because you're gay." He put his hand gravely on Nick's shoulder. "You're a sinner because you're a slut."

They both lost it. Nick couldn't help himself. He opened his mouth and just laughed, drooling beer all over himself and the kitchen floor. Scott tried to cover his mouth, but it was no use. He was laughing out loud.

Trickles of beer ran down Nick's chest and into his underwear. He abruptly understood how Theo must have had felt at dinner.

Darren suddenly yelled from the bedroom. "What're you doing?"

Neither Nick nor Scott could answer him. Both were trying to stifle their relentless laughter, and almost suffocating themselves in the process.

"What're you doing, you freak?" Darren bellowed. "What time is it?"

Almost in answer to him, the alarm erupted a second time.

"Motherf...!" Darren wailed.

Laughing out loud in the kitchen, the two lost souls sank to the floor, sitting on the cold tile as they listened to Darren whack angrily at the poor alarm clock over and over until it was finally bludgeoned into silence.

Nick raised his eyebrows at Scott. "Oh, dear god, he killed it."

They both roared.

They tried in vain to be quiet. Regrettably, the damage had already been done. Laughing, shaking and smiling, trying to keep hold of their newly opened beer bottles, they sat helplessly on the tile kitchen floor.

"I have beer in my socks," Nick said, pointing to his feet and guzzling half his bottle.

"It's all over the floor too." Scott shook his head, resting with his back against the dishwasher, flashing his big white-toothed smile like a billboard advertising porcelain facial implants.

Nick, still guzzling what was left of his beer, began to mop up what they'd spilled with his socks.

Scott burst with laughter. It no longer mattered, though. He didn't bother trying to stop it. His deep, sexy bellow rang through the apartment, which made Nick laugh out loud. He sprayed beer a second time and had to re-double his efforts on the kitchen floor with his socks/foot-mops.

"I knew you two little girls were destined to get into trouble," Darren said. He'd appeared in the archway to the living room, dressed only in his own dark-gray boxer briefs and a pair of thick athletic socks. He stood there squinting through the dregs of sleep, scratching at the top of his head. His hair was standing up in the back like half of a broken halo.

"Nick, what are you doing?" Darren asked, absently rubbing his bare chest. "You've got beer all over yourself."

Scott looked up at him. "Hi there, pretty man."

Nick covered his eyes with his free hand and laughed. He rested his head against the refrigerator door and giggled like a ten-year-old.

"Okay, it's time for you two to get some sleep." Darren carefully stepped into the kitchen, trying not to mop up any beer with his own socks, and took the beer bottle, now just about empty, from Nick.

"How long have you been here, Scott?" Darren asked.

"Oh, my gosh." Scott shook his head solemnly. "Centuries and centuries."

Nick howled and doubled over, now covering his face with both hands.

"Oh, jeeze," Darren said. "You're a mess. Can you get up and into the bedroom? I am not going to fuckin' carry you. Did you hit the vodka too? You're going to be sick, baby."

"I'm fine." Nick pushed himself up off the floor until he was sitting again, still laughing. "You're not the boss 'a me."

"Thank goodness!" Darren rolled his eyes, taking the beer bottle from Scott as well. "You two aren't, like, kissin' cousins, or anything, are you? Scott, it's okay if I leave you here to watch him, right?"

"Yes." Scott nodded. "Don't worry your gorgeous, blonde head there, Mr. Jealous Boyfriend."

"All right." Darren sighed loudly. "I'm going to go and get dressed now and pretend you didn't say that. That way, I don't have to punch you." Darren reached down toward Scott. "Give me your hand."

Scott lifted his arm into the air and Darren pulled him up off of the floor.

"Help me with him, please," Scott said, nodding at Nick.

"Did he have anything besides alcohol?" Darren asked, grabbing

Nick by the arm.

"Knock it off!" Nick pulled away. "I'm fine, you dork. And shut up. I couldn't sleep, unlike you, Coma Man. So, I had some vodka."

"Okay," Darren said, grabbing a dishtowel and trying to wipe up Nick's face. "It's night-night time, though, baby love."

"Are you going to work?" Nick asked, grabbing the towel from him, "or are you going to put me in my jammies too?"

Darren raised his hands in surrender, chuckling. He gave the towel to Nick and turned to walk out of the kitchen. "I'm getting in the shower."

"Good!" Nick blurted after him. "'Cause, ya know, you should see your hair!"

Darren walked back down the darkened hall. Nick heard him close the bathroom door and then flick on the light.

"You're not going back to the hotel, are you?" Nick looked at Scott, trying to finish the job on his face with the towel. Then he started to dry off his chest.

"Fuck, no!" Scott smirked. "You have a *huge* bed." He started down the hall toward the bedroom.

"I get the right side!" Nick yelled.

"Whatever," Scott threw back.

The floor was still a mess of spilled beer. Nick stooped to wipe up what he could. He heard the door to the shower slide closed and the water come on.

The kitchen was still very dark. So, he mopped up the spots where he thought he was most likely to slip, as he knew he'd get up later and forget that he'd sprayed Corona everywhere.

After he was relatively sure he'd gotten the dangerous portion of spilled beer off of the floor, he stood and turned on the water in the kitchen sink to wet the towel a bit.

Darren issued a terrible shriek from the shower.

"Oh, crap." Nick turned off the sink faucet. "Sorry!" he yelled.

He could hear Darren yelling back, but couldn't make out all of the words. Something about Nick's ass and kicking it and blah blah blah blah blah.

Throwing the towel into the sink, Nick left the kitchen and passed the bathroom, where he heard the shower and Darren's familiar humming. Apparently, he wasn't too pissed off.

Scott hadn't turned on the bedroom light, but the morning had crept in enough so that Nick could make out his denim shorts and the X-Files/Powerpuff Girls T-shirt, which had been neatly folded and set atop the side dresser. There was a long lump under the thin summer comforter on the left side of his bed. All that was visible of Scott was a thick tumble of wavy black hair, pressed in a lump against the headboard.

Nick slid into his regular place in the king-size bed and lay back contentedly, lacing his fingers behind his head. He listened to the sound of the shower in the next room and to Darren's faint but familiar humming and was happy.

Many of the countless mornings Nick had spent with Darren were less than entirely pleasurable. Still, his humming, along with the quiet rumble of the water on the shower wall, was always a soothing sound.

"He loves you very, very much, you know," Scott whispered.

Nick looked at him. Scott was facing away, on Darren's side, curled snuggly underneath Nick's comforter.

"Darren loves you very much," Scott repeated.

Nick didn't reply. He listened instead to the rhythm of the shower and to Darren's soft, happy humming.

Scott sighed, sounding very close to sleep; a yawning, sleepy demon.

"It really scares him, though," he said, "and he hates you for it."

CHAPTER IV

†

Closer

Who is he that saith, and it cometh to pass, when the Lord commandeth it not? Out of the mouth of the most High proceedeth not evil and good? Wherefore doth a living man complain, a man for the punishment of his sins? Let us search and try our ways, and turn again to the Lord.

- Lamentations 3:37-40 (KJV)

West Hollywood, California
The lobby lounge of the Hyatt Hotel
The north side of Sunset Boulevard, just west of Hayworth Avenue

†

Bishop Patrick had only been in Los Angeles for five days and was already yearning to leave. The city was every bit as vile and corrupt as he'd ever heard, and more. It wasn't so much the crime, or the pornography, or any of the other standard transgressions found in a large urban area; he'd seen those many times before, all over the world. Nevertheless, there were two specific aspects that put this city in league with Sodom herself. One was the idolatrous dedication to wealth and appearance, which prevailed to a degree that was beyond any other city he'd known, beyond comprehension and which, frankly, turned his stomach. The second was the icing on that cake; the outright need to *flaunt* wealth and appearance, to parade every nuance of success and privilege.

His current home—being a very loose term, considering the degree of travel required of him—New York City, was not low on arrogance, by any means. Though, he didn't believe it possessed such an unbalanced focus on, not only the acquisition of personal fortune and a physical ideal, but the compulsive and constant overture, exhibition, and validation of those attributes.

Not only did the people of Los Angeles seem to need to be both rich and beautiful at a level that was surely *religious*, but they also needed to make sure everyone else in the world could clearly see just how rich and beautiful they were. It was to that end they allowed every other pursuit, noble or otherwise—predominantly the latter, he assumed—to decay into extinction. There existed nothing else within this city's boundaries but the desire to be better than your neighbor, and to be utterly certain that he, and everyone else, knew it.

The profusion of these vices, the domination of greed and vanity on such a scale, was made all too clear to the young bishop from the day of his arrival, as the conditions of his visit imposed upon him a need to operate in their accord. The essence of his mission, the manner in which information had to be gathered, dictated the conditions of his undertaking. These conditions left him vulnerable to the unmasked flaws of the populace.

The bishop was without the protections of his office, as he needed to keep his vocation a secret. Without his title, or even the most primary religious trimmings, there wasn't a foul word, inappropriate anecdote, miscreant conduct, or brash and insolent opinion that the dregs of this western community were at all ashamed to exhibit, right in front of him, and with profound splendor.

No one tempered their behavior around him when they didn't know of his vocation. He had to walk among them without the reverence to which he was accustomed. He had to eat with them without the respect he'd known since he'd first worn a collar. The endurance of this circumstance, he supposed, was a necessity of his mission. While he was in America, he had to alter his methods. It wasn't a widely known precept, but when one pursued demons, one did not do so while holding the Bible aloft in one hand and flinging holy water from the other—*that* was saved for the inevitable confrontation.

The Church, though awash in its prevalent vows of poverty, was nonetheless not without significant resources. Resources that could easily provide the trappings necessary to blend an individual, when the need arose, into virtually any environment, even one of such corrosive and eccentric affluence. That being the case, Robert encountered no hindrance in acquiring the trappings he believed would best suit his purpose. The fact was, Cardinal Matine was very enthusiastic about Robert's purpose in California and made sure it was funded properly, and without the scrutiny of the papacy.

For the time being, the bishop resided at a lavish hotel on the Sunset strip, for appearances only, of course. If the influence of the underworld was to be rooted out, it was necessary to begin looking where it most obviously operated and thrived. The poor were pious and unremarkable. It was the rich and famous who were both deviant and influential, and therefore more attractive. To demons, of course.

Robert had also arranged to lease an automobile, a silver, two-door Mercedes hardtop, which he thought would serve to instantly avert even the harshest suspicions toward the true nature of his task. Yes, it was wonderfully luxurious, but he didn't consider it a sin, or a transgression from his vows, to enjoy that perk, as long as it remained a necessity of his labor. He did, on the other hand, assert substantial effort to curb any unnecessary use of the car's considerable horsepower. Some of the time, he even succeeded.

Bishop Patrick discarded the simple clothes he'd worn in his day-to-day activities ever since he was in seminary and donned instead a collection of elaborate designer suits acquired with the help of a commissioned saleswoman in Beverly Hills who, incidentally, provided Robert with his first up-close look at general Los Angeles ethics in action. She'd initially been considerably abrasive. Although, once Robert's intentions to obtain almost an entirely new wardrobe, as well as his ability to pay for such a thing, had been clearly established, she became more and more amiable. The more items he stacked on the counter, the lighter her mood, the easier her manner, the more dutiful her attention, and the more gracious her deportment.

At the outset, Robert had thought of the men's store sales woman as an extreme, as an abnormal example of brazen ambitious manipulation, viewing her as a moderately irritating curiosity. However, the horrible behavior of the representative at the car dealership outdid the men's store saleswoman in a surprisingly short amount of time. Immediately after which the woman checking into the hotel before Robert treated the desk clerk in a manner that made both earlier examples of bad behavior look like the conduct of postulant nuns at a leper convention. When it was Robert's turn at the check-in window, the poor clerk still had tears in her eyes.

Still, the most exquisite examples of resident inhumanity were all around him and they were constant; he simply had to wander the city in a car. The disregard the people of Los Angeles showed for the rest of the human race was demonstrated as plainly as possible each day, over and over, on the roads. The drivers in LA, which consisted of ninety-six percent of the city's population, displayed their true character each time they discarded every directive of, not only the most basic traffic laws, but also the most basic human considerations.

The evil natures of those living in Los Angeles were made plain each time they pressed the accelerator into a left-hand turn, speeding intrusively across the path of an oncoming car that had no traffic behind it for miles, just for the rush of causing that driver to pound on their brake; each time they signaled a right-hand turn in order to pass to the side of a long waiting line of cars at a busy intersection, and then sped forward in front of them all instead of turning.

That was, of course, only a tiny example, out of far too many, of the ways in which these people were willing to risk, not only their own health, property, and very lives, but those of complete strangers. All that, merely to gratify their need to validate their own privilege, their own self-assigned entitlement, to satisfy a *me first* compulsion that was nothing short of an epidemic in the City of Angels. Their compulsions were even worse than a simple *me first* objective: in order to be satisfied that they'd gotten away with something, that they'd won the moment, the drivers in LA had to make sure that someone else was the loser. It wasn't enough to simply race down the roads in the glittering trophies of their success. No, someone else needed to be left in the dust.

These behaviors openly exhibited the worst of human wickedness. The name 'City of Angels' was a bad joke. As Robert was sure he was about to confirm, in its literal sense, he believed Los Angeles was instead the 'City of Fallen Angels.'

Robert found his surroundings more than just distasteful and disheartening; he found them repulsive to the point of nausea. He couldn't help but treat those with whom he interacted with an evident revulsion. However, they seemed only to interpret his contempt as nothing more than a homegrown attitude. His very disgust with the reprobate inhabitants had apparently helped him to blend right in with them. Well, hooray for Hollywood.

He'd contacted the cardinal two days after his arrival to inquire about his review of the materials that had been priority shipped back to Rome. Matine was absolutely inflamed after viewing the videotape made by Alex Monroe, and his first request of Robert had been to determine for whom the tape had been produced, and to contact that person, or persons, immediately.

Robert already knew the identity of those to whom the cardinal referred. They were Alex's college roommates, Jeremy Wilson and

Andrew Davis, both USC sophomores.

The boys had, of course, been thoroughly interrogated by the LAPD, for all the good it did.   It seemed that what the boys ultimately provided local law enforcement were the names of the employees of the club at which Alex worked; the identical leads supplied by the video itself—the only practical leads to be found anywhere, which struck Robert as ironic, considering the sheer absurdity the police associated with the rest of the recording.   The club employees had been subsequently interrogated, which yielded enough information to help with just a little less than nothing.

Though he realized his exposure to them was still fractional, Robert was not impressed with the LAPD.   He made that decision as he sat in the bar of the Hyatt West Hollywood Hotel, late Saturday afternoon sharing drinks and a small table with a young off-duty female police officer, and gazing out of the lobby's clear glass front at the view of the hotel across the street and the growing activity at the House of Blues, which was next to it.   It had only taken two drinks and a very modest number of lies—all white, of course—to goad her into divulging much, much more information than she normally would have provided.   Then again, in this city, it seemed everyone had a photograph of themselves—a 'head-shot'—along with a resume in the trunk of their car, and were more than happy to sit and gab, in a very public place of course, with a well dressed, young-looking, Mercedes driving, assumed, 'player.'

The good bishop never actually told the trusting young officer that he was the Director of Talent and Series Development at Fox Studios.   Though, his allusion to that idea was rather creatively and effectively implied.   Therefore, even if she was much more interested in talking about the new production schedule for the second season of Fox's Tuesday night sitcom hit, specifically casting, the woman was easy enough to divert after her second cape cod.

This was the fourth local peace officer, and the first female, to succumb to Robert's deft manipulations and end up supplying him with sensitive information regarding the Monroe case.   It turned out, luckily enough, that this particular officer had worked very closely with a senior officer who was directly involved.   She'd even been able to provide such wonderful details as the perceived intelligence levels of the victim's roommates, which were at a level that caused the investigating officers to not only completely rule-out the boys as suspects, but also strongly question the admissions policies of the University of Southern California.

As far as the involvement of Alex's co-workers—the ones also named by his roommates, as well as Alex himself on the video, the ones accused by the deceased to have been secret fire-breathing, boogie monsters—the gist of their reaction could be summed up quite accurately with the word 'denial.'

The two boys sharing Alex's dorm room didn't know what he'd been talking about. Yes, he'd worked at the club with them, but no, they'd never heard of Gil threatening him. No, they'd never heard that Alex and Gil had had any kind of altercation. No, they'd never heard of any 'shrieking' match between Gil and his employer, Laura Shah. Yes, she'd dated Alex briefly, but no, they didn't believe that Ms. Shah was ever aware Alex had been stalking her. No, he'd never confronted her. No, she wasn't Satan's slut, and no, to the best of their knowledge, she didn't drink blood straight from a bucket.

The police just didn't have their hearts in their work. Robert couldn't really blame them. Excuse me Miss, but after you broke up with your two-hundred pound boyfriend, did you by any chance toss him through a closed glass window? Does anyone you know have the ability to incinerate small electronic devices with your breath? Would you happen to know where your ex-boy-pal was getting his hallucinogens?

Robert would still need to speak with both of the roommates personally, of course—matching IQs and shirt sizes not withstanding. He'd need to speak to them just in case they could offer any additional information at all before he went to the club itself. Frankly, Robert wasn't in a hurry to throw himself in front of a moving train by going directly to where the alleged lamia made her mortal living and was currently preparing for the arrival of the world's most ancient icon-of-feminine-independence/killer she-demon.

Bishop Patrick had learned firsthand, in Pano Panayia on the island of Cyprus more than a dozen years ago, that it was unwise to take for granted any degree of divine protection from demonic power. One must not only be wholly prepared theologically, but also armed with unreserved faith, and perhaps even an automatic weapon or two, before considering the possibility of actually facing a manifested demon. Out of a team of seven, he was one of two that survived the lesson, and the only one to have done so with his sanity intact.

The entity with whom they'd tangled had been a smarmy incubus by the name of Brathwidth—Robert had come to believe—who, although no more than a common terrestrial demon, was maybe just a little more serious than an imp or a familiar. Though, he was certainly far, far shy of the class of demon that included Lamia, or, Lord help him, Lilith herself, whose power would yield only to that of Lucifer.

Still, that unfortunate incident would not repeat itself here. Despite being on his own, Robert was older and wiser. He was also the most senior bishop in the sect and the cardinal's favorite. Robert would be sent what he needed when the time was right. After all, the cardinal was counting on him, as was God.

Right now, Robert would concentrate on the task at hand. He just wanted to be sure to cover all his bases and simply find out where the USC boys had moved after their roommate's unexpected flight.

"How long have you been at Fox?" the slightly buzzed cop/actress inquired.

"Wait a minute," Robert said. "You've been on the lot before, haven't you? Weren't you one of the women who wanted to marry a millionaire?"

"Oh god, no!" she giggled.

"Are you sure?" Robert smiled. "I'm trying to figure out where I've seen you. Have you modeled for Donna Karen? You have, haven't you? That's it! I knew I'd seen you somewhere!"

The off-duty officer grinned, giggled, and vigorously shook her head, letting her hair swish around in a manner Robert supposed was meant to be seductive. Though, she didn't exactly have voluptuous hair. It was somewhere between Annie Lennox and Fabio.

"Really?" Robert feigned surprise. "I'll bet you just don't want to tell me. What was it? A bad sit-com? Did you get a bad review? Oh, my gosh, did some idiot fire you?"

"No, no," she giggled. "Really, I haven't worked at Fox."

"Oh, I know! What about *Cops*? I'll bet you were on that show, huh?"

"No. Not me." She sighed. "I wanted to do it, but they don't let you just sign up. It's random, sort of. Though, they do a lot of work with the sector brass to get everything ironed out before they film, or tape, I guess. So, we know in advance when they're going to do it, but they won't let us just change precincts, just to be on the show. One of the 'rules.' I'm sure you understand."

"What sector are you in?"

"Well," she said, closing her eyes, nodding, "I've been in Hollywood for six months now. Smack in the heart."

"Like it?"

She shrugged. "It's interesting."

"I'm very impressed that you're assigned to such a high profile area. You must be quite an officer."

"Why?" She tried to swish her almost-Fabio hair. "'Cause I'm a woman?"

"Oh, no. I didn't mean it that way. I'd be impressed with any officer that managed to navigate such a challenging arena."

"Well, I can certainly say it hasn't been easy," she said, putting down her drink, wearing a sycophantic smirk.

"I'm sure. Isn't it terribly dangerous?"

"Can be." She nodded, smirking some more.

He grinned at her.

"What?" she asked. This time her grin was suspicious.

"I'm just trying to picture you in a uniform."

"Ugh," she grunted. "Don't go gettin' all weird on me."

He laughed. "Why not? Weird can be fun. No one's ever asked you to don your badge for them?"

"Robert, really, I see weird everyday." She smiled. "You can't imagine how much. And if you're talking about the kind of situation I think you are, then that's the last place I'd ever 'don' my badge."

He smiled back at her. "Fair enough."

"Please tell me you're not a weirdo. If you are, you're the best dressed weirdo I've ever seen. But they come in all kinds, I suppose."

"I'm sure that's true. However, I'm not a weirdo. At least, I don't believe I am."

"I don't think so either." She smiled again, swished the Fabio-do. "And doing what I do, I'm getting pretty good at recognizing weird."

"What's the weirdest thing you've ever seen?"

"The weirdest person? Believe me, there've been a lot, even though I've only been on the street for a year."

"Uhm." He grinned, shook his head, and tried to reword the question in a way that would open up the category and move her toward the right subject.

"It doesn't have to be a person, exactly" he said. "Just tell me about a really weird, Hollywood-ish situation. It might be good for a script."

That did it.

"Well, hands-down, it'd have to be last weekend," she said.

"Just this past weekend?"

"Yeah. Very, very early Sunday morning."

"What happened?"

"Well, there's a gigantic nightclub about eight blocks from the station. A real posh-pit, open after-hours, very young clientele, fake IDs, that sort of thing. It's one of those snooty, celeb-hives, you know what I mean?"

"Lots of stars? How big is this club?"

"Mostly just wannabe stars," she said with a hiss. "Very young trust fund-ers who don't need to hold down regular jobs and can go to twelve auditions a week. And I think it's the biggest club around. By that I mean literal size and popularity. Three stories, tiered dance floor, private VIP room, all that. I'd be very surprised if you hadn't been there a few times yourself."

"A little self-indulgent?" he asked, trying to keep her attention off of him, though his pulse was quickening. She was obviously talking about the very same club at which Alex Monroe had worked.

"You have no idea," she drawled at him. "It's open all night for the same reason all the other after-hour clubs are open all night. Everyone's on drugs. We hit that club occasionally, but we're not talking about the type of crowd that'd kill their mothers for the price of a crack-pipe. Besides, the people that go there are either lawyers themselves or have about nine of them on retainer. The rest, the young, high-brow ravers, they only know one attorney, but they call him 'Daddy.'"

"There was a drug bust there last Sunday morning?" So that's what the kids were doing instead of attending mass, Robert thought, trying to keep a cynical smirk off of his face.

"No." She shook her head, raised her eyebrows. "It wasn't even inside the club. Down the street, about a block and a half, there were these giant lion prints in the alley."

Robert almost choked on his cranberry Calistoga.

"You okay?" She frowned at him.

"Yes, yes." He nodded, wiping his mouth with a cocktail napkin. "That's incredible! 'Lion' prints you said?"

"Yeah, well, enormous paw prints or tracks," she said. "They were feline, though, but that's not even the weirdest part." She gave him a little Mona Lisa smile, leaned back, and sipped her cape cod.

He tried to retain a look of mild curiosity. "What was it?"

"The paw prints…" She was attempting drama.

Robert continued his façade of placid interest. "Yes?"

"They were made with *blood*." She sat back and crossed her arms with the look of one who has just pitched *ET the Extraterrestrial II: The Revenge of Elliot* to Merchant Ivory.

"*Human* blood?" He was saying a silent prayer that his poker face was holding up. He had no way of knowing.

"It turned out to be." She shrugged. "Though, the paw prints were fake."

"Really?" he said, finally able to exhale and sit back in his seat.

"Yeah. We had some expert guy from the LA Zoo come to the station to take a look at the photos. He was pretty impressed. He said they were very good fakes."

"Fakes of what?"

"Well, big cat tracks, I guess. A tiger or a lion, he couldn't tell. The thing was that they were just *too* big. We gave him the measurements along with the pictures and he said that an animal with paws that size would have been between seven-hundred and fifty, and nine-hundred pounds, and that just wasn't possible."

Robert suddenly felt very disoriented, as if someone had spiked his sparkling water. What she was saying was just too good to be true. It was too much. She was telling him the trail ended here. She was saying the goal was in sight.

"The blood came back as being real, though," she continued, "but no dice with the tracks. This is Hollywood, after all. Someone was playing a very sick joke."

"A joke?"

"Well, yeah. The alley had been cleaned and there was puke and blood everywhere, which, to throw an even bigger wrench in the works, the lab said was from the same person."

"Wait… The alley had been cleaned, but there was, what, vomit…?"

"Yeah, bile, or vomit, yeah. And blood. It looked serious enough. Like someone had a pretty severe problem. The thing was that it looked too staged. What tipped us off was that there wasn't a speck of dirt in the whole alley, it was clean as a bone, from end to end, except for a dumpster, the puke, the blood, and the tracks. There was nothing else at all. Most importantly, though, there was no body."

"Staged?"

"Okay, imagine this thin alley between two large industrial buildings, and there's not a speck of dirt or trash or anything to be found. I mean, it was Disneyland clean. There were all kinds of the usual junk in the street and in the back-alley at the other end, but nothing at all in the side alley where we found the tracks. The captain said it looked like someone had taken a leaf-blower to the scene before they staged it. If that's what happened, they didn't do a very good job, or they changed their minds about what they were doing, because it also looked like they tried to clean it again."

Robert suddenly knew what it must feel like to sit in front of a slot machine and see each window bring up a cherry. He knew what she was going to say. He'd heard the description of the same sort of scene many times before. Though, it was still very important that he not reveal even a hint of his knowledge.

"Wait," he said. "Okay, now you've lost me completely."

She laughed and Robert smiled back, resisting the urge to shake her violently and maybe smack her a little.

"Okay, here, listen." She tilted her head, smirking. "The alley has, like, no dirt in it, right? Nothing, at all. It could have been swept clean even, maybe. Then, after it was cleaned the first time, that's when the blood and the puke got there."

"Blood and puke? How?"

"We don't know, but that's the distressing part, because all that stuff was real enough."

"All right, but then it was cleaned *again*?"

"Sort of. Then some wacko walked through the whole mess of blood and stuff wearing some fake giant lion shoes."

"Lion?" Robert hoped his face didn't appear as bloodless as it felt.

"Or a tiger, or something, but it would have been one of the biggest cats ever, we're talking *Guinness Book* here, and there's no way an animal like that could have ever gotten into the city without someone knowing about it. First of all, an eight hundred pound tiger would be huge, even if it were a Siberian tiger. They're the biggest, I guess. And lions, well, they just don't get that big. See, the zoo guy told us a big Siberian tiger would outweigh the largest lion by a few hundred pounds. Never mind any other kind of big cat, like a panther or a leopard."

"Right." He nodded at her.

"So, we decided it had to have been staged. Had to be. It just didn't make any sense otherwise. Maybe someone wanted to try to pull off some sort of hoax, like a giant loose monster tiger or mutant lion in the city or something like that. They swept the alley, planted the blood, maybe made themselves sick doing it, and then walked through the whole mess with their mega-lion shoes.

"The problem I see is that the blood and the puke came from the same person, and they'd be hocked-up on several party drugs at the time. The captain didn't think that was a very big deal, though, which was pretty stupid if you ask me. It doesn't really make sense if someone were staging the scene. If that were the case, they'd probably have gotten the blood from somewhere else."

"Maybe it could have been a gunshot or a stab wound?" Robert asked.

"No," she shook her head. "We never got an M.E. out there, but there would have been more pure blood and it would have been patterned very differently. No, it was nothing like that. We don't think there'd been any kind of an attack. There'd have been more evidence than just the blood. No, someone either just puked it all out, or poured a little blood onto the ground and then ralphed on it."

"What a lovely picture."

"Sorry," she said, blushing.

"You keep saying 'lion,' but the zoologist couldn't tell?"

"Well, yeah, he said they looked more like lion tracks than any other cat, but they were just way too big to have been made by a lion. They were more than twice the size of a regular full-grown male. So they must have been fake, and if they were fake, they could almost have been modeled after any big cat."

"Right. Go on. This is fascinating. Now, you said the alley was cleaned *again*?"

"Oh, yeah. See, after the fake paws were tracked through the mess, someone used a leaf blower. The blood and the pu—uh, vomit, whatever, were spread across the pavement, like there'd been a very strong wind. The only thing is that it was spread in *both* directions out of the alley, starting from one point, near the west end. The wind couldn't have done that, unless it came straight down at a single point. How many times have you heard of something like that happening, right? It would have had to be someone with some kind of big leaf blower. Maybe the wacko changed his mind about going through with his hoax and tried to clean everything up again."

"Doesn't this all sound terribly unlikely to you?" Robert asked. "Wouldn't the person with the leaf blower have ruined any tracks left behind?"

"Sure." She nodded. "If he'd been really thorough. Some of them were pretty smeared, but there were certainly enough left over that would have needed to be washed away, not just blown away."

"It still sounds so farfetched."

"Yeah, well, remember this is Hollywood. If some crazy goon gets the idea to try to pull off some kind of a stunt, some kind of a hoax, like a giant monster lion running around eating people, this is the city where he'd most likely be able to give it a serious go. The materials to perpetrate something like that are probably not that difficult to obtain here in the movie capital. Plus, with that enormous club right down the street, no one was going to hear anything like a leaf blower."

"That's remarkable." Robert was stunned, but not for the reason the young officer might have thought.

"Yeah." She nodded briefly. "The news got wind of something going on and sent a van, but the captain felt that, if it was a prank, the worst thing we could have done was give it press. So, he taped off the alley and didn't let the reporter near the mess. We just told the crew that we didn't know what had happened and couldn't let them on the scene. They put up a fuss, but... you know." She waved her hand in the air, shook her head.

"But you documented all of it, I assume?"

"Oh, sure, but right after we got the photos, we washed down the alley. The captain didn't want to give that one incident too much attention. He said we should wait to see what kind of injuries had shown up at the hospitals that morning and if there was a follow up scene. You know, if the weirdo did it again, then we'd have much, much more to go on from pattern evidence. See, if it had hit the tube, we could've seen repeats all over the place, or copycats." She laughed suddenly. "No pun intended."

"And if it wasn't a prank?"

"It was." She nodded knowingly, took a gulp of her drink.

"What if it was just a movie being made?" Robert thought he should throw one or two more wrenches into the works. Unlikely or not, this was one case where heavy police attention could encumber him. Maybe he could divert some.

"With real blood?" She tilted her head at him. "No way. Plus, no permits had been issued, and you can't just sneak in a film crew in the middle of the city and shoot a scene without being noticed. Even in the dead of night. Well, actually, especially not in the dead of night."

"What if it was just a small crew with a hand-held camera, or a student film? They could have been using some kind of huge cat-ish costume and maybe someone got hurt, or sick, or there was an accident and they were the ones who tried to clean it up?"

"Ooh..." She raised her eyebrows, stuck out her bottom lip, and nodded slowly. "Maybe. Though, it wouldn't have been a cat costume, because the tracks were way too detailed. A small production team wouldn't have gone to that kind of trouble."

"No, I suppose not."

"But if the tracks themselves were what they were filming..." She grimaced.

Robert leveled a gaze at her. "Did someone check with any of the film schools?"

"I don't know. That's a good idea, though. The students are

supposed to apply for permits too, but they can be expensive and, with insurance and all that, you know how stuff like that goes. Especially if they don't think they'll disrupt traffic or anything. Maybe you're right and they tried to film without a permit in the middle of the night and someone got hurt."

"All right, maybe I should be the one with the badge."

She picked up her drink. "Maybe so." She nodded, smiling. "Maybe so."

He sat with her for another half hour, although it seemed an utter eternity. When he finally did leave, he hoped she hadn't been too horribly devastated that he excused himself without asking her to star in a new series or even offer her so much as some measly walk-on part.

Her story had to be substantiated, of course, but the characteristics were simply too precise to be anything but genuine. Robert hoped his suggestion about the film students would further redirect any police attention that might hamper him.

This was just too incredible. Robert had to get the cardinal on the phone right away. It was five o'clock on Sunday morning in Rome, but that didn't matter. The cardinal would want to be informed without delay.

He almost couldn't believe it himself, couldn't believe his luck. Surely, the hand of God was at work here to help advance his task. There were giant lion tracks found in LA, and it had only taken him four interviews and a little over five days to hear about it. Add to that the fact that the paw prints were found not two blocks away from the very club where Alex Monroe had worked. Robert couldn't entertain the notion that it was just coincidence.

The police had assumed a leaf blower was responsible for the clean alley. That was a new one. Leaf blowers weren't common enough in the other small countries he'd worked to have been considered. He hadn't even heard that idea while he was in New York. Though, no matter where he worked, no one ever suspected the truth either. No one ever suspected that the materials in all those crime scenes all over the world, which had been blown around as if by some weird and isolated gale force wind, had actually been disturbed by a very large pair of wings.

The cardinal would contact Bishop Sigovia in Greece and send him to help Robert. Young Bishop Sigovia, Robert thought, was a twit, but still the most promising apprentice—a depressing thought—and the most obvious choice to bring Robert what he'd need. Bishop Sigovia would have to go to Rome first, to get the artifact, but that shouldn't delay him too long. Besides, Robert still had a lot of work to do.

Now it all made sense. Lillith was coming and now he knew why.
She'd found him. He was here. The skotos was here in Los Angeles.

Of course, Robert would have to get to him first.

†

Managing any nightclub was difficult.   Managing the largest
nightclub west of the Mississippi was nearly Herculean. Managing the
largest nightclub on the west coast when you were a woman was
matchless. She ruled.

Karen Alanson placed a freshly signed stack of timecards in her
out-box. Then she poured a little more Bacardi into her Diet Coke, put
the bottle back inside the file drawer, and picked up the phone. Only
two more things to do before she could lock the office, race home,
make herself even more remarkably beautiful, run her special errand,
and be back at the club before the A-list started to ask for someone to
unlock the room upstairs.

The first thing she had to do was to get Troy on the horn and make
sure he was going to be at his apartment and that he was stocked. It
was no good finding time for a special errand if the store's shelves
were empty.

The second thing was to meet briefly with Laura and explain to her
why she had to fire Gil.

"Hello," Troy's familiar voice buzzed through the handset.

"And how's my very favorite specialty-vendor doing today?"
Karen cooed. "Busy?"

"Oh, sweet mother of marble, Karen, what the holy gondolas do
you need now?"

"Did we get up on the wrong side of the cave this morning?"

"If you think I'm going to let that tiny arrogant turd into my home
again—"

"Really, precious, how many times do I need to apologize? How
about you let me make it up to you?"

Troy didn't reply.

"Honey?" Karen sang. "Sweetie? How about I stop by and make
things right?"

"What are you gonna do? Bring me Scott Wolf?"

"Wow, you're funny. Tee hee. No, but I'd like to do a little
shopping and I'm feeling both like being generous and also causing
myself some serious biological damage."

He paused, then, "Continue."

"I was thinkin' I'd stop by between home and my way back to the club. You got goodies?"

"Inventory is high."

"And hopefully, I'll soon be as well. So, honey, if I can't manage Mr. Wolf for you, you wanna try some Karen burger?"

"Jeez, Karen!" Troy whined. "Don't you get enough from your harem?"

"I'm just kidding, Troy. My god, you queens are touchy."

"What time are you going to be here?"

"I dunno. Seven-thirty? Hey, baby, I know what you really want, though."

"Yeah? What's that?"

"Some Reynolds wrap. You want yourself some Nicky Reynolds wrap, don't 'cha baybah?"

"Bitch..." Troy chuckled. "Are you purposely trying to—?"

"He's coming tonight, by the way, have I mentioned that yet? Does that help make up for things at all? Darren called me last night to make sure they'd be on the list for the upstairs room. And get this, he asked me to get a black card for a relative of Nicky's."

"Wow," Troy droned, yawning. "Nick's mother wants to be a regular at the club?"

"Ooh, amusing zinger there, babe. Tee hee. No, honey. Apparently, the dish is that Nicky has a cousin in town and he's not only gorgeous beyond reason, but he's got more money than Ross Perot."

"I hope he's taller too."

"Bet on it."

"Does he indulge?"

"I'm assuming. You want an intro? Wanna say upstairs at one-thirty? I told you I could make things up to you."

"Double-click on that."

"Done. Okay, then, I'll see you first, though, at the Troy Palace, between seven-thirty and eight. Maybe eight-thirty. Nine at the latest. Unless I get there at nine-thirty."

"I'll turn on some soft lights for you."

"It's so nice that someone loves me."

"How *is* your dog?"

"Ciao bella!"

"Um, yeah, aloha."

She hung up. Karen absolutely adored Troy. Actually, she absolutely adored just about any guy who wasn't constantly trying to taste her. Since Troy not only fit that bill, but he also was the source of just so many other pleasures, he was currently her number one guy and the longest functional relationship she'd had with any man since her father. Karen's father had fallen from a nine-story scaffolding when she was eight.

She had a boyfriend at the moment, a flavor of the month, so to speak, who was certainly yummy. Raphael was one of those major male supermodels that made perfect arm-ornaments, when he was in town, which was never for very long or very often. He kept telling her that he had to take advantage of the attention while it lasted. Boy, did Karen ever understand that.

Raphael didn't like to be out in public when he was in LA, which was a shame, because Karen simply lived to show him off. Especially at the club on Saturday nights, when having him in tow made all the queens in the room so green with envy that the dance floor looked like a field of bouncing broccoli.

She knew why he didn't like to go out with her, though. His best friend had told her. He didn't like that people looked at them and wondered who was prettier. It should be obvious. Wherever Raphael went, *he* wanted to be the prettiest flower in the meadow. Normally, he never had even the slightest problem. However, at the club, even Michelangelo's *David* could be intimidated.

Karen certainly didn't mind guys with egos. They were much easier to understand than those without them. At least a guy that was all about himself wasn't going to expend unwelcome energy on her, energy that maybe focused on her every move, that maybe told her what to wear or who she could have as a friend, that dictated how she was to behave or how to get him off or that she needed to drop a few pounds or gauged just how hard he could backhand her without making the kind of a mark that might land him in jail.

Karen was twenty-two years old before she'd realized, wholeheartedly, that men really weren't supposed to hit their girlfriends and that she had legal recourse in that area. The fact had certainly never been explained to her while she was in Tennessee, and certainly never by her mother, whose own string of boyfriends often seemed to consider both of their faces to be fair game. It wasn't until one of them began to consider several other areas of Karen's body to be fair game that she finally left. She was sixteen.

Karen didn't hate men, though. Even now, thirteen years later, she didn't look back at her somewhat turbulent beginnings with any kind of resentment. Although, she hadn't always felt that way.

It wasn't very long after she'd arrived in Los Angeles before some of the guys she dated began to hit her too. There were guys that didn't hit her, but they weren't the ones that stuck around for very long. It wasn't easy for Karen to come to the conclusion that the problem wasn't with her, that she didn't deserve, or wasn't destined, to be with a man who didn't have any reins on his temper. Eventually, though, she'd allowed herself that suspicion and was finally able to put it to the test. She remembered with a sturdy clarity how violently her hands had been shaking the first time she called the police. She could barely dial the phone and actually had to try several times just to manage nine-one-one.

Of course, the guy was out of jail before the bruises were off of her face, but he never bothered her again. More importantly, the entire experience had somehow transformed her. Just taking that action, finally accepting that things didn't have to be that way, had made all the difference, as though a switch had been thrown and she'd suddenly been powered-up.

Included with her inner change was a new energy, a new vibe, which emanated from her and did most of the work as far as screening the men she met. The shitty ones just didn't feel comfortable around her anymore; she was dangerous.

Karen had met the club's owner, Maxwell Hertz, four years ago and she adored him too. He'd recognized something in Karen besides her almost unconsciously glorious sexiness. He decided to foster that more unique aspect of her, which was a decision for which Karen would always hold him in esteem. If he wasn't so enthusiastically homosexual, she might have even fallen for him completely. Still, that was something she could say about nearly all the men in her life.

They worked very well together, Karen and Max. She'd started as his personal assistant and within a year, even though she'd still been in business classes at City College, Max was so impressed that he made her the club's Monday through Thursday manager. Eight months after that she was the Friday night manager, and a year after that, Max gave her Saturdays.

Saturdays in Los Angeles were the magic nights. Everyone that wasn't dead or in jail went out on Saturday nights. Max allowed her to concentrate what she'd learned from the School of Hard Knocks on that spectacular night's potential. Karen managed to make Saturday nights more successful than Max had ever seen them.

It was on Karen's watch that the major celebrities had started coming. It was Karen who was responsible for the entrance line staying at least a block long for well into the wee hours of the morning. On holiday weekends, if you weren't on somebody's list, forget it, you weren't getting in.

She'd managed to create an elite type of value where there hadn't been all that much value to begin with, and that was really the name of the game, wasn't it? Suddenly, just being in the club meant you were a player. Being allowed into the private room downstairs meant you were a star. Being in the room upstairs, well, that meant that somewhere there were temples built in your honor and statues in your image.

She'd been the club's general manager for six months now, a position created for her, as Max had handled those specific duties himself prior to Karen's rise. She displayed even more insight and sheer good business instinct in her hiring and delegations. It certainly wasn't as stressful as producing a high-profile party for twenty-three hundred people once a week. Let the new Saturday manager sweat that out for a while.

There were now six managers working under Karen, twenty-one bartenders, eighteen bar-backs, fifteen door and security personnel, and nine maintenance employees. Add to that the special talent she brought into the club on an independent contractor basis, such as DJ's, sound and lighting engineers, interior designers, and nationally known party promoters.

Then there were the unofficial members of her team. Unofficial, yet indispensable, members, such as Troy.

Karen was a confident woman. She'd had to struggle for her confidence, to trust that she really could take care of things, but once she had that, it was time to give herself permission to be happy too.

She hadn't spoken to her mother since she'd left home and didn't want to. Karen had created a life in Los Angeles beyond anything she'd ever imagined while she was behind the fences in Maryville, Tennessee. She planned to leave every reminder of the person she'd been taped up in a dusty box, high on the top shelf of her walk-in closet, along with her high school yearbooks, her Madonna-wannabe paraphernalia, and the un-cashed check for a hundred dollars that her mother had given to her the day she left home. Screw the meek whiney bitch. Karen hadn't needed her then, and she didn't need her now.

With the relentless assistance of a speech coach, people guessed Karen was a native Californian, which suited her just fine. The person she used to be had a southern twang that could split marble.

Karen had a new family now in the form of some intimately close friends. Although managing the club consumed a significant amount of her time, she was able to cultivate some very close relationships with a few of the club's regulars.

Darren Jacobson, one of the moderately successful promoters that the club occasionally engaged—Karen would *never* use the phrase 'moderately successful' around Darren, however, praise Heaven, no—although at times a jerk, was really just a scared kid at heart, something Karen recognized instantly. She loved him. He really was a lovable guy, once you got to know him, once you got past his Mr. Charming façade, complete with the need for his sexual orientation to appear ambiguous. It wasn't, though, but no one had the heart—or the eggs—to tell him. He was basically a good guy trying to do the best he could. He just didn't know it.

One of the most ideal examples, though, of a good guy trying to do well by the people he loved, was Theo. Now there was an angel on earth if ever she'd seen one. She couldn't get enough of him, and although Theo occasionally required some mild discipline—he wasn't the brightest bulb in the chandelier—she did absolutely everything she could to see that he was kept happy and healthy. Anyone that hurt Theo would have to answer to Karen, which included Theo himself.

Eddie took wonderful care of Theo, for which Karen adored him as well. And although he too was maybe a couple of members short of a committee, together, Theo and Eddie, well... they were almost functional.

The most fun Karen ever had, the biggest perk of her fierce devotion to the club, was when she got to bring the guys into the private room upstairs and watch them light up like toddlers on Christmas. They got to rub elbows—and sometimes other body parts—with celebrities that most people wouldn't ever see that closely without a concert ticket and some very strong binoculars.

The whole group still just about cried with affectionate laughter every time they told someone about the night Theo and Eddie followed Toni Braxton around like puppies for four hours. She was very sweet to them. They kept fighting over who got to run to the bar for her or take messages to her manager in the downstairs room. Before she left, she let Karen take a picture of the three of them. Max paid to have an enlarged print professionally framed, which he hung in the office, right in the middle of his own collection of visiting-celeb photos. Everyone loved Eddie and Theo.

These were the kind of men Karen liked in her life. The Raphaels were nice, much better than the testosterone riddled beer-zombies she used to date, but still too unstable and unpredictable. Not only that, but they tended to be miserably unobservant and, although she didn't mind them being self-involved—to a degree, of course, let's not get silly—one thing by which Karen could not abide was being unobserved.

She adored her boys, the magic five, Troy, Darren, Nicky, Theo, and Eddie. They not only indisputably adored her right back, but they also observed her to the point where they noticed whenever she so much as had her bangs trimmed. Now what woman on Earth wouldn't kill to be surrounded by men like that? So they never put out. Big deal.

On Saturday nights the club was a magic land and, although it certainly had its resident queens, Karen was their goddess. The other kind of guys, well, they were sometimes fun as toys. Let Raphael hang out in London as long as he wanted. All the pleasures that the magic five couldn't personally give her were easy enough to obtain on a sample basis.

There was a knock at the door and Laura Shah peeked inside.

"Sorry I'm late," she said with a wince and a smile.

Karen waved off her apology. If Laura ever entered a room with any other three words, Karen would accuse her of being a pod-person.

"No problem." Karen reached over to Max's desk and pulled out his chair. "This'll be quick. Here, sit down for a sec."

Laura gave Karen a nervous look when she came into the room, which Karen didn't understand. Laura had been working with Karen and Max for almost two years and was one of the best promoters around. In fact, she'd been instrumental in the deal Karen had made with Lauren Isseroff.

Although Karen managed a world-class nightclub, Los Angeles wasn't exactly a hotbed of opportunity for contemporary DJ's, and she had trouble booking the bigger names. Junior Vasquez, Hex Hector, Frankie Knuckles, Victor Caldrone, Teri Bristol, Brian Ikon, David Knapp, Tony Maserati, Angel Moraes, and even Boy George, had all spun at the club at least once, but they were nearly impossible to book, and their visits were exceptionally expensive.

Lauren Isseroff had been a European DJ deity for years before she ever agreed to come to the States. Even then, she only came as far as Miami and New York. The idea that she spin in Los Angeles, even at its most notable hot spot, was never something she'd been willing to discuss. Still, Karen had tried, through the mail, over the phone, and in person.

"Do you want a Diet Coke?" she asked Laura. "They're in the fridge."

Laura took a soda out of the mini-fridge and sat in Max's chair. She looked nervous, which, again, Karen thought was silly. She was very valuable to the club. Somehow, Laura had arranged for a direct phone conversation between Karen and Lauren Isseroff. Not only that, but she'd even been able to seed the ground a bit about the notion of a booking on the west coast. Then she pumped the club enough to Lauren's people that they were able to convince her to discuss the possibility. The resulting conversation had been intense, invigorating, and brief: Lauren had promised to spin at the club on none other than New Years Fuckin' Eve, and in return, Karen had promised her much, much more than she could possibly deliver.

"Is something wrong, Karen? Did Lauren cancel?" Laura looked genuinely distressed. Even when she frowned she hardly had a wrinkle on her face. She was all of twenty-eight, but looked like an absolute baby, the bitch. Karen sincerely tried to decide if she genuinely disliked Laura, or was just jealous that she looked like a cover-model for Ageless Chicks with Perfect Tits Magazine.

"No, nothing like that," Karen said. "Your hair looks great, by the way." She meant it too. Laura had the thickest, shiniest, and most beautiful hair Karen had ever seen. It went way beyond stunning. Auburn-brown and very straight, except for the subtlest curve, which gave its extreme volume a kind of fluid grace. She always wore it off her face, flowing behind her ears and down her back, creating a wide and gorgeous frame for that flawless baby-face of hers.

It was quite important that the employees at the club be very attractive, especially bartenders and promoters. This was a key detail, and one that Karen took very seriously. She was more than rewarded with the turnout at Laura's events; the lines were always packed with hundreds of delectable men who were practically slipping in their own drool to get close to her.

Regardless of that, Karen rarely stayed very long at Laura's events, even when they were ragingly successful, and they were all ragingly successful. She just didn't like to hang out with her for some reason. She hated to think it was because Laura made her feel like an ugly stepsister, which she did, but Karen still hated to think it. Then again, such things had never stopped her before. Funny.

"Thanks," said Laura, relaxing a little bit.

"Babe, I need you to cut Gil loose." Karen got right down to business. Troy wasn't going to wait forever and she still had to primp.

"What?"

"Listen, I'm really sorry, but he's just not reliable. You have to know that."

"Karen, I—"

"Before you start, let me just say that I think this is the best thing for you. Now, I know I have no legal right to ask you to do this, because he's technically your employee, but while you're under contract with us, you represent this club. I, personally, think that you're the absolute idyllic image of professionalism and glam-spunk. But, sweetness, Gil is draggin' you down."

"I agree." Laura nodded.

"You do?" Karen's eyes widened. "Oh, hot damn, I'm so relieved." She smiled, laid her hand on her chest, and gave a few dramatic heaves.

"He's a twerp." Laura shook her head, giggling.

"Oh, blessed mother, you're an insightful girl. I knew there was something I liked about you." Even having said it, Karen couldn't quite make herself believe it; there really wasn't much that Karen actually liked about Laura. It made her ashamed, as it was obviously some kind of petty issue, but there it was, just the same. In fact, she didn't just dislike Laura: Karen almost got physically ill at the thought of her. It just didn't make any sense.

"Listen, Karen," Laura started, "the truth is I've been thinking about getting rid of Gil for a long time."

"Beautiful *and* smart." Karen forced a grin. "Can I pick 'em, or can I pick 'em?"

"So, I have no problem with that. I guess I just didn't have the nerve to do it myself, but now that you've said something, I feel much better about it. I'll tell him today."

"Oh, glory days, I'm so glad we could work this out. To tell you the truth, Laura, I never understood why you hired him in the first place. You're always fighting, he's never around when you need him, he pisses everyone off, he's got a chip on his shoulder bigger than he'll ever be, and he *never* smells very good. Not to mention that the police were utterly convinced he had something to do with Alex dying."

Laura started to respond but Karen raised her hand and stopped her.

"Now, I'm not suggesting that he did," Karen said. "Lord knows I don't think Gil could dispatch a cockroach without wobbling a bit in the final rounds, but I know that you both lied to the police about the way all of you got along. So, I really don't know what's going on there, but Laura, I think you're going places, and that little guy, please forgive me, is nothing more than a liability."

"I couldn't agree more."

"Why, on earth, did you ever, *ever*, hire that boy?" Karen giggled, shaking her head as she reached for her spiked Diet Coke.

"He introduced me to Lauren Isseroff."

Karen clutched her necklace. "No! He did not do any such thing! You just pack your shit up and get the fuck outta here!"

Laura laughed, nodded, and patted her leg with her open palm for emphasis. "No, no, I'm not kidding! He did!"

"That elf introduced you to Lauren? Right! Next you're going to tell me you're really a man." Karen grinned. "Or that Gil is!"

Both women screamed with laughter, eyes bulging. They rocked in their seats, threw their heads back, and clapped their hands.

"Oh, my god," Laura said after a minute, wiping at her eyes.

"I do not fucking believe you!" Karen was beside herself.

"No, it's true." Laura nodded again. "In New York a couple years ago. It was while Lauren was spinning at Specter."

"How the hell did Gil get into Specter? Through a mouse hole? You're shitting me."

"He used to work for Lauren."

"Okay, now I know you're on drugs."

Laura shook her head, smiling. "It was mostly in Amsterdam. I don't think it was for very long, because she seemed to really want to get rid of him too."

"This business is just filled with intelligent women."

"Anyway, I was visiting New York, you remember?"

Karen nodded.

"So," Laura continued, "he was hitting on me at Specter and he tried to impress me by introducing me to Lauren. Well, naturally I took advantage."

"Naturally." Karen closed her eyes, nodded.

"As soon as the intros were done in the booth and she had a second, I pitched her. I tried to get her to come out here and spin."

"My girl." Karen touched the corner of her eye, wiping an imaginary tear.

"Shut up!" Laura laughed, reaching over and slapping Karen's knee. "Anyway, she laughed in my face."

"You too?"

"But…" Laura raised a finger at her. "She said she'd *maybe* think about it, and told me to get her card from downstairs. I was just about to leave when she stopped me. I thought she'd changed her mind, so of course I gave her my attention. She told me that Gil had been assisting her, but he'd always wanted to live in LA. You know, the whole 'actor' thing. He'd need a job, of course, and maybe he could sort of keep her informed about the good clubs, and the next thing I knew he was out here working for me and I can't tell you how many times I've wanted to hit him with my car."

Karen giggled, but was having trouble shaking the feeling that Laura had just made up that story on the spot, right in that office with her, lounging in Max's executive chair.

Karen threw it off. What difference did it make? She didn't care if Gil was Laura and Lauren's love-child. Laura was willing to get rid of him and that was all that mattered. He wasn't going to be running around the club pissing everyone off anymore. Karen thought about the time he'd pointed at Sally Field and, well within ear-shot, said *Oh, look! It's the flying nun!*

Karen shuddered.

"So, good, we're agreed," she said. "Make sure to have a final check ready for him, you know, labor law, blah, blah, and tell him that Max would like it if he didn't come to the club for a while. Now, you understand, Laura, that when I say 'for a while,' I really mean, 'never, ever, ever, never again.' "

Laura smiled, giggled. "Yes, I understand."

"That might be a bit touchy, and I can just see Gil giving the guys at the door a hard time and making a scene. But Laura, Brad and Matt will happily break both his little arms if he shows up here, so try to make that work, okay?"

Laura took a deep breath. "I have an idea for that, but you'll have to agree to it."

"What?" Karen's stomach flipped up into her ribs.

"Well, first, do you mind if I put a little of that Bacardi in this one too?" Laura smiled impishly, pointing at her soda.

Karen dropped her jaw in mock-shock and put her hands on her hips. "Now, what makes you think I have Bacardi in the office?"

"Oh, Karen, I could smell it from the DJ booth. You don't mind, do you?"

"Of course not." Karen reached for the drawer and the bottle, giving Laura a quick sideways glance. There was quite a nose on that girl. Laura's bionic sinuses picked up on the brand and everything.

"What if I toss Gil the pre-party in Nichols Canyon?" Laura asked, pouring the rum into her cola. "What if I let him sink or swim handling that bash all by himself?"

Karen was suddenly confused and very nervous. "I don't know, Laura. It's pretty important to Lauren that—"

"A good deal of the work is already done." Laura poured another hefty splash of rum into her soda and handed the bottle back to Karen. "What still needs to be done will keep him way too busy to be able to cause any scenes here at the club, which he wouldn't even think of doing if he thought he'd been promoted. If he screws up the private party, then Lauren's less likely to balk if we send him off. If the party's a hit, then we've sort of officially pushed him into independent party promotion. The club never has to use him again, of course, so he's out anyway." Laura smiled ghoulishly. "Win, win."

Karen raised her eyebrows and blinked rapidly. "You know Laura…"

"What?" she answered with a shy grin.

"If you had bigger tits I'd be all over you right now."

They laughed and clinked their soda cans to seal the deal.

†

Scott's room at the Mondrian wasn't the most lavish to be found in the city, but it was cozy, very contemporary, and had a view of Hollywood and Santa Monica that could mesmerize. High on the twelfth floor, the view was made even more magnificent by the position of the hotel itself, as it sat on a bluff with its back to the south west. The room didn't catch the direct rays of the sunset, but the sky over Century City still blazed with its fire.

"I want to look at condos in Santa Monica next week," Scott called from the bathroom. He was drying his hair after a shower.

Nick lounged on the single king-size bed, watching the sun's dying splendor race high above the city. Darren had gone to see Troy and hadn't gotten back yet. Troy was probably very busy. It was, after all, Saturday night again.

"You're what?" Nick scrunched his face at the bathroom door.

"I'm thinking that being close to the beach would be fun." Scott stuck his head around the corner, his wet hair flinging clear droplets of water on the carpet. "Or do you think there's a better place I should be looking?"

"No." Nick shook his head. "It's a great place, I guess."

Scott went back into the bathroom. "Hey, would you pop in that CD I like, please?" he asked, his voice echoing out off of the bathroom mirror.

Nick rolled over to the side table and hit 'play' on the mini-system stereo they'd brought up to the room earlier in the week. Since going out last Sunday night, Scott had acquired quite a taste for dance music and picked up some of the latest mixes. He was especially fond of Victor Caldrone and Brian Ikon.

The previous week had been about goofing off and playing the tourist game with Nick as the guide. Monday night had been dinner at The Ivy and then to the Century City Mall for an action movie showing lots of bare muscle—nothing was accomplished during Monday's daylight hours, as those were spent unconscious. They went for coffee at The Abbey after the dude-flick. Scott had been introduced to at least half a gazillion of Nick's friends and acquaintances, as well as, very likely, to more than a few he'd never met before. Scott was introduced as Nick's cousin "from back east."

It was back to the Sunset 5 Plaza on Tuesday morning for a workout at Crunch, where Nick taught Scott how to spot him. Although, he was almost crushed on the decline-bench when Scott was distracted by Rupert Everett, who was trying admirably to look inconspicuous while every person in the room watched him work through a set of cable crossovers. Scott was a little star stuck. He told Nick that he knew Rupert would be a major star ever since he'd seen him in *Another Country* with Cary Elwes.

While they were there, Scott didn't work out. He explained that his body "just comes this way."

After the gym was shopping on Melrose. Scott made Nick have lunch at Johnny Rocket's, of all places, and insisted on consuming almost every flavor of milkshake known to man, complete with toppings of whipped cream as high as traffic cones. This prompted a male model at a nearby table to stop and bond with Scott over the perils of bulimia.

The afternoon found the dynamic duo scavenging the Beverly Center and then Rodeo Drive, stuffing Nick's car with bags and boxes of treasures for, not only the both of them, but Darren, Theo, and Eddie as well. Apparently, Scott had some actual accounts at actual banks, each of which had issued him actual credit and ATM cards, under various pseudonyms, of course. Unlike the previous Sunday, when all the banks were closed, he didn't have to lick anything.

Darren met them for dinner that night at PF Chang's where they managed to drink themselves silly. They crossed the street afterward to see a late showing of the current Eddie Murphy comedy, which helped to ease the process of sobering up.

On Wednesday morning Darren skipped working and Nick skipped working-out so they could take Scott to Universal Studios. Scott turned out to be a major source of film trivia, which made Nick and Darren wish they'd sat in the back of the tram, where Scott might have been less likely to correct the tour guide as frequently.

They met Eddie and Theo for dinner at Gaucho Grill, and were so tired afterward the three of them fell asleep on Nick's couch right in the middle of a very entertaining rerun of the latest of popular nighttime dramas.

Thursday morning brought Nick and Scott back to Crunch where he was star stuck again, this time by Ryan Reynolds, initially of *Two Guys and a Girl* fame, now a movie star. Scott walked right over to the guy and introduced himself. He shook Mr. Reynolds's hand, and then told Nick that, even though they had the same last name, there was no biological relation. Nick couldn't get Scott to tell him anything else he may have gleaned during the brief instant he'd touched the handsome young star besides, "He's Canadian, and the rest is really none of your business."

After Crunch came brunch at Hugo's, where they saw Kevin Sorbo arguing with someone who they assumed was his agent. Nick asked Scott not to go over and touch him; he didn't need to know why the conversation was so heated or anything about Mr. Sorbo's lineage.

Then, they hit Hollywood Boulevard itself, where Scott had to be literally dragged across the sidewalk to keep him from stopping at each and every star on the Walk of Fame. They went into the Hollywood Wax Museum, Mann's (née Grauman's) Chinese Theatre, where they indulged in a matinee, and then Scott had to literally drag Nick into the *Ripley's Believe It or Not Odditorium*.

Just driving down the strip dazzled Scott as he recognized landmark after landmark. He was charmed into sheer melancholy by the Hollywood Roosevelt Hotel, for some reason. Later, at Scott's urging, Nick went through all the trouble of finding a place to park so they could walk around Hollywood and Vine "just for the heck of it."

Scott had spent thousands of years in the Mediterranean, Asia Minor, the Near East, Africa, and all over the European continent, but was jaunting through Los Angeles like a kid on his first visit to Disneyland.

Nick had made a mental note to take Scott to Disneyland.

On Thursday night Scott treated Nick and Darren to a performance of *After the Fall* at the Fountain Theater, but when they asked him what he thought of the show he replied, "I didn't get it."

Back at his hotel, Scott had a message at the desk that put him on the phone for what turned out to be the rest of Thursday night and a hearty portion of Friday morning. Nick and Darren had fallen asleep.

Each time Nick woke up, Scott said he'd only be another minute. He was still heavily involved with numerous financial institutions, first in Hong Kong, then Russia, France, England, and finally New York. Each time Nick woke up, Scott was speaking a different language.

Over a continental breakfast at the hotel, Darren made the mistake of inquiring about the all-night phone calls and had to stop Scott after twenty-five minutes of ranting on "rates of exchange," "international market guidelines," and "those brainless assholes at the Bank of London."

Nick and Darren had ended up going to Crunch while Scott stayed at the hotel to take a late morning nap. When they went back to pick him up he wasn't there. Nick used his key to get into the room when Scott didn't answer the door. They waited for forty-five minutes and were about to become seriously worried when he finally showed up. Scott explained that he'd have been back sooner but he had trouble with the salesman at the car dealership.

He'd gone down to BMW, because he liked Darren's new car. He ended up driving back in a tiny, two-seat number that appeared worthy of a grand prix. When they asked what kind of trouble he'd had with the salesman, Scott just said, "You know how they can be." Nick had a feeling the salesman's first mistake was shaking Scott's hand.

They decided to have a quiet evening at home, meaning Nick's place, but Scott wanted to spring for dinner first, so he called and invited Theo and Eddie. They met them at Mark's on La Cienega where they took up a table on the patio for two and a half hours. The restaurant staff didn't seem to mind though; it's good for business to have an attractive group of boisterous young guys having a great time where everyone could see them. Also, to say that Scott was a generous tipper would be the textbook definition of 'understatement.'

The five of them stopped at Blockbuster on the way back to Nick's, where Scott got to see another star, Sasha Mitchell, who was with a very tall woman. Scott asked Nick fairly loudly if she was "the one that he, you know…" and made the international gesture meaning 'smacked around a bit.' Nick laughed and shook his head furiously, while at the same time shushing him and trying not to trip over the other three boys, who were on the floor in near hysterics.

They settled on the most recent James Bond film, in honor of Scott's new car. Theo later suggested the film would have been much better had it been in 3-D.

The guys pulled out the hide-a-bed in the sectional and stacked it with pillows before starting the videos, as they knew one or more of them would be fast asleep long before the movies were over, especially since, during the films, they finished off all the booze that was in the apartment.

In the morning, Nick and Darren found Scott, Theo, and Eddie in just about the same positions they'd left them, with the exception of Theo's arm, which was draped over Scott. However, they were all still fully dressed and otherwise unmolested.

Theo actually ended up being the one who woke the other two because he wanted to watch some Saturday morning superhero cartoons, and insisted he simply couldn't do it without the sound turned up.

After breakfast at Eat Well they all decided to go to the gym. Theo was thoroughly insulted when he learned that Scott had been to Crunch with Nick and hadn't even considered asking him to be his trainer. Scott hired him on the spot — which Nick, of course, knew was an extra nice gesture, considering the amount of effort Scott actually needed to apply to maintain his perfect body, the bitch — for an amount that neither of them would disclose to Nick. However, when Scott first whispered the number to Theo, it actually made him look dizzy.

Well, dizzy-*er*.

Theo and Eddie usually worked-out at Gold's Gym, where the five of them ended up spending that afternoon. Scott bought memberships all around, upgrading Eddie and Theo, and promising them both memberships to Crunch as well. Scott explained that now they could choose their gym from day to day "depending on our moods."

It was unanimously decided that they would all go out together that night. Theo and Eddie went off to their homes for a disco-nap and then to get ready. Nick, Darren, and Scott went to the Mondrian to clean up.

After turning on the mini-system in Scott's hotel room, Nick made sure the music wasn't too loud for the neighboring rooms, but high enough so that Scott could hear it over the hairdryer. He laid back on the cool sheets and stretched. The window was open and a breeze, smelling faintly of the sea, rushed tenderly over him.

He'd had his own disco-nap right when they got to the room. It was an accident, though. While Darren got into the shower, Nick had lain down and promptly fallen asleep.

Nick woke an hour later. Darren had already gone off to see Troy on behalf of the whole group — bulk was just so much cheaper.

Nick hadn't put on a shirt yet after his own shower, and was lounging comfortably in just socks, boxer briefs, and a favorite treat that Scott had gotten for him during one of their afternoons on Rodeo Drive: a brand new pair of Versace pants.

There was a soft knock at the door and Nick rolled over again, then lumbered up from his lethargic sprawl to open it. He'd been very comfortable, so it took him a minute. By the time he opened the door, Darren was already staring at the carpet, but hadn't yet started to lick his teeth.

"Were you still asleep?" Darren asked, smiling, brushing inside.

"Just about." Nick shut the door behind him. He noticed that Darren had gone home and changed.

"I thought we were going to stop at your place on the way to get the guys," Nick said, "so that you could change then."

"Yeah," Darren said, crossing the room and turning up the music, "but it's such a fuckin' mess, I really don't want anyone seeing it. I haven't been home since Thursday afternoon."

Nick knew by 'anyone,' Darren meant he didn't want Scott seeing it. That made Nick smile. Despite liking Scott so much, Darren still wasn't comfortable enough to allow him into his apartment, which would have audaciously revealed the fact that Darren was a pig.

Darren had changed into a plain white t-shirt, a pair of laced Hogan ankle boots that Nick picked out for him in Beverly Hills, and some Halogen cargo pants, which fit very, very nicely.

Darren looked at what Nick had put on. "Are you trying to show me up?" he asked with a grin.

"No chance of that." Nick smiled back at the compliment. "Besides, we don't wanna look like somebody's back-up singers, do we?"

Darren sauntered across the room, ran his hands around Nick's waist and laced them together, pulling him close, whispering into his neck. "I dunno. Do we?"

Nick laughed and scrunched his shoulder up to Darren's ear. "You're tickling me, you freak."

He brushed his cheek against Darren's, who'd just shaved and smelled like menthol. "What'd you bring me?" Nick whispered.

"Some Missy…" Darren purred into Nick's shoulder, swaying him playfully to the music.

"Uh, huuh…"

"And some Gina…"

"Oh, my."

"And some coke-alina, in case Missy is in a bad mood, or only so-so."

"You're such a boy scout."

"What size are these, my little model-man?" Darren asked, tugging on Nick's back belt-loop.

"Thirty-two."

"That's the way, baby."

The hairdryer stopped and Scott leaned out of the bathroom. "Hey, Romeo, excuse me."

Darren leaned back over his shoulder sarcastically and threw Scott a playful smirk. "Yeah, what?"

Scott laughed. "What time are we dropping?"

"I dunno. What time do you wanna drop, baby?"

Scott shrugged and went back into the bathroom. "I dunno."

Nick let go of Darren while he was still leaning, causing him to fall back on the bed with a startled gasp.

"Oh, you're so tricky," Darren said mockingly, throwing a pillow at him.

"Yeah, you were scared," Nick said, crossing around the bed and turning the music back down. "What kind did you get? Missy, I mean."

"Troy didn't have any more of the red ones, so I thought we'd try the new white ones with the little half-moon on them."

"MDMA?"

"Supposedly. We'll see."

"Lovey-dovey?"

"Hopefully. That's what the Troy-Man said."

"Were there a lot of people at his place?"

"Yeah! My god, I thought he was having a party. I called from the car, though, so he had a bag ready for me. 'Ten baseball caps, a carton of juice, and a case of cola.' I told him I did not want fries with that."

"Ten?" Nick raised his eyebrows at Darren, who had rolled over and wadded a pillow under his chin as if he were going to nap.

"Yeah," he said. "That's two for each of us. I didn't want to dip into my reserves. We *know* those are sweet. We should leave them in the sock drawer for a private occasion." He winked at Nick, who actually blushed, which made them both laugh out loud.

"Hey, Romeo?" Scott bellowed from inside the bathroom.

"What Scotty?" Darren yelled back. "Ain't you done fixing your mascara?"

"What do I owe you?"

"A big wet sloppy French-one, baby!"

"Dream-weaver!" Scott came out of the bathroom, his hair was dry and fell in thick, jet-black swirls down the back of his neck and behind his ears. He was in a pair of simple Tommy jeans, but still looked like he just stepped off a fashion runway.

"Oh, good, someone else is going low-glam," Darren observed.

"Nick was layin' around in his boxer briefs, so I made him put those on." Scott smiled at him. "We did that so you wouldn't suspect we had sex."

Nick laughed. Darren, shaking his head and smiling, chucked another pillow at him.

"What if," Nick said, picking up the pillow and laying on his stomach next to Darren, "we talked to Gina for a while, then started talking to Missy around ten or so, and maybe the second one, if we need it, at one or two?"

"You'll probably need it by eleven," Darren said, probably only half jokingly.

Missy had stopped being nice to Nick on a consistent basis several months before. It seemed she didn't really like hanging out with him anymore. She began to be very fickle when it came to Nick.

"Touché."

"We'll give Missy an hour to be good," Darren suggested.

It was rare they found a good batch, unless someone brought Nick something from Miami or New York. The pills he'd gotten from Florida were cheaper and less potent, but he could take two at one time and he'd get off the same way he used to on just one Californian hit.

Missy was one of those types of compounds to which a tolerance could be built, and Nick's tolerance was becoming very challenging. He'd only been indulging with her for a couple of years, but it was fairly regularly. Still, lately even when she was moderately polite to him, she still only kept him happy for half the time she afforded to Darren. Even after four years, he and Missy were still going strong, the bastard.

Even when Missy wasn't at all nice to Nick, he still had to pay the piper in the form of some very listless and dreary recovery time. It used to be only a day, but when the depression sailed into including a 'suicide-Tuesday,' without even so much as two good hours on Saturday night, it was obviously time to explore other options. Since Missy was being such a bitch, Nick had to find other friends.

"If Missy isn't being nice by then," Nick said, laying his head close to Darren's, "I'm just gonna go with Gina and a coke chaser."

"That'll be Plan B," Darren suggested.

Gina had been Nick's apparent savior. Nick wanted to get away from hanging out with Missy altogether, but it wasn't easy to just ignore her euphoric recall; they'd had some very sweet times together. It was tough to accept that the relationship was over.

The plan was to avoid suffering the horrors of sobriety by hanging out with someone else; someone who maybe wasn't as volatile as Missy, with so many mood swings, or as physically abusive. After a night with Missy, it wasn't uncommon for her to slap Nick around quite a bit.

"So," Nick said, "I won't drink at all, just in case Missy ditches me and I end up hanging with Gina."

"Good man," Darren said. "You get to be the boy scout now."

Although for quite some time Gina, GHB, was legal and could be obtained through sources no more exotic than General Nutrition Center, Nick hadn't thought about trying to use it to wean him off ecstasy. No one had that idea until after Gina had become a Schedule I compound. It became a Schedule I compound when its dramatic reaction to other depressants, such as alcohol, suddenly made it headline news.

"What about until then?" Darren asked. It was only eight.

"Scotty?" Nick turned to Scott, who was going through T-shirts, comparing.

"Yeah?" Scott said, not looking up from the open drawer.

"What time do you think you'll drop?"

"I dunno." Scott shrugged.

The irony was that Nick never drank alcohol until very recently. Gina seemed so much better, in that all the studies he'd seen from Europe and even the majority in the States claimed it was non-toxic on the liver and kidneys, a naturally occurring chemical in the human body, and wouldn't produce physical dependence.

So, Nick had taken the leap with Gina a few times in the comfort of Darren's home with no problems. Quite the contrary actually; those were superbly delicious evenings.

It wasn't until he tried to purchase and use it on his own, without a better understanding of its properties, that he encountered Ms. Gina's highly sensitive nature.

"Should we have a G-cocktail?" Nick asked. "After we get the boys, I mean?"

GHB could be the safest compound you could get, *if* it was manufactured, dosed, and mixed properly. It certainly wasn't for beginners.

"Why don't they just come here?" Scott asked, looking up, trying on a tight black v-neck that made him look like Scotto, the God of Hot. "Call them, tell them I'll take care of parking, and we can lounge here with Gina for a while, then cab over to the club."

As Nick had learned, if G was mixed with another depressant, such as keteset, it could make you sick and even kill you. The same was true of alcohol, of course, but this meant nothing to those who didn't drink. To them, GHB looked like the perfect diversion from a great many harsher chemicals.

"You know," Darren said, closing his eyes on the wadded-up pillow, "that Gina-lounging doesn't sound like a bad plan."

"Do you have your cell?" Nick asked him. "Scotty, do you have soda? You know, to mix Gina with."

Things only started to get really ugly when uninformed club kids started dropping unconscious on dance floors, either from taking too much Gina, in which case they just woke up later unscathed—however, no one ever heard about *that* part in the news papers, they just heard someone left the club in an ambulance—or from mixing it with something hazardous, in which case they sometimes didn't wake up at all.

Finally, when a couple of unscrupulous college students slipped some GHB into a girl's beer in the hopes of getting lucky with its influence, and instead ended up killing her, things went totally nuts.

"Crap," Scott said, "I don't have anything in the fridge except water. Wanna call downstairs?"

"We'd better," Nick said, dialing Theo.

Consequently, the genius government officials decided it would be more effective to tell a whole generation simply, *No! Bad! It is forbidden!* than to say, *Sure, take the stuff, but use it irresponsibly and you could easily be raped before it kills you.* Just like they said, *Sure, drink alcohol if you must, but do so in a highly controlled manner or the price could be life as you know it.* Just like they said, *Sure, smoke if you have to, but do it outside, so you don't poison your family right along with you.*

"Hey, Sleepy," Nick said into the cell phone. "What's your ETA?"

"Ask him what he's wearing," Darren said, "Is he going high-glam?"

Of course, there were others who were upset about GHB being on the market. Drug dealers for one. It was not only very cheap to manufacture, but very easy as well. When folks started making it themselves at home it began taking a major bite out of the dealers' ability to move the more traditional, and more lucrative, products.

After all, why spend twenty-five dollars or more for one hit of ecstasy that would last for five hours when you could spend the same amount of money to produce enough GHB to last you through every Friday and Saturday night for six weeks? Why snort cocaine and risk a nasty chemical dependency, not to mention jail, when G was so easy and didn't require a single minute of recovery time? It looked like the introduction of GHB into the American nightlife scene was going to take a bigger toll on drug dealers than the DEA. Sure, it could be abused, but so could a bottle of cough medicine. Sure, it wasn't something any idiot could handle safely, but neither was a weed-whacker.

"Are you going to get Eddie?" Nick asked Theo over the cell.

"If he shows up here in D&G's, I'm going home to change," Darren said to the air.

"Well, Scott wanted me to tell you to park here so we don't have to drive," Nick said to the phone, ignoring Darren. "Right. And Gina is going to hang with us for a bit before we mosey."

GHB went on the DEA's list of scheduled compounds right alongside heroine and PCP. Schedule I, which meant there were no medicinal uses for the drug at all, despite the fact it was being widely used in Europe as a sleep aid, an anesthetic at high doses, and as an alternative for alcoholics at small ones.

The DEA, though, was no stranger to dictating to the American people what they couldn't handle, no matter what was said by any other source. Ecstasy itself had been hailed by psychotherapists as a very useful drug, and even ruled in court to be a medicinally viable compound. Then the United States Drug Enforcement Agency decided on its own to overrule the court and ban the substance completely and in every regard; some people were abusing it, so no one was allowed to use it, researchers included. Never mind the legal ruling of some federal judge. What do they know?

"Yes!" Nick laughed into the phone. "He got it for you. Down boy!"

"If he shows up in those white things Scott got him," Darren whined, "I swear I'm going home."

The risk of possessing GHB had become substantially greater, so after only the first few goes with Darren, Nick had turned to alcohol. It was legal, and better than going cold turkey, the thought of which made Nick want to cry. Anyone who couldn't understand why letting go of these compounds was so tough had only to tell a group of snow skiers that they were never allowed in the mountains again, because some idiot fell off a cliff. They'd quickly appreciate their lack of empathy just before they were run down and impaled on ski poles.

"Darren," Scott said.

"Yeah?"

"I'd wear the pants you're already in, if I were you."

"Really?"

"Have you even *seen* your ass?"

Eventually though, through its fundamental appeal, GHB was worked back into the nightlife scene and the boys were tempted by its allure. However, it was back to being an item that was *much* more expensive, and any information about its safe use was *much* more difficult to obtain, which made it *much* more dangerous.

Although the guys didn't want to use it very much, due to it being so non-PC even among drug users—if you can imagine that—they nevertheless tried to incorporate it into the regime again to maybe help keep more control over the more physically costly drugs, such as ecstasy and cocaine. So, now they tried to balance their lives with ecstasy, cocaine, keteset, alcohol, and GHB, instead of just GHB.

Well, at least the drug dealers were happy.

"Nick, how's my butt?" Darren asked.

"What?" Nick said, clicking the phone shut.

"Do these pants make me look fat?" he said, rolling onto his stomach and wiggling his tush.

Nick and Scott shook their heads, both of them rolling their eyes.

†

There was a line already. Nick looked out the car's window and was amazed. It was only ten-thirty and there was a line already.

Scott had called downstairs after Theo and Eddie arrived and arranged for a car so that none of them had to drive. Nick hadn't realized it would be a limousine, much less one that seemed to be longer than a city bus. As they passed by the entrance and the waiting crowd, he was almost embarrassed. They'd eventually need to get out of the car in front of everyone, which would no doubt bring a barrage of questions when they got inside. *So, is it your birthday or did you win an Emmy?*

The line wasn't too long, but it was impressive. In another half-hour or forty-five minutes it would be twice its current length, and after an hour and a half, it would be so long that most who saw it would turn around and go somewhere else. Not that there *was* somewhere else. It was a good thing the four of them just happened to be part of that oh-so-rare elite, the holders of the club's super-exclusive, black membership card. No matter how long the line, they wouldn't be waiting in it at all.

It wasn't a holiday weekend. Nothing special had been advertised to be happening at the club; no guest DJ from Miami, no pop dance-diva strutting her stuff to a DAT of her latest hit, no theme party with enormous decorations and banquet tables filled with free bottled water, cut bananas, pineapples, and strawberries. Sometimes these big nights just happened for no perceptible reason. Sometimes it seemed the whole community just got the itch to be beautiful and to be out and to be seen. When they all got that itch at the same time, it was like Pride Weekend happening twice.

This was one of those nights. It was somehow energized and the mood was ravenous and expectant. Love was in the air.

Darren picked up the phone to the driver. "Don't pull up yet," he said. "Go down and make a right on Melrose, take that down to La Cienega, make a left, down to Third, another left, then back up here. If the line isn't past the corner lamppost, do it again."

"Vitamins?" Theo asked, raising his eyebrows while he bobbed his head to Abigail's *Let the Joy Rise*. The music pumped out of eight expertly placed speakers.

"Yeah," Darren said, hanging up the intercom phone. "Now's good."

No one had dropped yet. Gina was being very nice and ten o'clock had come and gone, unnoticed.

Darren doled out a pill a piece, except to Nick, who whispered, "Just give me both of them."

"Are you sure?" Darren whispered back, under the music.

"Just like a Miami brew," Nick explained. "Maybe I'll be able to keep up with the class."

"Don't make me worry."

Nick grinned at him. If Darren had said that the previous weekend, Nick would've laughed. Tonight he almost believed him.

Nick pulled a bottle of water out of the otherwise untouched limo-bar and swallowed both pills at once. That would do it for him as far as Missy was concerned. Even if he found himself back down on earth too soon, a third hit at any point during the rest of the night would mean he'd be a miserable bitch all day Sunday and most likely all of Monday as well, perhaps Tuesday and Wednesday too. So, that wasn't even a consideration. If it came to it, Darren had coke with him. They'd leave Gina in the limo, where Nick could retreat if the world became too boringly solid and engage in her oh-so-soothing company.

Theo had the entire rear seat to himself. Nick and Darren sat behind the closed shield to the car's cab. Scott was on the side, across from the bar and TV, drumming on Eddie's shoulders, who was sitting on the floor between his legs. When he drummed on top of his head, Eddie would laugh, pitch forward out of reach, and smack Scott playfully on the calf.

Nick knew the night wasn't going to get any better. He couldn't imagine anything that was any better than this. No one was speaking but every face held a pregnant grin, every head swayed in unison, every heart was hammering with the natural adrenalin that rushed through them in anticipation of the night to come. Anticipation, Nick knew from a good amount of experience, could be very, very sweet.

They'd split up once they got inside, especially if it was going to be as crowded as Nick imagined. They'd try to stay together for a while, but it was difficult enough to keep even two or three people from being separated in crowds of that density, and five was just too much. They'd meet up again in the upstairs room, of course, either spontaneously or at a predetermined time, but there'd be no other moments like this one.

There'd be developments; someone wandering off alone, someone mad at someone, someone hitting on or hooking-up with someone else. The night would gain its color and distinguish itself with the unique patterns of its drama, all within the frame of the customary formula. There'd be surprises within the predictability, there'd be moments of drastic loss within a throng steeped in brilliant joy, there'd be unchecked laughter, unhampered bliss, secrets learned, stories told, and maybe a tear or two would fall as the night puffed itself up and pretended to be a week.

But none of it would measure together to rival Nick's moment. They were young, they were beautiful, they were together, and there was nothing else; no issues, no interruptions, no crowd, and no tomorrow.

The heavily tinted glass surrounding their wandering haven showed only the faintest blossoms from the streetlights outside, blossoms of light that would stop and then move again in harmony with the car.

Nick didn't know where they were, what street or what corner, and it didn't matter. When the car eventually stopped and the door opened it would all be over, just as it all began.

CHAPTER V

†

The Smelly Imp

And Saul's servants said unto him, Behold now, an evil spirit from God troubleth thee.

- I Samuel 16:15 (KJV)

Los Angles, California
On the street next to a stretch limo,
idling outside the club on Highland Avenue

†

By the time there were enough people waiting in line, in front of whom Darren wanted to be seen getting out of the limo, they'd circled through his little detour route three more times and fifty minutes had passed. By then, Missy had shown up in all her glory and was promising Nick an evening together that would be just like old times. She was in a splendid mood and making a real effort toward reconciliation. It looked like rolling the dice and taking both pills at once might have been worth the risk. Of course, the needle was still moving up, but Nick wasn't worried about an overdose, not from only two hits.

As Nick stepped out of the car, he completely forgot to be embarrassed by what he thought of as its superfluous lavishness. He was looking instead at the group of beautifully dressed boys who were standing immediately behind the velvet rope. They had their arms crossed, obviously annoyed at having been forced to bear the indignity of waiting in a line, but Nick could only focus on how great their biceps looked when they stood that way. He had to remember to cross his arms more.

Nick didn't know any of them. They were probably from out of town. If they'd been local, Nick would have certainly noticed them before, seeing as they were put together so nicely.

"Baby?" He tapped Darren's shoulder. Darren was talking to Theo and the limo driver.

"What's up, schnook?" Darren said, turning toward Nick.

"Do you know any of those guys standing in the front of the line?" Nick asked, without looking back at the subjects in question.

Darren squinted at the line for a moment. "Nope. Nice, though."

Now Nick *knew* they weren't locals.

"Why?" Darren asked, smiling down at him. "Do you want one of those?"

"No!" Nick pretended to be shocked. "They were just staring at us. I thought they might know you. That's all."

"Well, if it makes you feel any better, I think the whole line was staring at us because we just stepped out of a rolling condominium."

"Are they still looking?"

Darren glanced back. "Yes, and they're positively salivating," he said, "but not at the car, or either one of us." He grinned abruptly, nodding to indicate that Nick should look behind him.

Nick turned and saw that Scott had just gotten out of the limo and was straightening his t-shirt, pulling it down toward the front pockets of his jeans. The shirt already fit so tightly it could have been paint.

When Nick glanced back at the crowd, he saw that Darren was right. Every eye was fixed in an unblinking, hypnotic gaze right at Scott. He couldn't have commanded more attention if he'd been Sharon Stone.

Nick smiled, crossed his arms, backed up, and stood against Scott's front, laying the back of his head on his shoulder. Scott wrapped his arms over Nick's as Darren turned back to Theo and the limo driver.

"You've been here all of nine seconds and you're already more popular than the fabulous Miss E. herself."

Scott pressed his lips to Nick's ear and sighed.

"I'm not sure we should be here," he whispered. "It might not be safe."

Nick turned to face him in alarm. "Oh, my god, what's wrong?"

Scott put his hands on the back of Nick's arms and pulled him close, whispering, barely breathing out his words. "Nick, I'm sorry, I didn't know where Darren was planning to bring us tonight. I thought we were going to one of the little places we went on Sunday night, or to someplace new. I'm not all that sure we should've come back here."

Nick saw that Scott was frowning and squinting up the street, toward the alley were they met.

"Okay." Nick quickly nodded, somewhat startled. "We'll go. Just you and me. We can get right back in the car and cruise up the coast if you want. I'll just tell Darren that I'm sick, or that you—"

"That might be premature." Scott shook his head slightly. "Don't panic. I'm just a little worried. I'm sorry. I should have gleaned this. I should have looked. I was enjoying the suspense, though."

"Don't be silly. You shouldn't need to go around touching everyone and reading everything in their minds."

"I love you too, you know."

"What?"

"I'm sorry, Nicholas." Scott grinned sheepishly. "Sometimes I can't help it." He rubbed Nick's bare arms where he'd been holding him. "It's very strange but, most of the time, when I touch you, I'm easily able to block everything, every thought, every image. But once in a while you have a thought that's like a scream in a deep canyon, echoing over and over. It overwhelms me before I can stop it. One thought, in your voice, over and over."

"I thought you needed permission to—"

"Just the first time."

Nick nodded. "I see."

"I usually don't listen. Really, I can block just about any—"

"Shhh, man," Nick said softly, pulling Scott slightly away from the rest of the group.

Missy did this to some people every now and then and Nick recognized it. Whatever was on their mind, whatever heartrending secret lay over their thoughts, had a tendency to be given free and easy voice. On top of that, affectionate emotions were radically enhanced; feelings of love and intimacy especially, even just the level between close friends. That sort of thing was very difficult to keep to one's self.

Nick glanced over at the other guys. Eddie had just gotten out of the car and joined the conversation between Theo and Darren. The driver closed the limo door behind him.

Darren turned suddenly and looked at Nick and Scott with questioning concern. Nick pressed his hand in the air back at him, mouthing silently, *It's okay*. Darren nodded silently, then turned back to Eddie and Theo.

"Just now," Scott went on, "when you looked at me, it just bellowed out of you like thunder. It's been brought to the surface by the drug, I know, but it's real just the same."

"I don't know what to say." Nick shook his head, pressing his cheek to Scott's, listening to his familiar whisper.

"You don't have to say anything" Scott said quietly. "I'm guilty.

I'm guilty, because I saw it coming and I allowed it, even though I know you're confused and I know what you feel for Darren. I know the distinction between us is blurry for you right now, at best, but Nick, it's there and it's profound, and I can help you see it. I have to be something altogether different for you, and I know you know that, in a way. I know that your whole view, your grasp on your life, has been jolted by what I am, by what I've been telling you, but I can fix this—"

"Shhh." Nick shook his head, smiling, and again pressed his cheek to Scott's, whispering into his ear. "Let's not talk about this now. Not here. Let's just go. We can talk in the car."

Scott shook his head and sighed, stepping back a bit. "I'm not sure that would be the wisest move. 'Cousin' story or not, Darren wouldn't understand. And I want to help him too."

"Oh, jeez, don't worry about him. He'll get over it. He's done far, far worse than just ditch me with a relative. Believe me."

Nick waited until Scott looked him in the eye before going on.

"What's wrong?" Nick asked him quietly. "Can you explain it to me? Is there something about the alley being so close? I didn't think about it before. I should have said something."

"No, it's not the alley." Scott shook his head. "It's this place, this club. It might be dangerous. I just want to get a better sense of things before we go in."

"What is it?"

"Nick, I don't know. I'm sorry, I just don't know. There might be others around, but I have little chance of learning that from out here. It might be a gamble to go in."

Nick's mouth went a bit dry and a stinging shiver ran up his back and across his shoulders.

"Remember last week," Scott went on, "in the dark, in the alley, I told you I'd been fighting. I told you that I was drained."

Nick nodded.

"It was with another demon. Last weekend I had a confrontation with a powerful hunter. She's a very high member of the Legions. She tracked me down in New York and brought me here. She captured me, and dragged me here, to Los Angeles."

"Why?"

"I don't know."

Nick's stomach sank and his throat felt as though it would close.

"She?" he whispered.

"There's so much to explain. There's so much I should have said before tonight, before right now. I was just enjoying..." He stopped, shook his head. "I will, though, I promise. I'll tell you everything I can, but we should be careful. This place may be a little dangerous."

"You think some other demon, that she—"

"I don't know," Scott said, leaning in, speaking again, very cautiously into Nick's ear. "I really don't know, but this place looks like a hub. It could be a hub of influence. I'll explain it all later, but for now just know that a hub of influence is where the demonic power within a city, or even an entire country, comes together. This is the type of place where their work is done, at the ears of men."

"Well, wouldn't that be downtown or something? Wouldn't that be City Hall, or the Civic Center, or some place like that?"

"Sometimes. Though, most often it's a place just like this one. It's where the most dynamic, most influential people gather regularly and in significant numbers. In every hub, in every one of them, all over the world, one may very easily find demons at work."

"Oh, my god."

"This could be... it feels like ..." Scott shook his head again slowly. "I just don't know."

Darren suddenly called over to them. "Hey, is everything okay?"

"Yeah." Nick nodded back at him. "Just give us a sec."

Darren turned back to Theo and Eddie, squinting his eyes a bit before taking them off of Scott and Nick.

"I saw this club in Darren's mind," Scott whispered. "I couldn't recognize any significance through his eyes, but I did see the inside of it. I think I saw a room where we may be all right for a while. At least long enough for me to figure out if it's too dangerous here."

"Holy crap, you think there could be other demons here?" Nick huffed under his breath. "My god, Scott, we really should go."

"Nicky, don't panic."

"*Are* there any here? Do you see any? Are there other demons here?"

"Right now? I don't know. There aren't any out here, right now, outside. Nick, really, I'm sorry, I didn't mean to unnerve you. It's just a possibility. I thought I should tell you, just in case. I'll look inside, though, quickly, as we move to the room."

"What are you talking about? What room?"

"On the first floor, there's a private room. Darren tricked a young girl last Saturday into going there in order to avoid her."

"You mean the big VIP room? Behind the back-bar?"

"Yes." Scott nodded. "I think that's the one. We should go there.

Just for a while. Just long enough to keep Darren from getting too upset, which will happen, if we leave just now."

"Scotty, I know it's supposed to be private, but a lot of uninvited people still easily get into that room. The bouncers aren't, like, CIA agents, or anything. If we're going to stay for any time at all, I think we'd be better off upstairs."

"There's a large window in the bigger room downstairs, though," Scott said. "It's mirrored on the outside so that no one can see inside, right?"

Nick nodded.

"The room upstairs is more exclusive, yes," Scott explained, "but if a demon gets in, and identifies me, there'll be a problem. There's very little chance I won't be able to handle it, but if not, if I'm seen by one of the Fallen, or a high member of the Legions, then there will be no way out. If we're downstairs, I can watch who's coming into the room. Plus, there'll be a lot more people around and a demon will be far less likely to reveal themselves."

"Okay, Scotty, listen, um, I'm just a bit freaked out right now. I have my ID, and my membership card, but fuck it I remembered to score any holy water before we left."

"We won't stay long, but it might be better if we find out about this place either way. There are better ways, though. There are easier ways. It's just so close to the alley, I'm just not sure—"

"I got away with accidentally bumping into one demon, and I'm not too excited about playing *that* lottery again. You know, Scotty, a limo-ride up the coast sounds just so much better right now than going into this club and hiding in the back-bar. Fuck Darren."

"Yes, we'll go. You're right. But not now, not immediately. The driver will wait. The car will be here. If we wait a bit, we'll be able to take Darren with us. I'm not comfortable leaving him here. We'll bring Eddie and Theo too, if they'll come."

"Why don't we just take them now?"

"I could be very wrong. It might be a coincidence that I ended up so close to this place last weekend." He sighed heavily and shook his head, which made his face bump softly against Nick's. "I don't want to spoil this night. There's a lot at stake."

"What are you talking about?"

"We'll sit for an hour, maybe two. We'll let this chemical do its work. Darren will be more at ease. In just a little while, he'll be happier, and then we'll go. While we wait, I'll tell you what I can. I'll tell you what you should know. No matter what happens, though, remember, I will let nothing harm you, and I will not leave you." Scott touched Nick on the chin, lifting his eyes to meet his. "Remember that, Nicholas, always. I will not leave you."

Nick could feel the tension through Scott's fingers. He could almost see the turmoil that spun within him, the anxiety, as he struggled to make the right choice and communicate his sincerity. Scott nodded toward Darren, Theo, and Eddie. "I will protect them as well," he whispered. "With every bit of my power, I will protect you and those you love."

Nick took a deep breath. Scott's eyes were very blue and very resigned. Nick didn't know what he was looking for, what he thought he'd see in them. He didn't know how he'd gotten here, to the door of this familiar place, a place he loved, a place that suddenly held more than a little foreboding.

"Scotty, why is my heart pounding so hard?"

Scott looked back at him shyly, apologetically. "Because you're alive."

Nick was thinking about pressing his objection and maybe pulling Scott back into the limousine, but Darren walked over. He was looking at them sheepishly, approaching with respectful caution. It was apparent to the other three boys that something was wrong. They'd obviously been trying to be patient while it was worked out, but Missy was not at all a patient girl, and so she had passed along her annoyance.

The whispering had gone on too long. Scott and Nick's private conversation had taken a little more time than would have indicated just a minor issue. So Darren, being the most appropriate choice, walked over, bringing them back to the moment at hand by silently offering his support.

"We're cool, babe," Nick managed, even though he knew Darren could tell he was lying; Nick could feel that the flush had left his face. Worse, Scott wouldn't look at Darren at all, hiding his face behind Nick's.

"What can I do?" Darren whispered, stepping in close.

Nick made a quick decision. "Go ask Matt who's on the door behind the back-bar. We're going straight in there."

"You wanna go behind the back bar?" Darren asked, raising his eyebrows.

"Scott wants to watch the dance floor."

Nick knew this whole situation was making Darren very uncomfortable. He wasn't good with any kind of drama, much less being in front of a lot of people in what wasn't the most masculine of scenes.

"You okay, Scotty?" Darren asked, touching his shoulder.

Scott turned to him with a tepid grin, but Nick was happy to see that there was blush in his cheeks and his eyes were clear. "I'm not as used to Missy as you disco-studs. It's been a strange week for me too, being with a family member that isn't evil." He smiled. "There's a lot that's on the surface right now."

Darren smiled back. "I know how that can be."

"I know you don't like it as much," Scott went on, "but I don't feel like being smack in the midst of all the action just yet, or being completely hidden away upstairs. So, is it okay if we hangout downstairs for a while? It'd be nice if you sat with us in there too. We'll stay in the corner, in the dark, where you won't be seen."

"Will I get my big sloppy French one?" Darren grinned down at him.

Scott smiled broadly at that. Nick couldn't help but grin right along with him.

"Hey," Scott said, "I pay my debts."

They were all still smiling as Darren took Scott by the hand and led him to the entrance. Nick watched them go until Theo walked over, took his hand, and they followed them inside. Eddie looped his finger into Nick's back pocket and sauntered along.

Nick turned back to Eddie with a grin. In true Eddie fashion, he touched Nick's smile with a kiss, which, like so many other things in life, was graceful, very sweet, and much too brief.

†

Although there was a line, the crowd inside was still a touch on the sparse side. Nick knew the club sometimes did that, held a group outside just for appearances rather than in accordance with any fire codes—which would be utterly ignored later anyway. The comfortably meager assemblage wouldn't last, though. It was a fleeting phenomenon that few ever saw before five, six, or even seven o'clock in the morning.

They'd passed in front of the line, as they always did, and sailed by the entrance counter with no problems. Matt was on the door this week, and he knew all four of them very well. Well enough not to question the presence of their party's fifth member, their unfamiliar guest. When they passed him, Matt gave a melodramatic nod to the kid sitting at the end of the hall, stamping the wrists of incoming patrons with the ink of acceptance, and they walked right past him without so much as a smile or a *Thanks, we appreciate it.*

Once they got inside, they had to move briskly to keep up with Darren as he maneuvered toward the back-bar with Scott in tow. Nick wasn't close enough to the door of the downstairs VIP room to hear what Darren said to the security guy stationed outside. He didn't recognize him. Boy, this place went through security guys pretty fast. Whatever Darren said, though, seemed to do the trick. The unfamiliar security guy nodded quickly, opened the door, and motioned for Theo, Nick, and Eddie to hurry inside.

At this early hour, the room was empty, with the exception of four guys hunkered together over the coffee table. They were taking turns with a bullet, tapping it while it was upside down to help fill the tiny chamber in the cap, then turning it right side up and snorting the contents. In here, there was no need to hide it under the table.

Nick recognized them all, though they weren't really his friends, just acquaintances of varying degree. Two were regional directors for the entire west coast for an enormous marketing firm, as well as being one of the longer-term male couples around. One of the remaining two owned a very successful and very exclusive private training gym in Studio City, and the last had spent his entire adolescence and most of his teens with a major part on a nighttime soap. Typical back-bar boys.

The five new arrivals, crossing the room toward the booths on the far wall, nodded their hellos at the resident bunch. Soap Opera Boy smiled at Eddie when he passed by, which made sense. Nick happened to know they'd spent a lot of time together naked.

"Why are we down here?" Theo asked as they reached the largest booth in the corner. From its cushions, one could watch the whole room, see most of the considerable dance floor through the glass and over the bar, and watch to see everyone the security guy stopped outside the room before he either let them in or turned them away.

The crowd had already grown noticeably, just in the minute or two it had taken them to travel around the dance floor and behind the back-bar. A second bartender stepped into view to help with the tiny line that was forming at the well. Everyone in sight was moving to the music, which was gaining momentum, moving into more compelling rhythms.

Darren turned to Theo. "What's the big deal?" he asked. "Hey, do me a favor and go tell Karen that we're here."

"You don't mind being in here, do you Theo?" Scott asked, scooting behind the cocktail table. "I know it's not your usual spot, but I just like this booth, that's all. I like to watch the dance floor."

"That's cool." Theo smiled. "You gonna dance with me later?"

"Do angels have wings?"

Theo grinned. "Well, you don't."

Nick looked up sharply, which made Darren give him a funny glance.

"I think he's hitting on my cousin," Nick explained. Theo blushed.

"But I certainly *do* have wings, big guy," Scott said with a wink. "I just didn't wanna wear them tonight."

"This place is gonna be swarming in a couple minutes," Eddie said, looking around.

"I was going to meet Karen upstairs at one-thirty," Darren said. "I guess we don't have to tell her we're here. She's not expecting us until then. She might still be in the office anyway."

"I'll check," Theo said. "I don't mind."

"Hey, see if Max is there too, would you?"

"I might not be back right away. I'm sort of starting to roll kind of hard."

"Me too," said Eddie, absently rubbing his stomach.

"What about you guys?" Darren looked at Scott and Nick, who'd both settled next to each other in the back of the booth. "You rollin' yet?"

Nick took a slow, and deep breath, grinning, rubbing his hand down his chest. "Like thundawh," he drawled.

Eddie giggled. "That's the way, baby."

He started to get into the booth with them, but when Nick saw the look on Theo's face, he leaned over the table at Eddie. "Why don't you go upstairs with Theo for a bit, Beauty Boy? I'm not being a bitch or anything, but..." He rolled his eyes over in Scott's direction, hoping Eddie would get the silent, fabricated excuse. *We just had a little drama outside, and we'd like a few more minutes to finish working things out.*

"Oh, sure." Eddie nodded. He looked disappointed, though.

"We can snuggle a bit when you get back." Nick grinned at him. "Wanna?"

Eddie smiled. "Do angels have wings?"

Scott turned and giggled at that. "Don't be long."

"We'll run," Eddie said, backing out of the booth, motioning for Theo to follow him. "C'mon, muscles."

Eddie took Theo's hand and they walked briskly out the door. Nick watched them through the glass as they moved into the dance floor's fast-growing crowd and were lost.

†

The music never bothered Karen while she was in the office. In fact, it did a great deal to pick her up while she was working. Since tonight she'd already *been* picked up — Troy was not motherfucking kidding about his inventory — it only served to further liven her artificially enhanced euphoria.

This was going to be a special evening. She was dying to meet Nick's cousin. No less than seven different sources had told her that, despite having a hairstyle that screamed, *Help me! I'm stuck in an episode of LA Law!*, he was about the sweetest eye-candy around.

The intercom buzzed on her desk and she hit the button. "Speak, darlin'."

"Karen, it's Matt," said a familiar, masculine voice. He must have been calling from the desk in the entrance hall, which meant something unusual had happened or was happening; he should have been out front.

"What's up?"

"Brad just thought he saw that runt guy. What's his name again?"

She slammed her pencil down onto the desktop. "Oh, my god! Gil? What? Brad saw Gil?"

"Yeah, that's him."

"Where? At the door?"

"No," Matt continued. Karen could hear the murmur of the crowd at the entrance behind him. "Down the street. He thought he saw him watching the line. When Brad spotted him, when he spotted Gil, whatever, he ducked into the lot behind the music studio."

"Oh, man…" Karen ran her hand through her hair, forgetting about the hour she'd spent working on it, which wasn't made any easier by the hefty line of coke she'd done beforehand. "What the hell is he doing?" she said, thinking out loud.

"Karen, that's the guy Max wants totally eighty-sixed, right?" He sounded a little too enthusiastic.

"Matty…" Karen murmured, putting her shoes back on. "Do not kill him. I mean it! If he comes to the door, do not kill him!"

"Okay, okay, whatever," Matt droned out of the phone. "Boy, Max was pretty harsh today, though, when he was tellin' us about him. He doesn't like this guy at all."

"Matty, really, I'm in no mood to deal with the cops tonight, okay? That would suck. Seriously! Oh, god, don't break any bones! Please, Matty! Go tell Brad too. No bones! Don't kill him and don't break any bones!"

"Hey, we're professionals, babe."

"He knows he's not supposed to be here, evidently, or he wouldn't be hiding like a weasel. Man, this is all I need."

"So, what, we just watch him?"

"Okay..." Karen sighed. "One bone. You can break one. But then *you* have to be the one that talks to the police, 'cause I don't want to. You can break one, but not a big one. Don't break his leg, or anything. And if you break his arm, you can only break either the radius or the ulna, *not* both of them."

Matt laughed heartily. "Karen! Down girl! He disappeared, really. I just wanted to make sure, if he comes back, or shows up, do you want me to buzz you?"

"Yeah, babe." She relaxed a little bit, but left her shoes on. "I'll either be here in the office or on my headset."

"Only one bone?" Matt whined.

"If you stick to just fingers, you can do two or three."

"Right on. I'm headin' back out. Smooches."

"Oh, Matt, don't hang up!"

"What, chica?"

"When we get to capacity, make sure to hold the line until I get down there."

"You mean, what, ten minutes ago?"

"You're kidding!" Karen slapped the desk with her open palm.

"Nope."

"Crap, where's it at?"

"About a three-quarter block, I think."

Karen sighed again. "Okay, hold it as of right now. I'm just gonna primp a little and I'll be right down."

"Takin' care of a line of your own?"

"As thick as my arm and never you mind."

"Save me some."

"Matty, baby, you know I've always got you covered."

"Charming, generous, and luscious, you are," he purred in his Robert Redford voice.

"Okay, Matty, honey, you know not to say shit like that unless you've converted."

"Well, I'm at least good for a kiss."

"And you know I want it. At least Bradley's still straight, ain't he?"

"Last I checked. Want me to find out?"

"Don't you fucking touch him, Blanche!" She laughed. Matt and half the bar crew had been teasing poor Brad the Security Guy about switching over to their team for weeks. Yeah, as if that sort of thing *ever* really happened outside of porno movies.

Over the speaker-phone, Matt was cracking up, along with a few other people at the desk who happened to be close enough to hear Karen's exclamation blast through the handset.

"So, get down here and gimme my smooch," Matt said.

"Keep it in your pants, party boy. I'm comin'."

"Okay, I'll hold the line, and you snort one." Matt laughed again.

"Don't crack wise," she said, smiling, as if she hadn't heard that joke four-hundred times. "If Gil shows his little elf-face, try and stall him until I get there. Maybe I can talk some sense into that golf ball brain of his."

"Ten-four."

"Hey, make sure Bradley knows too! Just the ulna, or a few metacarpals!"

"Got it."

"But wait 'till I get there!"

"Check," Matt said. "Can I go back out now?"

"When I say so!" She giggled.

"How 'bout now?"

"Wait."

"Okay."

"All right," she said, laughing. "Now, you can go."

"Smooches."

"Yeah, lick me."

Karen could hear Matt giggling as she hit the speaker button again, hanging up.

All right, where was Laura's number? Karen needed to get her on the phone if she could. Maybe Laura could get down there and find Gil before Brad and Matt turned him into ground chuck. Sure, it was Laura's night off, but motherfuck, she'd promised to talk to the elf and work things out. It wasn't like Laura not to take care of things. It wasn't like her to leave shit for Karen to clean up.

She dialed Laura's condo, then her cell, but hung up when she just got voice mail at both numbers. Of course Laura wasn't home. Karen really didn't expect her to be there. When you were single, and looked like Laura Shah, Saturday nights were not spent inside your own apartment.

The club wasn't having an event tonight, much less one of Laura's, so there was no reason for her to be anywhere near it. Therefore, there was no chance Karen could stroll downstairs, give her a dirty look, and forego dealing with Elf Boy altogether.

Karen was going to have to handle this herself. She was going to have to go stand at that stupid counter for who-fucking-knew how long and make sure that her door guys didn't tear Gil's arms off and use them to beat him to death.

Karen gritted her teeth at the thought. Flakiness simply wasn't a characteristic Laura had ever shown before. So, that couldn't possibly be the reason that Karen had a sudden and sickening feeling of dislike for the woman. That would have been irrational, wouldn't it?

†

Darren really did hate being in the room behind the back-bar. It was okay for the first ten minutes or so, but then he couldn't help but think about wandering. Jeez, what did Nick expect? The club was so full of people now that the window to the dance floor looked like a writhing human zoo exhibit.

The DJ was no one famous, but someone had obviously given him a very, very good hit of something very, very groovy, because he sure was up there making a very, very nice name for himself.

The dance floor was no longer even visible behind the solid wall of bodies at the bar, but Darren could hear it calling to him just the same. He was rolling hard and this hang-out-in-the-booth-behind-the-back-bar biz was getting tired. He was itching to make his rounds. However, the way Nick was rubbing the back of his head, lightly brushing the tips of his fingers in dancing swirls through his hair, sending rivers of contentment down his back, Darren didn't know if he even *could* get up at the moment. Despite that, he was going to try.

"I haven't even said hello to Matt yet," Darren blurted, turning his head, speaking over the music right into Nick's ear.

"He's going to be off at two," Nick said. "What'd you do, walk right by him at the door?"

"Isn't that Jeremy, over by the wall?"

"No." Nick closed his eyes, shaking his head. "Jeremy moved to Boston."

"Well, who's that on the couch, over by the wall?"

"I dunno."

"Do you want some water?"

"Not yet."

"What about Scotty?"

"Darren?" Nick said, taking his hand off of Darren's neck.

"What, Schnook?"

"Go already."

Oh, crap, now he'd done it. "I'm just gonna get some water."

"Whatever, babe."

"Are you being bitchy?"

"I dunno." Nick chuckled. "Am I?"

Darren sighed. You'd think dating a guy would exempt a person from having to play games like these. When you dated another guy, you shouldn't have to notice every little haircut, pretend to give half a rat's ass about what they did that day, stay awake after you came any longer than it took to toss the towel toward the bathroom door, or ever, *ever*, have to answer a question like, *What are you thinking?*

"You know I can't just sit for too long, baby."

"Darren, I'm totally fine. Just go."

It wasn't as though Nick behaved like such a girl all the time. It wasn't like he called twice a day, or dropped little hints about what he wanted for his birthday, or even *when* it was his birthday. When was his birthday again?

"This feels great and everything, but I'd just like to—"

"We're cool." This time, Nick outright laughed. "What do you want me to say? Just go. We'll be here."

Scott sat up. "Darren?"

Darren raised an eyebrow at him. "Yeah, babe?"

"Bring me back a water, 'kay?"

"That's it?"

"Well, if we're not here when you get back, then we're out in the limo."

"The limo?" Darren squinted.

"Yeah." Scott smiled at him. "Fucking."

Nick and Scott both laughed. Darren couldn't help but shake his head and laugh a little too. Scott clearly loved giving him a hard time about Nick. Evidently, it was his favorite joke.

"You got it," Darren said, still smiling. "You sure you don't want a bottle of water too, baby?"

Nick shook his head and grinned. Darren just looked at him for a moment. Damn, Nick was beautiful. "You sure you don't need anything at all?" Darren asked.

Nick half smiled, then with a slight giggle, puckered up for a kiss, as if Darren would lean all the way back into the booth, in front of all these people, and plant one on him. Nick was almost smiling too hard, apparently finding the idea of Darren doing such a thing completely hilarious. He even began to outright laugh a bit.

Well, screw him. Darren leaned in, and the look of shock on Nick's face was so severe, so close to genuinely startled fear, that Darren began giggling too. But that didn't stop him.

When Darren reached Nick, they were both laughing. He kissed him full on the mouth, full on his parted lips in the middle of their stunned smile. They laughed together through their teeth. Darren struggled to press his lips to Nick's.

He rocked back, biting his lower lip, looking Nick in the eyes.

Nick was still smiling. "You freak," he said.

Damn, Nick was beautiful.

Darren leaned back in, but this time neither one of them laughed. He lay his mouth on Nick's with a tender brush of his lips, and pressed with gentle firmness as Nick kissed him back.

They were the same lips Darren had spent hours kissing on countless nights, alone in the darkened quiet. They were familiar and comfortable lips, yet blazing with something Darren suddenly didn't recognize. It was like kissing someone new, kissing some forbidden, dangerous stranger. A forbidden stranger that Darren just happened to know very, very well.

†

There was no longer any question about the turnout at the club. The building didn't have any rafters, but if it did, it would have been packed to 'em.

Eddie had a tough time keeping up with Theo for two reasons. One was that whoever Theo passed that recognized him was bound to see Eddie trailing behind and insist upon at least a hello, if not offering a complete *So, what's up?* to which Eddie would be obliged to respond on behalf of both Theo and himself. The other reason was that Theo was able to nearly race through the dense assemblage because, since he weighed two-hundred and sixty pounds, people got out of his way.

"Sorry, dude, I've gotta keep up with Theo," Eddie explained to the latest *So, what's up?* Eddie tried to amble through the milling people before they closed back into Theo's wake.

He didn't have to worry. Theo had been stopped by Ponytail Guy and was talking to him while they leaned against the wall at the bottom of the stairs to the second floor.

Bettina was pumping through the twenty-five thousand dollar speaker hanging over the corner of the dance floor, singing to everyone she just needed *Time to Move On.*

Eddie pressed through the last barrier of bodies between him and Theo.

"I was finally able to kick the crystal habit," Ponytail Guy explained.

"Cool, man." Theo nodded. "How'd you do it?"

"I switched to cocaine."

"Hey, sweet pea," a soft, female voice said behind Eddie as a manicured nail ran seductively down his triceps. He turned to see a very attractive and very young looking girl pass by in tow of a very tall and very unattractive man. Eddie nodded a smile at her as they disappeared, just barely recognizing her as someone to whom he'd spoken several weeks prior. He couldn't remember her name. Eddie was really bad with names.

"I mean," Ponytail Guy continued, "it's a little more expensive, but I'm worth it."

"Right on, " Theo bantered back, clueless.

Eddie looked at him, inhaled deeply, his eyes wide and his smile wider, which was their private signal to each other meaning, *Oh, my god, I am so high!*

Theo chuckled and grabbed Eddie's shoulder, bringing him into his arms and turning him around to face outward. They stood that way, Eddie's back to Theo, Theo's back to the wall of the stairs, Theo's arms wrapped around Eddie, Eddie's arms wrapped back up around Theo's, as they listened to Ponytail Guy explain why coke was so much better than crystal. They were both rolling with the first waves of Missy's considerable influence and it didn't matter who was speaking to them or what was being said as long as they had each other, as long as they were together.

Ponytail Guy just talked on and on. He was obviously on crystal.

†

"Have you seen any?" Nick asked.

"No." Scott shook his head.

"Would they recognize you?"

"Some."

"Who would?"

"The ones that knew me before."

"Before the Fall?"

"Yes."

"They'd recognize you like this?"

"Immediately."

"The others… ?"

"They wouldn't know me just by looking at me. I'd have to let them touch me."

"And you, you'd recognize them?"

"I can smell them."

"Why can't they smell —?"

"They're a specific kind of creature. They have a very distinct odor. Though, very few humans are able to detect it."

"The ones that didn't know you before?"

"Not all demons are fallen angels."

"No?"

"There are only a few of us left."

"What —?"

"Most of the Fallen have been destroyed."

"Oh, my god. How? By God?"

"No."

Nick rested in the crook of Scott's shoulder, Scott's arm draped behind him, his hand absently massaging his forearm.

Nick turned, looking up at Scott.

Scott explained. "They were destroyed by the Beast."

†

It was still relatively early and none of the guys had yet taken off their shirts. It wouldn't be long in this crowd, though.

Darren wasn't happy about the idea of waiting in the line at the bar, much less paying half a month's rent for the bottle for the water he'd promised to bring back to Scott in the wannabe room.

He stood against the wall in the front room, his favorite spot away from the dance floor and the frantic milling between it and the back-bar. Here, he could watch the double-sided front-bar for anyone he knew who happened to be standing in line and was maybe close to the bartender. If said acquaintance was able to slip Darren's drink order in with their own while they were saying hello, after Darren just happened to notice them—therefore avoiding any time that Darren would have to personally spend in line—well, then that would be a lovely little coincidence, wouldn't it?

No one yet, though. Packed though it was, the club was still only filled with the B-crowd. No biggie. Maybe Darren would just slip around the corner and saunter down the darkened hall to the front lounge. It had a much smaller bar, but maybe its line held an early A-lister with whom he could team up to score his waters.

Now that he'd wandered away from Nick and Scott, Darren felt a little less like being on his own. He pushed away from the wall and

THE FALLEN
229

began to navigate through the traffic into the hallway.

After he kissed Nick, Darren had half expected to turn and see the majority of the VIP room's occupants gaping in shocked silence before they broke into a sprint in order to be the first to start the buzz around the club. But nothing had happened. Nothing at all. Darren was trying to explain to himself why he was disappointed.

The harsh fact was that, even though the room was crawling with wannabes, it hadn't looked like anyone even noticed. Not even That Straight Guy, who was hanging out with Nose Hair Man, Soap Opera Boy, and That Straight Guy's Friend. He at least expected to get a little shock from That Straight Guy, who was even kind of a jerk.

They all had to have seen it. The second kiss at least, which had lasted a good ten or twenty seconds. Darren shook his head and half smiled in confusion. He'd kissed Nicky, right on the mouth, right in front of a room full of B-crowd babies, right in front of a slew of wannabes that no doubt knew who he was, and Darren hadn't even gotten the hint of shock from anyone. No one at all, not even That Straight Guy. Go figure.

Darren knew the whole world wasn't all about him. He knew everyone in sight of him wasn't captivated by his every move. Sometimes it felt that way, though.

Sure. Sometimes it felt like the whole world was all about Darren. Certainly not at the moment, however.

†

Ponytail Guy excused himself and disappeared the instant he thought he recognized his pharmacist. Even though they were supposed to be finding Karen, Eddie didn't have the motivation to rouse Theo and head up the stairs. They were very comfortable where they were, out of the way of traffic and snuggled against the wall where they could both see and be seen.

They weren't making the rounds or looking for Karen but it hardly mattered. The world was passing them by. Tall Unattractive Man sauntered back the other way, back toward the back-bar, towing the same young girl, who gave Eddie another little wave. Eddie smiled back with genuine affection, but he was feeling so good he would have smiled fondly at Jesse Helms.

Three guys who all lived in his building bounced by, each beaming a raucous smile as they recognized him, then leaned in with a kiss and a *Hey, Pretty Boy!* to both Eddie and Theo before bounding up the stairs. They were followed by a very attractive male couple holding hands. They caused Eddie to stifle a burst of laughter into Theo's arm, because they were not only in exactly the same outfit, but also had exactly the same haircut, Heaven help us all. Blue Shirt Guy threw a peace sign and a wink at Eddie as he followed That Guy with the Huge Package onto the dance floor.

Three not-so-aesthetically-blessed guys each slowed to appreciate the sight of Theo and Eddie, who smiled politely, which was their initial response to unsolicited attention. Once the three unfortunates were out of earshot, though, Eddie and Theo, sympathetically shaking their heads, recited their usual mantra: "I hope they at least have money."

Theo swayed happily to the music, rocking Eddie in his arms, singing along with Whitney Houston in his ear.

"*I learned it from the best, I learned from yooooou!*" he crooned just north of the pitch. Eddie laughed, patting Theo's arms in time with the beat, laying his head on his bicep, which was the size of a grapefruit.

They must have been a pretty picture, standing there together, swaying to the music, obviously rolling hard on ecstasy, because all the passers-by grinned at them. Everyone smiled, friends, acquaintances, tricks, and even those to whom they had no connection whatsoever. Everyone smile, that is, except That Really Short Guy, who didn't even glance in their direction as he charged to the stairs with a purposeful stride. Eddie had seen him around before, but no one ever had anything nice to say about him.

For such a little guy, he had a huge attitude.

†

"Do you think we're safe?" Nick asked.

"I don't know how to answer that," Scott explained into Nick's ear. "I think we're safer than we would be in that tiny room upstairs. Though, we're also safer than if we were alone in the limo cruising around town."

"Why?"

"Well, it's just a question of being found. If I'm going to be found, the best place would be in a crowd. A demon will not reveal itself within a crowd of people."

"Why not?"

"It's one of the rules. Nothing would drive a human directly and permanently into the arms of God faster than the genuine sight of a demon, manifested in its true form. Most humans don't live very long after they've seen a demon's true form because the demon must kill every human that witnesses its true face or risk being destroyed himself by the Beast."

"What's that about?"

"Well, you see, the Beast can't afford to have people shocked into the service of Heaven simply by the true sight of his brethren."

"Is that why you wouldn't let me see you before?"

"You mean in the alley?" Scott asked.

"Yeah."

"Well, actually, no. It doesn't really matter where I'm concerned. I'm already marked. In fact, nothing would thrill me more than to charge around in the light of the sun, in my true form. Nothing would be better than that. I wish I could. I wish I could be the means of so much human revelation.

"I can't, though, for the same reason I couldn't let you see me. Most mortal minds can't handle that kind of revelation. Sometimes it's not even really necessary to kill the human because their mind just snaps at the sight. Their sanity breaks in the instant of understanding and, very often, after they go mad, they can do nothing else but take their own lives."

"But you said you would have killed me if I'd seen you," Nick said. "Why not just let me go crackers? Why not just leave me to it?"

"Well, that's a little simpler. I would have killed you because, had you seen me, you would have screamed."

"Um… okay."

"Nicholas," Scott said, shaking his head slowly, "I was sitting there, without even the energy to phase out, trying to hide from her. I was trying to stay out of sight, out of her detection, until I could be certain she was gone. So, the last thing I needed was for a mortal witness to send a shriek into the night that would've alerted her as efficiently as a flare. Actually, I almost killed you immediately, the moment you came around the corner, but I could tell that you were sufficiently, um… out of it."

"If I'd been sober, you'd have killed me then?"

"If you'd been sober, you wouldn't have been heaving your guts out in an alley."

"Funny how things work, isn't it?"

"Now that's as keen an observation as has ever been made."

They giggled a bit, then sat in silence for a moment, rocking their heads to the music as Regina Belle's voice rang through the room.

Nick's heart was pounding and a warm wave of heaven rolled over him. Every breath was a treat. It felt so good, so remarkably wonderful, to be close to Scott, to be resting with him, against him. The deep resonance of Scott's voice was incredibly soothing and achingly familiar. It made Nick think of Darren and the same intimate comforts he had in his company.

Still thinking of Darren, Nick turned his head toward Scott's chest, faintly smelling the soap from his shower mixed with the fresh cotton of the black t-shirt.

"Why do you want to stay with me?" Nick asked softly.

Scott sighed. Nick could feel his own heart quicken at the question. Scott's hand stopped rubbing Nick's arm. He rested his cheek on the top of Nick's head, but didn't answer.

"Why are you still with me?" Nick asked again. He'd wanted to ask before. He'd wanted to say something earlier in the week, but he couldn't bring himself to articulate it. It was the same old question he had for everyone in his life. It was from the same quiet darkness into which he was so afraid to look.

"Do you want me to go?" Scott barely whispered.

Nick squinted against him. "No."

"You're not afraid? You're not afraid of what you don't know?"

"Yes, of course I am. Of course I'm afraid. But I chose to believe you. I chose to give you the power you asked me for, and now my love too, I guess."

"There's not much else Nick," Scott said quietly. "There's not much else to life besides what you have right now. And the rest of it you'll see soon enough.

"That's why I stay. That's why I'm with you, because I've seen so much and I know what you have is so close to what's pure. It's so much of everything that's beautiful and worthy. It's been a blessing to be a part of this. You and Darren, Eddie and Theo. You're a family, you know. You're a family, not by birth or marriage, or thrown together by necessity. You're a family through choice and blessing. Blessings aren't easy for me to ignore."

"That doesn't sound like my life."

"Bet me," Scott said. "Bet me that you're not blind as a bat."

Nick closed his eyes and listened to the beat of the demon's heart.

"And," Scott continued, "I stay because I can hide here. I can hide within this life and it's easy to leave everything else alone. I can rest in your world, in every facet that shapes itself from your touch or that of those you love, those *we* love, and forget. I can forget what I am, what I've seen and what I know. I can pretend that everything is simple and pain is little more than an afterthought, a passing observation."

There was laughter in the room with them. It echoed into their corner, despite the ring of the music. It echoed into them and Nick took a sumptuous breath, feeling it send Missy dancing through him. He pressed his face to Scott's chest, closing his eyes tight, listening to Scott's heart, listening to the repetition of his breath.

"Why aren't you an angel anymore?"

Scott sighed again with a smile and a chuckle.

"I'm sorry," Nick offered. "It's Missy. She's terrible at keeping quiet and even worse at being delicate."

"It's all right. I knew you'd ask me that sooner or later. I've had to answer it before. First to myself, of course. Though, try and remember, I'm just guessing. I don't really have an answer. Nothing with any real certainty."

"Fair enough."

"Well, obviously, I made a mistake. I took the wrong advice, followed the wrong lead, and thought about making a choice. Just the thought of making my own choice outside of the direct service of God, just the thought of that... well, it settled into my being and changed me. It changed me to a form that was more suitable of my chosen purpose, and yet incompatible with Heaven, it would seem. And so I fell."

"That's all?"

"That's all it took."

"No deals with the Devil?"

Scott laughed again. "Well, not *the* Devil, no. I've never met him, though I've seen him from afar. The Beast fell a very long time before I did."

"There's more than one devil?" Nick asked with a smirk.

"Yes." Scott nodded, smiling. "Sort of." He pressed his face close to Nick's, whispering. "We're getting into semantics again, definitions, interpretations. Technically speaking, anyone, any entity, can be labeled 'a devil.' It's not terribly difficult to be a destructive force."

Nick rested against him, listening, the room's laughter and voices echoing and dancing around them.

"Scotty?"

"Hm?"

"Have you seen any? Or, excuse me, *smelled* any? Tonight, I mean."

"No." Scott took in a deep breath, but did not sigh. "No, I haven't.

I haven't seen or smelled anything."

The cushion beneath them thumped along with the music, which the building itself seemed to have absorbed into its structure. Nick watched the well-dressed throng of beautiful people shimmer before him as if in a steady, glamorous dream. His skin tingled, his heart pounded, his breathing powered and amplified the euphoric haze, and the sound and feel of Scott's heart against his ear sent swells of delight through him, which found sudden flight from his lips.

"Wanna dance?" he asked.

†

The music was primo and Karen made a mental note to check again who it was she'd hired to spin. She'd have to engage him more often.

She fumbled with her keys until she found the one that would lock the office behind her. It was well after one o'clock and she was supposed to have met both Troy and Darren in the upstairs room. She'd left it unlocked with one of the new security guys at the door. The boys were most likely already inside.

Karen realized she'd forgotten to grab a black card for Nick's cousin. "Oh, crap," she whined, turning and fumbling again with the keys to get the damn office back open.

By the time she'd gotten inside, unlocked Max's drawer, snagged a black membership card—no one's name was ever printed on any of the cards; if you lost it, you were a loser—and primped herself back to peak, she decided she deserved another couple bumps to get back into gear. After all, she still had to run down to the entrance and make sure there weren't any dead elves stuffed behind the counter before she could go to meet the boys. Karen would need her energy.

There was an extra long vial in her bag, which made it easier to fish out; the small ones always got mixed up with her other stuff and she had to practically shine a light into the bag to find them.

She tapped out a wonderfully chubby bump of coke onto the back of her hand, on the skin between her thumb and forefinger. Then, watching in the mirror to make sure she got all of it, she closed her right nostril and sucked the lovely little pile of powder off her hand and into the left side of her nose.

Knowing that now the right nostril was going to be terribly jealous, she tapped out an equally attractive bump onto the other hand and repeated the process for that side of her face.

Leaving the office for the second time, she turned to pull the door shut behind her, giving it a hefty jiggle to make sure the lock had caught.

"Hey, watch it there, Tattoo!" a young, male voice whined behind her.

She turned to see a small group of B-crowd babies, huddled at the base of the stairs to the third floor. The alpha-male was obviously a little miffed at some outsider who'd just pressed through them on his way up. Served the stupid B-crowders right. They shouldn't be gathered around a high traffic area like that. It was a fire hazard, after all.

Ignoring the little group, Karen crossed the landing to the top of the stairs leading down directly to the main dance floor, stopped at its peak, and took in the sight below her.

Karen never got used to the glorious image of wall to wall happy, healthy, dazzling people. From the base of the stairs, stretching across the expanse of the immense main dance floor, and disappearing out of her line of sight below the overhang of the DJ booth, the first floor rippled and writhed with the faces, shoulders, and waving arms of the dancers below her. It was a sea of mirth, of sexuality, of decadence, and abundant affection. It was an urban nirvana, the struggles of living falling away at their feet to be trampled in a delightful dance.

Grinning, running her fingers over the top of her ear, enraptured with the elevation provided her by the drug, and enthralled at the sight before her, Karen descended.

†

Scott led Nick through the crowded back-bar, around the lounge, and toward the dance floor. Nick held him at the waist, stepping in time, close enough to catch the scent of shampoo in his hair.

"So, you let a human see you? In your other form, I mean? That's why they're looking for you? That's why you're marked?" he asked.

"No, not specifically," Scott said back over his shoulder. "I've been marked for a very, very long time. After that, it didn't matter if I was seen or not. Since then, I've been seen by quite a few people. In both forms."

"Did they go nuts?"

"A few."

"You're *that* scary lookin'?" Nick asked, with a sarcastic grin. "You're so ugly that you think I'd go crazy?"

Scott laughed. "I don't know. I don't think I'm scary looking at all, not compared to some of the others. In fact, I don't even believe my image would be all that unfamiliar to you, not in this 'modern' age. Though, some people still lose it just by looking at me. Maybe it's the shock. I'm sure it's not easy to have your worldview altered in such an instant and permanent way."

Scott reached back and took Nick's hand. They wandered at the crowd's edge, watching, enchanted. Nick was amazed by the density of the crowd.

Nick leaned toward Scott's ear. "It can't be any worse than the sight of Darren on Monday mornings."

"True." Scott giggled. "That boy can be frightening before noon."

"You should see him late at night though, when he's wet, like in a midnight Jacuzzi."

Scott turned and grinned. "Sexy?"

Nick nodded enthusiastically, rolling his eyes. "Oh, saints protect me, yes!"

Scott smiled, nodding.

They were wandering just at the outskirts of the dense dancing mass, allowing themselves to be half maneuvered by the current of people. Nick could feel all the eyes on them. He could feel the weight of all the glances that were enraptured by Scott's beauty, and his as well.

"Why were you marked then?" Nick asked. "Why are other demons looking for you?"

"Oh, boy, that's a tall order. My crimes against the Beast are far too many to list."

"You're kidding!"

"He's such a control freak!" Scott rolled his eyes. "There are people we're not allowed to go near, spells we're not allowed to cast, places we're not allowed to go—"

"You must have done something huge, though. Something big enough to get his attention."

"Yeah." Scott nodded solemnly. "Yeah, I did at that."

"Well?"

"I really crossed the line, I guess." Scott gently pulled Nick through the crowd with him, turning to speak into his ear. "I broke just about all of his rules eventually, the directives set forth by the Beast for the Legions and for the other fallen angels, so that we, not so much as *help* him really, as simply stay out of his way. In so doing, I've become a means by which others may gain favor from him. Delivering me to him would be highly beneficial to any being, whether they're one of the Fallen, like me, or just one of his legions. It doesn't matter.

"But, Nicholas, you're right about one thing, I suppose. There was something huge. Almost immediately after I fell I, to use a contemporary phrase ...I got myself put rather high on his shit list."

"Scott, what did you do? Specifically, I mean."

Scott sighed. "Pretty much what I'm doing right now. I caused a ripple in his plan, a flaw in the tapestry, so to speak. Out of love, I enlightened a human soul."

†

"Is Nicky here?" asked Troy.

Initially, Troy hadn't seen Darren come into the front lounge, but it was quite lovely when he found Troy on the couch and singled him out in front of everyone. It got even better when Darren asked Troy to come stand with him in line at the bar and keep him company. Troy's entourage couldn't have been greener. Darren Jacobson was asking Troy to spend some quality time. *Eat your hearts out, schmucks.*

"Yup." Darren nodded.

"Where's he at?" Troy smirked at him. They weren't in too long a line. There was only one guy pouring, though, so they could still be waiting for a bit. "He's not lying in a ditch somewhere this week too, is he? Tell him the upstairs room is much more comfortable."

"Okay, let's not rub salt into that, shall we?"

"You were *such* a spaz last week." Troy shook his head, smiling.

"Hey, I was worried he'd poisoned himself or something."

"Or something." Troy smirked again.

"Anyway, um, nice weather we're having. How 'bout them Yankees, blah, blah, blah."

"You're pretty dangerous when you're protecting your boyfriend there, Rocky."

"He's..." Darren stopped. He closed his eyes, took a deep breath, grinned. "He normally takes pretty good care of himself. So, I'm not used to doing anything like keeping an eye on him."

"Let the love flow, man."

Troy had never heard Darren admit it before, but it seemed Darren and Nick *were* boyfriends after all. Troy didn't know whether to congratulate him or kick him in the balls.

"Anyway, tonight he's fine," Darren said. "I left him behind the back-bar with his cousin."

"Oh, yeah, that's right." Troy cocked his head. "You mentioned this cousin earlier. I thought you were just buying large. You know, giving me a story to cover the increase in your product consumption. You wouldn't believe the shit I've heard."

"No." Darren shook his head. "There's a real cousin."

"I know, I'm just hasslin' ya. Karen told me."

"Is she here?"

"Somewhere. So, can you tell they're related? What does this cousin of Nick's look like?"

"He's a total hottie."

"How descriptive of you."

"Yeah, I know it." Darren smiled. "I'm a poet."

Troy suddenly saw an opening for some hope.

"So, this good-looking cousin... um, any, uh... have you... you know..." he stammered, raising a questioning eyebrow. "Have you ...indulged? With him? Or whatever? At all?"

Darren laughed, shaking his head. "No, no, no. I've kept my hands to myself."

Crap. Troy hoped Darren wasn't suddenly going all monogamous. Now the tough question. Troy licked his lips. "What about them?" he said. "They knockin' boots, or what? It's not like they'd have deformed children or anything."

"Man, no!" Darren chuckled. "That's gross! They're like *cousins*. Hello!"

"Oh, please, Becky. If I had a dime for every guy I know who messed around with his cousin, I'd have a good dollar ten, maybe a buck twenty."

"They're not kids playing spin-the-bottle."

"No, no, they're big boys, playin' hide-the-salami during a game of leap-frog."

"You're a sick man." Darren slowly shook his head, clicking his tongue. "I suggest you talk to someone about that, before you become a danger to yourself and others."

Troy smiled and shrugged his shoulders. He felt much better, but he didn't stop. He loved giving Darren a tough time.

"Okay," Troy said, raising his hands in surrender. "If you're all set to be all happy and unruffled here—"

"Troy, dude, really!" Darren laughed. "Things are great right now. Nicky's not fucking his cousin. Chill, baby."

"Is the cousin even on our team?"

"Duh."

Troy wanted desperately to press forward in his inquiry, but they'd reached the bar, dag-nam-it.

The bartender was shirtless, of course, displaying yet another perfectly chiseled physique in this oasis of masculine over-development. He obviously thought it would bring more business to his bar and maybe even sweeten the tipping impulse to boot. Undoubtedly, Troy realized as he struggled to keep from staring at the guy's nipples, the bartender was correct on both points.

If only Troy wasn't so skinny, maybe he wouldn't feel so insignificant. He wondered if any of these guys realized that they'd never actually need all their giant muscles for any practical purpose. They probably wouldn't need a quarter of it. It wasn't as though the bartender was going to finish up at work and then go hunt his dinner with a spear.

Good lord, as if there weren't enough façades on every studio lot in town. No, there had to be human façades too, tending bar at the only real club in town, a thirty-five dollar pair of underwear sticking out of his elastic gym-pants, and smiling impishly at Troy as if he didn't see him as little more than talking piano wire.

Troy wished he had half an ounce of discipline to get himself into a gym. He also wished he wasn't afraid that taking steroids would make his dick fall off.

He looked around and tried to get past his thundering lust—mixed with raw jealousy—and see the muscle boys for what they really were: bags of all-too human tissue, pumped-up with horse testosterone, Decca, and temporary self-worth. What were they going to do on that not-so-distant day when all their self-worth wasn't so firm anymore, maybe hanging from their chest past their groin?

"Karen said she'd point out Nick's cousin for me," Troy said, handing a twenty to the bartender, and consciously averting his eyes away from the parts of him with nipples.

"Yeah, have you seen her?" Darren asked, squinting. "We were supposed to meet her upstairs, but I don't think we're gonna make it."

"She said she'd be in the upstairs room…" Troy checked his watch. "…ten minutes ago."

"I've gotta go collect the boys."

"Where are they?"

"I dunno." Darren shrugged, smiling. "Probably fucking in the limo."

Troy laughed right along with Darren and nodded his good-bye as he turned and headed back into the darkened hall. Troy suddenly wanted to kick Darren in the balls again.

†

"How's my big baby boy?" said a familiar female voice from

behind Theo. A set of thick, acrylic nails trailed a teasing path up the back of his neck.

"Karen?" Theo smiled with a jubilance only possible through genuine devotion and a hearty boost from the great and glorious Miss E. herself.

"Hi, baby," Karen cooed, kissing him on the ear. Theo let go of Eddie long enough to turn and embrace her.

"We were on our way up to find you," he offered.

"Yes." She giggled, returning the hug. "I can see that." Theo blushed.

"Hey, pretty lady." Eddie smiled at her.

"Ooh, precious," she chimed, turning to him, "you look sweeter than boysenberry jam."

Karen gave Eddie an equally loving embrace and a kiss that left a hint of crimson lips on his cheek.

"You look great, Karen," Theo said. He loved the way she dressed and the way she let her hair tussle around her shoulders. It was blonde, like Darren's, and she let it grow just past the base of her neck. He thought it always looked somewhere between oh-I-just-woke-up-like-this and oh-I-just-spent-my-retirement-money-at-the-salon.

"You know, you are just my little muscle-muffin!" She beamed at Theo, taking his chin in her hand and leaving the same shadow of crimson on his cheek. Theo giggled like an eight year-old.

"We really were about to come up, Karen," Eddie said.

"I know, honey." She nodded.

Theo leaned into her ear. "We're rolling, a little."

She patted him on the face. "Okay, um …duh, baby."

"Do you need anything?"

"Aren't you just the blessing from the sky? No, sweetness, I'm all taken care of. Now, you two really should go upstairs. I was supposed to meet Troy and Darren up there a little bit ago, but I have to run to the front and handle something first. Would you just let them know for me? Please, please?" She puckered into a pleading frown and a kissy-face at the same time.

"Okay. No problem. Is there something wrong up front?"

"Oh no. It won't take long and then I'll be right up. Listen, you guys are all on the list, so there shouldn't be any trouble. I kept the crowd small in there, and there aren't any major names. It's gonna be nice and intimate. I'll be looking forward to relaxing a bit and meeting Nicky's cousin."

"You'll like him." Eddie smiled.

THE FALLEN 241

"That's what I've heard."

"He's mine, though." Theo gave her a warning glance.

Eddie snorted.

Karen beamed her most motherly smile. "Whatever you say, darlin'."

†

Nick led Scott to his favorite spot on the dance floor, which was the only corner onto which the air-conditioning blew directly. It was the only place that didn't feel like Houston in July.

He pulled off his shirt, mostly out of habit, and because just about all of the other guys around them had already shed theirs, hanging them from their pockets like personal designer face-towels. He didn't even think about it until Scott followed suit. If the crowd sharing the dance floor immediately around them hadn't yet noticed their arrival, they did then.

Nick smiled at him and Scott grinned back, shrugging.

"When in Rome," he said.

"Do as the Romans do," Nick replied.

"Been there. Not always the best of advice. However, more than appropriate at the moment."

The DJ blared love and delight from the impeccable sound system, which engulfed them along with the cool air being pumped out of the enormous vent above. Nick watched Scott with a playful grin. He was moved as much by the crowd as the inescapable rhythm that saturated the very air and the glowing bliss of Missy's mood.

He rubbed his hand absently across his abdomen, which always triggered the ecstasy and sent brilliant bursts of tingles through him. He closed his eyes and swayed with those tingles, rolled with them, lost with them.

"Why aren't you an actor anymore?" Scott said suddenly, waking Nick from his trance.

"What?" he asked.

Scott smiled, stepping in closer, moving in time with Nick and the music.

"Since you're uncomfortable with me purposely gleaning from you," he said, "perhaps you can just tell me, in your own words. Why you aren't an actor anymore?"

Besides being confused, Nick was a little startled by the question. He looked around at the tightly packed mass; the bare-chested muscular men, the trim alluring women with their hair pulled up or falling in luscious ponytails, everyone smiling, everyone dancing, a water bottle in every other hand. No one was looking. No one was listening. No one was noticing.

"I'm still an actor," Nick said.

Scott raised his eyebrows and smirked. "When was the last time you worked?"

"A few months ago."

"When was the last time you studied?"

Nick took a deep breath. "A little over a year ago."

"When was the last time you spoke to your agent?"

"Don't pretend you don't know the answers to these questions, Scott. Don't pretend you haven't gleaned all of this from Darren or Theo."

"I know the answers, yes, as well as you. What I don't know, and what I asked, is why."

"I'm still an actor," Nick insisted again.

Scott pressed his lips together in an expression of disappointment. He touched Nick on the chin to force his eyes to his.

"Nick," he said, "a bodybuilder who hasn't been to the gym in six months can hardly call himself an athlete."

"What does that mean?"

"One is defined by one's actions, Nick, and by the intentions that influence those actions. What were you today? What were you besides the gem of Darren's life, besides the walls of my sanctuary? What were you besides Theo's confidence and Eddie's paragon? What were you for you? What does Nick mean to Nick?"

"Scotty…" Nick shook his head, pulling his chin from Scott's fingers. "I don't know what you're talking about." Though, he felt his throat close and his eyes begin to burn.

"You are their rock, you know. You're the center of their lives and almost a matriarch."

Nick giggled. "Are you calling me a woman?"

"No, of course not. There just isn't a word quite suitable for who you are to them. It's more than family. You're certainly more nurturing than simply protective."

"We're friends."

"Yes." Scott nodded. "Yes, you are."

"I don't know why I'm not working."

"No? Are you sure?"

"Theo and Eddie…? They…?"

Scott placed his hand gently back onto Nick's face, stopping his movement, moving in to whisper in his ear. "Nick, Theo doesn't really have any family in Puerto Rico."

"What?" Nick pulled back in surprise.

"Theo's from Garden Grove," Scott explained over the music. "His father left before his second birthday, and his mother threw him out when he was sixteen. She said it was because he was gay, but he knew if she didn't have that, she'd have found another excuse."

"Oh, my god," Nick uttered into the air. The crowd mixed and danced around him, unaffected.

"He's ashamed," said Scott. "He's embarrassed and he's broken, but you and Darren have given him hope. You listen to his dreams and you advise him on them, in all seriousness, as no one has ever done."

"We love Theo."

"I know."

"Why didn't he tell us this? Why didn't he tell us where he was from?"

"He doesn't want to talk about it. He doesn't want to remember or allow his childhood to define him, especially in your eyes. He wants to be someone else. He wants to be mysterious."

"Does Eddie know?"

"Yes." Scott nodded. "Some of it. Though, it's rough on Theo, so Eddie leaves it alone."

Nick shook his head. Scott smiled at him with unveiled affection.

"And Eddie is hiding," he said. "Just like me."

"Yeah." Nick nodded. "That I knew."

"His family never asked him to leave, but they might as well have."

"They're so rough with him," Nick said. "They have so much. They're so well off, but they still don't think they can afford to let him choose who he wants to be."

"But you do. You take him at his word and give him all he asks for."

"I love Eddie too."

"I know."

"What are you saying? What does this mean?"

"Happiness has two components, Nick. There are only two ingredients to its formula, both simple, yet essential. Without both of them, happiness will never be complete and constant."

Nick just looked at him.

"It takes both love and purpose to be truly happy," Scott said. "You've brought them together and given them hope because you love them. You love Theo and Eddie because they're yours without reservation, without condition. You love Darren, despite his flaws, despite the pain he causes you, because you know, when he holds you in the dark, when the world around you is quiet and his thoughts are at peace, when he's not bombarded by what he thinks are the pressures of the world, he loves you back. Darren loves you back, and with the same fervor, and the same validity, that streams so freely from your own heart, love for him and the rest of your family, unhindered by such tainted considerations as worldly acceptance. You've allowed them to be happy with you. You've allowed them love, for now, but you really need to find the other component that makes *you* happy. It's time that you found your purpose. Find what's beyond them. Find what delights your heart. Know the goal of your heart and move to it. Only after you've done that can you take them with you. Only then can you continue to keep them together, keep them with you, and keep them safe."

"Safe from what?"

"This is a passing refuge," Scott gestured around them. "Its magnificence is real and enlightening, but also narrow and unyielding. You can't tell me that you've never looked around and known that everything you saw was an illusion. These lights, these clothes, these faces, these bodies, these people are all a pretty, pretty show. This is a show that points to the truth, celebrates it, but cannot satisfy it on its own. Some of these people, even as they dance around us, some of them know the truth. Some of them are keenly aware of the futility in this world, in looking for substance only here. It's like trying to create a vast and grand mural with a crayon. The ones that don't know, the ones that dance and laugh here with whole abandon, with pure delight in their youth and beauty and money and fame, with this singular celebration of what is utterly foolish, they're *choosing* not to know. They're choosing not to see. They're choosing to see only what they think is of value, just as you have been doing. They're living inside a futility that they're barely keeping at bay. Just as you've done. Just as you've been living."

He stepped close to Nick abruptly. "This world, these excesses, will never change, but *you* will. You cannot stay the same. It is not possible. So, you'll either learn and move on, or cling to what you think you know, and be destroyed.

"If you came to this place to celebrate the truth, that would be one thing. But you don't. You come here to hide. You come here to hide from the truth, and that is something else completely."

Scott placed his hands on Nick's shoulders, pulled him close, and lay his lips near his ear, as if in a kiss.

"I will give you all I can," he said, "all I am allowed by Heaven and the angels who still know my name. As I stand here, touching you, faintly hearing the cry and the innocence in your heart, out of love, I'll give you the first of these gifts. You have got to find your purpose to save them, to save your chosen family. You have to not only get up, but also step higher than this place to which you've allowed yourself to fall, in order to save those three upon whom you've lain your trust, those with whom you've cast your hopes. You have more than just yourself now, and you need to see that. You're not alone, as you're so fond of telling yourself. You have a family and you are accountable to them. Regardless of their faults or their sins against you, you are accountable to them. You can save them from their own unresolved fear and intemperate indulgence. You can save them from what the world would make of them, out of its simple and bitter ignorance, and in so doing, in doing all of this for them, you will save yourself."

†

"Has anyone seen him?" Karen asked. She stepped behind the counter, moving immediately to its far end, near the front door. Matt had changed places with Bobby, sending him instead to check IDs, membership cards, and monitor the line with Brad. Matt wasn't actually behind the counter, though. He was sitting on its edge, gabbing with some regulars he'd allowed just inside the door.

"Nope," Matt answered. "At least I haven't heard anything."

"I'll be right back."

Once outside, out of habit, Karen looked immediately to the line of people behind the velvet rope. It had always been her direct indicator of the night's success or failure. Looking now, she was astounded to see the line stretching around the building's corner and into the side lot. She didn't want to go look into the side lot; that's where she'd see the really unhappy people.

"How's it inside?" Brad the Security Guy asked, seeing her step out.

"Delicious," she smiled. "Any exits?"

"Just a couple. Nathan brought out some dork that puked in the hall trashcan. The sick dork 'left' with the aid of a couple friends. Other than that, its been pretty one-way."

"And the natives?"

"Well, of course they're restless, but I haven't heard any actual war drums yet."

"Start a trickle. Don't select or show favorites. I'm going to be at the front counter for a few minutes."

Brad the Security Guy nodded. "Gottcha, babe."

She gave him a sideways glance.

He smiled. "It *is* 'babe,' isn't it?"

She smiled back. "Sweet pea, you keep smilin' at me like that and I won't care if you call me 'Matilda.'"

Brad the Security Guy giggled. Karen loved to a hear big beefy man giggle.

"Oh," she said, almost as an afterthought, "have you seen that little guy again at all?"

"Nope." Brad the Security Guy shook his head. "Not a sign. He probably bailed."

"Are you sure it was him?"

It was Brad the Security Guy's turn to give Karen a sideways glance.

She grinned. "I didn't mean any offence, big guy."

"None taken," he said, and grinned back.

Was he flirting? It looked to Karen like this big handsome security guy was flirting with her. She could only hope.

"I'm going to go back in, but Bradley..." She leveled a serious gaze at him. "I said 'trickle,' so don't let that turn into any more of a flow. And you know my rule. Don't let me catch either you or Bobby taking any grease. Remember the story of the goose that laid the golden eggs."

"Yes, ma'am."

"If you see the runt, just come and get me. I'll be right inside. Or, if you really need to, you can send Bobby in to get me instead ...if you really feel you need to ...you know, maybe detain the runt yourself and maybe accidentally punch him a few times. I hear that happens sometimes. People can sometimes run right into a person's fist on accident."

"Yes, ma'am. Thank you ma'am," Brad the Security Guy said with another giggle. Ooh, but he was delectable.

"Okay," she cooed at him, puckered up, and gestured with her finger to come closer. "Now, gimme a smooch, or else you're fired."

Brad the Security Guy also puckered up, then happily pursued some job security.

†

The security guy stationed upstairs, the one at the secret door around the corner from the coat-check—which was just the funniest

thing to see in a bar in California—didn't even glance at his list. He
just let Theo and Eddie into the upstairs room as soon as he recognized
them.

Inside, there were only a few people milling about. The music was
the same as was playing in the rest of the club, pumped into the VIP
room through expertly placed speakers connected to the room's upper
corners and hidden behind decorative furniture. It wasn't too loud,
which enabled to small assemblage to enjoy a level of conversation not
easily achieved on either of the lower levels.

Theo walked right in, hoping Eddie would just follow. He didn't
want to look like a dork by standing for too long at the door, scanning
the group for a familiar face. No, better to confidently march right in,
as if it were his own living room.

Luckily, he spotted Troy right away and didn't have to alter his
course by very much to get to him. Theo smiled, glanced quickly
behind him to make sure Eddie was there, and then ambled up to
Troy.

Troy was standing with his arms crossed, looking either confused
or irritated—Theo couldn't tell which—and talking to That Really
Short Guy.

"I don't want to try and control anything that comes into the
party," That Really Short Guy was quietly explaining to Troy. "All I'm
saying is, since Laura has essentially handed it over to me, I'd like to
open your options completely."

"Hey Troy." Theo nodded at him.

Troy winked and held up a single finger to indicate he'd just be a
minute. Eddie stepped up next to Theo and nodded a hello at Troy,
who winked again.

"So, no more of this 'no Gina,' bullshit?" Troy asked.

Before answering, That Really Short Guy turned slightly, giving
Theo and Eddie a condescending glare. Theo was taken aback. Mostly
because he'd never had someone look at him with such contempt, and
certainly no one who was so much shorter and barely weighed barely
weighed as much as one of his legs. Theo thought That Really Short
Guy must have some pretty heavy brass ones.

Troy shook his head and tapped That Really Short Guy on the
shoulder. "Oh, motherfuck, don't worry about Theo and Eddie.
They're regular clients. Not to mention extremely close friends of
Karen's. They'll probably be exclusively responsible for my profits at
your little function. I'm sure you'll see them there, bright and early
and with bells on."

Troy motioned for Theo to step closer. "Theo, this is Gil," he said. "He tells me that he's now handling a private pre-party to promote New Years Eve at the club."

"How's it goin'?" Theo smiled at Gil, noticing that the little man's condescending expression did not change.

Gil just nodded and shook Theo's hand. After which, for some reason, he giggled.

"And this is Eddie," Troy said.

Gil shook Eddie's hand as well, blinked rapidly, and abruptly smiled. "It's nice to meet you both. I've heard quite a lot about you from Karen and Laura."

"I don't actually know Laura very well," Theo admitted.

"I'm not surprised," Gil said. "She can be a bit aloof whenever she's around the unsophisticated."

"What?" Theo squinted down at Gil, crossing his arms and wondering if he heard what he thought he'd heard.

"Look, I don't like discussing business here," Troy said quickly. "So, why don't we talk a little closer to the date."

"Fine," said Gil. "I just wanted to make sure that you kept all your supply lines well inside the loop. I don't want any shortages. There'll be no denials at the house. It's a private residence, and I plan to take advantage of that feature."

"Your call." Troy shrugged.

"Yes, it is." Gil smiled. "It is at that."

Without so much as a nod or a glance, Gil walked straight to the door, opened it, pushed the security guy out of his way, and headed to the stairs.

"Nice guy," Eddie said.

Troy smirked. "I'm in shock that Karen's letting him handle that party. The guy's a total turd."

"When is it?" Theo asked. "The pre-party, I mean."

"Late December."

"Won't a lot of people be out of town?"

"Maybe." Troy shrugged again. "I don't give a shit. It's not my gig. Though, you'd be surprised."

"I've seen him around," Eddie said. "Who is he?"

"Some goob that used to help Laura Shah with her breeder-bashes." Troy closed his eyes and shook his head. "Apparently, he's handling his own now. I've been roped into catering. I'd never have signed on, but I thought I'd just be working with Karen. If this shit's true, I'm gonna kick her ass."

Theo shook his head. "Man, he's probably full of it. You'd better wait and see what she says."

"She was supposed to be here right now." Troy looked at his watch.

"She's at the front door," Eddie said. "Something about some trouble with the line."

"Mother—!" Troy gritted his teeth. "Look guys, no offense, but I've had my fill of Muscle Boy Central tonight. I'm gonna jet. I'll try to catch Karen at the door, but if for some reason I miss her, would you tell her to call me?"

Theo nodded. "Sure."

"And tell her she still motherfucking owes me Scott Wolf."

†

"This doesn't look like the limo." Darren snuck up behind Nick and startled him.

"Hi, pretty man." Scott beamed at him, swaying to the music. He took the bottle of water Darren brought for him. "Thanks, baby."

"We're already done doin' the nasty out in the car." Nick smiled over his shoulder at Darren. "We just came in for a short break, then we're gonna go back out and take turns chewing on the upholstery."

"Ha, ha, tee hee." Darren stepped around so he could face both Nick and Scott, the other dancers adjusted slightly to make room for him. "Still rollin', schnook?"

Nick just smiled.

"Oh, good golly, Miss Molly!" Darren said, grasping Nick and Scott by the shoulders and dancing with them. "I'm supposed to hook-up with Karen. She wants to meet Scott."

Nick didn't stop dancing. "Yeah?" he asked "When were you supposed to do that?"

Darren looked at his watch. "Twenty-five minutes ago."

Scott laughed. "Karen… she's the blonde girl you were so chummy with last weekend, right?"

"Yeah." Darren nodded. "She's upstairs with Troy. He's our pharmacist."

"You mean 'drug dealer?'"

Darren laughed. "You're about as fucking subtle as Eddie!"

Nick looked at Scott. "Do you think we could head up there?"

"Sure, I guess so," Scott said. "I think it's okay. Besides, I don't want to start sweating."

"How could you possibly start sweating?" Darren smiled, looking up at the massive air conditioning vent. "You're dancing right under this arctic wind."

"I just don't like to perspire too much," Scott said. Then he looked right at Nick. "It's more potent than spit."

"What?" Darren squinted.

Nick's eyes widened with his smile. "We'd better go then," he said, grabbing Darren by the hand. "Follow me big guy."

"Anywhere you go, baby." Darren smiled, dancing off the floor behind Nick. "Anywhere you go."

†

Karen busied herself by auditing the membership registration sheets. It was a completely superfluous task; one of the guys at the entrance always checked the forms before issuing any new memberships, but she had to try to stay at least a little busy or she'd start gabbing with one of the regulars and eventually abandon her post and sprint upstairs.

"I promised myself a long, long time ago," Troy said as he walked up and leaned against the counter, "that I'd never, ever again, be stood-up by a woman."

"Oh, Troy honey!" Karen blurted, setting the clipboard underneath the counter. "I'm sorry! I sent Theo up to let you know what was going on—"

Troy was already smiling. "Stop, stop! Don't worry about it." He waved a hand in the air. "I'm tired anyway."

"Please," Karen said, smirking, "don't tell me you can't take care of that."

"I don't really feel like taking anything to pick me up. Besides, it might also make me unbearably horny, which is a burden I simply don't need at the moment."

"Well, you're not leaving, are you?" She frowned.

"Yup." Troy nodded. "You'll either have to introduce me to Nick's reputedly delectable cousin at some other time, or deliver on your earlier promise of supplying me with Mr. Wolf. Though, I suppose I could be appeased with some other equally yummy bundle. Freddie Prince, Jr. comes to mind."

"I think he really is a breeder, honey."

"Fine, but you get the general idea."

"Sure, baby."

"And what's the deal with putting that detestable, vertically-challenged, bigot in charge of the New Year's promo gig? I'd get huffy and puffy about it, if I didn't think it'd get you all excited."

"Oh, shit!" Karen had completely forgotten to warn Troy. "I can't believe I spaced about that!"

"I told you I hated that guy. How come—?"

"Sweetie, you don't have to do anything. Really, it's fine if you want to back out. I totally understand." She clutched her forehead. "Oh, I'm such a dunce! Laura and I worked out a way we thought we'd be able to unload Gil without a mess. Tossing him a bone seemed like a very good idea at the time. I was just trying to avoid any drama."

"You were trying to unload him?"

"Yeah." Karen smiled awkwardly. "I don't know why I didn't just tell Laura to drop him straight off. I guess I should've. She made a lot of sense, though. She really wanted to keep things smooth, you know?"

"You handed him the New Year's promo bash just to keep him quiet?"

"I guess so, yeah." Karen bit her lower lip. "Do you think I'm a dumb-ass?"

"Oh, my god, shut up. Look, I don't care, really. I'll handle it. He's at least good for the invoice, right?" Troy raised his eyebrows at her.

"That'll be taken care of, my sweet. That, I can guarantee."

"All right. No harm, no foul, but if he calls anyone a 'bone smoker' again, I'm gonna rip his larynx out and serve it as pâté."

"Troy, honey, now it's not like you to go around poisoning people."

"You could have at least told me yourself, or had Laura call me."

"Laura didn't tell you?"

"No." Troy shook his head. "Tattoo did. I just saw him upstairs."

"What?" Karen heard the word drop from her mouth like a dried, broken cracker.

"He cornered me upstairs and gave me all these alterations to the original plan," Troy explained. "He said he wanted to make sure I had everything available, but I got the distinct impression he was just babbling bullshit to make sure I knew he'd been put in charge."

"You saw him upstairs?" Karen stared at Troy, unblinking.

"Karen, babe, I know I don't have to tell you how much this punk pisses me off. So, in the future, I'd be mighty happy if you didn't allow him access to any endeavors in which I might be interested. I'm seriously contemplating the idea of possibly considering the notion of maybe putting some effort into attempting to find out how to sort of have him shot."

"He was upstairs? Tonight? Just now?"

"Yeah." Troy squinted. "What's wrong? Am I speaking Latin, or something?"

"Oh, my…" Karen laid her face in her hands.

"What's wrong?"

"He's been eighty-sixed," Karen groaned from between her fingers. "Max decided he didn't want him allowed in the club anymore."

"Max is a smart man."

"Troy, that's why I'm down here." She looked up at him, wrinkling her forehead. "That's why I didn't meet you upstairs. Brad saw him outside and I came down to make sure he didn't get in. Are you sure you saw him upstairs?"

"Karen, I told you. I haven't indulged in anything."

"I know, I'm sorry." She shook her head. "I just don't know how he got into the club."

"Well, I can't help you with that, but he's somewhere in there."

"He's not upstairs anymore?"

"Nope. He left right before Theo and Eddie told me you were down here."

"I guess I could send Bobby and Matt to sweep—"

"Listen," Troy said, quickly patting her arm, "I'm gonna go. You might want to jaunt upstairs and let the guys know you haven't forgotten about them."

"Yeah, you're right."

"Call me tomorrow, if you want. Not early, though."

"What? Around ten?"

"Sure. Eleven sounds fine."

Troy kissed Karen on the cheek, patted Matt on the shoulder, and headed to the door.

"Troy!" Karen called after him. "If you're up when I call at noon, you wanna have lunch?"

"Sounds good to me," he said. "I'm sure I'll be up by twelve-thirty. One o'clock at the latest, unless I'm not."

"Okay, great. It's a plan. I'll talk to you at two. Smooches!"

He smiled, turned, and threw a friendly wave over his shoulder before the doors closed behind him.

†

Eddie didn't really like anyone that was in the tiny VIP room with them. He smiled and listened politely, as did Theo, to all the rapid chatter, but it was just the same old squawking as any other night. He couldn't remember who'd told him they'd just signed with William Morris, or who'd dropped David Geffen's name—who didn't anymore—or who'd been crowing about being a Who in Whoville with Jim Carrey in *How the Grinch Stole Christmas*. Really, freak, who cared?

There was no point in hanging-out upstairs if the VIP room was going to be throttled with B-crowd babies—or even worse: C-Crowd Wannabes. Not that Eddie considered himself any better. On the contrary; he admired them all for their seemingly undaunted and unflinching reach for the brass ring, despite the conspicuously overwhelming odds against them, which meant they were all either religiously fervent artists or complete and hopeless morons.

Once or twice he'd seen it happen for one of them. He'd witnessed an eager up-an-comer suddenly finding themselves slipping their fingers around the prize and yanking it hard into their possession. After that, however, Eddie still had to listen to them, only at that time what they talked about was their sudden custody of the prize. He'd smile and nod, though not at the standard and endless list of breakthrough projects or names of celebrity acquaintances, but at their thin philosophical theories as to what pulled them out of the crowd. They went on and on about what they thought it was that propelled them into the five and even six figure income range while their peers still had to scrape together enough cash for a dinner of Top Ramen and Gatorade. They'd weave out for him—and themselves—the logical explanation for their 'unique' success, which often included the acknowledgement of God, talent, tenacity, breeding, education, and instinct. They went out of their way to acknowledge everything. Everything but blind luck.

After Troy left, Eddie and Theo treated themselves to a bump or two of Special K, settled against the arm of one of the oversized couches, and bantered snide comments about Gil until the first of the tiny crowd stumbled over to hit on Theo. Eventually, all those casting their line at Theo would figure out there wasn't any mutual interest and either shift to Eddie, or move on. Of course, they were immediately replaced. The latest guy who'd set his sights on them was actually kind of cute. Though, in a stale, boy-band kind of way.

"I didn't really agree with the poll," Boy-Band Guy was saying. "I thought Suzanne Summer's book was much more helpful than Mary Lou Henner's."

"Really." Theo nodded. He looked at Eddie, pursed his lips, and raised his eyebrows, which was his Please-Save-Me expression.

"Oh, yeah," Boy-Band Guy continued, "but I wouldn't buy any of the products she markets. Especially not that stomach one, or whatever. I mean, throw a towel on a skateboard, for cryin' out loud."

"We should go check for Karen downstairs, Theo," Eddie said.

"Oh, yeah, what time is it?" Theo mocked alarm, grabbing Eddie's wrist and checking his watch.

"You guys gotta go?" questioned Boy-Band Guy.

"We were supposed to meet some people up here but I don't think they're coming," Eddie explained. "I think we should cruise a bit."

"That's cool. So, you think you'll be back up —?"

"It was really nice meeting you." Theo offered a tiny wave, held Eddie by the shoulder, and started him toward the door. "Take it easy."

"Yeah, cool, …ciao." Boy-band Guy looked a little lost.

"Let's see if we can catch Karen downstairs," Theo suggested as they walked out of the secret door behind the coat-check booth. "I'm rolling too hard to wait in there."

"Don't you want to go back and get his number?" Eddie smiled.

"You know he's not my type."

"Well," Eddie said, "at least you're nice to guys like that. I think you're the only person I know who doesn't take some kind of haughty pleasure in watching a guy suffer over you."

"Shut up." Theo nudged him and pretended to be above the observation, but Eddie could see that he was blushing.

They started down the stairs to the second floor, Eddie in front. He looked up over his shoulder at Theo. "Still," he said smiling hard, "you could have at least given him an autographed video or something."

Theo lowered his chin to his chest. "Don't make me slap you in public."

†

Trying to get off of the dance floor actually took quite an effort. The crowd had become so dense it was silly. Nick wondered if the strained shifting and swaying everyone was limited to doing actually counted as dancing. When they finally got to the edge of the swaying mass, he thought it felt like dragging himself onto the beach out of a rip current. It was even easier to breathe.

Darren and then Scott followed him out of the wall of people, though not immediately; there was just no way to stay together inside such a throng. Once they were all out, they headed across the club, Darren in the lead. The crowd, milling between rooms, through the lounges, and to the bars, was as thick as Nick had ever seen it. The building's capacity had obviously been exceeded long, long ago. He wondered what Karen would do if the Fire Marshal showed up, or worse, if there was a fire.

Almost right away, Darren turned back and took Nick's hand— shocking him stupid for the second time that evening—and headed toward the stairs.

Even after the kiss in the VIP room, Nick still looked down at his hand in near disbelief as Darren held it tightly and pulled him along. Missy was certainly working her magic, and he felt as wonderful and content as she'd ever made him feel. Even so, on top of all that, now with Darren's fingers laced through his, he was suddenly giddy with delight, immaculate and engulfing. All combined, the moment was nearly overwhelming.

He reached back with his free hand and took Scott's. Then, like a giddy, happy little train of toddlers, the three of them made their way through the first floor; Darren connected to Nick and Nick connected to Scott, through the main bar area, and around to the stairs.

The night was clearly in its prime. Clumps of stunning people stood together, emanating an irresistible charm, laughing without reserve, touching and swaying, kissing and smiling, enjoying their youth and beauty, languid in their confidence, thriving inside their star-studded haven, exempted from the world and suspended in time. If there was discontent, it was well hidden. If there was insecurity, it was earnestly tempered.

Obviously, Darren was in an especially splendid mood; he looked somehow taller, his chest broader, his smile immeasurably disarming. With only his grin, he seemed to part a path through the crowd as he sauntered along in step with the music, nodding his head and swaying his shoulders.

Nick smiled and watched the crowd give way before them. With an awareness that surprised him, he reached to embrace the moment, savoring it, preserving it.

Glancing back, he looked into Scott's ice-blue eyes, noticing his heavy grin and radiant air. He took note again of Scott's tranquil, parted lips, his flawless skin, his angled jaw. The waves of his hair framed him like polished ebony, highlighting features that were already beyond exquisite. Nick smiled again, thinking that beauty like Scott's could be called nothing less than divine.

All the while, Scott looked back at him with an intense understanding, every ounce an angel, every movement mesmerizing, his expression one of clear and open affection. They walked on and Nick was torn between marveling at Darren and indulging glances back at Scott.

While pondering his enchanting dilemma, Nick turned away from Darren again and caught Scott's eye. This time, he was somehow sure his new friend knew just what he was thinking and it made him blush and laugh. Right then, holding tightly to Scott's hand, Nick loved the idea that he might share his thoughts. The two of them could know that unusual intimacy, sharing a connection both innocent and profound. Then Scott smiled so abruptly that Nick blushed even more.

Moving closer to Nick, Scott brushed his lips across his cheek. "This is the brightest treasure in living," he said. "This is Heaven. Savor this instant and keep its memory where it may be quickly retrieved. It will carry you farther than you know. Hold tightly to Darren and appreciate this night without any thought of tomorrow. Every effort of existence strives only to achieve this joy, this contentment."

Looking at him, Nick felt a childish awe. He trustingly put one foot in front of the other, letting Darren slowly pull them through the crowd.

"How did you come to be with me?" Nick whispered, smiling. "How did I get to be so lucky?"

"I was yours all along." Scott leaned into him, brushed his cheek against Nick's. "As it was always meant to be."

†

"Gil got into the club," Karen informed Matt.

"Who?" He looked back at her quizzically.

"The runt!" she squeaked. "You know, the elf we've been looking for! Somehow, he got inside."

"No way." Matt shook his head. "There's no way he could've gotten past us."

"Look, Matty, sweetie, I'm not pointing any fingers. I don't know how it happened, but Troy just told me he had a fucking conversation with the creep upstairs, and in the VIP room, no less. Who's on that door?"

"Steven."

"Was he at Max's little briefing today with—?"

"Yeah, yeah." Matt nodded. He looked thoroughly confused.

"Okay, well, I think you and Brad should sweep the club."

"All right."

"Grab Andrew, Vince, and Brian. Put them on the back stairs. Get Neal, Brent, and Craig. They're on the dance floor stairs. Tell them to make sure Gil doesn't slip by them. Then, take Marco and Cindy, check the lounges and the restrooms, both men's and women's—"

"Why the—?"

"Babe, please don't argue with me right now. This is serious. Just check them both, okay? Then see if you can get Tim and Robin to help you sweep the dance floor. You know how to secure each section systematically, right? Make sure the alarms are active on all of the exits. When you're sure he's not on the first floor, station another person at each stairway and sweep the balconies. I'm going to call Steven and make sure that Gil's not back in the upstairs room or out on the landing."

"All right, we'll take care of it."

"Don't confront him Matt, but don't let him leave. I don't care what it takes. You make sure you give me enough time to get a squad car here. I want that little prick in handcuffs. This is fucking trespassing. Laura better have motherfucking taken care of her little conversation with him. She better have fucking handled this, or else it's her ass."

"I'm on it." Matt turned to leave.

"Matty?" Karen called.

"Yeah?"

"Don't instigate anything. But if he should make you feel threatened, you know, if you're put in a position where you feel you simply must defend yourself, forget everything I said about only breaking one bone. There's no limit anymore. He's obviously begging for it. Go to town, baby."

†

"Hey, baby, baby." Darren smiled at Theo and Eddie as they stepped off the stairs to the third floor onto the landing in front of the club's office. "Did you see her?"

Theo nodded. "Just for a minute, though. She had to go down to the front to handle some trouble and asked us to let you know."

"Who's up there? Anyone interesting?"

Theo did a spastic little shake of his head and frowned.

Eddie smiled at them as he came around Theo. Darren reached out, running his fingers up the back of Eddie's neck, who moaned.

"You're a pretty, pretty boy," Darren smiled. "Anyone ever tell you that before?"

"I am so slammed right now," Eddie said, his eyes closed, his neck loose in Darren's grasp. "We are fuckin' rolling downhill without breaks."

"Dance?" Theo suggested, beaming a smile and doing a spastic little nod.

"The first floor's a smelly, sardine hell," Nick said, resting his head back onto Scott's shoulder, who wrapped his arms around him from behind.

"Why don't we go back up," Eddie said, stepping into Darren's embrace. "I think we all need to lounge for a bit. There's a loveseat up there that looks just perfect for five."

Darren chuckled. "That sounds sweet to me."

"Me too," said Theo, stepping over to Nick and Scott. He rested his hands on Scott's shoulders, who shuddered suddenly and pushed himself away from both of them.

"You okay?" Eddie asked.

Darren's arms fell from around Eddie. His face, for the second time that evening, showed a curious concern.

Scott didn't answer. Instead, he started to cough. He patted his chest and braced one arm on his knee and coughed several times.

"Scotty?" Theo said, stepping over to him, his hand out, offering his help.

Scott immediately stepped away, shaking his head, still coughing, raising his hand toward Theo to stop him.

No one knew what to do and the four of them just looked at each other with an alarm that was heading toward panic. After a few seconds, though, Scott stopped coughing, but was still heaving out great bursts of breath in loud, rasping grunts.

"Oh, my god, Scott...?" Nick barley spoke.

Scott just nodded. His breathing became more regular and he straightened a bit, looking directly at Nick, nodding some more.

"We have to go," Scott said, still breathing heavily, as if he were winded. "We have to go right now."

"What's wrong?" Darren asked, letting go of Eddie completely.

"We need to go," Nick said stupidly.

"Nick, what's going on?" Darren stepped over to him, then looked toward Scott. "Scotty, are you okay? Do you need anything?"

"I'm fine," Scott said, nodding slightly. He was almost breathing normally.

"Is there anything I can do?" Theo moaned. He was holding his hands to his chest, his fingers laced, as if he were cold.

"No, baby, don't worry." Scott looked like he was trying to smile at him, but he didn't move any closer. "I just got a whiff of something and it caught me off guard, that's all."

"I don't smell anything," Eddie said.

"It's... um..."

"What do you mean by 'whiff?'" Darren asked. "Did you snort something?"

"Yeah!" Scott snapped his fingers. "That's it. That must be it. Someone shared a bullet with Nick and me while we were on the dance floor. That must be it."

"That was not smart." Darren gave Nick an irritated glare.

"Fuck off, Darren!" Nick snapped. "It wasn't K! It was coke!" Even though he hadn't really snorted anything at all, it still pissed him off that Darren assumed he'd make the same mistake twice. "We all know I'm too impulsive to be trusted, but I'm not a *complete* idiot!"

"Oh, come on, I didn't say that," Darren said, reaching over and lacing his fingers through Nick's.

Eddie was looking at Scott timidly. "You're not goin' all River Phoenix on us, are you?" he asked.

Scott shook his head. "No, baby. No, I'm fine. Really. I just want to leave. Let's go. Let's all go right now. The limo will be just as comfortable as the loveseat upstairs. I promise."

Nick looked at Darren with raised eyebrows.

"You really wanna go?" Theo asked.

"Yeah," Nick said, still looking at Darren. "I told him earlier that if he was at all uncomfortable here, we'd go. This isn't really his scene."

"It's not that," Scott said. "I just don't feel so great anymore. Why don't we just get in the car and cruise around? Darren, don't you have another hit for me out there?"

"Yeah," Darren said, "but don't you want to do that—?"

"I'd much rather just lounge with you guys."

"Can we just go?" Nick looked around at Eddie and Theo. He was starting to feel a little agitated. "You know, you guys are welcome to stay here, but I'm gonna go with Scott."

"Easy, tiger." Darren pulled him close and wrapped his arms around his shoulders. "We can all go. It's not a big deal. It's not like we paid a lot of money to get in. We just want to make sure everything's all right."

"Everything's fine," Scott insisted. "We'll curl up together in the car for a while."

Darren nodded reluctantly. "That's fine," he said.

"Theo?" Scott looked over at him.

"What, baby?"

"Go wash your hands really, really well before we go. Edward, you too."

†

"It was on their hands," Scott said. "The smell of it was on Theo and Eddie's hands. I didn't catch it until Theo touched me."

They were standing near the corridor that lead to the main entrance. Darren, Eddie, and Theo were in the men's room.

"You could smell it?" Nick asked.

Scott nodded slowly. "It hit me a little abruptly, like a stink bomb. I'm sorry I was so dramatic, but—"

"Are we okay? Should we head out to the car?"

"We're fine. Don't panic."

"Don't panic? Theo and Eddie were touching—"

"This is the best way to find out, Nick," Scott said. His voice was calm, deliberate. "There's been no direct contact. Theo and Eddie touched an imp sometime tonight. It was just an imp. No big deal."

"What the fuck is an imp?" Nick could feel his stomach begin to cramp and he had a sudden ache at the base of his neck.

"It's a very minor, terrestrial demon, usually very small," Scott said quietly. "They've also been called gnomes, gremlins, or pixies."

"They're not dangerous?"

"Well, yes, they can be somewhat dangerous, but—"

"Where do you think it is now? Does it know you're here?"

"I'm sure that it doesn't." Scott was still keeping his voice low and calm, but Nick could feel his heart begin to hammer anyway.

"Theo and Eddie only encountered it very briefly," Scott continued. "Most likely, it was just in passing. I only smelled it on their hands. It was just an imp, though. They're really no threat at all. At least not to me, anyway. I'd have no trouble handling an imp and making sure it didn't hurt you. Any of you. Also, this one seems to be particularly smelly, so I'm sure I'd know if it were very close. At least we have this warning. At least we've been given the chance to get out without a confrontation."

"I've brought this to them." Nick shook his head. "I've put them right into harm's way."

"I can go, Nick," Scott said. "I can disappear for tonight. I can leave right now. You could tell them—"

"Please don't leave me, Scott." Nick looked up at him suddenly.

"Nick..." Scott took a deep breath and knitted his brow. "Not unless you want me to. I will never leave you, unless it's what you ask."

Nick sighed.

"I know you're a little frightened," Scott said, "but there's nothing more to be done. We're going to be fine. All of us. You haven't put anyone in harm's way."

"I'm having a little trouble believing that."

"We'll work this out."

"I would die if you went away." Nick stepped closer so that he could speak only for Scott's ears. "At the same time, I'm afraid of what that means. I'm a little afraid now, I think, because I need you."

"Don't give up, Nick. We can't submit to whim. We need to decide together what's going to happen."

"I can tell you that," Nick said, chuckling. "We're gonna get the fuck out o' here, that's what's gonna happen."

"Yes." Scott smiled. "But no matter what follows, don't submit to whim. Don't sit back and expect fate to mold your life. You have choices, and I expect you to see them."

"It's just..." Nick shook his head, pursing his lips and shutting his eyes. "Can you tell me that I'm not an idiot?" He opened his eyes and looked into Scott's. "Can you prove to me that up isn't down, and right isn't wrong, and that I didn't completely lose my sanity a week ago?"

"Stop clinging to what you think you know." Scott sighed. "Trust yourself and see what's really in front of you, not what others have said that you should see."

"What if I can't tell the difference?"

"Then we're all in a shit-load of trouble."

†

"No one's seen him." Matt's voice came through the intercom from the upstairs VIP room. "All the exit alarms have been on all day, except the north alley doors, but they were only open long enough so that Andrew could get the trash out this morning, and he said Max locked the alarm back on before noon."

"He's got to be here somewhere." Karen put her face in her hand again. This was really pissing her off. She considered dismissing the whole thing; it could have been a case of mistaken identity, but that would've been a cheap and ultimately fragile relief.   Troy knew who Gil was, and Troy wasn't at all fucked up.   No, Gil had gotten inside the club.   Somehow, he'd slipped in right under her nose.   She wanted to wring the little fucker's neck herself.

"Matty, baby, do me a favor," she said, closing her eyes against the sobriety that was slowly creeping over her.   She wanted to send it away, to rip upstairs, tap out a line of bliss on her desk, and suck a better mood up her nose through a straw.   But she knew she had to handle this before she could indulge and leave Matt in charge of the club.   Also, that wasn't her style.   Drugs were never an escape for her.   She always promised herself she'd never use them that way.   "Just sweep the dance floor one more time, along with the back bar and the downstairs room.   I know it's a pain in the ass, but I'd really appreciate it."

"That's cool," Matt said.   "We'll check as many times as you want, pretty lady.   I don't know what happened, but if he's in here, we'll find him."

"Have I told you today what a pack of sugar you are?   Because if I haven't, let me just say now that you're sweeter than a bon-bon."

"I've still got two guys stationed on each floor at each stairway, so we'll start another sweep as soon as I secure the upstairs.   I'm gonna lock-up this room.   That all right?"

"You're so proactive.   I love that in a stud."

Matt chuckled.   "You're even cool under pressure.   You know, if I were a breeder, I'd be all over you."

"Okay, my heart just skipped a beat."   She smiled.   "You know better than to do that to me."

"I'll see you in a few."

"Thanks, doll."

She hung up and placed the phone back on the lower shelf.   When she stood up, Gil was standing in front of the counter, looking at her with a smirk and a twinkle in his not-quite-brown eyes.   She tried to stifle her scream, but was unable to stop an initial high pitched squeal.

"Ooh, did I scare you?" he crooned.   "I'm sorry."

"Gil."   She managed to breathe out his name, but that was all.   Her heart was in her throat, blocking any further communication.

"I'm on my way home," Gil chimed.   "I just wanted to stop before I left and say 'thanks.'"

Karen could only hold her fingers over her mouth and try to get control of her breathing.   She was alone at the counter, since she'd sent most of the guys to sweep the club.   Only Bobby remained, and he was outside holding the line until she gave him word to start letting people in again.

"Laura called me this afternoon," Gil went on. "I just want you to know that you don't have to worry for another second about the New Years promotion bash. It'll be sweet. Sweeter than a bon-bon."

"I'm sure," she said, trying to figure out how much of her conversation the little fucker could have heard. He might have been crouching in front of the counter to eavesdrop on her, which wouldn't have been a surprise, but she was sure she'd have seen him coming down the hall. Putting that aside for the moment, she tried to remember if she'd left her purse in the office and if her pepper spray was still inside it.

"Now," said Gil, drumming his fingers on the counter, "although I'm really very happy with this new arrangement, Laura did say something else that I didn't quite understand."

"Oh?" Karen raised her eyebrows and tried to look like she cared. Then she stopped, wondering why she even bothered.

"Yes." Gil smirked. "She said that you and Max asked that I didn't come out to the club for a while, which, of course, just didn't make any sense to me." He folded his arms and leaned onto the counter toward her. "You didn't say anything like that, did you, Karen? She must have misunderstood you, don't you think?"

"Um…" Karen took a step back and tried to glance at the lower shelves while she was thinking of something to say. "Actually, Gil—"

"You must have said that you thought I'd be too busy to help her here at the club for a while. Now, see, that would have made much more sense, but Laura still insisted you'd said you didn't want me around at all. What do you make of that?"

There was nothing on the shelves under the counter but the telephone and a box of membership forms. She'd left her purse upstairs. Oh, crap, she'd sent all the bouncers into the club to look for this walking booger, her pepper spray was locked up in the motherfucking office, and now she had to think of something to tell the booger to get him to go away.

Why hadn't she taken tae kwon do? She could have taken tae kwon do instead of that frickin' advanced accounting course. Since she'd gotten her degree, she'd never once, not for a blue-fucking-second, needed to use a single shred of the shit she'd learned in motherfrickin' advanced accounting, but now she was going to be assaulted by this detestable little elf and all she could do to defend herself was toss a plastic telephone at him.

Why were her palms sweating? Heck, she had to outweigh Gil by twenty-five pounds at least. Why was her heart beating so fast? She'd stood-up to guys three times his size. Why didn't she just step around the counter and dropkick the little gerbil down the street? Before she knew what she was doing, she put her hands onto the counter and smiled.

"Gil, honey," she said, hoping she wasn't talking through her teeth, "I'll call Laura. Of course there was a misunderstanding. She and I both consumed quite a few rum and cokes while we were discussing this. In fact, I don't remember half the conversation." She giggled nervously, thinking the whole time that she couldn't believe what she'd just said.

Gil grinned. "I thought it must have been something like that."

"Of course it was," she said, feeling a little sick. "You're more than welcome here. Though, I'm sure you really will be pretty busy with Lauren's party, don't you think?"

"Speaking of..." He glanced at the countertop, where he drummed his elfin fingers some more. "I spoke with Ms. Isseroff before I came over."

"How is she?" Karen smiled. Although it made a little voice in her head scream in alarm, she forced herself to reach under the counter and take hold of the telephone's handset. If she had to, maybe she could get in a good whack before he could reach her. That would do the trick. His skull probably wasn't very thick. It was only the size of a cantaloupe, for cryin' out loud.

But why would he try and get to her? He wasn't threatening her, wasn't saying or doing anything that could be viewed as hostile, aside from the maybe/maybe-not trespassing shit. Karen felt threatened anyway.

"Fine, fine." The smelly little leprechaun smiled back. "She's very pleased with all this. Not that she doesn't trust Laura, or you for that matter, but it makes her feel much more comfortable that the two of you are going to concentrate on the main party, New Year's Eve, here at the club, exclusively."

"Well, I'm glad." Karen smiled again. Smiles all around. Smile, smile, smile. Everything was hunky-dory. So why was she gripping the base of the handset and wishing it was a baseball bat? Why was she hoping the cord wasn't twisted so much that she wouldn't be able to pull it out quickly? Well, she thought, she'd hate for Gil to pull away and miss having his teeth knocked down his throat. She shivered at herself.

Gil stared at her but he wasn't smiling anymore, which was good. Smiling made him look like the Happy Dwarf from Hell. He exhaled heavily out through his nose, but Karen thought she could still smell his breath, a sour and rotten smell, like wet clothes left in a hamper for a week. She wondered, not for the first time, why she seemed to be the only one who thought Gil always smelled like he'd just crawled out of a dumpster?

"You're busy tonight, I know," he said. "I'm going to go and get out of your way. Though..." He looked around as if just now noticing they were alone in the hallway. "I'm surprised that you don't have more help down here with you."

Karen had the sneaking suspicion that Gil was baiting her. He knew exactly where all the guys were, and he just wanted to get her to make-up another story for him, something about why she was at the counter all alone, perhaps. He knew she'd told Laura to keep him out of the club, so he showed up for just this purpose; Gil wanted Karen to stand there in front of him and eagerly eat her dignity. He wanted to see if she'd squirm. He wanted to stand in front of her and make her dance. Gil knew everything, and suddenly Karen was certain of it. He wanted to make her dance for him and, fuck-it-all, she hadn't disappointed him, had she?

Karen was utterly disgusted with herself. She should just tell Gil to get the fuck out of her club and go suck himself. What was he gonna do? The strongest thing about him was his breath.

She had a firm grip on the telephone handset beneath the counter, and all she wanted to do was whip it out and bash him one across that smirking little jaw of his. She wanted to crack his head open, even though he wasn't really threatening her, even though all she had to do was scream and Bobby would run inside to help her, probably followed by enough muscular club regulars to challenge the entire World Wrestling Federation, even though all the rationalism at her command told her the elf was two seconds away from prancing out the door on his own and she should just let him go.

Karen swallowed, smiled, and shrugged. "I can handle anything that comes through those doors."

"I'm sure you can," Gil whispered, smirking some more. "I'm sure you can."

He gave her another few seconds to change her mind and assault him with her communication equipment, but she held her smile, stared right back, and let him step away, unbruised, and with all of his teeth.

He slapped the counter and nodded, sending Karen's stomach right up into her lungs. "Well, I guess I'm outta here," he bantered. "See ya. Wouldn't wanna be ya."

"Buh, bye," she said, completely through her clenched teeth. The telephone handset was covered with sweat from her hand, but she didn't loosen her grip.

Gil winked at her. The disturbing little piece of crap actually motherfucking winked at her!

He turned, pushed open the door, and left, still smiling, watching Karen over his shoulder, watching her squirm. Finally, the door swung shut and he was gone.

Karen stood there for several seconds, still gripping the handset, and willed herself not to cry.

†

"We should cruise up the coast for a while," Darren suggested. He'd just put his shirt back on and was waiting for the rest of them to put themselves together. "Maybe we could stop in Malibu for a bit."

"What about Venice?" Theo asked.

"I don't think Venice would be the best place to roll through this time of night," Darren answered. "Unless it's in a tank."

It wasn't even two o'clock and Darren was feeling quite a tug of anxiety. Why were they leaving already? Why was Nick acting like such a freak? Scott seemed fine. He wasn't messed-up at all. At least he wasn't showing any of the normal signs of being all that messed-up. He seemed wide awake, alert, certainly cognitive, even articulate.

The club was thriving all around them. Darren knew damn well from plenty of personal experience that they were probably going to walk outside and see there was still a line down the block. If there was a line down the damn block when they walked outside, Darren knew he was going to have to take some very deep breaths to help him try to keep from becoming visibly agitated.

Why the holy hell were they walking away from this great party? Something was going on. Something was in the air and everyone was out to enjoy it. Everyone was rushing to get together, to see and be seen, to find the source, to gather together and satisfy whatever craving was sweeping the night.

Everyone but them. They were leaving. They were adjusting their shirts and heading back out of the club, when instead, they should be dropping their second hits of ecstasy, pressing through to the dance floor, and, on the way, tossing their t-shirts in the trash.

He would have let them go without him. Darren would have given

Theo and Eddie a hug, maybe even kissed Scott and Nick on the cheek, let them all leave with a wave and a little white lie, something about not staying much longer, something about being home before the sun came up. He would have let them go, let them leave this unexpectedly radiant night behind and wander out to do who-fucking-knew what, except that there was something up with Nick.

There was something wrong with Nick, and for the second time in less than a week, Darren had a strong feeling that he needed to be with him. He'd taken Nick's hand to apologize for jumping on him. He'd taken Nick's hand, and Nick had been trembling.

The music rolled through the hall leading to the front entrance, tantalizing him, pleading with him not to go.

Darren turned to lead them all out and, once again, took Nick by the hand. They pressed through the final clique of partiers and headed down the darkened hall.

Nick was still shaking.

†

After a few very breathless moments and counting to ten several times, Karen turned to the wall mirror behind her to make sure there weren't any tears forming. Aside from a serious natural blush, she'd succeeded in keeping her face from giving away her lapse of control. The instant the door closed behind Gil, she'd been overwhelmed with such a wave of relief that she almost sobbed aloud. It felt positively childish in its intensity.

Although nearly overwhelming, the feeling had been very brief, and was almost instantly replaced, first by surprise, then confusion, and finally anger. The putrid runt had somehow terrified her, which was just about the most ridiculous notion Karen had ever had, and now she was livid. Why the fuck had she been so afraid of that talking action figure?

She reached underneath the counter and brought the phone up. Maybe one of the bartenders in the back bar could run out and grab Matt for her. She had to wipe the sweat from her hand before she dialed.

"Hey, baby!" a man yelled from down the corridor.

This time she did scream. She wailed a hearty blast of fear, threw her hands into the air, knocked the telephone over the other side of the counter, and then screamed again.

"Oh, my god, Karen!" Darren was walking briskly down the entrance hall, Nick in tow, followed by a guy who she assumed was

Nick's cousin, then Theo and Eddie.

Theo and Eddie were laughing.

"You pricks!" she yelled at them, trying to stifle a nervous smile. "That was not funny! Darren Ryan Jacobson, you scared the shit out of me!"

"I'm sorry!" He stepped up to the counter, let go of Nick's hand, reached over and took hers. "I didn't mean to."

"That's okay." She sighed.

Theo and Eddie were howling.

"You two can shut up at any time." Karen leveled a very serious glare at them. They both did their best to comply, but Eddie kept snorting.

"Karen, you really should switch to decaf," Theo said. Eddie snorted.

She just smiled at him, sure that her heart was pounding so hard her tits were shaking.

"Are you all right?" Nick asked. "Where's Matt?"

"I'm fine, sweetness, thanks." She cocked another glare at Theo. "It's nice to have someone, who actually cares, show a little concern."

Theo leaned over and mock whispered to Eddie, "Ooh, she's gonna get all bitchy now." Eddie snorted some more.

"Darren, darling," Karen said, wiping hair out of her face, "would you hand me the phone? It fell over the counter."

He picked up the phone and put it on the counter. It was in several pieces.

"There're some more bits of it over here," Darren said, staring at the floor.

"Oh, god!" Karen whined. "That's all I need tonight!"

"What's wrong?"

"I've gotta go find Matt. He's sweeping the club with most of the guys. They're trying to find some freak that slipped inside."

"I'll go get Matt for you," Theo squeaked, apparently trying to get back into her good graces.

"We can't!" Nick looked around at him sharply. "We've gotta go."

"You're leaving?" Karen looked at Darren in disbelief.

He blinked rapidly, smiled, and nodded at her.

"Are you sick?" She blinked right back.

"Scott is," Nick offered. "A little."

"Hi." Scott smiled and waved.

"Oh, so you're the gorgeous cousin." Karen leaned on her elbows toward him. "I'm Karen Alanson. I guess you and I are related, since

I'm all of these guys' mommy."

Scott beamed the most precious smile and chuckled. "Well, it's very easy to see where they get their good looks."

"Oh, lord help me, you're beautiful *and* charming."

"Don't forget rich," Theo added.

Karen sighed. "I wish, *oh* how I wish, that I could get to know you better right now, but I'm in the middle of some minor crisis-management and I've got to run upstairs."

"Another time, then." Scott smiled again.

"I can just run and do it really quickly, Karen," Theo said again. Nick shot him an irritated look.

"Thank you ever so... but that's not necessary, baby," she said. "I want to stop in the office for a couple minutes anyway. I'll get him."

"I'm sorry, Karen." Nick shook his head. "Maybe you could stop by the apartment tomorrow?"

"Sweetness, sweetness, don't worry about it! Go take care of your cousin. Though, honey, you actually look a little pale yourself."

"Sorry about scaring you," Darren said.

"You know what," Karen said, switching to her Helpless-Little-Girl voice, "you *could* do me a little favor, Nicky."

"What's that?"

"You could let Theo and Eddie watch the door while I run upstairs for a minute. The rest of you could go get your car and I'm sure I'll be back by the time you're out front."

"I'm sure that's a big fat lie," Nick said with a smile, "but I guess it's fine if we wait for a bit in the car. We came in a limo."

"I heard," she said. "Did someone get married?" She looked at Darren, who rolled his eyes.

"I'm gonna go find the car." Nick pulled away and started toward the door.

"Jeez, antsy-pants!" Darren looked at him in surprise.

"Darren, I'm just going to get the car," Nick said, opening the door. "I'll be right out front with it in just a minute."

"I'll go with him," Scott said, and before Darren could say another word, they were gone.

He turned to Karen and sighed. "I think Nick's on crack."

She laughed. "Baby, aren't we all?"

"You sure you don't want me to go upstairs?" Theo asked, yet again.

"Honey," Karen said, putting her hands on her hips, "I told you I have to stop in the office for a minute."

"I *knooow*," Theo whined, raising his eyebrows several times to indicate he was sending her a psychic message.

"Ooh! I want some too!" Eddie chirped.

Karen looked at Darren and sighed heavily, grinning.

"Take 'em." He smiled. "I'll wait here."

†

Nick walked briskly past the long line of well dressed, aspiring club patrons, who looked at him like he'd lost his mind. He barely noticed them, or looked up when someone called his name from the line.

"Hey, Nicky!"

He waved, although he didn't know to whom. Bobby had told them that the limousine driver took the car down two blocks past the gas station, since the lots that were closer to the club couldn't accommodate it.

"Would you feel better if we ran?" Scott smiled at him.

Nick let out a deep breath and almost smiled himself. He was feeling better just being out of the club.

"Don't tease me," he said.

"Everything's going to be all right, Nick."

"What would've happened if it found you? If that imp, whatever, found you? You're sure it couldn't have hurt you?"

Scott laughed hard.

"What?" Nick smiled. "I don't fucking know! You never said you were 'mighty,' remember?"

Scott was still grinning. "Yes, of course. Though, I never said that I wasn't, either."

Nick stopped. "Okay, wait a minute—"

"Don't you know him?" Scott was looking down the street.

Nick followed his gaze.

"Yeah," he said. "That's Troy, our pharmacist. He's the tall one leaning against the Lexus."

"Who's he yelling at?"

"That Really Short Guy."

"Yes, the shorter one. Who is that?"

"No." Nick giggled. "That's what we call him, 'That Really Short Guy.' He's just some dork that nobody likes. I don't know his real name."

"Nobody likes him because he's short?" Scott asked, looking puzzled.

"No, no, no." Nick shook his head. "Nobody likes him because he's an asshole."

Another block or so past where Troy was standing, Nick could see the front end of the limo sticking out from behind the building.

"Come on," he said, starting down the sidewalk again. "I'll introduce you to Troy."

"Nick—"

"Hey, Troy baby!" Nick yelled, smiling, picking up his pace. Troy looked up and seemed genuinely pleased to see him.

"Well, well, the wayward Nicholas Reynolds." Troy smiled. "Are you looking for a place to puke?"

"Shut up!" Nick smiled. He closed the gap between them and gave Troy a generous hug. "Are you two breaking up? You were getting kind of heated there."

"Nick!" Scott said again from somewhere behind him, more urgently.

"No, Gil and I were just finishing up." Troy threw a nasty look at the shorter man. "Weren't we Gil?"

"Hi." Nick nodded at Gil, who extended his hand.

"Nicholas!" Scott screamed.

"Why is your friend waiting all the way over there?" Troy asked.

Nick followed his gaze back up the street, where Scott was standing, about half a block from them, at the same time extending his hand out of habit.

In a fraction of an instant, Nick understood. He understood why Scott had asked about the shorter man talking with Troy, why he hadn't come the rest of the way down the street with him, why he looked so upset. Though, it was the next instant that really mattered. That was when Gil shook Nick's hand.

The first time Nick had snorted Special K was at a gay pride party in San Diego. He was already very well acquainted with Missy, and Darren figured it was all right for them to play with a compound that was reputedly very complementary to her. Nick had swooned with joy just a couple of minutes after handing the bullet back to Darren, and it almost felt like the dance floor was dropping out from underneath him and all his bearing seemed to be draining away with it. He'd grasped Darren around the neck, resting his head on his shoulder, the only solid object around, it had seemed. They both had laughed, not missing a beat, somehow swaying together with the music and the rest of the dancing crowd.

Now, standing on this Hollywood street corner, his hand clasped by this shorter man he didn't know, Nick felt his bearings drain away again. This time, though, it was not a pleasant rush. It was a sickening pull that tugged painfully at the back of his eyes, the joint of his jaw, and the whole of his throat. It pulled at him and crawled through his head like ants in a rotted melon.

Suddenly, this sickening feeling, this pressing, draining ache, leapt up through his face and popped from his forehead. He cried out and staggered back.

He could feel Troy's car behind him, and thought he could hear him talking. Though, he couldn't make out what he was saying. In fact, he could barely see or hear anything at all and thumped down on the hood of the car with a creaking thud. Feeling almost like he'd inhaled an enormous amount of nitrate, he reached back with one hand, trying to steady himself and to keep from falling completely back onto the hood.

His vision was clearing, he was beginning to feel the curb beneath his feet. A soft, less violent throb pushed on the back of his eyes, and his throat felt incredibly dry, as though he'd swallowed a swatch of felt. He began to cough.

"Nicky!" Troy was patting him on the back. "Nicky are you okay? Nicky get the fuck off my car."

"What happened?"

"Crap if I know. Can you get off of my car?"

Nick stood up. The wooziness wasn't too bad and he only needed to take a step or two to keep his balance.

"Who was that?" Troy asked. "Was that your cousin? He's cute."

"Um, yeah, that's Scott, my cousin. Where is he?"

"He took off. He ran up the street after Gil. I think they went around the corner down past the video store."

"They what?" Nick looked up at Troy, who was a little fuzzy, but otherwise recognizable.

"Man, I don't know. Gil took one look at him and ran down the street. He's pretty fast for having those puny legs. Your cousin's no slow-poke, though. He took off after him like one of Charlie's Angels."

"Oh, my god, they ran down the street?"

"Hey, Nick, I don't blame him. I don't know how your cousin knows Gil, but I hope he kicks his ass. I wish the little coward hadn't run, I would've liked to see—"

"Did they go east when they turned past the video store?"

"Um… they went that way." Troy pointed and swooped his arm to indicate a left-hand turn. "Whatever way that is."

"Thanks." Nick patted him on the chest and took off after them.

"No problem."

Nick stopped after a few feet and turned back to Troy. "Oh god, Troy, can you do me a huge favor?"

"Nick, I have asthma and I—"

"No, no! Troy, would you please, please just pop your head inside the door to the club and tell Darren that we'll be right back? He's right there at the counter. Please?"

"Nicky, really, I don't think your cousin will have much trouble with Gil at all. You probably don't need to—"

"Thanks, Troy!" Nick waved, turned, and took off.

CHAPTER VI

†

Wings

The first was like a lion, and had eagle's wings: I beheld till the wings therefore were plucked, and it was lifted up from the earth, and made stand upon the feet as a man, and a man's heart was given to it.

- Daniel 7:4 (KJV)

Los Angeles, California
Headed east on Waring Avenue,
between McCadden Place and Las Palmas Avenue

†

The streets were dark. It was after two o'clock in the morning. Traffic was certainly sparse, especially on the residential streets within the neighborhood of small apartment buildings behind the club.

Nick jogged at a moderate pace, trying not to make too much noise. He wanted to be able to hear any unusual activity, such as a couple of guys running around — or killing each other.

He couldn't see very much. The streetlamps looked to him to be a little on the dim side. It was funny because every time he could remember sneaking out from the club to the car with Darren, on the nights they'd parked on these same streets, to either indulge in a bump or two of something scandalous, or to scandalously indulge in each other, the streetlamps seemed to shine down on them like set lighting. Funny they should seem so dim now.

He stopped jogging and stood panting a little, trying to listen carefully to the night around him. There were no sounds besides the buzz of the meager traffic along the main street three blocks behind him, and the faint thudding of the music from the club. The local residents probably loved that.

It was a warm night. Nick was reminded again, by the silence and the shadows, of the time he'd spent in an alley not far away, just a few days ago, listening to a voice from the darkness. Alone again, in the suspended hours of the morning, he stood just listening now to the sound of his own breathing and nervous thoughts.

He considered turning around. He thought about going back because, this time, he was painfully aware that there was a demon or two somewhere in the dark.

Nick's head was still swimming and an eastward breeze sent tingles across his ecstasy-sensitive skin. Resting against the corner of a short brick wall surrounding a small apartment building, he rubbed the back of his arms and gazed at the sidewalk, trying to focus his hearing, trying to pick up any clue as to the direction Scott had chased That Really Short Guy.

When, or if, he found them, he had no idea what he was planning to do. Probably nothing. What could he do? Pray?

Despite the brief temptation, Nick didn't turn around and go back. What was important was that he found Scott. Whatever was going to happen, he wanted to be with Scott. He needed to find him.

Of all the stupid things to do, shaking that guy's hand, not paying enough attention to even notice that Scott wasn't walking next to him anymore, two minutes after he'd practically dragged the guys out of the club for fear of bumping into whatever-it-was that Theo and Eddie had encountered. The exact whatever-it-was to which, he assumed, he'd extended his open hand like the King of the Brainless Dorks. All of it was frosting on what he considered his recently idiotic behavior.

Taking Scott completely at his word, and absolving him of any blame for this situation, meant laying it all on Nick. *Hey guys, let's go out to a demon hangout and take so many drugs we forget our names! That'd be cool!*

Yeah, he sure was the group's nurturing matriarch. Uh huh. Sure. *Bet me. Bet me that you're not blind as a bat.*

Still, Nick had tried to talk Scott out of going into the club in the first place. Once he learned that his favorite night-spot was also, very likely, an attractive playground for demons, Nick did attempt to avoid it. He reminded himself that it was Scott who'd said it was for some reason important they go inside for a while. He'd said there was a lot at stake, whatever that meant.

An urgent grunt echoed between the apartment buildings a few yards ahead of him. Nick couldn't tell exactly from where it had come, and was still staring stupidly across the expanse of parked cars and tiny urban lawns, when a motorcycle flew out from between two of the apartment buildings. It was literally flying, swiftly and silently, in a mild arch about fifteen feet over the street. It landed securely in the lower branches of an enormous pine tree just beyond the opposite sidewalk.

The creaking branches and ruffled leaves of the pine tree made a substantial ruckus, but nothing compared to the noise that would have come had the motorcycle landed on the street, or on a car, or slammed into the building instead. It looked like it was a Ninja, red and yellow, and in very good shape. Well, until it landed in the tree.

Once the branches had settled and no longer creaked with the weight of the motorbike, Nick distinctly heard the sound of running feet.

Racing up the sidewalk, he turned down a smaller street in the direction from which he guessed the projectile motorbike had come. In spite of the apprehension of the moment, Nick indulged in a grin, as he imagined the look on the face of the motorcycle's owner when he eventually discovered it. That was life, Nick shrugged; kids threw rocks at each other, demons threw motor vehicles.

He turned the corner. The little street on which he found himself seemed even darker. It was relatively short; after a single block, separated only by a thin alley, it dead-ended into a high brick wall separating the neighborhood from an industrial district.

Nick stopped when he saw that the street was empty. He listened for another moment and heard the patter of distant running to the east. It was echoing between the apartment buildings.

Great. More alleys.

Steadying his nerves and letting out a heavy sigh—nearly making him laugh, considering he thought he sounded just like the huffy demon he was chasing—Nick took off at a mild jog toward the eastward entrance of the alley. He didn't want to run too fast; whatever trouble he was getting himself into this time, he wanted to at least keep from slamming into it blindly.

The alley was very long and narrow, allowing just enough space for a single car to travel between the backs of the apartment buildings or maneuver into one of the oil-stained carports. He tried to jog quietly past the darkened windows and tiny cement porches, but he was wearing somewhat heavy, leather boots. Nick's boots were really designed more for achieving a look of what was commonly thought of as 'metropolitan masculinity,' than for anything even remotely functional, such as stealth.

The sounds of distant running had stopped, but Nick kept his pace.

After glancing in both directions upon reaching the next cross-street, he continued in the same direction down the alley through the following block. He passed through another almost indistinguishable alley and came to the next block, where he stopped, caught his breath, and listened intently.

He didn't hear anything.

When he got to the next block, through yet another lovely little low-rent apartment alley, he stopped again, realizing that the running demons must have turned down one of the residential streets. If they hadn't, he'd probably have at least seen them at a distance.

However, which way to go was a total mystery. The only route that really made any sense to him at all was back in the opposite direction, where he could wait for Scott to show up at the club. He glanced back through the thin alleys in the direction he'd come and considered retreat again.

He decided not to go back just yet. He'd listen for another minute or two, and if he didn't hear anything, then he'd head back.

Darren was probably fuming. Hopefully, Troy had told him what happened—or at least what he *thought* had happened—and Darren would know to just stay put. It would piss him off, sure, but if he had at least half the sense God gave grass, and Nick knew he did, then he'd settle everyone in either the car or at the front door, and wait for a little while. That's what Nick hoped Darren would do, in any event.

Of course, they'd need to have a very good explanation when Nick and Scott finally got back. They'd have to come up with a hell of a story to talk Darren back down from his temper. Though, Nick wasn't worried; Scott had proven to be pretty creative in that department.

A noise to the north caught his attention and he turned his head in time to see a cat, or a very big rat, running across the street and then up into a tree. Maybe something had scared it. Maybe there was something going on down there. Maybe there was another cat up in the tree. Maybe Nick was standing there like a doofus trying to figure out the motivation of someone's wayward pussy.

For lack of any other clues, Nick cautiously jogged to the other side of the street, from where the cat had come, and slowly up the sidewalk to investigate.

Everything was deathly quiet. He could no longer hear the sounds of traffic or even the faintest whisper of music from the club. Every few seconds, a light breeze rustled the neighborhood shrubs and trees, which only seemed to accent the silence underneath it.

You'd think the sound of a motorcycle landing in a tree would have disturbed someone.   Although, in these tiny, low-rent, Hollywood apartments, who knew what kind of sounds to which the locals were accustomed, and therefore ignored, and through which they made a habit of sleeping?

What Nick heard next wasn't the sound of footsteps, or the distant engine of a car.   What he heard was the flapping of a heavy tarp, a dimly familiar sound, echoing between the buildings.   Then, from the same general direction, a very low growl, a harsh rolling sound.   It was the rumble of warning from the throat of a very big animal.   Not a dog, though.   Nothing even remotely domestic.   It was a lumbering feline purr, menacing and enormous, echoing against the brick and plaster of the quiet apartments.

Not turning back when he'd last considered it now loomed as mistake number three.   The first of course being when he allowed what he assumed was the imp to touch him, the second when he sprinted into the night thinking he'd overtake Scott and say, *Hey, don't bother with that That Really Short Imp Guy.   Let's go snort cocaine in the limousine!*

The sound came again, unmistakably real and undeniably near, although the echoing made determining an actual location close to impossible.   Whatever it was could have been very, very close, maybe watching him, maybe chuckling at this fool who was standing vulnerably in the middle of the street like a retarded gazelle.

He could scream.   The thought flashed into his head like a beacon. Nick could scream like a woman and wake up every mortal soul within a three-mile radius.   The widows all around him would suddenly flood with light, dogs would bark, doors would open, maybe sirens would sing in the distance as the squad cars charged to his rescue.

Sure, he'd have to explain what he was doing, standing alone on a quiet street at two-thirty in the morning screaming his head off like a prissy little girl, but that was no big deal.   He was just chasing imps and demons through the neighborhood.

What the fuck is an imp? the police would ask.

It's like a gremlin, you idiot.   Duh.

A tox-screen would only find two hits of ecstasy and God-knows-how-much GHB in his system.   He'd be out on bail by Tuesday. Wednesday at the latest.

Nick crept across a tiny lawn into a quiet shadow to listen some more, out of the open, where he might be able to get his bearings and think things over without worrying about something sneaking up on him from behind.

He pressed his back against the cool wall of the building, nestled in the corner made by the chimney, and stared blankly at the empty street. He listened and listened but didn't hear a thing. He didn't hear any traffic, any breeze, any wayward kittens, any flying motorcycles, or enormous growling monsters. He was alone, fucked up, and feeling exceptionally stupid, which was only aggravated by that particular feeling's familiarity.

Was this really even happening? Maybe he was still lying against the painted brick wall of the side alley, out cold on the hard and filthy pavement, covered with his own blood and bile, hallucinating a dark-haired savior, imagining a fallen angel rescuing him from his barely reasoned suicide. Maybe Nick was merely lost in the grand and beautiful delusion of his life going on.

Maybe the past week hadn't happened at all. Maybe he was dead. Maybe the slow preamble to the realities of demons was only someone's attempt at an easy introduction into Hell.

Nick thought of Darren, and was enraged by the realization that he wasn't sure if Darren would be waiting for him if he went back. He didn't know for sure whether the man who supposedly loved him so much would have put his evening of fun on hold. He didn't know if, instead of waiting patiently, Darren would have bellowed in anger, barked instructions to the driver to take them all away, take them someplace else, and leave Nick to his fate.

No, he did know. Theo told him that Darren had swept the club the previous week, just like he'd said. He'd given Troy a very hard time and pressed all their friends into the search for him.

Nick realized he did know what Darren was doing. He was waiting for him. He was waiting in the idling limousine with his two closest friends, and they were probably worried sick. He was waiting for him while Nick dashed off into the darkness after Scott.

Why had Nick dashed off after Scott?

You have choices, and I expect you to see them.

Nick suddenly ran. He burst from his hiding place and crossed the street in an all-out sprint. He didn't care anymore if his footfalls made any noise. He didn't care if he heard the rustling of demons around him. He didn't listen for the growl of an angry animal that might have bounded from its own hiding place and was right behind him. Suddenly, he no longer completely believed those things were at all important.

He whipped back around the corner, into the alley out of which he'd come, and increased his speed. In the far, far distance, he could see what he thought was the place he'd first entered the alley. He'd make a right, jog to the main residential street, make a left, and oh my god, how the hell did he get this far into Who-The-Fuck-Knew-Land?

Before he made it halfway to the end of the first alley he fell. Aside from hitting the pavement with a sickening thud, and having the wind knocked out of him, Nick was unhurt. He laid there on his belly for a breathless moment while he listened for any sounds behind him. Though, thankfully, he heard nothing.

The wind had been completely knocked out of him, and when he tried to draw it back, it felt as though his lungs had flown right out after it. He choked as he struggled to draw breath and only managed a dry wheezing rasp.

It occurred to him again, laying there on the concrete, that his life seemed to be stuck in a time warp, playing out the same pattern over and over. Here he was, face down on the pavement, in the tiny hours of a Sunday morning, in another alley no less, and he'd probably ruined his second pair of Versace pants. Déjà vu, baby.

Nick tried again to breathe and gained just enough air to cough painfully. When he moved his arms to push himself up, a stinging at his elbows told him he may have donated some skin to the pavement.

He was thinking about the pavement, and how grateful he was that it hadn't been his face that made first contact with it, when he heard a soft footstep rustle some loose pebbles. He froze immediately and listened for another footstep, but none came. Instead, a hand grasped him behind the neck with incredible force, knocking him out of his frozen push-up position. It closed into a steel grip around the back of his head.

Lifted off the ground, Nick watched in stupid surprise as the asphalt fell away from him and he was pulled almost into a kneeling position and then dragged across the road.

He still couldn't breathe, and the pain in his neck was overwhelming his senses, but he heard the voice behind him distinctly.

"I've caught myself a bunny," the tiny voice whispered. "I caught myself a prize, scamperin' through the night. A big, clumsy bunny."

There was sweat running into Nick's eyes. He tried to shake his head but the grip on his neck was as solid as stone.

"Don't wiggle now," the voice warned. "Don't be squirming around and making any noise. You might be able to help me, but if it comes to it, I'll snap your neck like dried kindling, and hang your dead bunny carcass on a street sign. Maybe that'd slow him down. Maybe he'll stop and cry over you for a minute. Maybe I'll be able to get the fuck outta here while he's boo-hooin' over his dead bunny boyfriend."

An arm suddenly wrapped around Nick's torso and the grip on the back of his neck was mercifully released. The hand that had lifted him off the ground came around and covered his mouth instead, and he was pulled swiftly out of the light and into the black shadows between two buildings. He was held that way, his arms pinned and his head tight against the body of his abductor, his legs crumpled awkwardly against the ground, out of the florescent light of the alley, close to the mouth of the nook, where a view was possible.

The thought of attempting any kind of struggle didn't even have a chance to develop, as the arms and fingers holding him were unbelievably immobile, as though Nick had been trapped within the grasp of a statue.

He tried to breathe through his nose. Moving only his eyes to look down, Nick could just see the white skin and knotted knuckle of the hand that lay across his mouth. It looked like the hand of a corpse. The skin was heavily wrinkled and textured, especially around the finger joints, and albino white, with a grayish, matted hue.

A distinct odor was coming from the flesh. Despite the strength in the hand, its surface seemed as that of skin filled with phlegm rather than blood. A sickly, moldy stink rose from it.

Nick's head was pulled closer to the mouth of the creature and he could feel its breath on the back of his ear as it whispered to him.

"I thought I was a goner for sure," it said. "I thought he'd caught me. As soon as I touched you, I thought it was over. Wow, you know, man, I thought I was done. Stick a fork in me, baby! I'm done!" The thing holding Nick stifled a whispered giggle. "Just keep quiet now, though. Let's figure all this out."

The thing slowly leaned toward the mouth of the nook, Nick and all, until it got a better view and could see there was no one coming. Then it slowly leaned back.

It had to be the short guy holding him, who, of course, had to be the imp. Nick's legs were bent in an awkward angle, his knees less than an inch above the ground.

He could feel his heart pounding like a hammer and his whole body tingled with the most basic of fear, rampant and overwhelming. There was no thought of escape, or of Scott or Darren, only this creature and what it would do to him.

"I think I might have hurt you a little," it said. "Not just now, when I tripped you, but back there with your skinny drug dealer, back on the main street, when you let me touch you. You shouldn't do that, you know. You humans these days are so fucking stupid the way you just let any old freak touch you."

It stopped for a moment, listening.

"When I realized who you were," it whispered, "phew, man, I had to rake through your mind so fuckin' fast! That probably hurt, I'm sure. Especially when I pulled out and took off. Did that hurt you? When I pulled out so fast? You're probably used to that sort of shit, though."

More stifled giggling, which actually sounded like the thing was gargling mucus.

Nick was utterly disgusted that it had been in his mind, seen his life, knew his secrets, felt his desires. He was humiliated and sickened.

"Of course," the putrid smelling little creep went on, "he was the first thing I saw. It just took a little digging to get all the particulars and stuff, that's all. Holy shit, you are one stupid fucker!"

The thing panted for a moment, calming itself, then wiped its nose on Nick's shoulder.

"I gotta hand it to her, man. She must have known." It belched, then blew a silent and rancid whistle into the air. Nick didn't think it was talking to him any longer.

"She had to have known," it whisper-gurgled. "She had to have known he was still here, which was why the funky snatch didn't shoot back to New York and go all chortling that I'd lost him. That's why she's trying to get rid of me. She wants him. She wants him!" The thing was sort of whisper-singing to itself.

A sound from the other end of the alley, a cracking twig or stick, silenced the thing. It held its breath. It turned its head back the other direction and stood there, not speaking or breathing, just listening to the night. There were no more sounds.

Although the night was slowly creeping toward morning, the light around them seemed to be fading. From where they stood in the tiny alley-nook, one of the streetlamps several yards away abruptly dimmed and went out.

"Ooh, Nelly..." the thing whistled timidly in Nick's ear in what he almost thought sounded like rising alarm. "Oh, man, fuck! He's comin', man."

Another streetlamp dimmed and expired, this one closer to them. Four streetlamps remained within view, but their illumination seemed pathetic. Perhaps it was their sudden isolation against the encroaching darkness.

The creature's grasp on Nick had loosened a bit. Nick turned his head slightly, and with a shifting of his eyes, was able to catch a glimpse of what was holding him.

Nick of course knew he was being held by a demon, even before he looked. He even knew, thanks to Scott's warning, that the sight of the creature might be a considerable shock. Seeing it, though, actually looking at the thing with the smell of it choking him, the sounds of its damp and oily voice hitting his ear like a spoken loogie, had an impact that was barely cushioned by his preparation.

Nick could completely understand how some might lose their minds. The boogieman had him. That's all there was to it.

Every child could sleep easily that night. Every kid in the world could impress his parents with his sudden and stable bravery by going quietly to bed and to sleep without insisting his father check the closet, swish a broom under the bed, or even allow the tiniest light to remain shining. There would be no noises in the dark, no faint and glowing eyes blinking within the crack of the open closet door, no grimy claws to pitch forth from beneath the bed at little feet just trying to scurry to the bathroom. The boogieman wasn't going to be there. Instead, he was standing in the narrow crevice between two apartment buildings in Los Angeles, holding Nick in his grimy claws and wiping the drip from his fetid nose onto Nick's shoulder.

Nick screamed, and although the sound was completely muffled by the hand on his mouth, the thing holding him instantly jolted Nick back into a firm grasp, its lips right at his ear.

"You'd really better shut the fuck up!" it said in a louder, breathy gurgle. "You are so close to being a dead bunny! In fact, it's amazing I haven't taken a bite out of you yet. But don't you for a second think I won't taste your living skin before I snap your little fag neck and toss you at him!"

Nick had seen a somewhat small creature, which was why his legs were pressed clumsily on the ground. The thing was covered with the same sickly white skin, stretched tightly over a bald head. Gray lines and wrinkles covered the skull like dead veins, though they pulsed with a putrid life. The ears were high and pointed, like the thin white ears of a bleached elf, and the thing's mouth was filled with nothing but slender and yellow teeth, pitching forth from dark gray gums into very sharp, cruel points. Just above its eyebrows, two thick horns sprang from the skull itself, the monster's thin white scalp puckering around the bases. The horns were very near stereotypical in their Hollywood-demonic formation, curving up from the slope of its forehead, one directly over each eye. They looked like brown and furrowed bone, cracked and wind worn, like the bark of a tree. The eyes of the imp were a glowing, golden orange, without the contrast of lashes or pupils. They were two tiny bulbs of fire beneath lids the color of ashen snow.

"He's coming," it whispered into Nick's ear, barely breathing the words. "Crap! Oh, crap! Oh, crap, oh, crap, oh, crap, oh, crap, oh, god, fuckin' crap!" it chanted, bouncing slightly with each 'oh crap.'

The night grew darker as the shadows crept toward them. Two more streetlamps dimmed, one immediately after the other, and then died in unison. As though shrinking in fear, the last two streetlamps dimmed into uselessness. Only the moon reflected off the plaster buildings and bits of glass in the gravel.

"I know you're here," the imp abruptly said to the air, no longer whispering, standing stone still, speaking in a soft, casual tone. "Do you know what I have in my arms? Can you smell his Tuscany? It's makin' me wanna barf."

Again, Nick heard the sound of a heavy tarp, this time being cracked angrily in the air. Indeed, a gust blew through the thin alley, carrying litter and a cloud of dirt.

"What would you give me for his life, Marbas?" the imp asked.

A low, rolling growl lumbered against the closed garage doors and echoed back and forth with its heavy menace.

"Or, should I call you 'Scotty?'" The imp giggled.

Nick stiffened within the grip of the creature.

"That's right, huh?" said the imp. "He didn't know your name, did he? Only that cute little sobriquet. Well there it is, Fallen One, oh, great bane of the Legions. Will you explain it to him now? Will you enlighten him to your title? 'Marbas the Black.' 'Marbas the Bringer of Night.' Will you set him on your back and fly him to the lands you've brought to ruin? Will you cuddle him when he cries at the sight of your power, this timid, clumsy little bunny-boyfriend of yours? Has he heard yet of the rotting death that comes with your touch? Have you described how the cities and the centuries saw piles and piles of bodies grow from your passing? Well, big guy, I just happen to know that you have not. Been holdin' back a bit, have ya?"

Soft footsteps disturbed the ground just around the corner from their nook, and looking up, Nick saw the light in the alley had been almost utterly obscured by a massive shadow. Each streetlamp was not only out, but gone completely.

"He has but to ask," came a voice in response. It was painfully familiar. Huge and dark, profound and resonant; it was Scott.

Though, it wasn't the voice Nick had heard throughout the week. It wasn't the voice that had just exposed to him the secrets of his soul on a crowded dance floor, or laughed with him in the quiet of his darkened living room. It was the voice from the alley. It was the resounding baritone that had assailed him from out of the darkness, out of the pitch that surrounded him while he lay semiconscious in the dirt. It was the voice of the darkness, the voice of Scott's true form.

It was the voice of Marbas. The voice of the demon.

"And I suppose he may ask at that," said the imp. "If he has the chance. If he leaves this place with the skin still on his face and not falling in pieces from between my teeth."

"You will not harm him," said Marbas.

"You're so confident. You think you're so keen, so clever, hiding right under our noses. Did you see her too? Did you smell her? Was it the bitch's stench that brought you back to our grasp?"

"You would be wise, imp, to concentrate on this instant, and not the lamia. I assure you, your issue with her has just now become the very least of your problems."

"This isn't a mannequin, Marbas!" The imp shook Nick slightly.

"Yes, yes, I see." Marbas sighed impatiently. "You have Nicholas. How very original and resourceful of you."

The imp hissed loudly.

"You have him for the moment," Marbas went on, "which is why I've granted you this brief audience. Though, don't mistake it as any guarantee you won't be bathing in flames before the sun rises."

"Oh, fuck off!" the imp spit through his clenched teeth. "We'll see who'll be facing the flames! They've been stoked for your flesh for centuries! We'll see who meets them first!"

The shadow completely covered the mouth of the alley where their view had been. A soft rustling sound drowned out all other noises and even the air stopped moving. There was no light at all to help Nick see anything and he couldn't even lift his face to find the moon or stars.

The shadow spoke. "Nicholas, don't be afraid."

The voice came from right in front of him, as if he should see the lips that spoke, but there was nothing there, except...

"Marbas…" The imp breathed the name in a trembling whisper.

There was light in the alley. There were two points that were four or five feet off the ground. They were blue and gently luminous, and they were getting closer.

Nick saw that they were eyes. They were Scott's eyes.

But they were too big. As they came closer he could see the dense blackness of the pupils within the familiar radiant blue, but could tell that they were too big and set too far apart to be human eyes. And the pupils weren't round. They were feline.

Shapes began to form before Nick as his own eyes adjusted to the near blackness. Shadows began to take contour and the darkness itself took on texture and outline. There was a familiar image emerging from the gloom.

Nick was stunned with a childish wonder. It was a lion. Huge and entirely black, black as blindness itself, it was stepping to the opening of the alley's fissure. Its head swayed and rustled a thunderous shroud of wavy mane that lifted over the creature's head and fell behind its face like the darkest clouds of a moving storm. The animal was enormous and closed-off the mouth of the fissure, which might have provided the imp with some small sense of security; the giant lion wasn't going to be able to charge into the nook to get him. It was just too massive.

Lifting his eyes, Nick could see that the tumultuous black mane wasn't what was blocking all the light and wind. There were wings behind it, wings Nick had seen before, stretching beyond his view, covering any glimpse of the sky between the corners of the buildings. They were as black as the lion, and featherless, great rising wings with stretched black leather for skin. They were like a dragon's wings, lithe and immense.

"Do you see me?" The blue eyes touched Nick, isolated him.

Nick nodded slightly in the imp's now lax grip.

"I'm so sorry," whispered Marbas.

The imp began to back down the other end of the tiny crevice between the apartment buildings, away from the great winged creature. He wasn't holding Nick as tightly, who could feel the almost bursting tension in the creature's movements as he was forced to back up with it.

"Marbas," it said, "you could have use of me. You could still have an advantage should you allow my tongue to remain living and within my head."

"Release him," Marbas grunted.

"You haven't taught him," the imp staggered. "He doesn't know anything yet. You'd have nothing to gain by destroying me."

"Are you all right?" Marbas looked at Nick, who nodded.

"I haven't hurt him," the imp offered. "I haven't bitten into him. If the lamia had taken him, if it had been her to have touched him, you know she'd already have torn the flesh from him like strings of cheese!"

"Imp, I am not in the practice of issuing a command twice."

"I am Gillulim. I'm no mere imp."

"I know who you are."

"And I do not serve the lamia —"

"I know who you serve."

"I will release the mortal, I will free him, but you must let me flee. You must allow me that!"

"Imp, I don't owe you anything. There is nothing that I *must* do. You would be wise to cease giving me orders."

"He's shaking with fear, you know. Your love is trembling in my hands and yet you'd deny me?"

"Nicholas." The blue eyes once again fixed on him. "The repugnant little creature that's holding you is Gillulim. He's rather large for an imp, though."

"I am the *king* of the —!"

"Shut up!" Marbas rumbled.

Gillulim stopped moving.

"He's really no more than an overgrown fairy," Marbas snorted.

"Hey!" Gillulim yelped. "Who's the fairy, you limp —?"

"Enough!" Marbas rumbled. "Remove your hand from his face, imp!"

"I am Gillulim! You will refer to me in the —"

"Gillulim, then. Remove your hand from his face and allow him to speak."

"That's better," said Gillulim, and moved his hand from Nick's face. Instead, he put it on Nick's shoulder and held him tightly.

"Scott?" Nick whispered to the dark.

"Yes." The lion bowed its head. "You see me as I am, Nicholas. I am Marbas."

"What's he doing?" Nick risked a glance behind him.

"Wasting his breath," said Marbas, as he fixed his gaze on the creature.

Gillulim's anger flashed through his grip on Nick, shaking him slightly. "You don't know everything, pussycat! Your arrogance is like a mountain! It will bring your ruin!"

"Ouch!" Nick yelped as Gillulim's nails pinched into him like needles.

"Ooh!" Gillulim exclaimed in surprise. "Sorry about that." He brushed at Nick's shoulder as if he would wipe away the punctures.

"I'm not hurting him, Marbas. I'm not hurting him!"

"Gillulim," said Marbas, "don't force me to—"

"Just wait a second there, champ!" Gillulim was panting. "You really need to hear me out. You really do! I've got somethin' you've just gotta hear. Now, I'd let go of your boy-toy here but—"

Marbas shook his head in frustration. He grimaced and then opened his eyes at the imp. Their illumination brightened for an instant. Then he issued a grumbling roar, very low, like the warning moans of an earthquake, and blew a growl into the alcove toward them. He tilted his head to his right, sending a wave of heat across the building's side, heat without flame. The paint on the wall rippled and blistered along its path.

Nick could feel the heat, even as the roar began, and ducked instinctively. Crouching as much as he could with Gillulim still holding him, he was able to avoid the projected heat, but felt it fly past him and singe the back of his neck a bit.

Gillulim had tried to crouch along with Nick. Though, he wasn't able to maneuver in the small space, and being the target, he couldn't avoid it. He was caught high on his chest, between his neck and shoulder, and thrown back against the wall to their right.

Gillulim cried out and clutched at his chest with his left hand, still grasping Nick's forearm with his right.

"You motherfucker!" he hissed. "That fucking hurt, Marbas! Knock it off!"

"I merely blew you a kiss, Gillulim," Marbas whispered. "Though, you're still holding him. What am I to do with you? Need you be consumed, shrieking in an inferno, before you will release him?"

Nick turned to the imp. "I think you should just let me go."

"Shut up." Gillulim jerked him around clumsily and held him as a shield. "You have to listen to me, Marbas!" he grumbled from behind Nick. "I'm tellin' you, dude! You don't know every-fuckin'-thing! Knock off the fire-breathing shit! You're pissin' me off!"

"Scott," Nick said. "I mean Marbas, whatever."

"Are you hurt?" The lion looked at him again. "Did I hurt you?"

"No, um, not really. I'm okay. You owe me a few neck hairs, maybe."

"See!" Gillulim hissed, still hiding behind Nick. "See, ya big pussy! You're fryin' the kid!"

"What's going on, Scott?" Nick asked.

"He thinks he knows something important, some information for which I'll withdraw and allow him to flee."

"You gotta listen, man!" Gillulim insisted. "I'm not fuckin' with ya! You and this girly-boy are neck deep, you flyin' shit-wad!"

"Do not fool yourself, Gillulim." Marbas sighed. It was heavy and deep. "You cannot stand against me. Even in your grasp, Nick is not in any danger. You know that. I am one of the Fallen. Even holding him, you know you have no power. Stand aside. Put Nicholas aside and face eternity with dignity. If you do not, I promise you will suffer first. You will suffer, deeply. Then you'll face eternity just the same."

"Do you think he really knows anything?" Nick asked, not anxious to see what the winged demon was planning to do to the imp. "Maybe he does know something."

"It doesn't matter." Marbas shook his head, the dense black mane billowing around him.

"Oh, crap, man!" Gillulim whined. "You're so full of it! You don't even know, man! I am not kidding! They're playin' you for a fool, Marbas! They're holdin' the hoops and you've been jumpin' through like a chump!"

"Would he lie?" Nick said. "Has he been lying?"

"I don't know what he's been telling you, but all the imp has said of me is true. I have been a source of darkness and a bringer of death."

Nick sighed. "You told me."

"It's much, much worse than I think you imagined. Much worse than I implied. I am no small force, Nicholas."

Nick nodded. "I think I knew that. I think I knew it, even as he said it."

"Oh, facial!" cried Gillulim. "He knows, winged one. He knows you're a terror! Your little love-fest is over, fallen one! He's on to you!"

"One is defined by one's actions," Nick said quietly to Marbas, ignoring the imp. "Didn't you tell me that?"

"Yes." The lion nodded.

"We're not that different, you and me?"

Marbas shook his head, the mane of black waves billowing behind him. "We're not."

"I haven't killed anyone or anything, but I'm not proud of my entire life."

Marbas nodded, grunting.

"Scotty… ?"

"Yes?"

"There's a lot more to these things you've done, isn't there? Somehow, I think that there's a lot more I should know before I decide whether or not you're really a terror. There's much more to all of this, isn't there?"

The giant, black lion simply closed his eyes and all was blackness. "Yes," he said.

Gillulim leaned against the wall. "Oh fuckin' spare me! I'm gonna hurl."

"You looked me in the eye last weekend," Nick said, "and you made a promise to me."

"And I will keep it," said Marbas, his great, blue eyes snapping open. "What would you have me do?"

Nick thought for a moment of all the things he could say.

Then, "Just take me home."

Gillulim gripped Nick from behind on both arms. "Wait a second!" he screamed.

Marbas lowered his head. "Look into my left eye, Nick."

Nick looked, and Marbas stamped his front left paw hard onto the concrete. Ripples in the air, just above the ground, shot across the pavement and slammed into Nick's feet. He felt nothing but an engulfing warmth, which flew like lightning up through his body and filled his lungs, his throat, and his head. He felt the power gather, surging in his torso. He threw back his head, overcome.

Gillulim cried out and seemed to be struggling to hang on to Nick. His hands were clasped tightly around Nick's biceps, sharp nails digging, but somehow no longer able to break the skin. Nick didn't really feel them.

Nick felt as though he was standing in a great wind, a hurricane, it seemed to him in fact; all other sounds were completely drowned out. Even the pressure from the imp's grasping claws was abruptly gone. Nick's vision was focused, clean, and he could see the great black lion clearly. It was watching him patiently. The wind that Nick felt wasn't made by the creature's giant wings. They remained folded and had not moved.

Somewhere there was a campfire. Nick could smell a roaring campfire, and the ocean. In a swoon, he was engulfed by an urgent ocean breeze as it swept across a late afternoon beach, the sand still warm from the day. He was utterly at home, utterly at ease, in the arms of all that was natural and right.

With a flex of his arms, the power snapped from Nick, through him, and exploded, sending the imp flying backward, several yards into the air, far out of the little niche between the buildings at its other end.

Instantly, Marbas extended his wings, snapped them once with a great, cannon-fire crack, and leapt straight up. Nick lost sight of him for a moment; the winged lion was impossibly fast. Nick glanced upward, spinning around, just in time to see Marbas bound off of the rooftop and rise into the night, vanishing in an instant against the blackness of the sky.

Looking down to the other end of the alcove, Nick saw Gillulim getting up off the ground. He was burnt and blackened on the left side of his chest, and holding his hands out in front of him, which appeared to have no skin on them at all, no more than a skeleton's fingers. He was very far away. He must have been thrown sixty or seventy feet.

Gillulim looked up suddenly, first directly at Nick, then at the empty view of the alley behind him.

From high above them came the sharp, cannon-shot snapping sound of the enormous wings as the demon circled back. Nick knew the imp would have to break and run or, in an instant, Marbas would be on him.

With a great grimace, the burnt, white imp drew-in a deep breath. Even across the distance, Nick could see an inferno glowing in its eyes. Gillulim drew back, then pitched his head forward with a horrible shriek.

Like with Marbas, Nick could feel the heat before it ever entered the alcove. Immediately he threw himself face-down onto the concrete. Even before he did, he could see the paint on the walls begin to blister, ripple, and crack, as the imp's breath rolled toward him.

There was fire rolling over Nick's back. He screamed and flattened himself onto the pavement as much as he could. It seemed to go on forever, but finally stopped, followed by a cooling wind.

He raised his head and saw there were lights coming on around him. People were cussing loudly inside the buildings.

Risking a glance, Nick saw Gillulim running at breakneck speed out of his view, off down another street, into another alley perhaps. He was moving haphazardly, frantic and hysterical.

More lights were coming on, along with the sound of windows opening. Finally, the noise had gotten to the residents and roused them. In a moment, doors would be flung open and Nick would be seen.

He jumped to his feet, ignoring the pain down his back, on his ass, and down his legs. He took off in the direction he'd seen Gillulim run.

Glancing back, Nick saw that the alcove between the buildings had been completely blackened with the heat, as though an inferno had blazed there. The charred ruin ran up the sides of the structures three stories high. Whatever power Marbas had sent to Nick across the ground, it must have still protected him. Had it not, he would have been reduced to just so much ash in the path of Gillulim's breath. Nick would have been a long pile of ashen bones, scattered across the pavement. The outside walls of the buildings were still smoking and had erupted into large blossoms of flame here and there on both sides.

The silence was broken with the sound of screen doors banging against the outside walls of the buildings along with some very angry voices. Not wasting any more time looking back, Nick sped across the main street, ignoring where Gillulim had run or whether Marbas was following him, through the darkest alcove, and toward what he hoped was the club.

†

He was panting. It was all he could do. Just out of the light from the lamps, just a few feet from the main street on which the club sat, Nick rested against the brick.

Exhausted, he'd stumbled into one of the late-night parking lots that rented its space to the club, but by day was reserved for clients and employees of the recording studio in the building to the south. The lot was still full, still silent. There'd been no change in the night. Nick could very likely saunter a few feet to the sidewalk, gaze just a couple blocks north, and still see the long black limousine sitting in front of the club's entrance, the car's taillights bright red, its passenger door open, expecting him.

They'd all be sitting inside, maybe cursing his name a little, maybe laughing casually and watching the clock. How long had he and Scott been gone?

He could almost hear the limo's engine, even with the music from the club billowing down the street. Nick could almost hear it, despite his near total fatigue.

What would he say when he tripped around the corner and came into view? There'd still be a line to get into the club. Of course there, would be, duh. It would still be peppered with people he knew, people who'd look at him and shake their heads. Once they got into the club, they'd spread the word that they'd seen Nick Reynolds wandering around outside. They'd maybe also include the notion that he looked like he'd passed out on the street and was run over by a truck or two.

He was totally out of breath. Nick's shirt had fallen off somewhere down one of the residential streets, perhaps underneath the tree that still held an adult-size, Ninja motorcycle in its branches. His t-shirt had been burned off in almost a straight line down his back. Reaching around, he felt blisters the size of pennies that had already formed along his spine from his shoulders to his waist. Gillulim's final breath, his last anger, was apparently hot enough to seep through even the protective power of Marbas himself.

Nick had indeed ruined his pants again; there were burns down the back of the legs from his butt to his ankles, and they were shredded at his knees from being tripped by the imp in the first place.

The pain was exquisite. Blood was dripping from Nick's elbows and his shoulder, though he hardly felt those wounds underneath the scream of agony down the back of his body.

He knew he wasn't supposed to rest his hands on his knees when he was out of breath. He'd learned in junior high school to hold his arms above his head after a long run or a sprint, which would allow more room in his lungs. He didn't give a shit, though. It felt better to crouch over his bent knees, rasping all the air that he could, watching the black asphalt beneath him, watching and seeing its solid truth, its solid, normal, regular, mortal, everyday truth.

He leaned back and hit the wall of the building with his burned buttocks and hitched in pain.

There was no way he would be able to walk around the corner. There was no way he could walk down the street, exposed by the considerably brighter lights of that major Hollywood avenue, and just stroll casually past all those staring eyes to the limousine.

Even if Nick got to the car without drawing too much attention, what the holy heck was he going to say to the guys? How was he going to explain what had happened, especially when he looked like he'd just fallen off of the spit at a luau?

"What happened to your shirt?"

Nick looked up in panic, shocked at how quickly his heart resumed slamming in his chest.

It was Scott, though. Even before he saw him walking across the lot, Nick knew it was him. Even as the instinctive fight-or-flight impulses rampaged through him, he knew.

It wasn't Marbas. It wasn't the enormous, winged, black lion. It was Scott.

"Where is it?" Nick stammered. "What happened to it? It just ran off."

"Your shirt just ran off?" Scott giggled.

"No, butt-bag!" Nick half laughed, half sobbed.

"The imp?" Scott was completely naked, but Nick hardly noticed.

"Whatever, you fucker!" Nick hissed. "That white putrid—!"

"Shh." Scott ran his hand down Nick's face to his chin. "You're trembling."

Nick saw that Scott was right; his hands were shaking violently and, despite the night's considerable warmth, he was standing with his arms pressed together as if he were freezing.

"It was gonna eat me."

Scott shook his head. "He'd never have dared harm you."

"Bullshit," Nick hissed. "You should see my back, not to mention my ass."

"Shh," Scott whispered again, and Nick realized he'd been moaning too.

"My back..."

"What's wrong?" Scott stepped to the side of him and Nick turned silently.

Drawing in a sympathetic breath through his teeth, Scott took Nick gently by the shoulders, and turned him so that he was facing completely away.

"Hold still," he said.

Nick heard Scott inhale slightly, felt him step very close behind him. Scott's hands slid tenderly down his bare arms. Then Nick felt Scott's lips press into a kiss on the nape of his neck.

Shivers immediately fell in waves from his shoulders all the way to his heels. He gasped as powerful tingles erupted around the top of his spine, just beneath where Scott was kissing him, and began descending and spreading very slowly down his back.

All traces of pain had disappeared and now a strong exhilaration replaced it. Warmth, soothing and vigorous, ran like water down his body.

Scott held him around the waist, put his head on his shoulder, and just touched his ear with his lips. Shivers again.

"Take a couple of deep breaths," he whispered.

"I'm okay now. Thank you."

"Why did you come after me?"

Nick turned around. "What are you talking about? Of course I was gonna come after you! What the fuck were you doing, just up and running out on me like that?"

"I couldn't let him get away. You should have stayed with Troy."

"You just up and ran out!"

"Shh. It's all right, I'm sorry."

"There I was, all by myself."

"I'm going to take you home now."

"I was standing there, and you'd gone…"

"I want you to close your eyes for a minute, okay?"

"You were all gone." Nick closed his eyes, suddenly very, very sleepy. "I was just standing there. With nothing."

Scott's lips pressed to Nick's forehead, and the breeze stopped, the sounds of traffic ceased, and he no longer felt the pavement beneath his feet.

Nick dreamed that he was a rabbit—a bunny, actually— and he was being carried through the sky in the mouth of a giant eagle.

†

When Darren looked up, Scott was leaning into the limousine with a cautious grin and an expression of timid curiosity.

"Were are Theo and Eddie?" Scott asked, stepping into the car and sitting on the side seat, very near Darren, who was sitting in his usual spot in the very back. He crossed his arms. He'd been running his tongue across his teeth, quite absently, but, as he saw Scott, and just as absently, he stopped.

"Inside," he answered. "They went upstairs with Karen and then never came back down." Darren noticed that Scott was wearing a completely different outfit. He pressed his head back into the upholstery with a silent huff. "Where's Nick?"

"Didn't Troy tell you what happened?" Scott asked.

"You know…" Darren shook his head. "This really isn't like Nick. He's not the flaky one. He's not the troublemaker."

"You think I'm a bad influence?" Scott grinned.

Darren shook his head slowly, gazing at his knees. "I don't know what you are," he whispered.

Darren had waited patiently for quite a while at the front desk while Karen and the boys ran back upstairs. He waited, drumming his fingers on the counter, alone in the hallway, bits of broken telephone scattered across the floor, some seriously amazing music wafting out at him like a taunting siren. He waited there, he stayed put, while some crazy shit was certainly going on around him, and he wondered how the holy motherfuck he'd gotten there. He'd been happily kissing Nicky one moment, and the next they'd all left him in that disco-tomb.

Nick was acting like a freak. There was a change in him that, although notable, certainly hadn't been all that gradual. At first, it was nothing more than intriguing, maybe even a little sexy. Darren had sensed it off and on during the previous week, ever since he'd tried to lift Nick out of a puddle of beer on his kitchen floor, to maybe help clean him up a little, and been told off for his trouble.

Nick had seemed indifferent to him. That was it. Darren no longer felt that Nick needed or—and this really stung—wanted him around. The problem with that idea was the incredible hunger with which Nick went at him when they were alone. The way he behaved in the bedroom over the last few nights was a baffling contradiction to his casual independence during the day.

Now, though...now Nick had utterly disappeared. For the second time in as many weekends, Nick was gone totally, and this time along with his unreasonably beautiful cousin. A cousin who, not only showed up out of nowhere to begin with, but who also showed up alone, just this minute, in completely different clothing than when they'd first left his hotel.

The first time he'd seen him sitting in Nick's living room, Darren immediately put the two of them together. They'd corrected him, though, and a little abrasively at that. Since then, Darren hadn't for a second considered that Scott could actually be screwing around with Nick. Not even when Troy, in his far-less-than-subtle lunge at the inside information on Nick's fidelity, brought up the notion that the two cousins might actually be "knockin' boots".

Even sitting there in the limo by himself Darren couldn't imagine that was the case. It just didn't feel right. They'd all spent a lot of time together and, sure, they were affectionate, but that was really how it was with all five of them, just as it was for countless other groups of guys throughout their overall community. It was a facet of a gay clique. It was an unabashed physical affection that they all shared, but it certainly wasn't sexual. It was yet one more secret perk to this 'alternative lifestyle'; Darren got to enjoy the physical fondness of his closer friends without the constant pressure of maintaining some machismo façade.

Scott somehow fit right into that. He'd slipped right into their group as if he'd known them all forever, and indeed, he sure did seem to know them. He had the same sensibilities, the same mannerisms, the same tastes. Well, except in hairstyles. What was that about?

Darren knew that Scott felt very deeply for Nick, and he never got even the slightest impression that it was from any other source than a shared history and relation. More than that, Darren felt Scott sincerely cared about *him*. It hurt to think there might be something tainted to this whole situation.

Nick had screwed around before, and heaven knew Darren had written the book on screwing around, but this was different. Despite the unspoken liberation of any standard, contemporary American, relationship moral-ethical, whatever-the-fucking-crap it was called these days, that existed between Darren and Nick, this would be different; this would be a deception.

If there was anything carnal going on between Nick and Scott, Darren was going to be hurt. Although he wasn't sure he deserved to play the victim, the thought still quieted his mind and pushed his heart to pound with a fearful anticipation. Darren was afraid because there would be pain in store for him. There would be what he suspected was quite a lot of pain, and he maybe even deserved it. Nevertheless, deserved or not, he was afraid that such a pain would prove itself to be more than he could endure.

He'd stood in the hall of the club's entrance just as Karen asked, and she eventually came down again, although alone. She'd said that Theo and Eddie would be down in a minute or two, that they'd been accosted by someone, or whatever, and were gabbing like girls at a bridal shower.

Darren had turned the door back over to Karen, accepted her peck on the cheek as thanks, and went out, expecting to see the limousine idling directly in front of the club's entrance. The car hadn't been there, though, on the street outside. There had only been the still-lengthy line and sparse, moving traffic.

So, Darren had walked down the avenue in the direction Bobby indicated and found the limo parked along the side of a dark building. Darren had expected to find Nick and Scott inside, maybe getting into the GHB or the cocaine, maybe caught in that oh-so-common 'how-long-have-we-been-here?' thrall that those compounds were capable of inducing. They hadn't been there, though. The car was empty too.

Darren had thought then, for just a second, that Nick and Scott perhaps hadn't been bright enough, or lucid enough, to ask Bobby where the driver had taken the car, and were maybe wandering around looking for it, but he dismissed the idea immediately. Neither of them was an idiot.

However, sitting in the empty limo—Darren had asked the driver to move it across the street from the club's entrance and double park with the lights on, which was exactly what Nick was supposed to have done, motherfuck-it-all—listening to the loud hum of conversation from the crowd across the street, and still the taunting, melodic rhythm from which there seemed to be no escape, he kept visiting the idea that Nick and Scott were lost. It had been the only explanation that didn't break Darren's heart.

But now Scott was here and Darren couldn't find refuge in that thought anymore.

"I haven't seen Troy since I left him in the first floor lounge." He shook his head at Scott.

"I have a lot to explain then." Scott looked at the floor.

"You bet your fuzzy ass you do."

"Darren," Scott said, scooting a little closer, so they could talk. He was wearing shorts and a t-shirt again, with sandals and no socks. There wasn't any hair on his legs and Darren almost laughed because he was suddenly sure that Scott's ass wasn't even the slightest bit fuzzy.

"Why are you smiling?" Scott grinned too.

"Because I can't believe I'm thinking about your ass right now."

"Um…okay." Scott nodded.

"You're not Nick's cousin," Darren said. It was a statement. Not a question.

He looked right at Scott when he said it. He wanted to see the expression on his face. When you came right down to it, all of the rationality of his nervousness, all the confusion, all the unreasonable anxiety, rested upon that condition, that Nick and Scott were cousins.

The car seemed suddenly very small. They could have been sitting in the trunk, and Darren wouldn't have felt more cramped.

Scott's face didn't register a reaction. He only stared at Darren for a moment, then slowly shook his head. "No, Darren. I'm not."

"I can't…" Darren stopped, his throat closing up suddenly. What was happening? He certainly wasn't going to cry in front of this guy, whoever the crap he was.

"Darren," Scott started, "I don't believe I'm about to use this phrase on you, and please don't kick my ass just for the sheer lameness of it, but it's not what you think."

Darren laughed in spite of himself.

"There's nothing going on between Nick and me," Scott said. "I love him, but it's nothing like you're most likely thinking. It's nothing like—"

"You must think I'm the biggest fucking dolt in the northern hemisphere!" Darren burst. "You think you can prance around me for a motherfucking week, fucking my boyfriend right under my nose, tell me some whacked, lame-ass shit about the two of you being cousins,

cousins, holy-fucking-crap, *cousins*, of all things, and then expect me to sit here and swallow whatever you blow in my face?"

Scott sat back against the limo cushion and sighed. Darren just stared at him. The crowd had gone very quiet across the street; there was drama blaring out of the open door of the limousine and the guys apparently wanted to hear every word.

"Do you two just hate me?" Darren whispered.

"You know the answer to that." Scott looked him right back in the eye, unblinking.

"Oh, really?" Darren shook his head again with an angry grimace. Grunting, he pushed himself back into the seat, retreating back into the upholstery.

Scott slid to the edge of his seat and leaned toward Darren. He didn't speak, though. He just looked at him like some goob.

"What?" Darren barked.

Scott didn't answer, he just held out his hand.

"What?" Darren repeated, smirking.

But Scott just sat there, staring at him, his hand extended toward Darren like he wanted money, or something. The look on his face was utterly unreadable. He didn't look guilty or stoned or angry or anything. If Darren had to pick something, he'd say Scott just looked sad. That's it. He just looked a little sad.

Before he knew what he was doing, Darren had reached out and put his hand into Scott's.

The expression on Scott's face changed instantly, but Darren still couldn't tell what he was thinking. All the tension went out around Scott's eyes, and his mouth opened just slightly, his lower lip falling away from his upper just a fraction. He drew in a breath and Darren felt himself doing the same thing, with him, like they'd planned it, like they were doing some stupid lung dance.

Darren wasn't thinking about breathing, really, but he couldn't help noticing that he was exhaling right along with Scott. He would've thought Scott was mocking him, but it almost felt as if it were him that was doing the mocking. His breathing was following Scott's, his chest rising and falling in an eerie unison.

There was no mirth on Scott's face. There wasn't anything Darren could even remotely read, not even simple sadness anymore.

"It's hard to be an only child," Scott said.

Darren sighed. "Don't start that shit again."

"You were so afraid to leave home when you went to college," Scott went on, shaking his head sadly, staring into Darren's eyes as if

he were reading a cue card. "You were scared because you could feel
your mother walking on the brink of depression since your father died
and you thought, if you left, she'd fall in completely and it would be
your fault."

"Holy fuck. What—?"

"She doesn't know you," Scott said, squinting at him, looking as
though he were in physical pain. "Oh, Darren...to this day, she
doesn't know a thing about you, and you sit with her, over dinner, or
next to her in the living room, *Wheel of Fortune* or *Touched by an Angel*
blaring on the TV and driving you crazy, but you try to listen to it,
because the alternative is your mom, droning on and on about what
Susan Wherts served at bridge last Saturday afternoon, and how she
could make the same thing, probably better, if her arthritis didn't flare
up while she was trying to roll those little strips of flower tortilla.
She's going on and on about nothing, because that's all you really have
between you. Nothing. You have nothing."

"My mom?" Darren stared at Scott's expressionless face, his mouth
open, his breathing no longer locked to him, but heavily working on
its own.

"You'd love to just tell her what you do for a living," Scott said.
"You'd love to just share that little bit, give her that small part of you.
You want to let her know that you organize people and places and
egos and idiots just like a symphony conductor. You manipulate
them, and they come together in one night and work well enough to
keep thousands of people happy and smiling. You make them happy.
You make them forget themselves and the things that hurt them. You
do that. You do. You'd love to tell her that you like the work so much
that it hardly seems like work at all and the time goes by and you
barely remember to eat or sleep."

"She knows." Darren furrowed his brow. "She knows what—"

"She knows that you produce parties, but it's obvious to you the
implications of that make her upset and embarrassed, but you lose her
when you try to clear things up, or paint a respectable picture, when
you get into any details, because she shuts down if the slightest clue
comes to the surface about what could possibly be the realities of your
life."

"What has Nick been telling you? He doesn't know—"

"Your mother sits with you, and you try to be the son she wants to
think she has, and you let her go on, not knowing you, you let her
drone and talk and mumble, because it's easier anyway, it's so much
nicer than the confusion and the fighting that just went on and on

when you were a kid. Your mother couldn't figure out why it was that you didn't fit in to anything, get along with anyone, and you couldn't either. Not until much, much later." Scott took a deep breath. "Not until Jeff."

"Jeff? Oh, my god, what—"

"Jeff would stay with you, in the big house with you and your mother, because you lived closer to school and you could stay late at practice. His mom had arranged that he could stay with you, since you were friends, and you both could just go straight to school the next day, after a late night. It was easier. It was so much easier for Jeff's mom since she had so many other kids and couldn't drive all over the place just for him."

Darren could only stare at Scott now. He didn't know what was happening or how Scott knew any of this, because no one knew this. No one knew anything about Jeff or what had happened.

"He'd sleep with you," Scott said, his voice heavy and knowing. "He'd sleep right there, right in the same bed, which really wasn't meant for two people, but your mother didn't' think anything of it. You were both boys after all, and not even grown. You could easily share the same bed."

Darren looked at him with wide unbelieving eyes, and Scott placed his other hand on top of his.

"It went on like that for a while," Scott continued, "just sharing the bed, just laying there, maybe touching at the knee, maybe his arm resting next to your back, maybe your face close enough to breathe on his shoulder, but nothing more, nothing big, nothing unnatural. Then you noticed that he didn't pull away if you pressed your leg closer to his, and you thought maybe he was draping his hand on your arm intentionally, feigning sleep, pretending to move without purpose, but it didn't matter, you got closer and closer, night after night, and neither one of you remembered when it changed. Neither one made a fuss the first night that one of you let your arm fall over the other's chest, when your head rested on his shoulder and he didn't move away, when his lips touched the side of your face and you could feel his breath across your cheek, when your hand found his and he held it, running the other up your arm to your chin, when his lips found yours and you were so afraid to open your eyes, afraid to see that maybe he was crying too.

"There were so many nights, so much darkness and bliss and confusion and elation and tenderness and guilt and clinging, holding onto him, pressing your face to his and pretending there was nothing else, there was no world outside his arms, and no one would judge you, and no one would taunt you, and this would be all there was, for the rest of time, this warmth, this safety, this obsession, this love."

"But he," Darren started. "But, he..."

"But he left you. He left you alone. He moved away, and you were alone in that tiny, giant, empty bed, and you'd sit there, for an hour, two, maybe four, and you'd rock back and forth, and you'd smell him. You'd smell him in your room, and you'd cry and cry, and press the blanket to your mouth because you could smell him there, but mostly because you couldn't let your mother hear you. You couldn't let her know anything. You had to stifle your sobs, because she couldn't know you, she couldn't, not then, not now."

"I never saw him again."

"And you grew up, and you went out with girls, and you liked some of them, and you slept with them, but they never made you weep. They never touched you so that your breath would stop and your stomach would ache and your soul would scream."

"I tried to be... I tried to do what—"

"Your mother wanted you to meet a nice girl. She wanted to see you off to college, and a career, and a nice wife she could talk with, she could cook with, she could laugh with, and you wanted to give her that. You wanted to let her see the future actually coming just like she'd wished for you, for all those years. You wanted to put grandchildren into her arms and see her face as she looked at you, happy to have gone through it all, happy to have had you, happy you were hers, proud to stand with you and hold your children, proud to be there, proud to know you."

"I went out with girls all the time. I went out with a lot of girls, but—"

"You were aching inside. It was constant and awkward. Sometimes you didn't notice it so much, like when you were reading something interesting or were lost in a show on television, but sometimes it was overwhelming, like when you were walking alone or peering out a window, waiting for a class to end, when you allowed your mind to wander, you allowed your thoughts to fall where they would, like rain down the side of a mountain, but it always went to the same place. It always gathered strength and speed until it was rushing in a river and you couldn't stop it, but you really didn't want it to stop, and you'd let it flow, right to where you knew it was going, right to the same place you found your quiet thoughts so many times before, right to a huge and silent place, where you weren't alone, and you didn't have to pretend, and you could rest and talk freely, and someone would be there. Someone would be there to listen and to laugh with you. Someone would be there to lace his fingers through yours and press your face to his and whisper that he loved you. He'd say it, and you'd let him say it because, there, in that restful place, it wouldn't mean the end of everything you knew."

"I never let him say it."

"You'd gaze at Jeff in the dark. You'd stare, not moving. You'd stare at his face and feel trapped and enthralled. You could almost hear his heart pounding. Never mind that you could actually feel his heart against your chest, slamming like a hammer. Never mind that your own heart was thrashing inside you as well, and you'd see that he wanted to say it. You'd see his lips quivering as he mustered the courage, and you'd wait. You'd hear it in your mind, over and over, and sometimes you thought of saying it for him. You thought of saying it for both of you.

"You'd see him begin to form the words, but you always stopped him. You always saw your finger go to his lips and you'd whisper, so quietly, oh, my god, you'd whisper like the faintest of breezes, without even the breath to stir the lash that had fallen on his cheek, 'Don't say it.'

"And he'd look at you for an instant, and there was relief on his face, or was it agony? You'd nod slightly, just so slightly, and you'd whisper again, only this time you said, 'Me too.'"

Darren shut his eyes and held his breath, but he couldn't stop him. He couldn't pull his hand away and push Scott to the floor, screaming at him to shut up, to just shut the fuck up.

And so Scott went on.

"You didn't even get a chance to say goodbye," he said. "He never said they'd be moving. He never mentioned a thing, and one day he was just gone and you knew his father had taken a much better job in Minnesota. Jeff really liked to play hockey anyway, but that was what your mom told you. That was what your mom knew, which wasn't anything, because you knew that he left because you didn't let him say it. He left you there alone because everything that was real was locked in your bedroom late at night, well after dark, never spoken of, never acknowledged. Even inside that room, when it was just him and you, alone in that quiet, peaceful place, you still couldn't let him say it."

"It would have been wrong!" Darren heard his own voice. It almost sounded like a sob, but it couldn't have been.

"It would have been the truth," Scott whispered. "It would have been the very thing the biggest part of you was so afraid to hear, so afraid would shatter everything you ever thought you were, everything your mother ever thought you were, everything you thought she wanted you to be, that person would be shattered forever, and then what? What would you have had together after that, Jeff and you? What would anything mean after that? You would have had nothing, because that's what those kind of people had. They had nothing, because they *were* nothing.

"And so you walked around, day after day, and you laid alone in the dark, night after night, and you ignored the ache inside you. You didn't think about it. You let it have you. You were sure there was nothing you could do, sure that it would go away in time and you'd be normal again. You sobbed yourself to sleep, pressing the blanket that smelled like Jeff to your face. You sobbed yourself to sleep so many times, through so many horrible, silent nights, and you told yourself that the pain would go away. You told yourself that those feelings would go away. That everything would be normal, would change and be normal, that it would all stop and just go away."

"But, it didn't."

"It got bigger. It became abhorrent and devastating. It almost ate you alive."

"It wasn't just Jeff anymore."

"It was much bigger than you allowed yourself to consider. You tried to quiet the ache. You tried to sweat it out at the gym. You tried to banish it with the conquest of girl after girl after girl after girl. You tried to crowd it out by immersing yourself within the culture of popularity and the rigorous extremes of manhood that popularity expected of you every single minute of every single hour of every single day."

"And…" Darren shook his head.

"You tried to pray it away." Scott laced his fingers through Darren's, holding him tighter. "You tried to send a prayer to Heaven each day and each night, each time your thoughts began to gather strength and take you to that place, that forbidden place, you prayed that God would save you from them, save you from those thoughts, that He would touch you and alter you and make you right."

"I prayed every day. I prayed and begged, but it…" Darren wavered. "But…"

"It only grew. By the time you graduated from high school it was behind your every thought. Could anyone tell? Were they talking about it? What would you say if they asked? What if someone said something to your mother?

"That's why you went so far away to college. That's why you didn't keep in touch with anyone from high school. They didn't really know you and you didn't want them to."

"I kept trying."

"There were more girls in college, one after another. But—"

"There were boys too."

"A windy night during your first semester. The first transgression, hardly felt, hardly remembered, but afterward you still rocked at the edge of your bed for hours. Not because you could smell him. Not because you felt anything for him at all. You just sat there rocking back and forth because you hated yourself.

"Each night, over and over, when the studying was done, when the lights were out, you'd sit and rock, holding the blanket to your mouth, shutting your eyes to the tears, stifling your sobs and hating yourself more and more."

"But it happened again."

"And again and again, each time sending you into a crater, sending you into a depression you knew so completely when the lights were out and you were alone. You wondered if it was the same place your mother saw, after your father died, when she was alone, after you'd gone to bed and the day was over."

"Then the city…" Darren blinked. "After college…"

"The city promised to be so much easier. There were all sorts of people in the city and you thought they wouldn't really care if someone was a little different, if someone had a little quirk."

"But they did."

"You'd hear them, in the clubs, when you let yourself go out. Not to a gay club. No, never to a gay club. A normal club. You wanted to go out and forget everything in a normal club, and you'd hear them, the popular people, the A-list people, talking about someone, laughing over someone's clothes, someone's car, someone's accent, someone's life."

"Everything."

"Everything was under the microscope and you worked even harder to be liked, to be accepted. You made it your life. You made it your life to be the guy next door, to be the one nobody bagged, to be perfect and charming.

"You'd make them dance. You'd make everything so much fun that there'd be nothing else, nothing outside the club, and no one would judge you, and no one would taunt you, and this would be all there was, for the rest of time, this warmth, this safety, and this obsession."

"I couldn't hold onto it. I couldn't keep it going, but—"

"The drugs helped. The drugs took you to that beautiful place, over and over, easily and without pain, without scrutiny. You could let go, a little, and you could smile and pretend it all meant something, that you were building something real."

"Nick..." Darren gasped suddenly. "Oh god, Nicky!"

"Yes." Scott nodded. "Nick. Nick appeared in your life and it all crashed in on you the first time you looked at him."

"He knew. He knew all the time."

"You'd stand with him in the club, at the bar, in the lounge, dance with him near you, lean down to talk in his ear, lean down and maybe brush your face against his hair, maybe smell his cologne, say something in his ear, anything, something funny, something interesting. You'd put your hand on his shoulder, maybe his chest, and he wouldn't move away. He wouldn't give you a funny look. His chest would be bare, of course, but all the guys had no shirt on, and no one thought anything of it. You'd stand there, touching him, leaning down to him, saying something, saying anything.

"And he'd touch you back. He'd steady himself in the swoon of ecstasy by holding your arm, or by leaning against you, and you'd help him, you'd hold his arms, you'd laugh with him, letting him stay close, letting him be near you."

"Everything changed."

"He was just going to 'crash' for one night. That was the story. You lived closer to the club, and the cab ride wouldn't be as expensive. You could take him home the next day when you were both sober."

"I never thought... it was so surprising, so unreal."

"Neither of you slept. The deception you allowed yourself vanished behind the closed doors and all bets were off."

"In the morning—"

"You took him home. You didn't speak all the way there. You wouldn't look at him when he got out, and you could only nod in quiet acceptance when he waved from the sidewalk."

"I don't remember driving back to my place again."

"Just sitting on the edge of your bed, smelling him. How long did you sit there? How long did you picture him in your mind? How long did it take before your realized you weren't rocking mindlessly, and you weren't holding a blanket to your lips, and no one would hear, or care, if you cried, or if you laughed, or if you sang his name over and over and over and—"

"I called him."

"He sounded surprised. There was real surprise in his voice and you couldn't blame him for it, could you?

"What did you talk about? I can't hear it. I don't think you even remember. I don't think it mattered, what you talked about that first time you called him, but it was easy and sweet, and he was with you again, that very night, and the next, and the next."

"He never—"

"—needed anything. He never seemed to mind when you didn't call for a while. He didn't whine over the phone if you just wanted to be alone or if you weren't alone and lied about it. He had a life, and he was very popular, and he wasn't in town all the time, and you didn't have to cater to him. You didn't have to answer to him, but when he was there, when he was at home, and your thoughts left you alone, and you weren't working, or you didn't have a lot to do, you could call him. You could call and the conversation would be effortless and pleasant and he never said anything that would make you uneasy. He never tried to say anything that might shine a light into your dark bedroom, when you held him, late at night. You never had to put your finger to his lips and whisper, 'Don't say it.'"

"At the club, though, I—"

"—gave a little. You bent a little. You reasoned that no one knew anything. So what if you danced together? So what if he rested against you? So what if you talked with your arms around his shoulders? You did the same with Karen, didn't you? The same with Eddie and with Thelma and everyone else who delighted your senses. What could anyone know from that?"

"It didn't last."

"Because Nick changed. Something happened to Nick. You don't know—"

"—exactly when or what or—"

"—if he heard something, or learned something, or just grew tired. He used to be happy and he'd make everyone else happy. He'd make you happy. He used to be full of energy and life and nothing seemed to bother him. Then he stopped working so much. Something happened and he stopped going out of town so much, and he stopped going out to the club so much, and he spent a lot of time by himself, and he wanted to spend a lot more time just with you.

"His drug use started to grow. He started to have bad nights when it was difficult to get along with him. He started to get quiet."

"It was too late." Darren shook his head.

"You couldn't just stop calling. He was a part of you. You couldn't just free yourself from him. You understood that."

"I tried."

"You did more than that, Darren. You turned on him. Suddenly he wasn't so subtle anymore when you were out together. Suddenly he didn't spend as much time roaming the club, being popular, being seen, having fun, letting you have fun, and then just sneaking off with you unnoticed. Suddenly he was right next to you a lot. Suddenly he was right there, most of the time. People started to associate you with each other. People started making assumptions. Suddenly he needed you.

"So, you turned on him. You'd step away when his back was turned, or you'd make excuses why you needed to go home alone, or you'd give him an ecstasy or a bump of something stronger, and then push him at Karen."

Darren flinched.

"But you kept calling him, and he kept coming over, and the nights were still good, and you could still fall asleep with him, you could still rest and hold him and pretend everything was okay. You could pretend that Nick hadn't outgrown the boundaries of what you were willing to give him.

"Life outside your apartment, though, that still had to be yours and yours alone. He was just a friend, just a guy that hung around with you. 'See everyone, we're not together! See, he's dancing with Karen! See, he's dancing with Matt! We're not anything more than good friends. He's dancing with Thelma! He's resting in the lounge with Eddie!'

"How much time went by? How many times did you look at him, late, late at night, just the light of the streetlamps slipping through your blinds, holding back an apology? How many nights went by when you could see that he was slipping, he was going somewhere dark, somewhere black. He was letting go of something, something he needed, and you saw it. You saw him falling away, even as you held onto him, even as you brushed your fingers through his hair, but you couldn't do anything. You couldn't say what was beating so hard against the inside of your own head. You had to take drugs to keep it quiet. You had to take drugs to shut it up. You saw it, and you saw that he wanted to hear it from you. He wanted to hear you open the door, because he knew it was closed, and he knew it was all you had, and he knew you'd never open it on your own, just because he asked you to, he knew. He knew all along.

"So you'd go on and on, and you'd let him get up in the morning, and go out by himself to his car, and you wouldn't say a word. You'd nod and maybe smile when he waved at the door, when he left, and you'd just sit there and let him take everything that was unsaid out the door with him. You let yet another chance walk away from you. You let him take what was between you and walk away with it, unsaid."

Darren could feel tears on his face. Streams of them. He was squinting but they wouldn't stop. He wanted to wipe them away, to reach up to his face and brush them all aside, but Scott was holding both of his hands. Darren didn't remember when he had given him his other hand, but Scott was holding tightly to them both, and Darren was holding him right back.

"Now a stranger has come into your lives," Scott said. "Now there's another face at the table and another voice over the phone. There's a shift in your world and Nick is pulling himself up.

"Nick is smiling all the time, and laughing. He's not a bother at all. Suddenly he's not sulking. He's easy to talk to again. He's playful and he's passionate, and he could take you or leave you. You don't think he needs you anymore. Maybe he doesn't even want you anymore—"

"Oh, my god!" Darren sobbed.

"He doesn't need you anymore, and he's not a burden, and he's not hanging on you all the time and he's not next to you every minute. He doesn't need you, and you miss that."

"No! That's not right! I don't miss his need! I miss—!"

"You miss *him!*"

Darren sobbed again. He opened his mouth to protest and sobbed instead.

"Maybe they *were* talking about you," Scott went on. "Maybe everyone saw you two and everyone knew. Maybe you've been a joke all this time. Maybe they'd smile at each other as you passed, on your way to the exit, Nick behind you. Maybe it was obvious. Maybe everyone knew all along. But Darren... Darren, do you even care anymore? Do you care who knows what or what they think?"

There were tears dripping on the upholstery, on his pants. Darren could hear them, he could feel each one rolling down his face, each one faster than the last, faster through the track of the one before it. He squeezed his eyes tighter.

"Maybe you're afraid." Scott leaned closer, touching his forehead to Darren's, whispering to him. "Maybe you never really gave a shit if they talked, or if you were a joke, or if everyone knew. Maybe Mr. Charming was never meant to hide Darren from the world, or make everyone like him, or leave him alone. Maybe Mr. Charming just kept the important ones at bay, the ones that could hurt him, the ones that could leave.

"Maybe you still think you're standing behind what you want people to see, but you know they don't see that. You *know* they don't.

"Still, you hide there anyway, because if you stopped, if you let it all go, if you looked Nicholas in the face and said what was burning its way through you, maybe he'd know you. Nick would know you, and you can't have that, now can you?"

Darren gritted his teeth, still trying to stop the tears.

"He'd know you, and then it wouldn't matter. It wouldn't matter if your mother knew you, or if your friends knew you, or if you let Jeff tell you that he loved you. It wouldn't make any difference, because Nick would know you, and Nick would love you anyway, and you'd be forgiven, and everything else would fall away. Everything else would have been for nothing, all a waste of time and tears, and there'd be only him, and everyone could know, and everyone could talk. They could laugh or point and you wouldn't care. Nick would know you. He'd love you, and there would be nothing else, and you'd know that beautiful place, over and over, each time he fell asleep, each time you watched him breathing easily, content at your side, wanting to kiss him, wanting just to touch those innocent lips, but reluctant to wake him. Happy instead to watch him dream, to watch the contentment on his face as he sleeps on your shoulder.

"With Nick on your shoulder, you know there can be so many nights, so much contentment and bliss and understanding and elation and tenderness and innocence and clinging, holding onto him, pressing your face to his and knowing there is nothing else, there is no world outside his arms, and no one will judge you, and no one will taunt you, and this will be all there is, for the rest of time, this warmth, this safety, this obsession, this love.

"So, now you glare at me, and you wonder what's going on, even though you know it's nothing, even though you know that Nick is nothing if not yours completely. Even if I'm not really his cousin, even if nothing we've said about how we know each other is at all close to what's true. Still, you know there's no reason to start thinking of blame, because you know if Nick lied, it wasn't for his sake. It was for yours.

"If he lied, he wasn't protecting his interests. He was protecting you from your own insecurity.

"But you're still grasping at it anyway. It's another reprieve, another distraction from what you really feel. You're grabbing onto this little mystery as if your very existence depended on it, and you're trying to use it to assert power, but you're failing, because there's no power there to assert. You're raging over someone you've never acknowledged. You're raging about losing a love to which you've never really laid claim.

"You want to somehow cry foul when you've dodged all accountability for all this time. You want to expect Nick to honor a commitment that you've never made.

"And so you're blaming me, and you're letting your mind fill in the blanks, even if they don't make any sense, even if they don't feel right, even if you know they're wrong.

"We're sitting here, and you're letting yourself think that you're the victim because it makes the ache go away. It makes the real ache settle back to where it might not eat you alive.

"But the biggest gnaw of all, the heaviest weight upon you, is not that Nick's been saved. It's not the confusion that grinds at you because you can't understand why you aren't able to just be happy that he's happy.

"It's because you could have been the one that saved him. You could have been the one that picked him up. You *should* have been, but you weren't.

"You looked at me just now, you sat here and looked me in the eye, and you grabbed at the excuse to hate me.

"And now we both know why. We both know why you keep him at a distance and yet rage because you're apart.

"But I can't let you have it. I can't let you hide from him anymore. You're going to come with me now. You're going to sit back and relax, and the car is going to take us to Nick's. You're going to sit with me in his living room, while he sleeps, while he lays in his bed alone, dreaming of you, and you're going to let me tell you everything. You're going to let me bring you into the loop, so to speak, because now I can't save him all by myself.

"I saved him last weekend. I saved him from you and I saved him from himself. Now, though, we all need saving.

"You need to listen to all of it and then you need to make a decision. Once you've heard everything, once you've seen what you may need to see, once I've answered every question you could possibly have, you'll need to make a decision.

"Because now, I need you too. Very soon, you'll understand why. Just know that things have changed. Things have become much bigger than just the three of us, just our brief and beautiful encounter in this life.

"I need you to come with me and hold my hand while I look into his sleep, while I lay my hand on Nick's forehead and see his dreams. You'll see them too. You'll share his dreams with me for just an instant, for just the tiniest of moments, but it'll be enough. It'll be enough because you'll only see one thing. You'll see Nick's dream, and you'll see that it's of you.

"Through all of this, although it may be selfish of me, you'll know in an instant what is truly priceless. Everything else will fall away, and then you and Nick can make the choice. You can look openly at the burden I've selfishly brought to you and you'll be able to make the choice.

"I need you and Nick to help me."

†

Looking out from his hotel window, Bishop Patrick scanned the sky again. He saw nothing but its vast black emptiness. He kept looking anyway. He didn't care how long it might take him to see anything. He didn't care at all.

Bishop Sigovia was on his way from Athens to Rome. The cardinal would call when the little, twit bishop arrived. The cardinal would call again after all of the arrangements had been made. Then Bishop Sigovia would start on his journey to Los Angeles to help Robert. He'd bring Robert what he needed. He'd bring him the artifact.

Cardinal Matìne had wanted to come himself. Of course, that wasn't possible. He needed to stay and make sure that no one suspected the artifact had been taken. Needless to say, there existed a very convincing fake in the cardinal's possession. Even so, it was exceptionally important that no one examine it too closely. Thirty years was a very long time to keep a secret. Especially one like this. It would be unthinkable for the truth to surface now, when they were so close to making things right.

Robert dropped three chunky ice cubes into his glass and poured the scotch over them. It was very late, and his mind was racing. He needed something to quiet his thoughts or he'd never get to sleep.

Frenzied images were pounding inside him. Just a few blocks from Robert's hotel, the skotos had been active. Robert could've walked to the site in less than thirty minutes. Not that he would walk anywhere, especially not at night, good gracious no. To do such a thing in this city would only call undue attention to himself, as no one walked anywhere in Los Angeles, except the prostitutes at night and the postal service during the day.

No, when he went there, to the club—and he'd go soon—Robert would drive the new Mercedes. The Mercedes was now being leased instead of just rented. No one would look twice at that.

Robert had gone to mass that morning, at the enormous church on Highland and Franklin. It had all seemed eerily familiar, until he realized the interior of that church had been used in the film *Sister Act*. He'd said a silent prayer, as it seemed even the holy temples here had their agents and a video reel.

The cardinal had tripled his budget, as it seemed Robert would be in the city much, much longer than expected. Robert had gone straight back to the little shop on Rodeo Drive and purchased some additional clothing. There was a different salesperson, though. A man this time. Although, Robert considered the term 'man' to be a bit loose in this instance.

However, the exact same transformation Robert had first witnessed with the female salesperson occurred just as predictably with the 'male' one. He'd watched very closely, taking an almost disdainful satisfaction from the clerk's behavior.

There were plenty of other stores that would've been able to provide Robert with what he needed, all over the city, but he went instead to the only one at which he'd ever made any lavish purchases. He went to the one where he thought he might again see the hypnotic dance of corruption. That Robert might be manipulating the situation never crossed his mind.

Now that he knew he was going to be staying, he thought about finding another place to sleep. Wouldn't the hotel staff wonder at someone staying in such a lavish hotel for a month? Two even? Did they see that sort of thing very often?

He was disturbed by the idea of going anywhere else; Robert liked his room with its expansive view of the city. It made him feel on top of things. It gave him a sense of being linked and yet at the same time detached from Los Angeles. He could gaze down at the urban sprawl and develop his plan, review his materials, all the while keeping the City of Fallen Angels where he could easily make his lofty observations. Not to mention the fact that, however miniscule the odds, he just might witness the demon himself from this haughty position.

Another ice cube went into his glass and there was another tip of the bottle. He wasn't usually a drinker. However, he was stuck in his room waiting for the cardinal to phone, and he certainly had no intention of allowing the significance of this time to play havoc in his mind. He'd tried meditation and prayer, of course, but the sense of imminent discovery and conclusion was such a powerful distraction, even the Bible itself had only served to enhance his nervousness.

He'd kept turning to Isaiah 34:14, where the prophet proclaimed the judgment of the red soiled country of Edom, that it would become a wasteland, suitable as a resting place for demons and even Lilith herself. Though the prophet names her, he does so with a euphemism.

An ancient trade connection between the most southern Palestinian cities, Edom was a forgotten place. Today, its name's etymology stood as the only source of modern academic interest, if there was any surviving interest at all.

Lilith would make her home there, so said the ancient prophet, in the wasteland that was once a thriving city. What was it that drew her? Was it the destruction of the city itself, or was her presence a planned condition from God, one that would prevent the city's recovery, maintain it as utterly unclean? Or could her mention in the scripture have been just a figure of speech, used to elucidate the degree of ruin that would befall the city; so much devastation that the demons of the earth would be called to it like children to a sandbox?

Only the small bedside lamp was burning in Robert's room. Placed below eye level, it didn't cause any reflection on the glass, which might stop him from seeing the night.

He knew he had very little chance of seeing him. Robert knew that against the dark sky there could be a dozen winged monsters, but should they be the same color as their background, from the top of his window to the distant yet clear horizon, he'd never notice them. No one would. Yet he still sat and stared, as if he were a teenager expecting Jennifer Lopez to suddenly come into view.

In Rome, in the Holy City, there was a painting in the hall to the cardinal's chamber. It held the image of the creature captured in brilliant oils. The likeness was said to have been painted in the fourteenth century by commission from the first bishop to have been given responsibility for the artifact. The very bishop to have seen the demon himself and then capture it.

The painting took up the entire wall from floor to ceiling and humbled everyone who gazed upon it. It was indeed an inspired work. Such mastery saturated the canvas. So much as to suggest actual illumination from the raging fires outlining the dark beast, from the edges of its wings to the borders of the canvas. The roaring black lion seemed caught in the preparation of a leap, his great head and mane almost lunging beyond the borders of the painting itself.

In the painting, the demon stood atop a small burning mound that, upon closer inspection, became a heap of listless and broken human bodies, several of which were trapped and mangled within the clutch of his giant paws. The monster's wings were stretched back to their farthest point, ready to rip down through the air and hurl the demon with majestic force out of the blazing scene and onto whoever stood before the image, staring into the demon's eyes. He seemed ready to fly at any instant beyond the enormous frame. There was fury in his eyes. The blue eyes that also shined as though they had a light of their own.

The effect was disturbing to say the least.

The demon had been described to the painter by the medieval bishop as being "black as the darkness from which he came," and indeed the likeness was like a glittering nightmare, painted in something as black as tar, darker and deeper than the blackest paint, yet with a smooth and hideous resplendence.

Perhaps Robert would see him soon. Perhaps, if he watched the skies with enough tenacity, he'd glimpse the stars beyond his window as they were blotted out by the shape of a giant lion, a great black demon with wings that spread across the night to the very horizon. Perhaps the skotos, the darkness, would finally soar within Robert's view.

This story is concluded in
Demon Tears

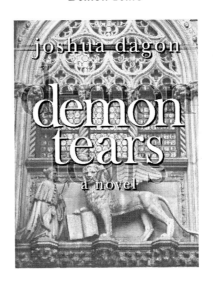

Joshua Dagon is a novelist,
playwright, and columnist.
He lives in Las Vegas, Nevada.